P9-DTP-669

WITHDRAWN

So, This Is Love

So, This Is Love

TRACY ANDREEN

WITHDRAWN

Viking

VIKING
An imprint of Penguin Random House LLC, New York

First published in the United States of America by Viking,
an imprint of Penguin Random House LLC, 2022

Copyright © 2022 by Tracy Andreen

Penguin supports copyright. Copyright fuels creativity, encourages diverse
voices, promotes free speech, and creates a vibrant culture. Thank you for buying
an authorized edition of this book and for complying with copyright laws by
not reproducing, scanning, or distributing any part of it in any form without
permission. You are supporting writers and allowing Penguin to continue to
publish books for every reader.

Viking & colophon are registered trademarks of Penguin Random House LLC.

Visit us online at penguinrandomhouse.com.

Library of Congress Cataloging-in-Publication Data is available.

Printed in the United States of America

ISBN 9780593525401

1   3   5   7   9   10   8   6   4   2

BVG

Design by Kate Renner
Text set in Sabon MT Pro

This book is a work of fiction. Any references to historical events, real people, or
real places are used fictitiously. Other names, characters, places, and events are
products of the author's imagination, and any resemblance to actual events or
places or persons, living or dead, is entirely coincidental.

The publisher does not have any control over and does not assume any
responsibility for author or third-party websites or their content.

For Walker

One

LAST HALLOWEEN

I regretted my decision immediately.

As I stood in the open front doorway of the Airbnb two-story mini-mansion rented by my classmate Bronwyn, I saw my new schoolmates dressed in attire that rivaled something out of a Hollywood costume party and I felt the plunge of dread.

They were audacious.

And impressive.

And I . . . was not.

I had come dressed as a burglar. Which was an outfit that required all the creativity of grabbing black jeans, a black turtleneck, black boots, black knit cap and gloves, and a five-dollar felt mask I'd ordered from Amazon so I could go low-key cheap for this event.

Which I had.

What I hadn't even done was grab a pillowcase stuffed with fake cash, because I only have two and they're both floral—which kind of throws off the whole "burglar" vibe—and I hadn't wanted anything to happen because Target didn't carry that set anymore.

It wasn't that I didn't care I had finally been invited to one of Bronwyn Campbell's famous parties, because I did.

A lot.

I also hadn't wanted to *look* like I cared. I mean, what if I'd shown up in some insanely elaborate costume—like, say, the throne from *Game of Thrones*—only to find myself faced with a sea of snobby expressions as my costume-free classmates sneered at my faux pas because dressing up for Halloween was for children and we were upperclassmen at the prestigious Barrington Academy. That meant we were *not* children. Even if I was still a few weeks shy of turning sixteen.

So, I'd fallen back on the tried-and-true strategy of "don't look like you're trying too hard," which had always served me well in the past.

Not tonight.

Because these people were dressed like they were at the freakin' Met Gala.

And I was one felt mask away from wearing an outfit already in my normal rotation.

Major miscalculation.

Not that anyone noticed.

No one paid me more than the most cursory glance before they returned to whatever it was they were doing, even if they weren't doing anything.

Was that a good thing? TBD.

My stomach roiled slightly and my second regrettable decision of the evening—sneaking a tiny bottle of pinot grigio from my roommate Thea's curiously impressive airplane wine collection, which she kept in the square fridge tucked in her closet—started to make its presence known.

She'd told me the first week of school that I could have one if I wanted, so technically it wasn't sneaking. In the ensuing weeks since then the subject had never been raised again and our interactions had dwindled to polite greetings on the rare occasions we encountered each other, so I couldn't be 100 percent certain. But I really wanted a dose of liquid courage before coming.

So, I grabbed one.

I'd only been at the Connecticut prep school since June, but my attention had been so firmly on trying not to fail any of my classes, both over the summer and now in the fall, that I hadn't made socializing a priority.

As a result, five months in, I didn't really have any friends, and I had to admit, I was more than a little lonely. Tonight was supposed to be my attempt to change that. After all, I'd received an emailed invite from Bronwyn, which was a first.

People didn't say "no" to Bronwyn.

At least not that I'd been able to witness.

She was the daughter of a wealthy real estate mogul, and she considered herself an aspiring beauty influencer with, as she liked to remind people, over twelve thousand followers. "And *counting!*"

I, on the other hand, last posted on Instagram two months ago. About my breakfast. It got four likes, including my mom's.

Sweat was starting to break out across my chest as my heart thundered with anxiety.

My eyes darted around the expansive living room, not quite sure where to land because there was so much going on. Noise from the deafening music. Smoke from a variety of cigarettes, some legal.

And the costumes. *Oof.*

I spied Josie Sutton in a shiny gold flapper dress with fringe galore, a headband, and a long cigarette holder drunkenly chatting with my mostly MIA roommate, Thea, and her boyfriend, Beaux, who were dressed like Claire and Jamie from *Outlander*. That astronaut costume sported by Gaines Alder looked potentially authentic, and, oh, God. I think Landon Sinclair really *was* dressed like the throne from *Game of Thrones*.

What was I thinking? I felt like a child attempting to migrate to the adult's table.

If I turned around right now and left, no one would know I'd ever come. I could give the whole "be more social" thing a try another time, when there was less pressure.

Like graduation.

"Hello, Finley."

I spun in the direction of whoever'd said my name and found myself face-to-face with—

I squinted.

"Arthur?"

At least, I *think* it was Arthur Chakrabarti Watercress? Unlike many of our other classmates, Arthur was dressed more sedately in a formfitting tuxedo that likely cost a pretty penny, his inky-dark hair tightly slicked back to the point of shining, giving him a very different vibe than I was used to seeing in our two shared classes or around our campus.

"Bond," he replied, utterly deadpan. An unlit cigarette dangled from his pouty lips and the faint scent of wine wafted off him, which surprised me. I'd never considered him to be the party type. More studious, like me. Then again, we were both at a party and I was already feeling the effects of the tiny bottle of wine, so I was in *no* position to judge.

"What?" I shouted in confusion above the thumpy music.

He pointed at himself and repeated, "James Bond. The Sean Connery version. From *Dr. No*, specifically. All others are imitations."

I almost rolled my eyes. What a dork.

Although, now that I allowed a second glance, he actually looked kinda—

"Arthur! *There* you are!"

He and I turned in sync and my stomach dropped because

Queen Bronwyn herself was descending on us like a pterosaur in a perfect recreation of the Lily James version of *Cinderella*, right down to the blonde wig over her gorgeous auburn hair and post— Fairy Godmother transformation blue dress.

Damn. She looked fantastic.

And she barely flicked a glance in my direction because her focus was securely on Arthur.

She handed him a chilled martini glass with a clear liquid and a curly slice of lemon peel at the bottom.

"Shaken, *not* stirred," she said, smiling broadly. "As requested."

I arched a brow. *What service.* Which was curious, because Arthur was hardly the social butterfly. At least that I'd observed. Not that I kept track of his comings and goings, because I didn't.

But now I had to wonder: *Was something going on between them?*

Last I'd heard, Bronwyn was together with some guy named Prescott, who was at Mayo Prep in Upstate New York, and the only reason I knew that personal tidbit about her was because she managed to work it into every third conversation I'd ever overheard her have. ("Prescott tells me he won't go to Lancaster Mountain to ski anymore, not since he's been to the ski resorts in *New York*." "Prescott sent me this box of candy from *Belgium*. Isn't it *amazing*?" "Prescott met *Drake*! At his *concert*! He sent me *a selfie*!")

"Many thanks," Arthur said, taking the glass from her. "Cheers." He took a sip. Nodded. "That's quite excellent." His crisp English accent lent an air of authenticity to his would-be Bond persona.

Bronwyn's smile grew coquettish. "Prescott says I make the *best* vodka martinis."

Ah. *There* he was. Good ol' Prescott.

Arthur turned to me, held up the glass. "Do you want to try a sip?" he asked, and if he hadn't been looking directly at me, I would have assumed he meant someone else. Arthur and I hadn't had many interactions these past few months. Well, other than him scowling at me because I took his favorite seat in class that first week.

I smiled politely. "No, thank you." The pinot grigio aside, I barely drank and wasn't going to dive into the deep end via vodka tonight.

He shrugged and took another sip.

Bronwyn was now looking at me, her blue eyes like lasers. "Finley?" I nodded. "I didn't recognize you."

My mind went blank with anxiety, but I knew I needed to reply, so I pointed to my head. "I hid my hair." Not the most insightful response, but at least it was accurate. My most recognizable feature—long blonde hair—was indeed tucked away beneath the knit cap. There was also the cheap mask I was wearing, which suddenly itched.

"I see that." She returned her attention to Arthur and smiled. "You look *great*."

He nodded once and repeated, "Many thanks."

She drew in a breath to say something else when Flapper Josie swooped in, grabbing Bronwyn by the upper arm, to Bronwyn's annoyance. Josie was too tipsy to notice.

"Come do shots!" she shouted at her BFF.

Bronwyn looked on the verge of shrugging her off when Astronaut Gaines and a boy dressed as the Mad Hatter who I was fairly certain was named Hawley Chen also appeared to pull her away, deeper into the house. All shouting, "Shots! Shots! Shots!"

As soon as she was out of view, I could breathe freely.

I turned to find Arthur watching me with a look of uncertainty. "Are you a mime?" he asked.

I frowned. "What? No. Mimes have white faces."

"Not all of them."

"I'm pretty sure they do."

"I don't think it's necessarily required."

"Are you a mime expert?"

"Are there such things?"

"There are experts for everything. Also, I'm wearing a mask. Mimes don't wear masks."

"Hmmmm," was his noncommittal reply before he nodded at me. "Ah. You're Wesley from *The Princess Bride*!"

"Wesley's the guy."

"I'm quite aware. But I can't quite ascertain what your costume is supposed to be." He waved at my attire.

"I'm a burglar, Arthur."

"Oh." He frowned. "Shouldn't you have a cloth sack? Preferably full of contraband?"

"Not if I haven't burgled yet."

"I don't believe 'burgled' is an actual word."

"It is, look it up."

He arched a single brow. "I'll get right to that."

Now I did roll my eyes. I considered walking away from him but didn't. After all, it wasn't like there was anyone else clamoring to talk with me, and Arthur didn't appear in a hurry to go elsewhere. Even if he did seem bored.

But that could've just been him.

"Why do you suppose we're here?" he asked out of nowhere.

I took an extra beat for him to provide context for the question, but realized none was forthcoming.

"At this party? Or life in general?"

"Either. Both. Though it could be said we're not."

"What?"

"Here." He waved his hand in general. "That we are, instead, mere simulations conjured up by our highly evolved descendants as they review what life was like in our time."

"Are you talking about Nick Bostrom's paper?" I asked, my gaze flitting around the room before I returned it to find Arthur's dark brown eyes boring into mine with a degree of, dare I say, incredulity.

"You know about that paper?"

I shrugged. "I read about it in *Scientific American*."

Sure, I knew my nerd side was showing, but this was Arthur, so I didn't particularly care. Plus, it was nice to have a moment when I could make a reference like that and not have the person I was talking with stare at me like I was speaking Latin. Which was basically every conversation I had with my ex-boyfriend, Brody Tuck, that didn't involve his hair, my hair, football, or food.

Arthur's stare lingered. "Fascinating," he murmured, almost to himself. Then he set the martini aside on the credenza and withdrew a silver flask from his pocket, pouring some into a short glass.

"I thought you wanted the martini," I said.

"Only for show. I'd already started with Chianti, and one should not mix the two. Trust."

Well, at least now I knew why he smelled like wine.

To my surprise, he offered the glass of Chianti to me and I automatically took it. Maybe he was tipsy and that was why he was being passably normal.

"The glass is clean," he assured me. "I brought it myself. I don't trust rental homes to have proper purification, particularly those which rent to teenagers."

He said it as if he wasn't a teenager himself. Then again, he seldom seemed like it. Granted I was always the youngest in the room thanks to my having skipped a grade, so everyone felt older than me.

Arthur took it to the next level, though, and not just because he was English. Wealthy English, at that.

I hesitated. The effects of the earlier wine were already racing through my bloodstream and I wasn't sure if I wanted to add to it with Chianti. But I also didn't want to look like a prude, so I sniffed the drink and was surprised. I'd never tried Chianti before. I was pretty sure Grandma Jo had a bottle or two for guests at the inn she owned, but she kept all the alcohol under lock and key.

I took a sip and, you know what? It wasn't terrible. Maybe a little sweeter than the wine I'd had earlier, and I could tell a little went a long way, but this was nice.

"Tignanello," he said, nodding to the drink. "My father is quite the fan."

"You drink with your father?" I couldn't fathom such a thing. Dad would kill me if he knew I was even holding this glass. Or at least send me "I'm very disappointed, Finley" looks. *Mom* would kill me. If Grandma Jo didn't beat her to it.

Arthur hesitated. Only for a fraction of a second, but it was there, and his posture stiffened. "Do you like it?" he asked, ignoring my question.

I decided not to push.

"Um, yeah." I took another sip to prove my point. It took every bit of control to not clear my throat against the tickle.

He seemed pleased. Took another sip himself. "Perhaps you were programmed to like it," he said, and I got the reference.

Shrugged. "Maybe. Though if my godlike future descendants were going to program me, I hope they'd have given me a more interesting life."

"Don't you hail from some sort of magical holiday town?" he asked.

My grip on the glass tightened at the casual reference to my hometown of Christmas, Oklahoma, which was decidedly devoid of magic.

Not that he needed to know that. In fact, no one needed to know that.

Ever.

"Mmmmm," was my reply. I've done better. I covered by taking a sip, then mentally noted I probably needed to be careful. Nobody wants to be the drunk new person who pukes in the bushes at the party they were barely lucky enough to be invited to.

"Christmas," Bronwyn said, and there she was again, by our side, in our conversation, only this time she was looking at me.

My heart clenched right along with my stomach.

"Isn't that where you come from?" she asked. "In Kansas."

I couldn't believe she remembered that, though I knew I'd told her once, early on in the school year, the singular time she'd taken a moment to engage me in a conversation I realized afterward was more for her to assess whether I was worthy of her time.

A test I'd clearly failed.

"Oklahoma," I corrected automatically.

She shrugged, dismissive. "Same thing."

No, it really wasn't, but I didn't want to correct her further, so I shrugged, too. One thing I'd come to realize soon after my arrival at Barrington was that East Coast people's attitude toward Middle American states was typically either one of collective trivialization or kitschy curiosity. It didn't take a genius to know which was Bronwyn's.

So, that's why no one was more surprised than I was when I followed the shrug with, "You should go there sometime. It's awesome."

I blinked.

Twice.

In rapid succession, because my hometown was many, *many* things. None of which were awesome.

Bronwyn laughed. And not in a good way.

Interestingly, Arthur didn't.

I glanced at him, only for a second, and when I glanced back to Bronwyn I found her eyes on me once again. Only this time there was a gleam to them, almost as if she were coiling, preparing to pounce. On me. Like a cat on a wayward cricket that happened into the house by accident and wound up missing a leg.

I was definitely the cricket in this scenario.

Which made no sense. We barely knew each other. And yet I suddenly wanted nothing more than to turn around and get the hell out of there. Fast. Before I lost a limb.

"Are there decent places to stay in this town of yours?" Arthur asked, sipping his Chianti.

"Of course," I said, happy to turn away from Bronwyn. "In fact, my Grandma Jo owns an inn. It's called the Hoyden Inn. It's in the heart of the town."

Bronwyn snorted. "Grandma Jo. How cute." Her tone was anything but.

My blood started to boil. Now she was treading on dangerous territory. My family meant the world to me. I wasn't going to let anyone mock them, not even Bronwyn Campbell.

That's why I kinda went off.

"It's an *awesome* place, and my grandmother's inn is an *awesome* inn, and everyone who stayed there thinks so. It's won awards. And folks come from all over the world to experience Christmas at Christmas. It's something they'll never forget!"

Bronwyn was not impressed. Instead, she aimed a gloved golf clap in my direction. "Yay for *you.*"

Maybe I would have said something then, or done something I regretted. But before I could respond, Gaines Alder slid up to Bronwyn, distracting her.

"Bron-Bron, purely out of curiosity, how important *is* it for you to get your deposit back on this house's rental?" he asked, stroking the approximate area of his chin were it not blocked from view by the space helmet.

When Bronwyn's pale face flushed with irritation, I knew this was my opportunity to bolt and took full advantage.

"Here." I handed Arthur my glass of Chianti.

It's possible there was a flicker of something—surprise?—in his dark eyes but I didn't bother to stick around to find out. Instead, I pivoted without bothering to say another word to him, Bronwyn, or anyone else.

I walked back out of the house. Destination: empty dorm room.

I did pause at the doorway to glance back. Bronwyn was yelling at Gaines, who took it remarkably well, like he'd had to deal with her berating him many times before.

And Arthur was watching me, his expression impossible to read.

Whatever.

None of it mattered.

So, less than thirty minutes after my arrival, I left, certain the whole thing had been nothing but a colossal waste of my time. *What could possibly come from it?*

Two

Winter break was over and Barrington Academy was exactly as I remembered: a thousand acres surrounding imposing neo-Gothic stone buildings, constructed in the early twentieth century, complete with a towering spire for the chapel and a planetarium built in the 1950s that had recently had upgrades. The dorm buildings were separated by binary gender designation, a leftover from when the school was initially an all-boys institution before being forced to go coed in the mid-eighties.

And the quad, with its pine trees and social spaces, where most of the students hang out between classes. Weather permitting.

That's where I was for my lunch hour on the second Monday since returning from my hometown of Christmas, Oklahoma.

There *were* some changes since I'd left the private prep school. Three big ones.

First of all, I was now together with Arthur Chakrabarti Watercress. Or I think I was. We hadn't actually defined our status since our first kiss on Christmas Eve, or the many that followed, but I felt that was a reasonable definition.

Second, Ayisha Lewis was now a full-fledged Barringtonian

(don't blame me, I didn't make up that name) as of nine days ago and she hadn't even experienced a speed bump in terms of popularity. Being unfairly attractive with flawless dark skin, long black braided hair, and a bone structure made for modeling definitely helped, if the expression on most guys was a clue. But Ay was much more than a pretty face. She was smarter than just about everyone in the room. Including me. She was also way better at navigating people. It was a relief to have her by my side considering how my first semester went.

And third, I had a new roommate who, as it so happens: "Never. Leaves. Our room."

I could picture her perfectly. Shoulders held in erect posture even while seated on her bed, reading. Always reading. Her red hair pulled tight into a perfect ponytail, thick-rimmed glasses sliding down her nose.

I was irrationally annoyed just thinking about her.

Ayisha gave me a look. "What do you mean?" she asked, tossing her long, dark braids over her shoulder.

The sky was dusty blue and windless. The early January sunshine made it feel warmer.

We were both in our uniforms—skirts made up of dark green, navy, black, and yellow plaid, tights, flats, navy sweaters with the Barrington crest on the left, embroidered over the heart, and a dark navy jacket—though Ayisha somehow managed to make hers look effortlessly stylish, even the tie, while I was fighting the urge to scratch against the wool.

"Exactly what I said." I sighed.

"She has to go to class," Ayisha reasoned as she rearranged the contents of her book bag.

"Right? You'd think. But she doesn't."

Her frown was skeptical. "You're telling me that, in the last nine days, your new roommate hasn't left your dorm room once?"

"Not that I've seen!" I threw my hands up in the air, attracting attention from a couple of Barrington freshmen seated on a nearby bench in the quad. I lowered my voice. "I get up in the morning and there she is, on her bed. I come back from class, there she is, on her bed. I go to the library to study, to the laundry room, to go for a run, any time, day or night, and she's always there when I leave and when I get back. Same place on her bed, too! I know her name's Petra, but I didn't realize it was because she was made of actual rock."

"You know Petra's a place—"

"Yes. I know. But *you* know what I mean." I leaned back against the concrete wall behind me, crossed my arms. "She barely talks, either. Just sits. And reads. Actual books, not on a Kindle or on her laptop."

"That sounds like a good thing," she said. "The no-talking part."

It's possible she sent me another look. Which I ignored.

"Maybe. Except it's also kind of unnerving. At least when Thea was my roommate, she felt like a normal person, who was also never there. Total bonus. I never thought I'd miss her." I leveled a look at Ayiaha. "I wish you were my roommate."

She remained suspiciously silent on that matter.

Ayisha had barely made it into Barrington this term. Not because she wasn't academically qualified—she was; more so than me—but the push to get her officially accepted (again) and enrolled had come very late, less than two weeks before school started, and when most everyone in charge was out for the break.

It was nothing short of miraculous she managed to get in at all, let alone jump through all the hoops needed to make the trek from our hometown of Christmas, Oklahoma, to the boarding school in Connecticut.

It was probably asking too much for her to also be my roommate, but I had been hoping.

Instead, I got Petra Bergerac. Who was in her junior year, like I was, though seventeen years old and had been at Barrington since she was a freshman. However, she had an open dorm spot and I guess it was determined by the administrators that me moving into her room was easier than her moving into mine. At the time I thought it was because Petra had been on campus longer and was thus more established.

Now I think it was because they knew she was basically immobile.

Ayisha grinned at me knowingly. "I think I know why you're really cranky about her."

"Why?"

"Because your boyfriend is coming back today and you want to be alone with him."

My face flushed with embarrassment. "That's not true!"

We both knew it was partially true.

Arthur had missed the first week back from winter break, which had been unexpected. For him and for me.

Today was January 12, and the last time I saw him in person was on December 28, when he and his aunt left at the end of their extended stay at my grandmother's inn. Arthur had returned to London with his maternal aunt, Esha Chakrabarti, for the remainder of the holiday.

I'd been secretly hoping his aunt would change plans to stay in Christmas at least through New Year's Eve, since she was now openly with my grandmother.

But no such luck.

Instead, Grandma Jo spontaneously hopped a plane to England—leaving my mom and dad in charge of the inn—while *I* wound up on two FaceTime calls with Arthur to celebrate the changing year in both our time zones. The second one—mine—was brief since Arthur's body clock was "at sixes and sevens" and his dark brown eyes were half-lidded throughout. But it was the thought that counted and Arthur was proving to be thoughtful.

Or, at least, he *had* been.

The last week, however, there'd been . . . a shift. Slight at the beginning, just him seeming distracted on our calls. But that led to shorter talk times. And the last three days had been texts only.

If I mentioned this to Ayisha, she would logically point out that I was in class while he was preparing to fly back from London, so there were fewer opportunities for conversation and I shouldn't worry.

I was kinda worried.

Not enough for me to vomit-text my feelings and fears, though that tipping point was inching closer. Yet enough that my mind kept swirling around little things like the length of our conversations and the tone of his voice, attempting to decipher what might exist only in my imagination. It was exhausting.

"When does he get here?" she asked.

"Today."

"I know that part. You've mentioned it a hundred times."

"Not a hundred."

"Close enough. What time?"

"He should be here by now."

It was almost one p.m. Arthur's flight got into JFK by early this morning and he was being driven from New York City to Barrington.

Which was yet another reminder that Arthur's family resided in a stratospherically different tax bracket than my own.

He'd also mentioned his plan to sleep on the ride over and then head straight to his dorm room to get it organized. I think he also wanted to see his room's condition since for the past several days it'd been left in the unsupervised care of his own annoying roommate, Landon Sinclaire, who was renowned for being a slob. Apparently that translated into a less-than-tidy dorm situation.

"He'll reach out once he's settled. Jet lag is a pain. Trust."

"Have you traveled abroad?"

"Once. To Spain, with Señora Sanz my sophomore year. When I came back, I was practically hallucinating, I was so tired."

"Oh, I remember that trip now. I wanted to go."

"Why didn't you?"

I shrugged, noncommittal. The truth was I'd been scared to travel abroad without my parents, even if it was a dream of mine.

A voice called, "Hey, Ayisha."

She and I glanced up at the same time to see a tall, curly-headed boy in the boy's version of the Barrington uniform—same colors, slacks, a jacket and tie—walk past us, his focus entirely on Ayisha. He gave a small wave to her.

She smiled. "Hey, Caldwell."

"See you at the meeting tomorrow?"

"You will."

She beamed at him and he seemed to blush with pleasure as he kept walking.

I frowned at her after he was out of earshot. "You know him?"

We both stood.

"Yeah. You don't?"

I shrugged. "I mean, I've seen him around, but we've never spoken." I think he was a senior, but I was bad about keeping up with those sorts of things. Who was in what grade, or the ever-shifting intricacies of who was friends with whom.

No interest.

Besides, they tended to change often and there were only fifty of us in each grade, two hundred students in the whole school. Then add in faculty, board members, advisors, important parents, groundskeepers, drivers . . . you get the drill. It was a lot.

"Caldwell Harrington," Ayisha said as we walked toward Tattersfield Hall. "We have Trig at first period together. He's nice." Her brow scrunched thoughtfully. "Have you noticed everyone here has names like a law firm?"

I had noticed, actually. But that wasn't what was on my mind.

"You're already making friends?" I nodded in the direction of Caldwell's retreating form.

She arched a brow at me. "Yeah."

"You've only been here a week."

"So? It's not that hard to meet people, especially when you're new."

On that, it was my time to remain suspiciously silent.

We passed a dozen more people on our way to our respective classes, Dr. Oswald's Astronomy and Astrophysics for me, and Visual Communication Design for her. About half the people we passed nodded or smiled at Ayisha, but not at me. I chose to ignore the tiny pang of what could very well be envy.

Instead, I reminded myself that I had made the decision to return to Barrington of my own volition with the goal of making my experience better this time. Of course, I hadn't envisioned what that looked like yet, but I was confident it didn't entail harboring resentment for my one friend's uncanny ability to socialize like it was her superpower.

"What meeting?" I asked instead. "That you're seeing Cadwell—"

"Caldwell."

"—at?"

"Valentine's Day Dance Committee."

I blinked. "You . . . you're already on a committee?"

"Not yet. First meeting's tomorrow at four." She smiled confidently. "*Then* I'll be on a committee."

The familiar surge of failure started to well up within me. I was a part of exactly zero committees or clubs since I'd arrived here.

Back home in Christmas, I'd been the extracurricular-activity queen. It was one of my biggest assets when applying to Barrington. Then again, things were easier back then. Homework had been a breeze, even the AP classes.

No more. All thoughts of anything other than studying had been placed firmly on the back burner as soon as I started my summer classes a few months ago and realized things had definitely changed.

But, you know what? Good for Ayisha. She had been hesitant to come to Barrington after her mother initially denied her attempts (which included being accepted!), telling her it was out of the question since Ms. Lewis needed help watching Billie and Linda, Ayisha's twin younger sisters. However, once they'd been accepted to their own music-oriented prep school not too far from here, that freed up Ayisha to pursue her own dreams.

And boy, did she!

It was a close call but there was a whirlwind of activity in the Lewis household in the days after Christmas to get her back into Barrington. And it had been a success!

Selfishly I was pleased to have my new friend with me. It had already helped ease my loneliness in a big way.

"You're really embracing the whole experience," I said.

"I worked hard for it, so, yeah." She nudged my shoulder. "You've worked hard for it, too."

I nodded, but the idea of joining anything here brought with it a queasy uncertainty that would have set off another round of self-questioning—one of my talents—but Ayisha and I had arrived at the split in the hallway where she went to her class and I to mine, making plans to grab coffee after our shared sixth period in Mr. Poisson's (pronounced PWAH-suhn) World Literature.

As I walked down the hallway to Dr. Oswald's classroom, I checked my phone to see if I'd received a text from Arthur.

Nope.

Maybe something had happened to his flight.

Or the limo that had picked him up from the airport had engine trouble or there'd been terrible traffic—always a possibility, especially on such a long drive. It wasn't the weather, unless there'd been a freak storm on the east side of the state. I hadn't checked the weather this morning. An oversight. Then again, he could have easily sent a message if that was the case.

Unless he dropped his phone in the toilet again. Was this a thing with him? I didn't know. There was so much I didn't know about him.

Which just made me excited about the opportunity to find out.

It still surprised me, how much I liked him. How thinking about him, which I did a lot, filled me with an electric sort of joy that was different from what I'd experienced while with my first boyfriend, Brody Tuck. That, I realized now, had been more about ego and pride. *Hey, everyone, look! I'm with the best-looking guy in our school! Me, the brainiac nerdy one!*

Arthur wasn't like that.

He was good-looking, but not in the way that turned heads. With him, my attraction had been more gradual, so much so I hadn't seen it coming until it smacked me over the head and left me reeling in disbelief in the middle of a reindeer ranch gift shop.

Once I'd settled in, though, I found myself falling for him more and more. I wasn't sure exactly how to define my feelings yet. I just knew it was way more than a mere crush.

Which was why not having heard from him in such a long time had me in a bit of a tizzy. Not proud of it, but there you go.

As I neared the doorway to Dr. Oswald's classroom, I took out my phone once more, sneaking in a quick peek at the screen to see if there had been any texts or voicemail messages I'd failed to catch, despite my acute awareness of every possible phone alert sound or vibration.

Nada.

I sighed and was slipping my phone back into the side pocket of my book bag when I walked into the classroom.

And that's when I saw him.

Arthur Chakrabarti Watercress.

In person.

Standing right there in the middle of the rows of desks, dressed in his full school uniform—it felt odd seeing him like that again—with his dark hair neatly trimmed since our last video chat, but otherwise looking exactly as I remembered.

And talking with Bronwyn Campbell.

Three

It's probably not a surprise to hear that I've been in a lot of awkward moments in my still-young life—please see my last Christmas experience for any number of examples—so you'd think I'd be better at handling them by now.

But no. I was not. I? Was still a dork.

I stopped in my tracks and gaped at him. Actually *gaped*. Like a cartoon.

"What—"

I didn't get a chance to finish my sentence because someone slammed into my back, sending me barreling forward into the classroom, my book bag flying off my shoulder and spilling its contents onto the floor. (Side note, I need to get better about closing that all the way.)

"Whoa!" came the sharp voice behind me, and while I was aware that another classmate continued past me, my eyes never deviated from Arthur and Bronwyn.

Now, I'm going to stop here because I know what you're thinking: *They're classmates. Classmates talk. Chill out, Finley.* And that's a perfectly logical perspective. Except I *saw* something in

Arthur's gorgeous dark eyes that made my heart sink: he looked guilty.

Of what, I'm not sure. Yet there was no mistaking the fleeting expression I saw pass over his face or how his posture tensed as soon as he saw me.

Bad sign. No one wants the person they're most excited to see tense up when the moment actually happens.

Then Arthur moved forward to help me gather my spilled books. He handed one to me and gave me a hesitant smile.

"Hello, Finley."

I took the book from him and stuffed it back in my book bag. "You're here."

"I am, yes." He nodded, then handed me another book, which I also accepted without bothering to glance at it. Was I imagining things or had his cheeks darkened with a blush? "It's good to see you."

That at least made me feel better. There were questions, though.

"Why didn't you—" I stopped when I saw Bronwyn now stood—hovered?—beside us.

"Everything *okay* here?" she asked me with a smile that could be mistaken for genuine.

"Um, yeah." I was confused. Was she talking to *me*?

"Good." Bronwyn glanced back at the boy who had bumped into me. "Gaines, you should *apologize* to Finley."

Gaines Alder—he of the astronaut Halloween costume fame—tossed his own book bag onto an open chair. He was a lanky boy, with thick sandy-brown hair he kept cut close on the sides. Right now his green eyes showed his defensiveness.

"She stopped in the doorway," he said, arms out, and I had to agree this was a reasonable point. But apparently Bronwyn did not.

"Gaines." She spoke to him like a mother to a naughty boy.

Gaines rolled his eyes, but he also turned his attention to me. His "sorry" was mostly sincere, I think, before he took his seat.

This seemed to satisfy Bronwyn, who returned to direct her smile back onto me. Which was more disconcerting than a semester of being ignored.

"I was just asking Arthur about his winter break," she said. "In your *hometown*."

My eyes widened in a surprise I didn't bother to cover as I looked at Arthur. "You told her about that?"

"No." He shook his head for added emphasis and I instinctively knew that was for my benefit.

Bronwyn clarified, "Our fathers are *friends*."

My eyes widened further. "Really?" I looked back to Arthur, whose blush deepened.

"It's a new development," he explained, shifting his feet, though his gaze that reached mine was firm.

Bronwyn waved her hand. "They're business friends, you know how it goes." I really didn't. "They *met* up over the break and got to talking. That's how I heard about Arthur's little journey to Christmas for Christmas." She giggled at the last part.

"Only the fact that I went there," he assured me with a slight haste.

"Which is enough!" she said, laughing as she reached out to tug on the fabric of his navy sweater near his shoulder. "Was it just *awesome*?"

I swallowed nervously; this was it. We hadn't talked about what he would say if anyone asked what he'd done for the break, though several times when we'd talked I was tempted to ask him what he had in mind. Now here was Bronwyn getting straight to the point and I felt unprepared.

Arthur's eyes met mine and his expression softened, causing my heart to thump a little faster.

"It truly was," he said, his tone warm.

We held each other's gaze for a beat longer than necessary,

which didn't escape Bronwyn's attention. I saw her react, albeit slightly—a tick of the head—and a part of me wanted to reach out to take Arthur's hand and turn to her and say, "Yep. We're together now."

Except I still wasn't sure that was the case and I wasn't about to discuss relationship status in our present company.

What I said was: "We had a lot of fun." Keeping it as vague as possible.

She smiled. "I'll *bet*."

My eyes narrowed as I tried to determine whether her emphasis in this instance was deliberately implying something or part of that weird vocal tick she had where she randomly singled out a word in her sentences to stress.

I never found out.

Right then, Dr. Oswald entered the classroom.

"Bon après-midi. Good day, good day," she said with her typical lack of enthusiasm evident in her French Canadian accent as she strode to the front of the room and set down her briefcase.

The students who hadn't already claimed their chairs moved to do so, including me. I barely got half a step before Bronwyn's hand came down to capture my wrist.

"Come sit near me," she said.

It wasn't a suggestion, and I was too surprised to do more than follow her to the first row. Naturally she had the first chair. I took the second, behind her.

I glanced over to see Arthur take the seat behind Gaines, across from mine in the next row, where his book bag was already resting. He was watching me, and I again saw that unsettling look in his eyes that made my stomach dip with nerves. But he quickly covered with a flash of a smile that didn't quite achieve authentic. No cheek dimple.

"Faire taire." Dr. Oswald raised her hands like she was a conductor before an orchestra, and the class quieted.

Even though this was my first official class with her, I'd seen her around the campus more than a few times.

At six feet, two inches in heels, Dr. Oswald was difficult to miss even without her honey-blonde hair piled high into an antiquated beehive hairdo. She was somewhere over forty but dressed like she'd stepped out of a class photo from the 1970s, the teacher who never smiled, made jokes, or seemed to care about much of anything not related to either astronomy or physics.

She didn't raise her voice to control her students. No need. I was pretty sure we were all intimidated.

Arthur and I both shifted our attention to the front of the room. And Bronwyn, who was in front of me, her long auburn hair tumbling down her back, which was fully in my view.

What was up with that? With her acting like we were friends?

I didn't have time to dwell (too much) on the shifting of my social situation, whatever it was, because I had to pay attention for the next fifty minutes as Dr. Oswald began her lecture.

She had gone over our course load on our first day back from winter break—from the big bang to the evolution of our understanding of galaxies to our place in the Milky Way, and many points of discussion, with a quiz every Friday over the past week's lessons, two papers that counted for a third of the grade, and at least one trip to the school's planetarium.

That was the part that had me the most excited.

I loved staring at the stars.

Arthur had missed a lot in his absence last week. It put him at a disadvantage. Although, when your mother is a professor of astrophysics at Oxford University, how much disadvantage did one really have on the subject?

Nonetheless, I planned to offer to get him up to speed, which would naturally include a lot of "together time." I hadn't gotten around to mentioning it in the few spurts of communication we'd had since I'd returned to school. The bell rang, signaling the end of class.

As we prepared to exit, I caught his attention, hoping to ask when we could talk or connect. About this class or anything.

Two things prevented that. One was Dr. Oswald asking Arthur to stay a few minutes after so she could go over what he'd missed. The other was Bronwyn slipping her arm through mine as if this was not disconcerting and propelling us both to the exit.

I glanced back at Arthur as he approached Dr. Oswald, hoping to find him glancing back at me, too, before I left.

He wasn't. He was adjusting the book bag strap over his right shoulder and facing our teacher, who had his undivided attention.

Which left me alone with Bronwyn.

Out in the hallway, she didn't drop her hold on me like I thought she would.

Lucky me.

We had the next class together as well, which meant she could keep a firm grip on me for as long as it took to travel the fifty feet to our Contemporary History class taught by Mr. Mehdi.

And she did. The question was, why? I suppose she could've gone through a transformational event over her own Christmas break, one that helped readjust her perspective and inspired her to strive to be a better person. Maybe it even involved reindeer.

I doubted it.

Then she said, "Tell me *everything* about you and Arthur," and her objective came ever so slightly into view, though the motivation was still an unknown.

"Like what?" I asked, keeping it as evasive as possible. This felt like a trap of some sort and I needed to tread carefully.

Overly dramatic? Sure. It still felt prudent.

"Like did the two of you hang *out* while Arthur was in town?" Her eyes sparkled with an intensity that undermined the cheer of her smile.

"Um, I mean, he stayed at my grandmother's inn, so, you know . . ." I shrugged, my eyes catching on the doorway of our destination. It was still an unfortunate distance away.

"The one who's his aunt's girlfriend, right?" she continued.

I blinked once as I processed the fact she knew that information.

Grandma Jo had hidden her sexual identity from most of the world, including her own family, until a couple of weeks ago, and now news of it had somehow traveled halfway around the country to slip into the conversation of a private prep school student she had never met? She'd be mortified.

I decided not to share that with her next time we talked.

Instead, I said, "Yep," to Bronwyn, and calculated that we had about thirty steps ahead of us until we arrived at our destination.

Other students swooped past on either side, though most gave her more of a wide berth than they did me.

I realized I could've asked how she knew that infor—

"Aren't you going to ask me how I knew that?" she prodded.

Okay, fine. That was the question I *should've* asked. So, now I did. "Did your dad find out from Arthur's dad?" It was the most logical line of informational transference.

"Yes! They've become *such* good friends in the last few months. Isn't that funny?"

Hilarious.

"How'd they meet?" I asked, even as I noticed a few of the underclassmen give Bronwyn and me funny looks. Clearly, I wasn't the only one who found our new association odd.

"*Here*, of course. At Barrington. When Lionel—that's Arthur's father, but I'm sure you already knew that"—I didn't. It had never arisen in any of our conversations—"came over with his wife, Bishakha, at the end of last spring semester. Apparently, Daddy met with Lionel in London this Christmas and they're looking to go into *business* together."

I frowned while my heart unexpectedly started to skip faster at the idea of Arthur and Bronwyn having the slightest off-campus association.

"I thought your parents owned a restaurant in town."

She waved that aside. "They bought it together, but it's really for Mom to run. A hobby. But Daddy is into real estate, as I'm sure you know. He and Lionel have so much in common."

She was dropping Arthur's father's given name like it was her boyfriend's. Speaking of which, I couldn't help noticing she hadn't brought up Prescott in a while.

"By the way, I don't remember, what does your father do for a living?" she asked.

"He sells insurance."

She gripped my arm and smiled. "That's so *useful*. Perhaps Daddy or Lionel can hire him once their deal is done."

That would never happen, but that was her point. She was putting me in my place.

I moved away, forcing her to release me or risk looking like she was clinging instead of holding me in my place.

"Maybe," was all I said, and I walked the rest of the way to Mr. Medhi's class on my own.

Four

The bells marking the end of sixth period interrupted Mr.
Poisson's lecture about World Literature and his impassioned
belief that it was the secret to understanding all of humanity, if we
would only pay attention!

He was a small man, not much taller than I was, but he was never
one to go halfway about any subject that moved him. Inequality.
Climate change. Billionaires trying to one-up each other in the
most obscenely costly ways imaginable.

But especially literature.

Some teachers, the older ones in particular, had gone over their
chosen subjects so many times as to wear them smooth in their
hearts, seldom eliciting a bump of interest or excitement in themselves or others. Mr. Poisson wasn't like that. His enthusiasm was
endless. I was probably four decades younger than he was, but I
envied that about him.

"Don't forget we have a test on *Chronicle of a Death Foretold*
this Friday, so everybody read up! It's a masterpiece!" He raised
his small fist in the air to emphasize his point, a shine of near-
rabid certainty in his pale-brown eyes that he hoped convinced us
to agree.

Everyone ignored him.

The last half of the last class of the day was always a challenge to hold students' attention, myself included. I knew Arthur had read this book already—he was a voracious reader—so I could ask him for tips.

We weren't allowed to have our phones out when class was in session, so the bell was like a starting gun going off for everyone to grab their mobiles as fast as possible.

I fished my cell phone out of my book bag to check for a text from Arthur.

There wasn't one.

Yes, he was in his classes, too, and was probably taking the correct action of accumulating his missed assignments and lessons, so I tried not to be disappointed.

I tried to be rational.

I tried to channel Mr. Poisson's positivity.

But my efforts were weakening with every passing minute.

Honestly? This really was starting to suck. It almost made me miss Brody, who was possibly the worst texter I had ever met in terms of clear communication, but at least he *made the effort*.

"Anything?" Ayisha asked, nodding to my phone.

"Nope."

She remained quiet, but I could tell she was as puzzled as I was. Which made me feel worse.

Although ours was still very much a new friendship, I'd already grown used to her being the voice of reason when my anxieties started to build toward a full gallop, so when she didn't tell me not to worry, I began to worry in earnest.

Super fun.

Ayisha and I had already gotten into the habit of going to the café at the bottom of Quinten Hall to grab coffee and study. But in that moment all I wanted was to go back to my dorm room, even with Petra surely there, to hide for a while.

Before I could try to stumble on some excuse, another classmate of ours whose name was on the tip of my tongue—Dexter? Deptford?—approached Ayisha to talk about their sculpting assignments, and I slipped away with a quick "I'll text you later."

She nodded once before turning back to the other student.

I was halfway to the girls' dorm in Charity House, my head down, absolutely *not* looking for any sign of a green puffy jacket belonging to a certain boy, and absolutely *not* clutching my phone in my coat pocket so I'd know instantly if there was an incoming text, when I heard my name being called.

"Finley."

I spun around to see . . . not Arthur.

It was Gaines Alder smiling in my direction as he jogged to reach me. We continued on the concrete path that led from the collection of academic buildings to the residential areas.

"I really am sorry about bumping into you earlier," he said, cinching his book bag higher over his right shoulder. His nose was slightly red from the cold.

I felt a ripple of confusion again as he shortened his strides to keep pace with me. We weren't friends. He was Bronwyn's friend. That much I knew. He functioned almost as her satellite, swirling around her with an ease that told me he had been in her orbit for quite some time. That said, he didn't immediately set me on alert like when Bronwyn was playing the "bizzarro bestie" game earlier. He had never been overtly unkind to me.

He had never been anything at all to me.

"I *did* stop in the doorway," I conceded, feeling magnanimous since at least *someone* had sought me out.

He grinned back. "Okay, right? So, I wasn't being a jerk?"

There was a friendliness to him now that I chose to lean into, partly because I really needed it at the moment, despite practically sprinting from my one genuine friend at the school only moments earlier.

"In general?" I asked. "Or about this particular incident? Because if it's the latter, then no, not as far as I'm concerned."

He cocked his head. "And the former?"

"I have no idea since we don't know each other."

He pointed to himself. "Gaines."

"That much I do know."

"Yeah?" He was back to grinning, but this time there was a hint-of-knowing quality to it.

"We had three classes together last semester," I said, though I didn't want him to think for one moment I had noticed him any more than I'd noticed any other boy. Mainly because I hadn't, but also because anything more would have felt strangely disloyal to Arthur. The boy who had yet to reach out to me since his return to campus.

"True point." Gaines glanced at me out of the corner of his eye. "What else do you know about me, Finley Brown?"

"I know we've never spoken this much before."

"Another truth. But in my defense, you don't exactly get out much."

He had me there.

And it reminded me of my goal in returning: be more social. Which really wouldn't require much effort since I'd been a border-line hermit my first semester.

"I'll give you that." I looked at him. "I also know you're Bronwyn's friend."

"Yep. The Bron and I go way back, since we were knee-high to a grasshopper, as my grandpop would say."

"Congratulations, I guess."

We neared the bridge that arched over the pond, which acted as the line of demarcation between the girls' and boys' dorms.

Gaines made no move to break off from me to go his own way.

"I know she can be a bit much sometimes, but she's really harmless." *Debatable*, I thought, but kept silent as he continued. "She's also a fantastic skier."

I frowned at him. "Random factoid, but okay."

"You'll see what I mean." He nodded with curious confidence. I frowned. "How would I do that?"

We reached the other side of the bridge.

"When you come this weekend," he said casually.

Finally, Gaines stopped walking and we faced each other.

He said, "Martin Luther King Jr. weekend. The ski trip? Everybody's talking about it."

"Not everybody, I haven't heard about it."

His surprise seemed genuine. "Didn't anyone tell you about the Barrington tradition?"

"Apparently not."

"Then, no wonder." He smiled like he'd solved a riddle. "MLK weekend is the only holiday between New Year's and Valentine's Day that we get off, so everyone heads over to Lancaster Mountain to clock in some quality slopes time."

A heaviness sank over me. This felt too much like another slight somehow, like when Bronwyn had invited every student at Barrington to go to her parents' restaurant in town to celebrate the birthday of her BFF, Josie Sutton. Well, everyone except me.

It had crushed me. Josie's birthday was the same day as mine, but also, who likes to be the one left out?

I told Gaines none of this. I said, "Oh."

"How were you planning to spend it?"

"Reading 'I Have a Dream.'"

He laughed. "No, really."

"That was really."

He blinked. "Really?"

"Really."

"Huh." He scratched his chin. "I don't think I've ever read that."

I didn't know enough about Gaines to know if this was a surprise. Was he studious? Or a goof-off? A legacy student or one who had earned his way through hard work? Did he want to be here? Did he want to learn and grow? I snuck in a glance at him now, at how the waves in his sandy hair at first appeared careless, but upon closer examination there were gleams of gel close to his temples and on their tips.

He cared more than he let on.

"You should," I told him. "It's not that long. And it's also quoted by half the world's speechwriters, so . . ."

"Bring it with you."

"Bring it where?"

"Ski trip. For the weekend." He said it so easily, but that didn't mean it made sense to me.

"I don't ski."

"They have instructors. Besides, it's about the parties and après-ski anyhow. That means 'after ski.'"

"I got that."

"You looked confused." He waved his index finger in the direction of my brows, and I realized I'd been frowning at him. I tried to stop.

"Not about the 'après-ski' part. It's about why you're telling me about the trip. We don't know each other that well."

He smirked. "You are in four of my classes *this* semester." Then he pointed at me. "And you're from that holiday town."

"Christmas, Oklahoma."

"I thought it was Kansas."

"Nope."

"Too bad. I think Christmas, Kansas, has a nice ring to it."

I sighed. Tired all of a sudden. "Gaines, why are you telling me about this trip?"

"So you'll come, of course." He jerked his head in the direction of my dorm, which was behind me. "There's a sign-up sheet for available rooms on the social board. Check it out. I promise, it'll be endless fun."

I nodded but made no further assent.

With one last grin, Gaines spun and loped back in the direction of Waller Hall, the boys' dorm.

I entered the first floor of Charity House and took a left into the common room.

It was a large, impressive space spanning most of the first floor. Wood-paneled walls. Tall windows. A scattering of tables and chairs for studying. Chocolate-brown leather chesterfield sofas and chairs that had seen a good amount of use over the years. They faced the concrete gas fireplace, which had been lit since the arrival of autumn.

I loved this area. It was one of the places that had exceeded my admittedly grand vision of what my prep-school life would be like before I arrived on campus.

The sign-up sheet was on the social board—an old-fashioned corkboard bolted to the wood-paneled wall closest to the elevator, as if the technological revolution of the twenty-first century had yet to arrive here—exactly as Gaines said it would.

The paper had a photo of a large ski lodge surrounded by snow on mountains typical of those found in New England with a white woman and man in red and light blue ski attire smiling at the camera. Probably from the Lancaster Mountain Ski Lodge website. *MLK Ski Weekend!* was in bold letters at the top.

At the bottom of the sheet were tear tabs with a printout of a website's address. The source of more information, should one be interested.

Entertaining the idea was not normal for me, which was why I was entertaining the idea. I promised myself to try harder this time around. To push myself beyond my comfort zone. Like a meme or poster or T-shirts for skydiving businesses often professed (JUMP BEFORE YOU THINK!).

The class trip to Spain that Ayisha took popped back into my head. I remembered how much I had wanted to go along.

But I hadn't.

At the time I justified my staying behind by telling myself our family didn't have the money, but I knew Mom and Dad or Grandma Jo would have found a way to make it happen if I'd really wanted it.

The truth was, I was scared. No. More like intimidated.

Kind of like I had been the first few months I spent at Barrington. Feeling as if I didn't belong, going to parties for less than a half hour before I turned around and left.

Well, no more.

This time I tore off a tab.

Five

Shocker. Petra Bergerac was seated exactly where she was when I'd left our dorm room almost eight hours earlier.

I shouldn't have been surprised. It was the same scenario every day last week. Yet I was in a bit of a mood, so it still bugged me. Especially the part where she didn't bother to look up when I opened the door and entered.

Or when I accidentally shut the door behind me with more force than was necessary.

She simply continued on with her reading, eyes focused on the pages in front of her.

Her books and her attire were the only variables she changed. Sometimes she was in plain, boxy pajamas. Going solely by the covers, her books were mostly paperback science fiction or mysteries. Always the bigger paperbacks, and she never broke the spines as she read. Once done, she placed the finished books in the large purple steamer trunk she kept at the foot of her bed and locked it up with a small gold padlock.

As if I'd steal them.

It did make me wonder what Arthur did with all the books he

read. Did he ship them home in a crate to join the no doubt stately Watercress library? Every time I pictured it, it got more and more like something out of *Beauty and the Beast*.

I kept that to myself.

I also kept at bay the part of me that wanted to say, *Hi, honey. I'm home!* in a singsong voice to Petra when I would enter our dorm room. And if we'd been friends, I would have.

We weren't friends, though.

I knew her reading habits, her sleeping habits—she seldom moved and made no noises, which was unnerving—her affinity for heather-green socks, and her plan to call home to her mother and stepfather every Sunday afternoon at two p.m. Always over the phone, never video. I'd made it a point to step outside for the first one, hoping to be seen as friendly and considerate.

She made no acknowledgment, then or yesterday, when I'd done the same again. I'd keep doing it, regardless. It was only polite.

Once she'd mentioned a stepbrother, and that her mother divorced Petra's father three years ago and remarried four months later. Presumably to the stepbrother's father. The way her lip curled when that tidbit of info had slipped out, I figured she wasn't a fan of either.

That was about it. That was what I knew.

I set my coat and backpack over the back of my chair then flopped across my twin bed, phone (with its blank screen) in hand, contemplating the wisdom of reaching out (again) to Arthur. I looked back over our past several texts, the most recent ones being perfunctory and more informational, not unlike the ones from when we first started texting each other back in Christmas.

When we were pretending not to like each other as much as we did.

"Are you friends with Gaines?"

I blinked and sat up on my elbows, not sure I heard right. Today was apparently the day for unexpected conversations.

"What?"

Petra lowered her paperback about an inch so our eyes connected across the space that separated our beds.

"I saw the two of you talking," she said, raising her index finger to point at the window facing the front of the dorm.

My new room was one floor above the one I'd shared with Thea.

"We're not friends," I told her. "But we're not *not* friends. That was pretty much the most we've talked." I sat up fully, curious. "Are *you* friends with Gaines?"

She shook her head, back to being done with me, and returned her attention to her reading. *All Systems Red*. It looked intense.

But she'd opened up a door—or portal, given her preference for sci-fi—for conversation, and I had a perverse desire to walk right through.

"Did you know about the ski trip on Martin Luther King Jr. weekend?" I asked.

"I'd heard." She turned a page.

"Are you going?"

She paused to look back at me, her auburn brow arched in what I could only interpret as a "no."

"You don't ski?"

"I ski."

That caught me by surprise. The idea of Petra being in motion to the extent of flying down a mountain seemed impossible. The idea of her walking beyond the confines of our shared living suite also seemed impossible.

She lowered her gaze yet again and turned the page, her tone impersonal. "I simply find it monumentally disrespectful to the legacy of Dr. King to engage in a wild bacchanalia on a holiday established to pay homage to one of our country's greatest humanitarians."

Well. When you put it like that . . .

I suddenly felt like a giant jerk for even considering the idea. Although "wild bacchanalia" was moderately intriguing.

My phone buzzed against my left palm. The vibration and noise startled me and I glanced down to see I had a new text.

From Arthur!

It was like a shot of adrenaline.

Ten words stared back at me: Hello. Would you like to get coffee in a bit?

I snatched up my phone and read the text four or five more times.

He wanted to meet up for coffee. How perfectly normal was that? How often had we had tea or coffee together back in Christmas?

Plus, it made sense, too. He would have returned from his classes, like I had, and maybe put away some of his belongings. Tidied up the place. He liked to keep things neat. Which meant he now had time to meet up with me. I wasn't sure how I felt coming in second to him doing chores in my imaginary list of priorities.

I'd address that later.

My thumbs flew over the screen: Sure. Quinten Hall?

He texted back: How about by the bee bridge? I can stop by Quinten Hall to retrieve a tea or coffee for you if you'd like.

I frowned. It was an odd request for a meeting spot. Then again, I wasn't sure if I was ready for the "coming out" as a couple that meeting in the full light of the coffee shop would create, so I didn't blame him for suggesting a more discreet location.

I texted: Sounds good. I'll have a small decaf coffee. Americano.

I saw the three gray bubbles on the screen pop up immediately and I bit my lip, anticipating some snarky remark about my "typical American" drink of choice.

Instead I got: See you there.

Okay, so he wasn't the most romantic texter on the planet. No *I miss you* or *It was great seeing you earlier*. But at least he had finally—*finally!*—texted me. I practically sagged with relief.

"Was that your boyfriend?" Petra surmised more than asked.

"Huh?" I asked automatically.

"You've been checking your phone every thirty seconds for the past few days, with occasional flurries of text exchanges where you smile a great deal." She shrugged. "I assumed it was your boyfriend."

"You're very observant," I said. She didn't reply. "Are you planning to be a spy for a living? Like Villanelle?"

"I'm assuming you're referring to the character in *Killing Eve*."

"That's the one."

"Villanelle is an assassin, not a spy."

"She's sort of like a spy."

"No, she isn't."

I didn't remember enough about the show to debate with her much further.

"Is it Gaines?"

And now I was back to frowning in confusion. "Who?"

"The boy you like."

I laughed. "No. I told you, what you saw was the most we've spoken. And that's mighty heteronormative of you, by the way. Assuming it's a boy. I could be gay, you know. Or bi. Or pan. Or ace."

"I suppose that's true." Her tone was impossible to read.

"Aren't you going to ask me if I am? Any of those?"

"I'll presume you'll tell me if you want me to know."

"I'm straight."

"Congratulations," she murmured, and turned another page.

I wanted to ask her how she identified, but I got the feeling my question wouldn't be well received. If she ever wanted me to know, she'd tell me. But that didn't mean I couldn't ask her another question.

"Do *you* like Gaines? Romantically?"

She met my eyes yet again, and I was reminded hers were a swirling mix of mostly greens and some browns, her mascara-free eyelashes a pale auburn that matched her brows. Normally on the occasion when I met her gaze, she was bored. At this moment, her gaze was downright piercing.

"No."

She was very firm about that. Then she reached over to take up her noise-canceling headphones and put them on, returning to her book.

I got the hint. The door to us talking further was now very much closed.

Six

There wasn't a bee this time. Maybe because it was considerably colder on this evening as opposed to the one only a month ago.

The lower half of my face was dipped against my winter scarf to keep warm but my breath was visible in tiny puffs, even against the lights from the bridge that arched over the dark pond.

I'd arrived early, mainly from nervous excitement. But that meant I was standing there a full fifteen minutes as the temps continued to drop. Rookie mistake. I had both of my gloved hands tucked under my armpits and was doing dorky little high kicks to generate warmth when I heard Arthur say:

"Hello."

I spun around to see him approaching from a different direction than I'd anticipated.

He held two steaming paper to-go cups in his gloved hands. For a moment I was reminded of when he came swooping in to my rescue at the Christmas Christmas Parade when I'd found myself cornered by Brody and my ex–best friend, Mia. It brought a smile to my face.

He brought a smile to my face.

"Hey."

For a long moment he just looked at me. Then he swallowed once and proffered my cup to me. "Here."

I took it, holding it with both hands to feel the heat through my own knit gloves, the same ones I'd worn as part of my burglar costume all those months ago.

"Thanks."

It felt wonderful and smelled equally so. But behind the aroma of coffee, I could also detect Arthur's distinct sandalwood soap and it made me want to be nearer to him.

I didn't move. This was the first real time we'd seen each other in person, alone, since the day he left Grandma Jo's inn, and I felt a surprising wave of shyness.

"It's good to see you," I said.

"You as well," he replied, his expression difficult to read.

I couldn't help noticing he made no move to step closer. Maybe *he* was feeling shy, too. Maybe he was waiting for *me* to make the first move. It wasn't unheard of.

So, I took a step forward.

Instead of softening his stance, or moving toward me in return, he dropped his gaze to the ground and tightened his hold on his cup.

It wasn't inviting, that's for sure, and I suddenly had an unsettling reminder of that look in his eyes when I saw him earlier today.

Guilty.

I felt it, though I didn't understand it.

All the giddy excitement within me vanished and suddenly a sense of alertness came over me that I tried to ignore, and failed.

I blew into the plastic lid's opening, struggling to think of something to say before landing on, "How was the rest of your day after Oswald's?"

"Good. I have all of my missed assignments. I'll go over them later tonight, arrange my schedule in order to get caught up as fast as possible."

"Sounds like a lot of study time is in your future."

"Indeed, yes. Quite a bit."

Good lord, we might as well be talking about the weather. I tried to nudge it back on track.

"Do you need a study buddy?" I asked, hopeful.

He shook his head. "No, thank you."

I was close enough to give him a tiny, teasing push against his arm. "You're supposed to say because I would be too much of a distraction."

"That's actually the point," he demurred. "I study better alone."

A long beat of silence followed, filled by a tidal wave of confusion on my part, mixed with irritation and a flutter of dread. *What was happening?* Something was off, no doubt. Panic sent my heartbeat into overdrive, like a hummingbird.

I stuffed one hand in the pocket of my coat so I could discretely ball my fist in agitation. "This is going awesomely," I managed to mutter without betraying my surge of fear.

He sighed. "I'm sorry, Finley."

He sounded contrite, which I'd only seen once from him, when he was responding to a gentle rebuke from his aunt Esha. It wasn't natural for Arthur then, but at least I understood the dynamic. Here and now? Between him and me? My warning sirens were now BLARING!

"What's going on, Arthur? You're back to being all socially awkward around me."

A bad attempt at injecting some teasing into all of this. When he bristled, I found it almost reassuring.

"I'm not socially awkward," he retorted, standing taller. "I'm British. You Americans often confuse the two."

"Harry Styles isn't socially awkward." It was the first thing that popped into my brain, don't ask me why. I wasn't a particularly big fan of the guy.

Arthur's eyes narrowed. "Have you met him?"

"No." I frowned. "Have you?"

"Once. In passing. At the British Airways first-class lounge in Heathrow. I stand by my statement." He smirked, which felt both familiar and painful.

"I feel like we're getting way offtrack here," I pointed out.

"Sorry," he repeated, his shoulders re-slumping.

Dammit.

I decided to be brave. I didn't want to be, but I also didn't want to talk about homework or Harry Styles. "And it feels like you're avoiding something. Or avoiding . . ." I took a deep breath. ". . . Me."

His answer should have been a swift *Of course not!*

Instead, he sighed. Which hurt. A lot. As did the way he dropped his gaze yet again and stuffed his hand deeper into the pockets of his puffy green jacket.

"I'm going to interpret your sigh as a 'yes.'"

I wanted to be cool in this moment, not let him know how fast my heart was racing or how tight my throat had become. However, my facade was blown when I spoke. "What did I do wrong?" And my voice broke slightly at the end.

He must have heard that. He looked up quickly and said firmly, "You've done *nothing* wrong, Finley."

"Then what is going on? We had such a good time together over Christmas. I mean, eventually. After the reindeer." I bit my lower lip. "Didn't we?"

His dark eyes softened. "We did."

"And I really liked video chatting with you once you were back in London."

"As did I," he agreed.

"But you've been distant the past few days. And today. And now. Ayisha thinks I'm being too sensitive." I watched him closely. "But I'm not, am I?"

He took a very long time before he swallowed and shook his head. "No."

Oh.

My breath left me then and I felt a slight trembling in my chest that resembled being chilled, though it had nothing to do with the winter cold.

Having my worst suspicions confirmed felt like a blow. Right up until that moment, I'd had hope. That I was being dramatic. Or insecure. Or wrong, somehow. Now I knew for certain I wasn't.

And it was awful.

My first instinct was to turn around and run away as fast as possible, before I humiliated myself by crying. A real possibility. I could feel it threatening.

I didn't, though. I stayed rooted to the spot. Hoping I could get through whatever came next with some dignity.

"I know we didn't define our—our . . ." He waved a hand between us. *Relationship* was the implication. He couldn't even say the word.

"It's only been a couple weeks, Arthur. I mean, my birthday was just a little over a month ago, when we saved the bee, over there." I pointed to the spot by the pond where I'd waded barefoot into the water and he'd helped me rescue the tiny creature.

"Ah, yes. The bee." A tiny smile quirked at the corner of his mouth in a way I adored.

Correction: *used* to adore.

"Christmas Eve was only two weeks ago. Ish," I said.

"Nineteen days, to be precise."

I almost laughed then. "You would know that off the top of your head."

"I counted."

"You counted. Because you were so happy? Or because you were . . . ?"

His expression grew hooded. "I am . . . many things." He took a sip of his coffee; it seemed like a nervous tick. I waited for him to elaborate further, but he didn't.

I did. "Including evasive."

Dark eyes flashed then. "*Including*"—he emphasized the word in a Bronwyn-like fashion—"graduating in fewer than five months." He fixed me with a pointed look, the meaning of which eluded me.

"Okay . . . ?"

"Did you realize that?"

"Honestly? I never thought about it."

"No." He shook his head to himself. "And why should you? We were barely cordial to one another before our Christmas escapade."

"So? We're in the 'getting to know you' phase of things. Or at least I thought we were, before you went all Danny Zuko to my Sandy." I tightened my grip on my own coffee, which I had yet to touch.

He scowled. "Am I supposed to understand that reference?"

"It's from the movie *Grease*. My mom loves it. Watching it with Grandma Jo is one of the few things they do together."

"I still fail to understand—"

I rolled my eyes. Naturally, the guy who'd needed help buying a pair of jeans also didn't know classic American musicals. "Danny and Sandy have a summer romance, but when they wind up at school together in the fall, he acts all cool and gives her the cold shoulder. Come on, Arthur. That movie made it to England, you have to have seen it."

He drew back as if offended. "Well, I haven't. And is that what you think I'm doing?"

"Isn't it?"

"No. Not at all!" His expression turned stormy.

"Feels that way."

"Well, I'm not."

I decided I had nothing to lose, so I came right out with it. "But we're also not going to, like, be together, are we?"

That stopped him. Hard. I felt a bitter twinge of satisfaction at watching his jaw clench shut. Not that being "right" on this subject was what I wanted, but I felt less crazy. I hadn't been imagining things.

Man, I wished I had been.

Arthur rubbed a gloved hand over his face and looked miserable. "I'm mucking this up."

"No, I think I get the picture pretty clearly," I countered, veering into babbling, an old standby of mine when anxious or upset. "The 'getting to know you' phase will forever remain cloaked in mystery, like D. B. Cooper. Or Roanoke. And that's totally fine."

"Finley—"

"Really, I'm okay. It was only nineteen days. No biggie, right? I'm cool, everything's cool." My head bobbed with nodding. "It was a holiday thing. Those never last. Well, except my grandmother and your aunt. They seem solid." My eyes narrowed. "Unless you know something I don't."

"No. Auntie is still quite keen on Ms. Brown."

"Good. Same with Grandma Jo. But that doesn't mean anything for us." My tone hardened. I waved between us. "We're not them."

"I'd like the chance to better explain—"

"Is the end result going to still be us not together?" He remained quiet, and I nodded once to myself. "Then I think we're good here." I backed several steps away from him, keeping him in my sight as I started creating the physical distance that reflected our new reality.

He made no move to stop me or to follow.

He just watched me go.

I got about ten yards before I took the hand not holding the to-go cup of Americano I would never drink out of my coat pocket and, with far more bravado than I possessed, pressed my index and middle fingers together in a jaunty salute. "I had a lot of fun with you over Christmas, Arthur. But Christmas is now officially over."

Seven

Ayisha stared at me in surprise.

"You didn't stay for more explanation?"

I flopped backward across her bed, staring up at the smooth ceiling in misery.

"What's the point?" I said, leaning heavily into my maudlin side, my voice thick with emotion.

"Explanation!"

I swiped at a traitorous tear that slipped out of the corner of my eye and lolled my head to one side so I could see her. Arms crossed, dark eyes boring into mine.

"It doesn't matter."

She raised an eyebrow. "I'm looking at your puffy face and the red splotches on your pasty skin and I'm thinking it totally does."

"He doesn't want to be with me, Ayisha. That pretty much sums it up."

Saying it aloud made it more real, and the pain hit me again like a knife right through my heart. It'd been two hours since my official dumping, and the only positive I could find was at least I'd managed to hold off from crying before I made it back into my dorm room. Where, of course, Petra was seated on her bed, reading.

As ever.

I was too upset to acknowledge her. I entered and went straight to my bed, where I lay for an hour and sniffled, stuffing down my urge to weep and longing to have my own room, even that temporary one from Grandma Jo's inn, so I could unleash the full force of my feelings in solitude. Which was impossible.

After a while, I rolled off my bed, grabbed some extra tissues, wiped my face, and went in search of my now one remaining friend at this awful place.

Ayisha had opened the door, taken one look at my face, cringed, and pulled me into her—thank you, God!—empty dorm. (Her roommate, Sable, was at a Monday church service in the chapel.) In under fifteen seconds, I had been given a bottle of water, an ice pack, and a box of exceptionally soft tissues, for which my nose was most appreciative.

Now she sat beside me on her bed. "Did he say those words? That he didn't want to be with you?"

"No." I sniffed. "He let me say them for him."

The chickenshit.

Ayisha handed me a clean tissue. "I would pay to see a replay of that conversation because I'd be willing to bet you reality-TV'd yourself into a worse situation."

"I don't watch reality TV, so I don't know what that means."

Her eyes widened in disbelief. "You don't what?!"

"It's all fake," I reasoned.

"*The Amazing Race* isn't!" Her eyes narrowed. "I may have to rethink this fledgling friendship."

Even though I was very nearly positive she was kidding, I sat upright. "No, please, Ay. I can't handle two breakups in two hours."

"Chill," she said easily, waving between us. "We're back on. But at some point, we're going to have to have a serious discussion about your choices in entertainment. And I basically said you probably caused yourself more drama than if you'd let things happen."

"Maybe. I don't know. I have a headache. I think I'm dehydrated," I complained, moving into the whiny stage of my sorrow. I took a drink from the water bottle.

Ayisha hit me with a steady gaze. "He liked you, Finley. I saw it. He even drove back in the middle of a blizzard for you. You don't do that just to end things two weeks later for no reason."

"Nineteen days," I replied, almost to myself, putting the cap back on.

"Whatever." She tapped a long, perfectly manicured nail (navy blue this week) against her lower lip. "*Something* happened after he went home and I think you should find out what it was."

"No." I shook my head in firm refusal. "I didn't come back here because of Arthur and I'm not going to let him distract me from what I want to accomplish. I came back here for *me*, to be successful on *my* terms. If I can. Somehow." I balled up the now wet, snotty tissue, tossed it in the trash can, and grabbed another.

"That's very empowering," she said as she eyed the near-capacity trash can.

"I feel like you're maybe mocking me a little."

"No, I'm serious. I mean, most of what you said is probably a lie but given everything, I get it." A small smile started around her eyes. "I also have an idea."

My suspicions grew. "For which part?"

"How to distract yourself from this trauma-drama that totally doesn't matter to you, but really does, *and* get more involved in school."

"I don't remember saying I wanted to get more involved in school."

"You do."

"I do?"

"You do. The best thing for heartache is activity. You get going on a million different things and you won't have the time or energy to wallow in feeling bad."

That made sense. And I'd certainly used that strategy before. Heck, it was part of the reason I'd agreed to help take Arthur and his aunt around my hometown, as a way to not think about what had been going on between my parents as well as Brody and Mia while I'd been away.

Great. Now I was thinking about Arthur again.

"Fine. I'll bite. What do you have in mind?"

Ayisha's smile turned klieg light bright, fueled by self-satisfaction.

"Valentine's Day Dance Committee!"

Barrington had three official big events organized by students (with some guidance from a designated member of the faculty): Homecoming in the fall, Prom in mid-spring, and the Valentine's Day Dance.

I'd missed going to Homecoming entirely, using my time to work on a paper instead.

Total excuse to not go?

Yes. But I'd just received a midterm C in Microbiology and hadn't cared about missing an important social event. Given how I barely managed a B by the end of the fall semester, I probably could've gone to Homecoming without much effect on my overall grade. Who knows? Maybe I would've made more friends then. Afterward, I heard other people talking about what an amazing time it was, with the room decorated to look a football field, complete with staged areas with real orange and yellow leaves strewn about to create the perfect autumn backdrop for photos.

Bronwyn had led the committee in charge of creating the dance and by all accounts it was the best anyone had ever experienced. Rumor had it that her parents had helped pay for some of the more spectacular parts (live DJ, pots of actual apple trees still bearing fruit, photos with the head coach of the UConn Huskies football team, et cetera). She had not been shy about accepting full credit. Of course. The thought of now helping her put together a Valentine's Day event made my stomach sour.

I stared at Ayisha. For a long time.

Full of dread.

She rolled her eyes at me. "Finley, there are two thoughts when it comes to learning how to swim: Take your time easing into the shallow end until you get comfortable before slowly moving into deeper water. *Or?* Dive in the deep end and learn real quick. You already tried the first way and we both know how that wound up." She reached over to drape her arm across my shoulders. "Now you're gonna try mine."

Eight

So, that was it. I wasn't together with Arthur anymore. Not that we'd officially *been* together, mind you. But we definitely weren't now.

And I was fine. Totally fine.

No, really.

I'd once read breakups were so painful because the brain produced so much serotonin while in love that it was like being a drug addict, and the end of love was akin to an addict going through withdrawals. It hadn't made sense to me at the time. Boy, did it make sense now.

Not that what Arthur and I had was love!

I think.

Maybe.

It was too soon for that . . . wasn't it? To be saying "the 'L' word"? Of course, how many songs and poems were written about love at first sight? And we hadn't had that. We'd known each other for months first. Hadn't particularly liked each other for those months.

Or, more accurately, *I* hadn't liked *him*.

Turns out, he had been crushing on me since Bronwyn's

infamous Halloween party, specifically when I had mentioned knowing the Nick Bostrom paper. He'd dropped that surprise nugget of info on me when we were still at the Hoyden Inn over Christmas break, sitting out in the back by the firepit. It had been our go-to for alone time, especially later in the evening after everyone else had gone to sleep. We would sneak into the kitchen, make cups of cocoa or tea, then grab a couple of fleece blankets and snuggle closer together beneath the sky full of the moon and stars.

"*That* was what made you notice me?" I asked with a laugh after his confession.

He was adorable in the flickering glow of the firelight as he shrugged. "I'd never met anyone else who'd even heard of Nick Bostrom," he told me. "Let alone knew his theory well enough to grasp the reference."

Snuggling even closer, I whispered, "Our future overlords clearly designed it as a modern-day glass slipper."

"Our future overlords are quite mad," he whispered in return, leaning in until our lips were only a couple inches apart.

"Our future overlords know us very well."

"They should; we are their creation, after all."

I laughed again, softly. He touched his nose to mine.

"What do you think they have in mind for us right this very minute?" I murmured, deliberately leading him.

"I have something of an idea," was his reply before he kissed me.

It had all been so perfect.

Which made his abrupt breakup even more of a mystery.

Ayisha was right, I should have stayed to find out what had happened to change things. It had been too humiliating, though. In the white-hot horror of the moment, all I'd wanted was to hit "release" on the proverbial escape pod and jet the heck out of there before I made a fool of myself by bursting into mortifying tears.

That was for later.

Now I regretted running away. I couldn't do anything about it, couldn't come up to him and say, "I know we just broke up but could you maybe provide some more details as to what led you to make this decision?"

I leaned my head against the wall at the back of Mr. Poisson's classroom and sighed for quite possibly the thousandth time that day.

I don't know what I was doing here. Well, that's not entirely true. I was here because Ayisha said distraction would help. I had reservations on that point since my "distraction" was centered around Valentine's Day, a day dedicated to romance and love.

But I did have one friend who was trying to help me and I would be there for her like she'd been there for me. This committee was important to her. I could tell by the gleam in her eyes any time she'd mention it.

When I asked her yesterday why, she'd been blunt: "Finley, you're white. It's different for you. I have to be twice as good, work twice as hard, achieve at least twice as much before I'm considered half as accomplished. You know way too many of these people here think I only got into Barrington because of some damn quota."

I wished I could argue against her point, but I knew she was right. Look at Michelle Obama. She was brilliant, beautiful, accomplished, poised, and amazingly scandal-free all eight years in the White House. Yet as soon as she suggested kids should eat better food and get moving more—which was totally basic—some people lost their minds. Hopefully that would one day change.

Until then, committees and extra classes and connecting with as many people as possible were part of her plan to make something of herself. To be better. To go further than people expected a girl—a Black girl—from Christmas, Oklahoma, would go.

Today, this meeting, was another step.

The desks had been rearranged into a circle and I had an empty seat on either side of me. There were about ten students from various grades already gathered. I knew most of their names but not much beyond. That included that Caldwell guy, whose attention was firmly on the doorway. I knew who he was hoping to see. And I knew when Ayisha arrived by the way his face lit up.

A perverse pride went through me when Ayisha only waved to him when he indicated the desk beside him was open and instead chose to plop down in one of the two beside me.

Ayisha slapped a flyer onto my desk. It was identical to the one in our dorm tower about the ski weekend.

She looked at me. "What do you think? You wanna try to get a room at the lodge and go?"

"Together? You and me?"

She set her backpack at her feet. "Unless you have one of those magical credit cards that your parents pay off for you without any questions and you want to get us two rooms."

"Only law-firm-named kids have those."

She snorted in amusement and I felt the first lightening in my heart since the Arthur Abandonment.

"I have some money saved up from working at your grandmother's place," she said.

"Me too."

"Cool. So? You wanna go?"

"I don't ski."

She shrugged like it was NBD. "Me either. We'll hang out at the lodge bar drinking hot drinks."

"You think we'll be allowed at the bar?"

"Only one way to find out. And this isn't Oklahoma. Near as I can tell, folks aren't as uptight about things like teens in bars, or alcohol in grocery stores."

"Again, you've been here for a hot second and you already know these things. How?"

She tapped her temple. "I pay attention, little one. Like when Mamma took me to La Belle's when she brought me up here. That's a local restaurant," she explained.

She didn't need to. I knew my expression darkened when I said, "Yeah, I know. Bronwyn's parents own it."

"It's nice."

"*That,* I wouldn't know," I said with more bitterness than I intended.

She arched a perfectly sculpted brow at my tone. "Do you want me to continue with this story, or would you rather mope about how you were dissed on your birthday?"

"Proceed." I rolled my hand.

"Thank you. Where was I?"

"It's 'nice.'"

"*Fancy* nice. You can tell they didn't skimp on the decor. And they don't have a problem with people around our age hanging out in the bar. Kellen Henry-Woods said it's the same at the lodge."

I had no idea who Kellen Henry-Woods was but they were apparently in the know.

Being able to hang out in the bar area pre- or post-skiing wasn't my concern, though. "Are you sure about going this weekend?" I asked.

"What do you mean? Everyone's going."

"I know, but . . . I mean, it's kinda . . . disrespectful, don't you think?"

"Why?" Then her face lit up with understanding. "Oh, you mean because it's Martin Luther King Jr.'s holiday?"

"Yes . . . ?"

She shifted to face me fully, one arm on the back of her desk chair, the other on the desktop. "Do you stay home on Memorial Day?" she asked pointedly.

"Sometimes."

She scrunched up her face in contemplation. "Okay, yeah, you would. But not always." She pointed at me knowingly. "Like last Memorial Day, when you went to the lake to celebrate your coming here early."

"You remember that?"

"Mia posted a lotta pictures," she said drolly in supreme understatement.

My former best friend, Mia Gurdowitz, was renowned for her love of selfies, with or without others. That particular weekend she'd made a point to throw me a party before I went to Connecticut and ultimately Barrington and she had gone to town on the pics. Later she'd gone to town on my ex-boyfriend, Brody, but that was another story.

"Point I'm making is, that holiday was created to honor the military members who've died for our country, and I'm gonna bet y'all didn't do any of that when you were hanging out at the lake, did you?"

I bit my lip. She nodded, self-satisfied.

"So, you don't think we should honor Dr. King?"

"Yes, we absolutely should! That man is a huge part of why I get to sit here right now and I will be forever grateful. But"—she held up a finger—"that doesn't mean I can't *also* go *not*-skiing this weekend with my friend who seriously needs a diversion right about now." Her eyes danced with merriment and I had never been more grateful that she had taken that job at my grandmother's inn over Christmas.

I felt better, one smile at a time.

I could do this.

"Okay," I said, determined. "Let's go *not*-skiing together this weekend."

She reached out and we fist-bumped, sealing our deal.

Then we both faced forward as Josie Sutton and Gaines Alder (who waved and smiled at me) both entered the classroom to take two of the last three chairs in the circle. I unconsciously braced myself because I knew that where those two were, a certain someone would likely be nearby.

When Bronwyn failed to appear after almost a full minute, I started to relax.

Big mistake.

I heard her laugh from all the way out in the hallway, and, foolishly, I glanced out the open doorway.

And there she was, laughing with her hand on Arthur's arm. What was worse was the fact he was smiling in return.

With cheek dimple.

Nine

As it turns out, it's difficult to pay attention to the jabber of a meeting centered around a Valentine's Day dance while your mind is a swirling hot mess of emotions, ping-ponging speculation, and the heart-pounding rage that comes with a newly realized sense of betrayal.

What. The actual. Fuck?!

That was flirting! I knew what flirting looked like, and that was absolutely, most definitely flirting! At least on Bronwyn's part. (Seriously? What happened to that Prescott guy?!)

When it came to Arthur, though, it was more ambiguous, if I was willing to overlook the cheek-dimple smile, which I 100 percent was *not*. I felt that was something that should have been reserved for *me*.

Apparently, it wasn't. Apparently, Arthur was now being liberal with his smiles.

Or maybe he wasn't. Maybe he did only reserve them for the girls he liked, and now Bronwyn was one of those.

While I wasn't.

Not anymore.

Back in Oklahoma, he'd been crystal clear about his disdain for Bronwyn. I wasn't sure how or when his opinion had changed, given he was in London since the end of December and I knew for a fact she had been here in Connecticut since most everyone returned on January 4. But given what I'd just witnessed, coupled with how things went down last night, it was obvious some sort of change had taken place.

Right under my nose.

Having Bronwyn enter the meeting as if she had been the one to instigate it and assume a leadership position over the proceedings did NOT help my whirling dervish thoughts and anger.

I stared at her for so long without blinking that when I did blink, it hurt. My eyeballs were Sahara-level dry. Couldn't tell you what she said. Her words came out indistinct and irrelevant, like she was a teacher in a Charlie Brown cartoon. At least to my ears. To the rest of the group, she was speaking coherent sentences, and if Ayisha's darkening expression was a clue, she was being her usual imperious self.

"Excuse me, Ms. Martinez?" Ayisha said, interrupting Bronwyn and drawing attention. Which was what brought me back into the moment. "Isn't this the first meeting of the Valentine's Day Dance Committee?"

Ms. Martinez sat in a desk opposite me and Ayisha, beside Bronwyn.

Sonya Martinez was a pretty woman in her forties. My guess was on the early side since she still tended to smile often. It made her seem youthful. She kept her long, dark hair in a neat plait down her back, favored colorful pantsuits, and was easily the most popular teacher at Barrington.

She smiled warmly. "Yes, Ayisha. It is."

"So, that means we haven't actually chosen the person to lead this committee, correct?"

A silence fell over the room followed by a flurry of wide-eyed glances as her implication became immediately clear to all.

I sat up straighter in my desk, newly interested.

"That's true, we haven't," Ms. Martinez agreed.

Bronwyn leaned forward with the intention of nipping this potential insurrection in the bud. "You're super new here, so you don't *know*, but I was the co-leader of Homecoming, the Valentine's Day Dance, and the Spring Formal my *freshman* year, and the *leader* of all three last year."

Josie added, "And she led, like, *the* greatest Homecoming this year."

A couple of other students nodded.

"But now we're in *this* year," Ayisha pointed out, unfazed. "And I've led more committees than I can count. Including Homecoming and Valentine's Day."

"Yes, but there's a substantial *difference* between Podunk, Oklahoma, and Barrington."

Ms. Martinez raised her left index finger in the air. "Tone, Ms. Campbell." She may have been one of the more well-liked faculty members, but she wasn't going to let that fly.

"Sorry," Bronwyn said, clearly not at all sorry.

"It's Christmas, Oklahoma," I interjected.

"Oh, that's right. You two"—Bronwyn waggled her finger between Ayisha and me—"are both from that *awesome* holiday town. How fun."

Guess the lovefest between me and Bronwyn was officially over. *Thank God.*

Ms. Martinez focused on the group. "Ayisha brings up a good point. We should take a vote as to who will lead the dance committee."

"But—"

"It's fair."

Bronwyn crossed her arms and huffed in irritation, not interested in "fair."

Josie and Gaines exchanged surreptitious "yikes" glances.

I smiled internally (and possibly externally, too).

Ms. Martinez addressed us. "By show of hands, who would like to be the leader of the committee?" As expected, Bronwyn and Ayisha were the only two with hands in the air. "Okay. Hands down. Now, let's make this simple. Who would like to see Bronwyn lead this committee?"

Only five hands went up: Bronwyn, Josie, Gaines, and two students I barely knew (Pashley Pashei and Hawley Chen). This was as much of a surprise to Bronwyn and her clique as it was to the rest of us who'd assumed a lopsided victory in Bronwyn's favor.

Ayisha smirked.

Ms. Martinez nodded. Hands were lowered. "And who would like to see Ayisha lead the group?"

Again, five hands—me, Ayisha, Caldwell, Nolan Zhào, and Eadrich Pinto—went up. Which meant we had:

"A tie."

Gaines muttered softly, "Uh-oh."

Which earned him a searing glare before Bronwyn huffed again. "Clearly, then, *seniority* should prevail."

"We're the same age," Ayisha pointed out.

"I mean 'seniority' in terms of *experience* leading committees."

"We pretty much have the same experience there, too."

"Here." Bronwyn waved her hand over her head. "At Barring*ton*."

Ayisha cocked her head. "Oh? Like a legacy advantage? Just because you were here first, you get to lead? How not surprising."

Bronwyn turned red and Ms. Martinez held up her hand.

"We will have co-leads of the committee. Bronwyn and those who voted for her will be in charge of securing the venue and acquiring the agreed-upon decorations as well as agreed-upon beverages. Ayisha and all those who voted for her will be in charge of the music, the agreed-upon food, and party favors. *Both* groups will work together to come up with the theme and types of food and beverages, as well as types of decorations and ticket sales. Is that clear?"

We all nodded our heads.

Twenty minutes later, we were all frustrated. Including Ms. Martinez.

We hadn't even agreed upon a theme for the dance, which couldn't be blamed on the power struggle between the Dueling Alpha Girls. That happened when ten people tossed around ideas that everyone else shot down because they wanted their own instead.

"Love Is in the *Air*," Bronwyn suggested without it sounding like a suggestion. "We can put heart-shaped balloons in baskets, like *mini* hot-air balloons, on tables throughout the venue and have people put their Valentine's Day cards *in* each one and people have to find the ones with their names on the front envelope."

She smiled like it was genius, but received looks of confusion from the group, including Josie and Gaines.

I was relieved not to be the only person who didn't understand any of that.

Ayisha forged ahead into the silence. "I did some research into ideas about love"—Bronwyn snorted. Ayisha ignored her—"and the ancient Greeks had eight words they used for different types of love." She glanced down at her notes, because of course she had notes. "Eros, pragma, philia, ludus, agape—"

Bronwyn leaned forward. "We're trying to find a theme, not do homework."

"And, like, no one speaks ancient Greek anyhow," Josie added, waving her hand.

"Obviously." Ayisha glared then looked at the rest of the group. "I was thinking we could give their meaning and maybe add other definitions of love, too, all around." She made a swirling gesture with her finger. "And make the theme about the different types of love."

I thought that could be kind of interesting—I had never heard of different types of names for different types of love. But before I could voice my support:

"It's too complicated," Bronwyn declared with conviction. "Dance themes should be basic." She said it like the verdict was final.

Then Gaines jumped in with, "Love Rocks!" and Ayisha's idea fell by the wayside.

"Boring," countered Bronwyn.

Gaines deflated, ever so slightly.

Nolan, a plain boy with a birthmark vaguely shaped like Florida on his left cheek, said, "Sweethearts Dance." His brown eyes shone with excitement. "We can have the sweetheart candies everywhere."

"That was last year, Nolan," Bronwyn said with a dismissive wave.

"But it was really good," the now dejected Nolan muttered.

"Wine and Roses," Josie tossed out.

"No alcohol," was Ms. Martinez's quick reply.

"Stupid Cupid," said Pashley, after my own hurting heart.

"Let's keep it positive," Ms. Martinez redirected.

"X-O-X-O," was Gaines's new suggestion. "Like in *Gossip Girl*."

"Reboot or OG?" asked Caldwell, genuinely curious.

Gaines frowned. "It's in both, isn't it?"

"I only watched the original." Caldwell volunteered, focused on Ayisha. "For Isabel Coates."

"Stay on topic," said Ms. Martinez.

"Love Bites," Ayisha tried again, ignoring Caldwell's dreamy gaze. "We can make it a love-themed food tasting, have local restaurants donate dishes and have all proceeds go to a shelter."

"Messy and expensive." It was Josie's turn to shoot Ayisha down.

"I like the idea of food," I said, backing Ayisha.

"It's a *dance*, not a fundraiser," Bronwyn countered. "Plus, we don't have enough time. If we were going to do that, we should've started last semester."

Ayisha and I exchanged glances.

"Crush," was Pashley's next sad suggestion. "Or 'Crushed.' Or 'Crushing'."

"Those could be taken *two* ways," said Bronwyn.

Which was probably Pashley's point, Bronwyn, I thought in silent defense of the girl with the slouchy shoulders.

"Let's keep going," said Ms. Martinez.

We kept going.

"Valentine's Cards, but with poker!" Hawley grinned. "Get it?"

"No gambling." Ms. Martinez shook her head.

Hawley slumped.

"Red Hots," Nolan tried again, sticking with the candy theme.

Josie scowled at him. "That's it?"

He shrugged. "They're delicious."

"Love *Is* Beautiful," Bronwyn tried again.

"Speaking of vague and obvious," was Ayisha's retort, earning a fresh sneer.

"Love Is Love," came the suggestion from Eadrich Pinto, a tall boy with red earspools, a rare self-adornment outside of earrings that the school reluctantly allowed after threats of lawsuits a few years ago on the basis of gender discrimination against boys. He ran the Barrington Queer/Straight Alliance.

"A theme already used back in 2015," Bronwyn informed us with a special look for Ayisha. "That's why it's *important* to have committees led by someone with experience."

Ayisha rolled her eyes.

"Love Is Blind," Gaines said. "Like the reality show."

"Love Is a Battlefield," said Pashley. *(Who hurt you?)*

"Love Is You." Caldwell looked at Ayisha.

"Love Is Like a Box of Chocolates." Guess who?

"We'll be here all day at this rate," Josie groaned. "Everyone's got their own version of 'Love Is . . .'"

That was when I felt a curious tingle of what could be inspiration. "Maybe that's it," I said. "Have the theme be *Love Is . . .* And let everyone come up with their own answer?"

Full disclosure, I was as much trying to bring this exercise to its conclusion as I was inspired.

But a smiling Gaines snapped his fingers and pointed at me. "I like it!"

"And we can wear name stickers with the word we choose," Ayisha mused.

"Within reason," said Ms. Martinez.

Perhaps sensing the shifting tide in the group, Bronwyn offered, "We'll have someone from faculty prescreen the answers."

"Yes. That could work," Ms. Martinez agreed, earning a smile from Bronwyn.

And the next thing we all knew, our Valentine's Day Dance had its unanimously agreed-upon theme: *Love Is . . .*

Personally, I already had a favorite word for the fill in, but there's no way I'd earn the teachers' approval.

Ten

You know that thing where you don't want to meet someone, so you keep seeing them everywhere, which sucks to high heaven, as my great-grandmother Beryl used to say (the "high heaven" part, not the "sucks")?

Well, it becomes infinitely worse when you literally *run into* that person you're trying to avoid. To the point a soft "oof" comes out of your mouth and you step away smelling the spicy/woodsy scent of his expensive soap. Caswell-Massey. Sandalwood, to be precise. (I *may* have asked Arthur about the brand once, with the idea being to buy a bar of my own to have handy when he was away, and yes, that's borderline creeper, but it's also a really good soap.)

I had just walked out of Yarley Hall, post–committee meeting, planning to wait for Ayisha to finish getting details from Ms. Martinez, and was not paying attention to where I was going when: *Bam!*

Arthur and I both staggered backward. Thankfully there were no other students to see the collision.

"Finley." Arthur said my name almost as if it were part of a

gulp. He knelt to pick up the well-worn book he'd been holding: *One Hundred Years of Solitude*. He had Mr. Poisson for a different hour, in the morning, and probably was on a Gabriel García Márquez kick after ripping through Poisson's other assignment.

That would be so like him.

Maybe.

How would I know?

What I *did* know was adrenaline was shooting through me. Always a straight ticket to the "Finely's going to act like an awkward dork now" part of a conversation.

I did not disappoint.

"Yep." I tucked the same strand of blonde hair over one ear. Twice. "That's my name." I legitimately bit my lip to keep from adding a wholly unnecessary "woo-hoo!" at the end there. My cheeks burned all the same.

He swallowed and appeared uncertain before he said, "Hello."

"Howdy." I jerked my thumb over my shoulder, in the direction of Yarley Hall and Mr. Poisson's classroom. "She's in there," I said. "Finishing up some things with Ms. Martinez."

"Who?"

"Bronwyn." Christ, was he going to drag out the agony for me by making me say her name? It was hard enough to maintain some semblance of cool while being this close to him. (Or at least I was pretty sure that's what I was doing.)

"Ah." He frowned for a long moment. "I'm sorry, but why are you telling me this?"

I shrugged to keep it casual. "Just being polite. Making conversation. As two people do."

"I see." His gaze slid off to one side and his frown deepened. "I feel as if I'm missing something . . ."

"Really? That's funny. Because *I* feel the same way. Like I missed a lot." *Why you felt the need to break up with me when I thought things were going great,* I added to myself. *And how Bronwyn managed to paint herself into the picture.* "Not that it matters." I deliberately sounded bored as I gestured between us. "Because we don't matter."

He went rigid.

I felt immediate remorse. That *had* been harsh. And I didn't want to be harsh with him. Despite being really, really upset, it was still Arthur. With his soulful eyes and great hair and—

"Fin!" a voice called out.

Arthur and I turned at the same time to see Gaines jogging toward us, a big smile on his face. He nodded to Arthur. Friendly.

"Hey, CW."

If looks could kill, I'd have to call 911 to have someone carry away Gaines's lifeless body. Smoke was practically coming out of Arthur's ears.

"I've told you before, Gaines. Don't call me that."

"Relax. It's just a nickname."

"I'm well aware. Now would be a good time to please note that I've not used one with you."

"Uh-huh, okay. Good talk." Gaines pivoted his attention fully on me. "Hey, nice job in there, Fin. You saved the day."

I smiled. "Thanks." Now was *not* the time to also mention I hated being called "Fin" by people who didn't know me well.

"Your idea was easily the best. Simple. And no association with cheesy TV shows." His smile was self-deprecating, and, sure, my sudden coquettish swaying might have been somewhat (completely) for the audience of a certain Chakrabarti Watercress, but I felt as if I'd earned the right to lay it on thick.

"For what it's worth, I liked X-O-X-O." I smiled.

"Right?" Gaines laughed. "But your idea was much better."

Arthur cleared his voice. "And what idea is that?" he inquired, glancing between us.

Gaines looked back at Arthur. "Oh, now we're having a group chat?"

Arthur's jaw hardened. "You did interrupt my conversation with Finley."

There was a protective way he emphasized my full name, as if he knew it was my preference, though we had never discussed it. And if the circumstances had been different, I might have found it pleasing. But the circumstances were not different. And I didn't.

"I don't know," I said. "I feel like *our* conversation was already headed toward its natural conclusion."

Gaines grinned in triumph. "See?" It was a little smug.

I wasn't expecting Arthur to have a reaction. Not really. He was the one who ended things. That implied a certain "doesn't care anymore" outlook to our former . . . whatever.

So, imagine my surprise when I caught sight of a slight wince before the walls came up and he covered it with an unreadable expression.

A tiny arrow of sympathy pierced my heart, spurring the need to make amends for causing him any maybe-pain before I could stop myself.

"Gaines and I were in the Valentine's Day Committee meeting," I explained. "We were coming up with ideas for the theme."

To his credit, Gaines smiled amiably to Arthur. "And Fin here saved the day by thinking of a theme that we all actually agreed on. A Valentine miracle."

"What is it?" Arthur asked. "The theme?"

"*Love Is*, dot-dot-dot." Gaines rolled his hand. "You know, like—"

"An ellipsis, yes, I grasp the concept."

I took over. "The idea is each attendee can add the word they think completes the sentence at check-in."

"Provided it clears faculty approval, which takes a lot of the fun out of it." Gaines grinned.

Arthur slowly nodded, processing.

I decided to keep the lighthearted tone going. "This gives you three weeks to come up with something clever," I told him.

Right then Bronwyn approached us, having just exited Yarley Hall, casually interjecting, "He's not going to be at the dance," as if she were the keeper of his schedule. That and the smile she directed at him made my already stressed-out heart start to beat faster than ever. "Unless you can be in two places at the same time," she added with a chuckle.

There was an implied intimacy in how she spoke to him and that tiny arrow of sympathy from a moment ago abruptly shattered into a thousand pieces.

"What does she mean?" I asked Arthur, unable to fully keep the extent of my ire out of my voice. If his sheepish expression was any indication, he'd heard it.

"I have . . . plans. For, um . . ." He cleared his throat again. "Valentine's Day."

Perhaps you've heard the phrase *Well, knock me over with a feather?* That was me.

"Oh. Okay." I bobbed my head like a nervous cockatiel. "Well, huh. Congrats. I guess." That last part was accompanied by a hand wave in his direction.

"Congrats for—?"

"Having an actual date on Valentine's Day, instead of going to a stupid dance. Totally the better deal. I mean, I know if *I* get a boyfriend between now and then, I will *absolutely* ditch the dance to do something with him."

Arthur drew back slightly. "Oh, will you?" His tone was positively frozen.

Which, how dare he! This was all *his* doing!

"Yes. I will," I said. "Because that's what you *do* when you're officially together with someone, you spend time with them."

"Thank you for the elucidation," he shot back.

"Anytime, since you apparently need it."

His eyes flashed. "I'm sorry? I need to be told how to be a proper boyfriend, is that what you're saying?"

"I wouldn't know since you're *not* my boyfriend." I turned to Bronwyn, who, along with Gaines, was watching the back-and-forth between me and Arthur like we were participating in a game of lawn tennis. Which people in her daddy's tax bracket probably grew up playing at their summer house in the Hamptons. I pointed. "Maybe *she* can answer the question."

"What do I have to *do* with this?" she said innocently. Too innocently, in my mind.

"Oh, please. Like you two weren't engaged in high-octane flirtation right before our committee meeting." Somewhere in the foggy back row of my consciousness I had enough self-awareness to recognize I'd just successfully blown past my earlier attempt at "semblance of cool." *Might as well double down*, said no one without later regrets. "I'm just impressed with the speed you managed to accomplish the seamless transition. Bravo."

I applauded in his direction.

"There has been no transition!" Arthur snapped. "And 'high-octane flirtation'? Really?"

"Just calling 'em as I see 'em."

"Then you, Finley Brown, had best get your eyes examined."

Gaines raised his hand to point at Bronwyn and himself. "Um, should we go . . . ?"

"No!" Arthur and I shouted at him in unison, then faced each other.

"I'll go," he said.

"Not if I don't go first."

"It's not a competition, Finley."

"I didn't say it was. *Arthur.*"

Arthur rolled his eyes, spun on the heel, and walked swiftly away in the opposite direction from me without a backward glance.

I turned my glare to Bronwyn. "Happy?" I asked, but didn't bother to stick around for whatever reply she happened to give.

Eleven

It had been a long week. And I really wanted to get as far away from Barrington and Arthur Chakrabarti Watercress as possible.

So, when the predawn alarm rang on Saturday morning, I hit the "stop" button after the first volley of bells and rolled out of bed. Bags were packed. Travel clothes set out. Showered the night before.

I was ready.

Because today I was going skiing.

Or, you know, going to a ski resort where I would mostly observe *other* people skiing. And consider taking part. Maybe. It was still up for debate.

I'd warned Ayisha about the possibility of me taking the "not" part out of our "not ski trip," and she said, "You can. *I'm* not gonna to do anything 'fun' that has a hospital waiting at the end."

She had a point.

Yet a restless part of myself wanted to shake things up. Knew I *needed* to shake things up, to get out of my funk. Classes had gone well, so a plus. Sure, it was the second week back, but compared to my first weeks last semester I was in much better shape. Heartache helped my focus.

And the thought of getting away at the end of the week was a big perk, too.

I'd pre-bought a package where I could rent equipment from the lodge and get an hour-long lesson from one of their instructors.

Mainly I was going on the trip for the cozy. After the week I'd just had, cozy sounded freakin' a-mazing. Snow on a mountaintop? Me holding a ceramic campfire mug? A fire in a large fireplace somewhere?

Sign. Me. Up.

As one who grew up in the flats of Oklahoma, going skiing wasn't something my family did. Grandma Jo was always working or going shopping in Dallas (which will always have a new connotation for me now that I knew what—and who—she was really doing), and my parents weren't what one would consider "athletic." Skiing was something other people did.

Rich people.

Which the Brown family was not.

We were solidly middle class, not rich.

These people I went to school with? Most of them were rich in a way that felt made up. Like, people today really had butlers? And servants? That felt fake, like something out of *Downton Abbey*.

And yet here I was, going on a ski trip right along with them.

I was excited.

Ayisha had taken charge (surprise) of securing one of the last available shared rooms at the lodge. Thankfully it was just the two of us. If I'd tried to make arrangements, with the way my luck had been going lately, we would've wound up in a dormitory with a half dozen kids who farted and snored the whole time.

I wouldn't have worried about running into Bronwyn. Nope. She had announced in our World Lit class that she'd rented one of the cabins, which were stationed in a semicircle around the lodge's main building. Because of course she did. That meant she technically wasn't on a Barrington-sponsored trip and was thus not subject to the same rules as the rest of us.

Even the elite had their hierarchy. We "peons" were staying in the main lodge.

Ms. Martinez, Dr. Oswald, and Mr. Poisson were our official Barrington supervisors. I was kinda curious what Oswald would look like in a non-astronomy setting. It was difficult to picture. Gaines said she didn't come the last two years that he'd gone, so he couldn't help me get an idea.

Gaines had joined me at lunch in the quad the day after our dance committee meeting/Arthur argument. He didn't bring up the latter, thankfully, and gave me more of the lowdown about what to expect over the MLK weekend.

"Ski Saturday day, party Saturday night. Rinse, repeat until we head home."

"Won't the teachers catch us if we party?"

"They haven't yet," he assured me as he stole one of the fries off my plate.

That day Ayisha had been on her phone elsewhere when he stopped by, so it was just the two of us. He was being friendly but not flirty, so I wasn't bothered.

And he'd seemed more genuine this time. It probably helped that "the Bron," as he liked to call her, was "in a mood." He'd rolled his eyes and stolen yet another fry.

"Why are you friends with her?" I'd asked.

He shrugged dismissively. "Habit." Then he stole the last fry and grinned at me.

I'd laughed and felt a little better. Maybe it was because of his company or because I had the trip to look forward to.

Or maybe it'd helped that I wasn't on edge since Arthur hadn't been to the quad for lunch since our blowup.

I'd gone from seeing him practically everywhere to only encountering him in Oswald's Astronomy class, where we avoided each other like one of us was radioactive. He didn't even glance at me. I knew this because I was getting a strain from keeping my head forward while watching him out of the corner of my eyes.

He hadn't budged once.

I tried not to let it sting. Logically I knew this was the most obvious result of our public fight.

But try telling that to my still-bruised heart.

Maybe I should look up those ancient Greek words to see if pain was part of lov—

Wait!

No. Not "love." I *refused* to use that word for a guy who'd only been in my life romantically for nineteen days before ending things over an Americano coffee.

Which was why leaving Barrington for a long weekend was a fantastic idea. Even if I did have to fumble around in the darkened dorm room in an effort not to awaken my still-silently-sleeping, shadowy lump of a roommate as I got ready and slipped out to meet Ayisha.

I don't know what I expected the vehicle to be that would take us from Barrington to the Lancaster lodge, but an honest-to-goodness yellow school bus wasn't it. Yet that's what we got. Complete with unnecessarily hard seats and an unnerving lack of safety belts. Was that even legal? Like, if there's one place that *really* should have safety belts, you'd think it would be a large, lumbering means of transportation that typically ferries small children.

The predawn check-in was at the school's front circle drive. We waited with about twenty Barrington students and our teachers, who gave us an information packet that no one opened.

Gaines wasn't present. I suppose he was probably going up with Bronwyn.

I wondered what Arthur would be doing over the long weekend. I couldn't imagine him doing something as common as a school-sponsored ski trip. That felt beneath him. Knowing him, he was probably reading a biography of someone obscure yet wildly accomplished.

Stop thinking about Arthur!

Right. Gotta do that.

Ayisha and I sat in a middle row. The first hour, we'd both made good use of our travel pillows and slept. After a while I blinked my eyes open in time to see that the first rays of light had already made it over the horizon for what looked like a clear-sky day.

I glanced at Ay.

She was already awake and focused on her phone, her thumbs flying over her silent keyboard at an impressive pace.

"Who are you texting?" I asked while yawning, my ears popping as we continued to gain altitude.

The question was reflexive, not meant to pry. However, when I saw her jerk a little, then recover and casually tuck the phone— mid-message, unsent—into her coat pocket, I grew curious.

"Home," was her clipped reply.

Her posture let me know she wasn't in the mood to divulge anything even if I asked more direct questions, so I held off.

But now I was on alert.

Oklahoma's time zone was an hour behind Connecticut's. What was painfully early here would put a call or text firmly in the "Is this an emergency?!" time of morning back home.

Especially for Ayisha's mom. Ms. Lewis was a stickler for rules and propriety. Ayisha had made it clear her mother had firm ideas for when a person should make calls or texts, including her children, and this time of day wasn't it.

Unless something was wrong.

I glanced at Ayisha, trying to see if she seemed tense in any way, but she'd closed her eyes and leaned back against the uncomfortable headrest. Nothing seemed wrong.

Then I heard a faint buzzing from her emerald-green coat pocket where her phone was. Which she ignored. That's when I knew for sure it wasn't Ms. Lewis. She would *never* ignore a call from her mother. Her twin preteen sisters were now at their own prep school out east. Though I seriously doubted it was either Billie or Linda.

Then who was blowing up her phone? So much so, she reached into her pocket to flip it to silent. All without opening her eyes. Or uttering a word.

Interesting.

Our friendship was still very much in the early stage. We had spent far more time as adversaries, but ever since our encounter at the raging Christmas Eve Eve party of our mutual ex, Brody, things had changed. Especially after she'd agreed to try to get back into Barrington. Once she succeeded, our communication had amped up and blossomed.

Still, what I didn't know about Ayisha dwarfed what I did.

Like who could be texting her at such an early hour.

Maybe it was Caldwell? He'd been the opposite of subtle in his fuzzy-eyed crush on her.

I shifted around to peer back to his bus row. One glance at him, however, ended any idea that he was the mystery texter. Sure, he could be faking that mouth-open deep sleep, but the drool on his chin was real. Strike Caldwell.

A quick perusal of the rest of our mutual travelers revealed nothing. I sat back in my position by the window right as I caught a faint light flash from her pocket, signaling the arrival of yet another text.

She ignored that one, too.

Very interesting . . .

Twelve

Lancaster Ski Lodge wasn't quite as magnificent as the website photos led one to believe. Then again, I wasn't in a position to bag on any person or business who chose to "enhance" their on-line presentation.

I made mental note of which areas I was going to show Grandma Jo when I called her later. As an inn owner, she was always curious about how other places presented themselves, to see if she could pick up any ideas, and she'd asked me to give her a "quick peek."

The two-story, palatial lobby was designed to impress, though I couldn't help noticing whatever shimmering elegance it may have had when it was first constructed back in the 1960s had faded. There was a smoothness in the wooden floorboards that showed the path from entry doors to front desk most folks chose to take. But it had massive windows overlooking hills covered in evergreen trees and snow and a fire in the central fireplace.

Dr. Oswald and Mr. Poisson had taken charge of distributing our room key cards while Ms. Martinez gave each of us yet another overview of the rules most of us had every intention of breaking.

"Curfew is midnight. No drinking, no drugs—"

"That includes pot!" Dr. Oswald interjected, her accent making it sound more like "poot," and yes, there was snickering.

Ms. Martinez continued. "Be respectful of the other guests *and* each other."

Dr. Oswald raised her finger in the air. "No hot tubs!"

That earned several disappointed groans.

Not from me; I was focused on the ski part of the trip. Those slopes looked *mighty* high.

"And if you need anything," Ms. Martinez said. "Either Dr. Oswald, Mr. Poisson, or I will be in the lobby at all times."

"Until midnight," Mr. Poisson noted.

"When you should all be back in your rooms," said Dr. Oswald. Firmly. Like that would somehow make it come true.

"After midnight," Ms. Martinez said, "if there's an emergency, you can also contact any of us via our own rooms or our cell phones, which are in your trip packets."

"But it must be important." Oswald again, eyes narrowed. "No nonsense." *Nunsense.*

Ms. Martinez maintained her official smile. "Please know you can come to us at *any* time if you have questions."

With that, they freed us.

For a moment after Mr. Poisson cheerfully declared, "Have fun, kids!" we lingered, like rehabilitated animals being released back into the wild. Looking around, uncertain. Everyone took an extra beat to register our sudden lack of constraint.

Then we were off!

Teens in every direction.

Ayisha tugged on the elbow of my black coat. "C'mon. We're in room twelve."

I followed as she headed for the grand staircase, which curved around the entry and led up to the second floor. We both had luggage, so we took the elevator tucked beneath it.

Room 12 was on the small side with two full-size beds and an en suite bathroom with a solid door, the kind that masked all sounds. Which, let's be honest, was a relief. New friendships had limits.

Ayisha took the bed closest to the window and the wall heater. She rolled her large floral luggage to her side of the room, then flung open the curtains.

Light flooded in.

"Sweet!" she said with a big smile.

I joined her at the window and with the smile.

Our view was excellent.

We could see the ski lifts and snow-covered trails that cut through the trees and up the side of the mountain. Both were swarming with activity.

Located closer to our lodge was the half circle of rental cabins, though not close enough for us to be able to see any details like the coming and goings. Enough trees obscured that, granting them privacy. But I could spot hints of activity already at a few of them.

Perversely, I wondered which one was Bronwyn's. Not that it mattered. We'd probably find out at some point over the next couple of days. Gaines had said there was always a party on Saturday. Whether Ayisha or I received an invitation was uncertain but also unlikely, given how the Valentine's Day Committee meeting on Tuesday had gone.

Which reminded me.

"Did you want to talk about ideas for music and party favors and stuff for the dance?"

Her look was incredulous. "Finley. We just got to a ski resort. Relax a little." She patted my shoulder like I was a toddler.

"Fair enough."

Ayisha's phone buzzed. It was atop her small bedside table, where she'd set it.

Her eyes darted over to it then to me then away. Like she didn't care. Which showed me that she did. The phone was turned over, so I couldn't see who was contacting her.

We both pretended nothing happened and unpacked.

There are efficient packers in this world. I was not one of them. By the looks of it, neither was Ayisha. There were two low wooden sets of drawers and despite the fact we'd only be here for slightly more than forty-eight hours, we managed to fill all four drawers. Takes talent.

She lay across her bed and grabbed her phone. "What time do you go learn how to *not* die while hurling yourself down a mountain?" She smirked.

I raised an eyebrow. "My *lesson* is at noon."

She arranged pillows against the headboard. "If you survive, let's meet up after. Maybe three p.m.? Then we can go grab some food and explore."

I was about to ask her what she planned to do while I was gone, but she was already perched with her back against the pillows, her attention on her phone.

I chose not to press. Whatever was going on with her, she would either tell me when she was ready or she wouldn't and it wasn't my business.

Even if I wished she would.

With a glance at the time—a little after eleven—I decided to head out to the concierge to figure out how the whole ski-lesson thing worked. Knowing me, the experience would take longer than I expected and I wanted to be on time for my first attempt at skiing.

I left our room and made my way back to the first floor, choosing the grand-staircase route for the view, which really did rock.

That reminded me about my promise to Grandma Jo that I'd show her an overview of the lodge's setup.

I fished my phone out of my coat pocket. Unfortunately, my AirPods were probably back at my dorm room. Somewhere.

I opted to keep the volume down and stay away from others so as not to be "that person," then placed the FaceTime call.

She answered after a couple rings.

"Finley, dear," she said with a full smile as she stared back at me.

It was after ten in the morning and she was in her office at the Hoyden. Smartly dressed with perfectly coiffed blondish hair and a generous application of lipstick. All of which, combined with the sparkle in her hazel eyes, told me everything I needed to know about the state of her relationship with her new girlfriend, Esha Chakrabarti. Arthur's beloved aunt. If the lipstick and hair were on point, things were going well. I'd seen what she looked like when they weren't, and the difference was unmistakable.

"To what do I owe this honor?" she asked, shifting papers around on her desk. She was a multitasker.

"You asked me to give you a look at the Lancaster lodge," I reminded her.

"That's right! How is it?"

"Look."

I turned the camera on my phone away from me to give her a good view as I finished descending the stairs into the front lobby, turning to make my way farther into the common areas, which were partially obscured by the huge 360-degree stone fireplace that dominated the room.

"Lovely," she said, then noted, "though they really need to refresh the flooring."

Of course she noticed that.

I turned the camera back onto myself, keeping one eye on where I was going as I continued our conversation.

"How's Ayisha?"

"She's great."

"Tell her that we miss her here at the inn."

"I will." I waited a beat. "Do you miss me? I worked there, too, you know."

"Your absence isn't as new," she said with a wry pull of her lips. "But yes. You're always missed."

"How are Mom and Dad?" I continued as I walked around the first floor of the lodge. There were several guests milling about. A few were from my school, in some form of ski attire. Which reminded me to go to the front desk to figure out where I needed to go for my lesson soon.

Grandma Jo answered, "They're both doing very well."

I refocused my attention on her image. "You'd tell me if something was going on, right?"

After the events of last Christmas, all four of us—Dad, Mom, Grandma Jo, and me—had vowed to not hide things from each other anymore. A Brown family pact. And though both of my parents looked radiantly happy the two times we'd video chatted since I'd been back, I was still wary. Total honesty was a new thing for us.

"Yes," she said with a smile. "I promise Skip and Dana are in a *very* good place."

"Okay, good."

I headed for the less-crowded side of the huge fireplace, where it was quieter.

"What are your plans for the day?" she asked.

I rounded the fireplace, getting so far as "I was thinking about—" when I stopped abruptly. A ripple of surprise went through me. "No!"

Arthur warmed his hands before the fire.

He wore his familiar puffy green jacket but the knit cap was new. Navy blue and a heavier wool. A shock of dark hair peeked out the front. And he had the audacity to be wearing a pair of dark Wranglers. Ones I'd helped pick out!

"Dammit!"

At the sound of my voice, he turned his head and met my incredulous stare. Which was when I realized I'd said that last part out loud.

"Seriously?" I said in frustration.

He arched a dark eyebrow in reply, his brown eyes hooded.

"Finley?" I heard the concern in my grandmother's muffled voice.

"Um, I have to call you back, bye." I lowered the phone to glower at the boy before me. "What are you doing here?"

"Well, it's a ski resort, so feel free to do the deduction." His tone was droll.

Ugh. He sounded like he was seventy again. That wasn't as cute as it had been two weeks ago.

"You weren't on the bus," I said. It came out accusatory.

His jaw twitched. "It was a last-minute decision. I came by car."

"Must be nice."

He smirked. "It is, rather."

He was deliberately goading me, which I perversely appreciated. Being mad at him helped me cover the fact that my heart was beating a million miles an hour and not entirely because of the anger. I was acutely aware that parts of me were happy to see him. The traitorous parts. I was mad at them, too.

"Do you ski?" he asked, his tone even, but I read his doubt.

I stood straighter. "I'm going to take a one-hour lesson. It's part of the package I bought."

"Ah. A lesson. That means you'll be relegated to the 'Bunny Slope.'"

"I think it's called 'Green Circle.'"

"Only if you make it off the Bunny Slope." Was that snarky?

Guess we were keeping our earlier fight going. Fine. We could do that.

"What floor are you on?" I asked. "So I can avoid it?"

He stuffed his hands into his jacket pockets. "I've made it easy for you as I'm not staying in the main lodge. I'll instead be staying at the Franz Klammer Cabin."

"The what?"

"Each cabin is named after a famous skier. Mine is Franz Klammer. Feel free to google him later."

"No thanks."

"Your loss. He's a legend."

"Good for Franz."

He nodded to my phone. "With whom are you video chatting?"

I straightened my shoulders. "That's really none of your business, now, is it?"

His upper lip curled into a knowing smile. "No. I don't suppose it is. However, you failed to properly end the call, so whomever it is likely heard the entirety of our conversation."

My stomach dropped as I glanced down to see he was right. The video was still going. Which meant . . .

Shit.

He nodded to me. "Have fun on the Bunny Slope."

"Green Circle," I countered, distracted.

"I shan't see you since I'm off to the Black Diamond. That's for the extremely advanced, should you be curious."

"Break a leg."

"That's not the correct—" He stopped, eyes narrowing in suspicion. "Never mind."

Arthur brushed past me on his way to the other side of the fireplace.

Out of sight. The spicy fragrance of his soap lingered, though. My throat tightened with emotion. I slowly raised the phone.

Grandma Jo stared back at me. Her smile gone, replaced by concern.

I cleared my throat and asked, "How much of that did you hear?"

"All of it. Just like Arthur guessed."

"Oh."

"What happened, Finley?" she asked gently.

Grandma Jo had been there for the evolution of my romance with Arthur, even as she was having her own with Esha. She'd seen me go from annoyed to crushing to hurt to deliriously happy. That last part was where I'd left her.

"Honestly, Grandma? I have no idea." I sighed and sat on the hearth's stony ledge. "Except somewhere between New Year's and last Monday, Arthur decided he didn't want to be with me anymore."

Saying it aloud again brought with it a renewed sense of loss. My heart clenched and I swallowed back against my emotions.

Her face twisted with sympathy. "Oh, honey. I'm so sorry."

"*I'm* sorry I didn't tell you," I said thickly. "I know we promised not to keep things from each other."

Grandma Jo's expression softened in understanding. "Within reason, sweetie. Not wanting to tell your grandmother right away about breaking up with your boyfriend is perfectly natural."

"I know, but . . ." I shrugged. My face felt warm. ". . . You're kind of invested, too."

"Because of Esha?"

I nodded. "I promise I didn't *not* tell you because of her."

"You're allowed to process your feelings at your own pace, honey."

Which was logical and made me feel a bit better.

"Did . . ." I bit my lip then continued. "Did Esha say anything to you? About Arthur? That might explain . . . things?" My voice sounded scratchy to my ears.

"Arthur didn't tell you why?" She was clearly surprised.

"No." I rubbed the back of my neck before admitting, "He was probably going to, but I basically cut him off in the moment, and yes, that was a very bad strategy. I'm aware. But . . . I mean, *did* she?"

"Esha hasn't said a word to me. In fact, the way she was talking last night, I don't think she knows."

"What did she say?"

"Just that she was looking forward to seeing you when she comes back to the States next month."

I frowned, puzzled. "Why would she look forward to seeing me? She knows I'm not in Oklahoma now."

"She's not coming to Oklahoma. She's coming to Connecticut, to see Arthur."

Now I was even more confused.

"Why is she seeing Arthur?"

As far as I knew, Arthur only spent time with his favorite aunt on special occasions, when his high-society parents were off doing their own thing. Like at Christmas. Or—

"For his eighteenth birthday," Grandma Jo told me. "On Valentine's Day."

Thirteen

I was a little in shock. Not knowing the date of my (sorta) ex-boyfriend's birthday felt like a huge oversight on my part.

Looking back, I couldn't believe I'd never found out. Granted, Arthur and I had barely talked before he came to stay in Christmas, the Halloween party and bee incident notwithstanding. That explained the months beforehand.

But afterward?

It felt impossible.

Clearly it wasn't.

After I ended my call with Grandma Jo, I remained sitting on the hearth, feeling the heat of the fireplace on my back. I went back over every conversation that we'd had since kissing on Christmas Eve to see if there had been any mention of his birthday. I found nothing.

Except . . .

The faint memory of an exchange tickled my background thoughts.

Arthur and I had gone for a walk around the neighborhood on Christmas Day, holding hands and taking in the vast amount of snow that seemed to cover everything. The streets and roads hadn't been cleared yet and everything still felt fresh. New.

Like we were then.

My mind had been racing all Christmas Eve night. In a good way. Thinking about everything that had happened that day and what it all meant. What I hoped it meant. Good scenarios. Great scenarios. Disasters. All points in between.

It left me tired. Thankfully the adrenaline of being with Arthur in that moment, walking through the snowy surroundings, kept me going. Our hands linked. How right it felt. The tingle of excitement every time our shoulders touched.

I'd blown out a breath. It fogged and floated on. Then I giggled. Happy.

I nudged him in the side with my elbow. Arthur instinctively understood and blew out his own breath that floated in the air after mine. Then we laughed together.

In that moment, he looked young. Felt young. Like the teenager he was. That wasn't always the case. Especially when he was upset. That day, though, he was happy. Almost silly.

"What's your favorite food?" I asked impulsively.

He answered, "Waffles." Which wasn't what I was expecting.

I decided to go with it. "Buttermilk? Blueberry? Whole wheat—"

"Buttermilk. With loads of Irish butter and toffee syrup. Dollop of real clotted cream."

"That's very specific."

"It's what Jost, our cook, would make every Christmas when I was very young, before I started spending it with Auntie."

My eyebrows went up. "You had a cook?"

"What? You do, too. Multiple cooks, actually. That terrifying small woman with the spoon for one."

"No, no. We have women who cook for the inn. It's not the same as having a Jeeves."

"Jeeves was a fictitious butler. Jost was our cook when I was growing up."

I remember thinking about what it must've been like to be Arthur when he was young. The melancholy rich boy whose parents sounded more focused on themselves and each other than their youngest child.

That raised more questions.

"Is Jost still there?"

"No, he retired several years ago."

"Do you miss him?"

"I miss his waffles." His eyes had twinkled with amusement. "Polly was partial to his egg white scrambles, with baked beans."

"That sounds disgusting." I made a face. Then became curious. "Where's your sister now?" He seldom mentioned her.

"London. With her husband. Edgar. He's an oncologist. Mildly tolerable."

"High praise. Any kids?"

"Not yet. Thankfully."

I playfully slapped his arm. "You don't want to be an uncle?"

"I'd love to be an uncle if it didn't involve Polly. I've yet to figure out how to make that happen."

I snorted. He grinned.

Then we stopped at the edge of a park to stare out at the wide sea of whiteness before us. A line of thick, gray clouds had rolled in. Covering us and bringing a hush to our surroundings.

"Do you like kids?" I asked. No, I wasn't going *there*. I merely wanted to know everything. Honest.

"You're asking a lot of questions," he noted, glancing over at me.

I tugged on his hand. "About you. I want to get to know *you*."

A smile flirted with the corner of his beautiful mouth. "What would you like to know?"

"What music you like. What books, besides science fiction.

What you want to major in when you go to college. When's your birthday? Do you like dogs? Cats? Ferrets? What are your feelings on hedgehogs?"

"Hedgehogs?" He was bewildered.

"Yes. We don't have them here. Not naturally. I think. At least not like you have in England. They seem like they're mythical creatures designed to be too cute to kill."

"They're not mythical. And I find myself neutral on the subject. They're indeed cute but also something of a nuisance. Like squirrels in that regard."

"But do you like dogs?"

"Yes."

"What kinds?"

"I had a beagle when I was younger."

"Named?"

His cheeks darkened with a blush before admitting, "Dobby."

"Shut up!" I turned to face him, grinning. "You liked Harry Potter?!"

"You say that as if it's a surprise."

"Because it *is*! I assumed you'd think it was too, I don't know, juvenile."

"Which it is. It was also the seminal book series of my young life. And it is *very* English. Do I get to ask questions about you?"

"Sure. But I'm going to keep asking you stuff. Like, what's your favorite color?"

"Newburyport Blue, with bright white trim."

"That's . . . okay. Back to really, really specific. Also, that's two colors."

"Both of which make up the color scheme of my bedroom back home." He gave a cute little shrug, but his brown eyes were sparkling with mischief.

I really liked this side of him.

"Okay, more questions. Your major? Which college do you want to go to? Favorite book? Birthd—"

He'd kissed me then, cutting off any further discussion. His lips were soft and tasted like peppermints, and we fell backward into a snowdrift. We made out until the snow seeped through our jeans and coats, becoming too much. We laughed when we both realized we shivering from the cold and hurried home, teeth chattering by the time we burst through the inn's back door, running upstairs to our respective rooms to change into something warm.

The rest of Christmas Day had been spent together with our families and I never gave another thought to the fact he only answered my obscure inquiries. Not the important ones. We had moved on to other subjects. Totally normal.

Except now I wondered if the kissing had been a distraction. A really nice one, and one I'd thoroughly enjoyed, I won't deny, but that's beside the point.

He'd done something similar when we'd been baking Christmas cookies and he hadn't wanted me to know the real reason behind him leaving his prep school in England to come to the US and to Barrington.

What if he'd done something similar about his birthday?

The more I thought about it, though, the more that seemed silly. What did it matter if his birthday was on Valentine's Day?

It didn't.

I actually thought it was kind of cool.

It also didn't matter because we weren't together anymore.

A point I felt obliged to keep bringing up to myself, because I seemed to keep forgetting.

Fourteen

"That's *it*?" I asked, moving my rented snow goggles up to my also-rented lime-green helmet, certain I'd heard wrong.

Boomer, the leather-skinned ski instructor who was like the human embodiment of the sea turtle in *Finding Nemo*, nodded and grinned. "Yah."

I looked around nervously. "I feel like I should have more in-struction," I countered, gripping my ski poles tightly.

Like, a lot more.

Other skiers were moving all around the penned-in practice area where Boomer and I were concluding the final moments of my hour-long lesson, but I paid them little attention. My focus was on figuring out how not to die. Mixed with a healthy reminder that I didn't *have* to ski down a mountain. It was a choice. My choice. I *could* say no. Ayisha certainly had. Honestly, that felt like the wisest course of action after what was unquestionably the fastest hour-long lesson in human history.

Boomer patted my shoulder indulgently. "Like my Uncle Pongo says, we learn best by doin'."

Boomer followed that pearl of wisdom from "Uncle Pongo"

with an undulating hand motion I assumed was supposed to represent the "doin'" part. Perhaps that was what I was supposed to look like when I skied down an actual slope, like Boomer had just told me I was free to do.

Green Circle, of course. My skill level.

Such as it was.

He gave me a look of encouragement. "You've stayed up the last four times you did the Bunny Slope," he said, nodding to the gentle incline not much higher than my parents' driveway.

My eyes bugged. "*That's* the criteria for sending another person up a mountain? Alone?"

"You won't be alone. There's plenty of other people up there."

He pointed up to the mountain with its multiple ski lanes of varying angles cutting through the pine trees. Dozens of people in bright gear were either slicing downward or taking the lift back up. No one seemed to be in distress. At least that I could tell from here.

"You totally got this," he said, nodding as he led me out of the fenced barriers of the practice area like a father guiding his reluctant child to the school doors on the first day of kindergarten.

While I was admittedly moving better than I had when I first began my lesson fifty-six minutes earlier, I still didn't agree with his assessment.

Before I could counter his certainty, however, a tiny flash of humanity streaked past us at a rate of speed I knew was not remotely safe.

It threw me off-balance, and I wobbled.

"Whoa," was Boomer's take as he steadied me by my elbow. Then he grinned a toothy grin and proclaimed, "Cannonball Kids." He pointed after the retreating streak that I only now realized was a child who was too far off the slope to be going that fast. "Gotta watch out for those little devils, they come outta nowhere and whamo-bandamo, you're slammoed!" He giggled.

Right as he said that, the kid in question nearly took out a couple, who cursed at him in fury. The kid never looked back.

I drew a breath to ask another question, but when I turned to Boomer, I saw he was already several yards away. Headed back to the practice area, where his next client had arrived.

Which meant I was alone.

For another couple minutes, I stood there. Ski poles in hand, icy wind against my exposed nose and cheeks. Determining what to do next.

Go up to a Green Circle ski lane—where many small children of the non–Cannonball Kid variety were slowly making their way downhill, with their parents close by.

Or scoot over to the gear rental area to return the gear and hop the shuttle back to the lodge, where I could join Ayisha for a lunch I'd already earned.

After much consideration, I decided I should at least make one legitimate attempt at skiing.

And yes, Arthur's earlier snark ringing in my ears was a deciding factor.

I hadn't seen him since I'd been here on the slopes. Not that I knew what his full ski gear looked like. Or had much opportunity to keep an eye out for him since my arrival. An instructor had escorted me from the shuttle drop to where Boomer was giving lessons. Still, I felt I'd somehow be able to recognize Arthur if I saw him.

I did catch a glimpse earlier of Bronwyn and Josie, recognized by their hyena-pitched laughter as they took a lift up a route for the more advanced.

Which was how, twenty minutes later, I found myself in the

opposite direction, atop the Bambi Slope (a Green Circle ski lane), as marked by a wooden sign with an actual green circle.

I felt almost proud.

I'd navigated my way from the spot where Boomer had left me to the Starbuck Ski Lift and waited until the very slow-moving lift raised me very high up into the air with only a flimsy metal crossbar providing negligible safety. Disney's Soarin' Around the World felt more secure.

I'd made it, though. I'd give myself credit for that.

Most of the other skiers taking the Bambi Slope didn't wait long after exiting the lift before they marched over to the top of the lane and launched themselves onto the slope.

It took me longer.

As I stood there, my mind spinning with what I should be doing—open skis into a triangle, keeping balance, turn the legs to steer the skis, et cetera—I could feel my heart thundering in my chest.

It wasn't that far, not in distance, not really. Plus, Bambi was one of the gentlest routes.

You can do this.

After about five minutes of a silent pep talk, and watching at least a dozen preteen and younger children go ahead of me, I finally pushed off. While it was an unspectacular first run down a low-grade slope, I made it to the bottom in one piece without falling, which felt like a victory. So much so I decided to try another run.

Happily, that one went well, too. It was even kind of . . . fun. Maybe a third—and final—run would be okay. I almost forgot about my schoolmates also being up here, too, when—

"He's ghosting *me!*"

Bronwyn's voice. Nearby.

Great.

I looked around, grateful my rented, snow-smudged goggles disguised me. I spotted her in her pale-yellow ski outfit walking ahead of me, in the same direction, carrying her turquoise skis. Her long auburn hair poked out of her helmet to swish perfectly down her back.

Beside her was Josie. Of course.

"Are you, like, a hundred percent? Sure?" Josie wore a bright pink outfit, including dark pink skis.

They were easy to spot.

"Not a hundred percent," Bronwyn said. "I just feel it here." She patted her flat stomach.

Now, I couldn't say for certain they were talking about Arthur, but of course that's where my mind went.

"Have you gone to his place?"

They moved toward the lift line I'd been using.

"Not yet. I want to run into him here, so it's *spontaneous*."

"Smart. He's gotta be here."

"Keep an eye out," Bronwyn instructed.

"Copy that."

They moved off to the Starbuck lift.

Which was why I changed my plans and walked onward to another lift line.

I was practically panting by the time I arrived—but it wasn't near Bronwyn and Josie and the guy they were discussing.

Whoever he was.

I looked around on the way up. At the treetops. The way the clouds clung to the sides of the mountains. Other ski lifts . . .

. . . which were where I spotted Arthur.

He was on a lift that ran parallel to mine before it veered off, going higher among the trees.

It took me a second to be sure. Red ski jacket and black ski pants, his face partially obscured by a blue helmet.

But I'd recognize that Queens Guard Posture anywhere.

Our eyes met over the distance right before trees rose up to divide us and I was almost positive he recognized me, too.

I was rattled. Not for any one particular reason, but for *all* of them. Because he was Arthur and I was mad at him even as I missed him and wished I didn't.

With my mind in such a whirl, I forgot to pay attention.

And missed my Green Circle exit.

I realized it after I was already farther up the mountain, where the only trails where Blue Square and Black Diamond.

So, not good.

Flustered, I slid off the chair lift at a point designated Treasure Trail—the sign had both a blue square and a black diamond, but the black diamond also had an arrow pointing upward and . . .

Let's just say, it was confusing.

I was pretty sure if I skied from this point, the slope would be for intermediate (which I wasn't) as opposed to expert (which I definitely wasn't).

I could have asked someone.

I didn't.

Glancing at some of the other skiers, I only recognized Hawley Chen goofing with two other guys in that shove-each-other-hard-in-the-chest-while-laughing-too-loud way guys often did when they're gathered in groups.

To my relief, all three launched down the slope, zipping and whooping and shouting.

I remained. Clutching and re-clutching my poles, trying to control my breathing while taking in the slope.

Oh. My. God.

It was way more twisty than the other ones, with areas having snowy bumps and thick clumps of pine trees at the edges.

Man, did I envy Ayisha right then.

She was probably sitting by a fireplace, sipping hot chocolate, texting with her Secret Texter. Safe. So, *so* safe. Maybe wondering when I was going to show so we could grab lunch.

If I was ever going to make it back to her in a timely fashion, I was going to have to go down that slope.

My mind was a jumble of all of the things I was supposed to do while I reminded myself that I had *just* successfully skied so I *could* do this. I simply had to be fully present, aware of my surroundings, and keep my skis in a wedge formation the entire time.

All very logical.

Five minutes later, I was in the same position. While a bunch of other skiers had arrived and launched and probably finished their run.

I might have stayed longer if I hadn't glanced over my shoulder to see an approaching skier from much higher up the slope. He wore a red ski jacket, black pants, and a blue ski helmet, and he was skiing very fast.

I knew who it was.

It was instinct. I pushed off.

Heading downward, my heart thundering, wind piercing the exposed lower half of my face, determined to keep myself upright at the bare minimum.

Do not humiliate yourself in front of the ex! Do not humiliate yourself in front of the ex!

Over and over, my thighs already burning as I clenched them to maintain control.

Within thirty seconds I knew—I was going to humiliate myself in front of the ex.

He was still behind me, so when I saw a curve bisecting the trail, I made the split-second decision to take it instead of continuing on the main course.

The terrain was instantly bumpier and the trees much closer.

I felt a swell of panic in my chest.

This was a stupid, stupid decision!

I didn't have time to berate myself.

In self-protection mode, I pulled the fronts of my skis closer into a tight wedge to control my speed. I needed to get over to the side and stop to reassess and the only safe way to do that where I didn't endanger myself or others was to get off the trail.

And that, ladies and gentlemen, was how I wound up in about four feet of snow in the middle of a pine tree grove, unharmed, but with the lower half of my legs buried in large drifts like I'd merged with the mountain itself.

Efficient in the most graceless possible way.

Panting, I planted both my poles into the ground and leaned the upper half of my body on top of them, wondering if my face was covered with spit or snot. No one mentioned that part of the ski experience. At least no one was around to witness my—

"What are you doing?"

I jumped and hollered, "Ahhhh!" as I turned to see Arthur at the edge of the trees.

Looking at me as if I was insane.

My hand landed over my racing heart. "You scared me!" I accused, trying to get control of my breathing. *Don't throw up, Finley.*

He lifted his goggles up onto his helmet. "That was not my intent."

"Well, you did." I whipped off a glove and wiped the moisture off my face.

It was spit.

Thank God.

He glanced around the surroundings before returning his attention to me. "I ask again, what are you doing off-trail?"

"Nothing."

He maneuvered into the pines, closer to me. "Nothing?" he scoffed as he went. "You simply felt the compulsion to hang out in the trees? Atop a mountain?" His gaze fell to where the lower part of my legs, from right below the knees down, were covered. "In drifts of snow?"

I stood straighter, jaw out, defiant. "Maybe."

"Brilliant," he said dryly.

"Thanks. Okay, well. Now that we've established what I'm doing, enjoy the rest of your ski experience." I added a cruise director wave.

He didn't wave in return. In fact, he looked quite stern. "I'm not leaving you here."

"Why?" I demanded, vexed.

"It's not safe. You started the day on the Bunny Slope, you're certainly not ready for the Black Diamond."

My eyes widened in shock. "Black Diamond?! I thought this was the Blue Square!"

"The trails merged."

"They can do that?"

He nodded. "And frequently do."

I huffed. "Well, that's . . . very bad planning!"

"Take it up with the management once you're safely back down."

"I will!"

"In the meantime, how do you plan to *get* back down?" he asked, arching his brow at me.

"By skiing. Not that it's any of your business."

He planted both poles through the snow into the ground on either side of his skis. "As a member of the human race with a healthy sense of decency, it *is* my business. I'm not going to simply leave you here to perish because you stubbornly refuse to ask for help."

"Who said anything about perishing?" My eyes went wider. "Is that possible?"

"A question to ask oneself before going to the top of a mountain."

I closed my eyes and let out a puff of frustration as I admitted the obvious. "Fine. I . . . may have gotten myself into . . . a situation." I held up a finger for emphasis. "But I do not need you to rescue me!"

"To be clear, my offering you assistance—were I to do so— is solely about capability, not gender stereotypes. My mother is a brilliant skier. I happen to have been skiing since I was around five years old. You, on the other hand, have been skiing fewer than five hours."

"Three," I mumbled, glancing away.

"Pardon?"

"Fewer than three hours. Not that it's important."

"It *is* important, Finley." He pointed to the slope visible through the pines behind him. "That incline is designed to be thrilling, but to those who are able to navigate it based on their advanced skill set. And while I have faith in your ability to eventually master the ski slope, should you so desire, you cannot convince me you're ready to safely tackle a Black Diamond–grade trail in under three hours from your very first lesson. Am I wrong?"

I bit my lip, wanting to argue back, but also having to admit, in the interest of honesty, "No."

He nodded once. "Then let's find a way out of this 'situation.'"

"Okay," I agreed because I wasn't suicidal. "Do you have any suggestions?"

Now it was his turn to sigh.

After a moment's consideration he reluctantly said, "One. I hold your hands and we go down together."

I frowned as I slipped my glove back on, uncertain how that would play out because, "Won't I need my hands for the poles?"

"We won't use the poles."

"Boomer said the poles are important."

His brows drew down. "Who is Boomer?"

"My ski instructor."

He scoffed, "The one who let you go on a mountain alone after an hour's lesson?"

"Yes, but I feel it's important to say that he thought I'd only be on the Green Circle."

"And yet you wound up on the Black Diamond," he pointed out dryly.

"Thinking it was a Blue Square."

"Which is also not a Green Circle."

"True."

He waved a circle around my general area. "How did this all transpire?"

I sniffed, wanting desperately to wipe my nose, which was in danger of being runny from the cold, but I wasn't about to risk it in front of him. "I, um, got distracted on the chair lift and"—I cleared my throat—"got off at the wrong spot."

"I see. Ski lift lesson learned. No thanks to Boomer." He practically rolled his eyes. "Now, back to the poles, or, in this instance, not using the poles. We can hold them as we go, if you prefer. Or I can strap them to my back. I have a pole carrier." He reached into his coat pocket to remove a fancy Nylon shoulder sling and held it up. "But what I ultimately have in mind is that I hold your hands and guide you down the rest of the trail."

"You'd do that?" I said in surprise.

"Of course." He attached his poles to the strap, glancing at me. "If it makes you feel better, my mother did it for me once in Switzerland." Then he took my poles from me and did the same.

"How old were you?"

"Five."

"Great," I muttered. "I'm going to fall back on the whole 'lack of experience' excuse so my pride isn't completely obliterated."

A tiny smile quirked at the corner of his mouth. "Wise choice."

He slung both sets of ski poles diagonally across his chest, the strap and poles making him look a bit like Robin Hood. Which was more than a little sexy.

And I couldn't even tell him.

Not right. Not right at all.

I sighed internally.

Now he faced me, focusing on my legs, which were invisible from below the knees down.

"First things first, let's get you out of this wonderful mound of snow you've so ably managed to become one with."

I tried to lift my right leg but it was difficult. Anticipating my impending imbalance, Arthur took my right hand in his. Steadying me. It was equal parts comforting and embarrassing. Flashes of him helping me rescue the bee flashed through my mind. Seemed like forever ago.

"I feel like a kid in their parents' shoes," I said, glad that the freezing cold hid the blush I knew was on my cheeks.

"Wait until you're done for the day and your legs feel like jelly."

"Jokes later, after we're off the scary mountain."

"I wasn't joking."

I looked up at him; he wasn't.

Awesome.

"Can we just focus?" I said.

"Here. Take my other hand." He held out his left hand covered by a black-and-gray ski glove. "We're both wearing gloves, so you needn't worry about actual contact."

"What's that supposed to mean?"

"Nothing. That *was* a joke, or a poor attempt at one." He frowned and I wished I could tell what he was thinking. "Come. You're going to need all your energy for the next phase."

"What's . . . the next phase?" I asked with no small hesitation, because apparently there were phases to this impromptu rescue?

"You'll help guide me as we go."

"Why would I need to guide you?" Try as I might, I couldn't picture what he had in mind.

"Because I'll be skiing backward."

And it definitely wasn't that.

My eyes widened at him. "What?! Arthur—"

"It's the best way to keep you stabilized, by using both hands."

"That seems super dangerous!"

The slope was imposing enough when facing it. But backward?! A pang of concern for him hit me, which he must have seen.

"I can do this. As can you." His eyes bore intently into mine. "I won't let us fall."

Crazy as it seemed, I believed him. To the point I felt some of the tension leave my shoulders. For a moment.

"Okay," I said.

He almost smiled then. I could see it. How his face relaxed, pleased that I was giving him my trust. It was all so confusing.

Though I had other concerns at the moment.

He supported me as I lifted my left leg up and somehow managed to get the ski over the snow drift. Followed by my right leg, with only slightly less awkwardness. My heart was pounding. From the elevation, the effort, and—who was I kidding—the company.

Step by clumsy step, we made it back to the edge of the woods and the start of the ski lane itself.

Other skiers were slicing downhill at varying speeds, but all much faster than I considered comfortable. None paid us any attention, and that was fine by me.

Arthur still had hold of both of my hands, his back already positioned to the direction we were about to go. He didn't seem concerned, so I silently vowed not to be either.

He nodded to the slope, his voice calm. "I'll step out first and get into position. Then, once you're ready, you'll step out and place your skis between mine. Keep them straight. We'll start slowly to get in sync."

"Are we going to do the squatty thing?" I asked, keeping most of my nervousness out of my voice.

He shook his head in confusion. "I'm sorry?" I demonstrated, bending my knees. "Oh. Somewhat. Mainly keep your knees from becoming locked and find a way to slightly shift your weight to the lower part of your body."

"So, the squatty thing."

He arched a brow. "However you prefer to call it," he said, before adding, "though never refer to it as such to anyone else with skiing experience if you wish to be taken seriously."

"I can pretty much guarantee that I'll never be taken seriously by anyone with skiing experience."

"Never say never."

I snorted. "You would find a way to get in a James Bond reference."

"To be pedantic, it's *Never Say Never Again*," he said with a hint of a smile. "But your point is made. Now, I'm stepping out. Are you prepared?"

"No, wait." He stopped at once, eyeing me in concern. "First this," I said, then drew in a deep breath and released it in a visible puff into the cold air.

He watched it drift upward into the trees, then met my eyes . . . before he did the same thing. Deep breath and released.

Like we'd done together before. On Christmas Day, in Christmas. We both remembered it. That meant something, didn't it?

I swallowed against the sudden surge of longing and he gently squeezed my hands then indicated his head toward the trail: *Ready?*

I nodded: *Ready.*

With his left leg, he stepped out onto the slope, angling his ski to keep himself from sliding too soon. Then I followed suit with my right leg, angling my ski between his.

"Well done," he said softly. "How do you feel?"

"Scared," I answered honestly. My heart was a jackhammer.

"Understandable. But we've got this. Do you believe me?" I locked on to his eyes, so dark and surrounded by such gorgeous eyelashes. I nodded. "I'm going to push off with my left leg first and you push with your right, then you push with your left so you maintain your skis between mine, and I'll follow your push with one of my own from my right leg. Does that make sense?"

"Yes."

"Excellent. We'll go carefully the whole way, even after we get going. I'll keep us stable and control our speed, but I'll need you to be on the lookout for anything unexpected."

Fear swooshed through me. "Unexpected? Like what?"

"That's the unexpected part."

"No jokes, Arthur! Are we talking unexpected like tornadoes or bears or UFOs?"

"Other skiers. We're almost to the long cruiser part—"

"The what?"

"It's a long, groomed run with few turns. It's up ahead, around this bend." He jerked his head back and to one side to indicate the direction. "From that point on our main concern is other people."

"That sounds like a life lesson." Apparently facing death made me quippy.

"Quite. Are you ready?" he asked.

One last puff of air for courage.

Then a single nod.

He pushed off with his left leg. I followed with my right. Then left. Then his right. And, what do you know? We were going backward down a mountain! Well, Arthur was backward. I could see everything we were approaching.

Slowly. Like, *really* slowly.

I was 100 percent on board with the strategy.

"You're doing a marvelous job," he said. I noticed his voice was just a smidge tighter, which made sense. His whole body was clenched as a way to keep in control of our movements.

"I'm just staying upright," I replied, breathless. My lungs ached.

"That's half the battle."

I hazarded a glance over his left shoulder to glimpse the upcoming trail, where I saw the bend he'd mentioned.

"Slight turn right," I said, then clarified, "Your right."

"Got it."

He angled his body so we both moved to his right.

I noticed we may be overcorrecting.

"Maybe lean slightly"—I demonstrated with my head—"so we don't go back into the trees."

"Like this?" He followed my angle and we eased ever so slightly away from the trees.

I nodded. "That's it." Another glance over his shoulder and I felt a bloom of relief in my chest as the view widened considerably where the run opened into the long cruiser.

"I can see the bottom of the trail!" I told him excitedly.

"How far?"

"A couple football fields."

"In English."

"Two hundred yards. Don't ask me to translate that into metrics."

"I would never ask that of an American," he murmured sardonically.

Which made me want to laugh. It was so very him. Mocking Americans was one of his favorite hobbies, even while in dangerous circumstances.

"It's a straight shot now," I said. "No skiers in front of us."

"Good."

We continued our steady pace down the slope. Moving in sync, albeit at the pace of a tortoise. I didn't even care about looking silly as other skiers whizzed by. Probably some from Barrington.

None of that mattered. I was with Arthur and we weren't fighting and things felt almost . . . normal. Despite the situation. Or maybe because of it. We were both so focused on surviving that the rest of the mess between us was pushed into the deep background.

"A hundred and fifty yards," I said, watching as the buildings of the base camp grew closer. Relief surged. "I think we've got it."

Arthur met my eyes and he smiled. "I believe we do." His voice, like his skiing, was calm and confident. I missed this version of him so much.

My heart tightened.

And suddenly I had to know. "Why did you break up with me?" I blurted it out before I could second-guess myself.

He blinked, startled. "You . . . want to have this discussion now?"

"I feel mostly safe now," I said, then admitted quietly, "and it's kind of all I can think about."

For several seconds, neither of us spoke. We just skied, the sweep of our legs still in sync. Other people passing us.

"A hundred yards," I mentioned absently.

He glanced back up into my eyes. "If we're going to be specific about it, I wasn't the one who officially ended things." There was an edge to his tone. "You were."

"Which we both know is a total cop-out. Fifty yards."

His shoulders slumped. "You're right. It is."

Another silence followed. Our pace slowed down further. Small children were passing us now.

"Though I didn't want to," he added, so softly I almost missed it.

My breath caught. Everything around us faded.

"You didn't?" He shook his head. I felt a thousand emotions hit me at once, like a logjam. "Well, now I'm . . . so confused. Because I didn't want to break up."

"Didn't you?" His dark eyes were vulnerable. I wanted to hug him. I also wanted to shake him. Were all boys so frustrating?!

"No!" I almost shouted. "How could you possibly think that?"

We stopped completely at the base camp. Neither of us let go of the other's hands. We remained facing each other.

"Why, Arthur?" I whispered, my voice close to cracking. "Please. Just tell me what happened."

I saw him swallow hard then. He released my hands and slid backward, gravity taking him several feet away from me.

By some miracle, I remained standing, even without the poles.

And held Arthur's gaze, not being the one to hit eject this time. No. I wanted answers.

When Arthur heaved a sigh and nodded, I thought that was exactly what I was going to get. Answers.

Finally.

He even got so far as, "You see—"

When: *WHAM!*

It was a Cannonball Kid.

Slammed right into him!

Arthur hit the snow-packed ground like a ton of bricks.

For a fraction of a second, I wasn't sure what the dark blob draped across him actually was. Until the little shit rolled off Arthur's supine body and muttered in a high-pitched, nasally voice, "Sorry, mister!" grabbed one of his ski poles, and swooshed off in the direction of an adult-size human.

The whole thing took less than five seconds.

Fear zapped through me. "Oh my God!"

With an instinct I didn't know I possessed, I grabbed the pole left behind by the Child Missile, popped out of my skis, and was at Arthur's side in seconds.

"Are you okay?" I said breathlessly.

He whispered, "Ow."

"Where?"

"Knee. Left. Twisted."

He pointed.

Yep. Sure enough, his left knee—which was still in its ski—was bent at an angle that was not natural. *Yeesh.*

"Do you want me to try to get you out of your ski?" I wasn't sure that was the best course of action, but, man, did that look painful.

His "That would be good" was strained.

I used the kid's pole to pop Arthur's booted foot of his ski, holding on to his leg as I carefully lowered it. I must've done an okay job, because he only clenched his jaw once, then sighed after the leg was on the snow-packed ground.

"Okay?" I asked anxiously. He nodded, eyes closed. "I'm going to get the medic."

"Ski patroller," he corrected; he was who he was. "I don't think that's necessary."

I scoffed, "It's a hundred percent necessary, Arthur! You hit your head, on top of your knee being messed up. You're getting looked at. Don't argue!"

He stared up at me, and, impossibly, his expression gentled. "I shall not argue," he said, voice strained but also quiet, and suddenly all I wanted to do was kiss him. I didn't, but my gaze dropped to his lips and back, and I saw him watching me intently and . . . yeah.

I stood up. Now was not the time.

"I'll be right back."

Fifteen

The Lancaster Base Camp medical clinic was bustling. In the hour that I'd been in the tiny waiting area, I'd seen two people carried in with knee injuries, one person with a dislocated shoulder, and one with head trauma. Intermingled were several bloody cuts requiring stitches and a guy puking into a plastic bag from altitude sickness. Normally that would've been enough, but I was too anxious.

Upon our arrival, Arthur had been placed in a wheelchair and rolled into the back part of the clinic, where a doctor was evaluating both his head and knee.

I remained behind to fret in silence.

Now standing near the hallway that led to the interior of the building, biting my thumbnail and hoping he'd be okay. I felt like he would, but I'd also read enough about random head injuries seeming to be of no consequence abruptly turning fatal that it didn't take much for me to conjure up any number of possible dramatic scenarios while I waited.

There were a few people besides me also waiting, so all of the hard plastic chairs were taken. I hadn't considered sitting. It wasn't possible. What I really wanted to do was pace, but there wasn't enough room without being obnoxious, so I settled for tapping the toe of my ski boot against the pale linoleum floor.

I still got looks.

Right after I'd arrived, I texted Ayisha I was going to be late, though I didn't go into full details.

I texted: Ran into Arthur. He had a collision (not by me!) and I went with him to the clinic.

Ayisha texted: OMG!! Are you both okay?

I texted: I'm fine. He's being looked at rn. Might be another hour. I'm gonna miss lunch.

Ayisha texted: NBD. I'll grab something. Txt me when you know more. 🙏

I texted: Will do.

That was fifty minutes ago. I wasn't sure how long an exam like this one was supposed to take, if I should be seriously concerned or not.

That left me plenty of time to consider what Arthur had said: *Though I didn't want to.*

It thrilled me! And confused me.

He didn't want to break up? Then why had he?

What was I missing?

A middle-aged Black man in a light blue scrub shirt, navy cotton pants, and a clear badge of some nature attached to a lanyard around his neck came out into the waiting area.

"Is there a Finley Brown here?" he called out.

I stepped forward. "That's me."

He smiled, though he seemed tired. "I'm Dr. Kelley. You're Arthur's friend?" I nodded. "He's asking for you."

"Is he okay?"

"He'll be fine in a few days. His knee is just sprained."

I wasn't sure "just" and "sprained" went together, but perspective was probably different for a doctor at a ski resort's clinic.

"Can I see him?" I asked, stuffing my hands into the deep side pockets of my ski jacket.

Dr. Kelley nodded even as his attention was already shifting to the chart one of the clinic's staff handed to him. "He's in bay three," he told me, then moved off down a different hallway.

I found Arthur at the end of a hallway where thin curtains acted as partitions between patients. He was sitting up on a hospital bed, now out of his puffy ski pants so his black base layer long johns were visible and, hello! How had I never noticed that Arthur had fantastic thighs? Like, really hot and—

Okay, I should absolutely *not* be checking him out right now. Bad form.

"Hey," I said, embarrassed and unsure where to look.

I glanced at his injured left leg, which was outstretched, his knee in a medical brace over the long johns with an ACE bandage holding an ice pack in place. He didn't look like he was in pain anymore. But he did look fatigued. There was even a stray lock of hair that stuck out a little wildly near the top of his head that he hadn't noticed or bothered to tamp back down. Which was unusual and spoke to his being out of sorts.

My heart melted for him.

"Hello," he replied in a weary tone.

"How are you feeling?" I asked. His boots were also off, and he only wore very thick ski socks. They were black with a light gray diamond pattern around the ankles.

"Like I was gang-tackled in rugby," he informed me with a wry tug at the corner of his mouth. "But I don't have a concussion."

"Are you sure?" I moved closer. "I mean, maybe someone should stay up with you and make sure you don't accidentally fall asleep and slip into a coma."

Random rom-com plots *could* come in handy, right . . . ?

He shook his head. "I'm exhibiting no symptoms. And I feel fine. It's mainly my knee."

"Do you need help walking?" I took a step farther into the space but made sure to keep a respectable distance.

"I have crutches." He nodded to an aluminum pair propped up against a mobile medical station beside me.

"Oh."

"But thank you for retrieving help for me." He smiled, and I felt my heartbeat pick up.

"Of course! I mean, you did rescue me off a mountain. The least I could do was return the favor ten seconds later. Not that they're equal, you know. Disaster-wise."

He grinned. "Well, they're certainly no out-of-control reindeer or sudden blizzard . . ."

That made me smile. "Don't pretend you don't miss the reindeer."

"I wouldn't dream of it."

There was a moment of silence between us, filled with all sorts of things we needed to discuss yet both of us knowing this wasn't the right place.

"How are you getting back to your cabin?" I asked. "I can go see about a rideshare, if you'd like?"

He shook his head again. "Actually, I've already called for a ride." He held up his phone, which I now noticed he'd been holding by his side.

"You have a chauffeur?" I teased.

A deep and distinct voice behind me said, "No. He has his father."

Arthur's entire bearing went rigid, and his eyes darted over my right shoulder.

I turned to see a gray-haired, slender white man in black slacks and a black cable-knit sweater with a white turtleneck peeking out from the collar standing in the opening between the curtains where I'd just been.

He was older, much older than my father, though Dad was always the youngest among my peers', so most everyone else's seemed older by comparison. But this man was at least in his late fifties, maybe early sixties. He felt even older. Honestly, if he hadn't just used the word "father" to describe himself, I would have pegged him more as Arthur's grandfather.

Arthur said he was an "oops" baby. We both were. Unlike my mom and dad, who'd gotten unexpectedly pregnant their senior year of high school, his parents were older when their surprise son came along.

I didn't realize how much older until now.

Yet there was no mistaking the posture of the man before me. It was pure Watercress. At least now I knew where Arthur got his uptight side.

What in the heck was his dad doing here?

Not just in this clinic but in the United States?

Arthur said his parents lived outside of London. In the fancy part. I couldn't remember the name of the neighborhood, which wasn't important in the moment, only that it was where the monied people chose to live.

"Hello, Papa," Arthur said, his tone formal.

Pa-*pah*.

"Arthur," was the acknowledgment he received in return. It was awkward. And cold. Not unlike the look the man directed my way.

Arthur nodded to me. "Finley, this is my father, Lord Lionel Watercress. Papa, this . . . is Finley Brown."

Don't think I didn't notice Arthur's slight hesitation before he said my name because I so did. I also didn't miss the way Lord Watercress's pale-blue eyes scanned me head to toe before he stiffly nodded in my direction.

"Ms. Brown." Then he turned his attention squarely back to Arthur. "Are you well enough?" His English accent was much crisper than Arthur's, which was a feat because Arthur sounded pretty darned crisp to my Middle American ears.

"Yes, sir."

"Good. Are you able to walk?"

"Yes, sir. With assistance, until the swelling subsides." He nodded to the crutches, which were a few feet away, out of his reach.

Lord Watercress looked from them to me, and I instantly realized what he expected. Before you could say *Hey, I'm not some hired assistant!* I had grabbed the crutches and handed them to Arthur, who said, "Thank you," while briefly glancing at me.

"There," Lord Watercress said. "Now you have assistance."

"Yes, sir," was Arthur's automatic reply as he carefully slipped his uninjured right leg off the bed and onto the ground, tucking his crutches beneath his armpits to help his balance.

Lord Watercress cocked his arm and flicked back the sleeve of his sweater enough to read his watch. "The car is waiting out front," he informed his son, and his tone got my own back up.

Maybe I was too American, but it pissed me off. The superiority of it all.

Before I knew it, I grabbed the hospital's plastic bag that held Arthur's ski pants and boots from where they'd been placed on the small chair and held it out to Lord Watercress.

He didn't make so much as a twitch toward it, didn't acknowledge it in any way, to the point it became uncomfortable.

I refused to lower my arm.

Pale-blue eyes met mine. Neither of us moved.

Full standoff.

Until Arthur gently took the bag from me with a quiet, "Thank you."

Lord Watercress stepped back out of the medical bay's space and into the hallway. With a final once-over directed at me, followed by, "Ms. Brown," Arthur's father exited.

Arthur shifted his weight on his crutches while gripping the top of the plastic bag in his right hand. He glanced at me, and I felt his embarrassment.

"Thank you for everything, Finley," he told me, his voice low.

My heart clenched and I reached out to touch his forearm, squeezing it once through his ski jacket, wanting some form of contact.

"Thank *you* for what you did for me," I replied.

We shared a smile.

Then, not able to stand it any longer, I reached up with my other hand to smooth down that one stray lock of hair back into place. There. Much better. But my hand seemed to have thoughts of its own as it slid down the side of his face. Our eyes met, and I suddenly felt the breathtaking pull toward him as we leaned—

"Now, Arthur," Lord Watercress's voice called out from farther down the hallway.

I dropped my hand and quickly stepped back. Arthur cleared his throat, shook his head once, saying, "Bye."

He maneuvered around the curtains, out of bay 3, and out of my sight.

For several moments after they'd gone, I remained standing there, my pulse racing, wondering over and over: *What. Just. Happened?*

Sixteen

"Y ou met Arthur's dad?!" Ayisha then whistled.

We were in our room. She laid across the width of her bed while I sat on mine, eating voraciously.

I'd gotten back to Lancaster Lodge a little over an hour after leaving the medical clinic. Too exhausted to go out to do a proper après-ski, which would probably entail hanging out in one of the lodge's restaurants with some of my classmates.

Thankfully, Ayisha had ordered ahead, so there was a cart with trays of food, including a club sandwich, loaded fries, mozzarella sticks, a banana, and an enormous slice of red velvet cake. I felt no guilt. Every calorie was earned.

Having caught Ayisha up on the basics of my afternoon, if not the more important details, I paused the act of scarfing yet another fry to make a face. "I'm not sure if 'met' is the right word. More like 'experienced.' Or maybe 'survived.'" I ate three fries in rapid succession, not even embarrassed that I was talking with my mouth full. "I swear to God, Ay, if there'd been thunder and lightning behind him, it would've totally fit the moment."

"Did you know he was going to be in America?"

"No clue," I said, dipping a fry into a tiny dish of ranch dressing. "What do you think he's doing here?"

"Your guess is as good as mine," I replied with a shrug. "But Arthur got super tense when he showed up."

"Really? Are they tight?"

I paused shoveling food into my mouth. "I don't know if that's the case," I said. "I get the impression Arthur respects his father."

I bit my lip and added for myself: *Or maybe fears him.* Because there had been a glint of something in his dark eyes when he realized it was his "papa" standing there at the edge of the bay and it wasn't familial love. And then there were the stories he told me about his parents when we were back in Christmas, stories that helped explain his deep affection for Esha and gave a glimpse into who his parents were.

"How are you doing?" Ayisha asked, watching me carefully. "You know, seeing Arthur again like that?"

I hesitated. I'd decided not to tell her about the maybe near-kiss. That still felt private. And confusing. But also exciting and wonderful and I wanted to hold on to it a bit longer.

"It made me miss him more," I admitted. "Like, I'd been trying not to go there, you know? About how much I missed seeing his stupid face."

"Cute stupid face."

"Cute stupid face," I agreed with a small laugh and blush. "But then he had to come swooping in like that and . . ." I sighed and pushed a fry around my plate a moment. Deciding. Maybe I wasn't ready to tell her we almost kissed, but I was dying to tell someone that, "He said he didn't want to break up with me."

Ayisha's eyes grew comically wide. "Way to bury the lede, Finley Brown!" I barely managed to deflect the pillow she tossed at me. "Tell me."

"There's not much to update. He dropped that bomb, and right as he was about to tell me is when he got taken out by the ski kid."

Her head dropped back in frustration. "Now I'm more mad at that brat."

I was so with her on that one.

"Where does Bronwyn fit into all this?" she continued. "I thought you said they were together."

"I *thought* they were, now I'm not so sure." I bit my lip. "I may have misread the situation." Though I didn't think I'd misread Bronwyn's part. Just Arthur's. Possibly?

Ayisha leveled me with one of her assessing looks. "Are you two getting back together?"

A rush of . . . something—excitement? Hope? Fear?—had me catch my breath.

That would've been the logical next step. He still liked me, I never stopped liking him. A lot. We should be able to get back together. But there was something that told me it wouldn't be that easy. I felt it.

Maybe it was that look in his eyes before he was bowled over on the slopes that seemed regretful. There was something more. Something I didn't know yet.

I struggled not to be fatalistic, but the truth was, "I have no idea."

"You want to, though. You're not pretending you're 'over him' anymore, are you?"

"Did I ever pretend that?" I said, leaning into playfulness I didn't fully feel.

She snorted. "Not successfully."

We both chuckled.

Her phone erupted with five texts in rapid succession.

She hastily put a pillow over it to mute the noise, but it was too late; my curiosity had been revived.

"I've been totally chill about not asking," I said, chewing a bit of greasy mozzarella stick. "But now I'm asking: Who's been blowing up your phone?"

She pursed her lips as she considered what—if anything—to tell me. "You're assuming it's one person," she evaded.

"*Is* it more than one person?" I asked, intrigued. Honestly, the way people fawned all over her, including me, the idea was plausible.

"Nah," she grinned. "I just like to keep you guessing." She winked, and I rolled my eyes, eating another fry. She sat up on her bed, grabbing a pillow and slapping it against her own midsection. Holding it like a shield. Her dark eyes grew contemplative for a moment before she said, "His name's Scotty Bu. He's half Korean and seventeen and I met him at that fancy restaurant Mamma took me and the twins to when I first got here."

I frowned. "La Belle's?"

She nodded. "That's the one. He was there with a friend, and he did that meet-cute thing where he bumped into me. Knocked my phone out of my hands, then made a big production trying to catch it before it smashed to the ground."

"Did he?" I asked.

A corner of her mouth tugged up. "He did. He's kind of athletic. Plays lacrosse. Anyhow, we only talked a little bit, not even a minute, before Linda came over to tell me we were leaving. Scotty managed to get that I was going to Barrington and my name—"

"How'd he get that?"

"Linda said it. And that was enough info for him to track me down."

I scowled. "That sounds creepy stalker."

"That's what I thought, too! But he grew up near Barrington and knows some kids who go there. He had Landon Sinclaire give me his name and number and socials. I checked him out for a while, made sure he's legit, saw what he's like."

"What's he like?"

"Do you know Dr. Nico Kim on *Grey's Anatomy*?"

"No."

She sighed and shook her head in annoyance. "Your pop culture needs a revamp."

"*Grey's Anatomy*'s been on longer than I've been alive!" I countered in my own defense. "There've been, like, thousands of people on that show. I'm surprised you know it so well."

"I watch it with Mamma; it's one of her favorites. That and *Bridgerton*. Which I do *not* watch with her." Her eyes widened in mock horror.

"Just show me his picture," I said, holding out my hand and making a grabby motion.

She scrolled through her photos on her phone until she found one in particular. She stopped and widened the image before turning it to me for my inspection.

"Whoa," I said at the handsome face staring back at me. Lean and angular, his jawline was impressively sharp and his cheekbones could cut glass. It was a posed photo, likely a formal one for class, if his dark coat and tie were any indication. That only made the fact he still managed to strike a dark-eyed smolder look even more impressive.

"Right?" Ayisha bit her lower lip.

"Are you guys a couple?"

She dropped her phone into her lap. "I've only met him for one minute!"

"Apparently you work fast," I teased, taking a bite of sandwich to hide my smile. "Spill. What's the deal?" I cajoled with a half-full mouth. Gross, but whatever.

She drew in a deep breath and told me, "He's here."

I did a double take and swallowed my bite. "Here?!" I eked out, my voice rising sharply. "At the resort?"

She shook her head. "At his parents' cabin. It's a half mile from here." She gestured behind herself, in the direction of the window.

"Are his parents there too?"

"Nope." She shook her head deliberately.

My eyebrows rose. "Oh?"

"Not like that." She made a face. "I mean, microwave popcorn takes longer to make than the amount of time we've spent together."

I snorted, then asked, "What about video calling?"

She held up two fingers and said, "Video calls. Otherwise, it's been text. His parents are kinda hard-asses about him getting good grades. Which, I can totally relate."

"But they let him go to a ski weekend and use their cabin?"

"They said no at first. But he got his stepsister to agree to tag along. He says she's crazy uptight, and I guess they're thinking she'll keep him in line."

"Will she?" Ayisha shrugs, hands in the air. "Where are his parents now?"

"Somewhere in South Korea. Scotty's dad used to be an assistant secretary there." There was a note of pride in her voice that she couldn't fully suppress.

"Impressive." I toy with a mozzarella stick, ignoring the banana. "And Scotty's nearby now?"

"Yep."

I watched her closely, realizing, "He's why you wanted to come here this weekend, isn't he? Why you asked me to come here with you."

She squirmed. "When you say it like that, it makes it sound like I tricked you," she countered defensively.

"Well, you didn't tell me the whole story," I tossed back, not accusing but not backing down, either.

She sighed in annoyance, but there was also a hint of chagrin. "Fine. I'm not exactly comfortable talking about him, okay?"

"Because of him, or because of me?"

She looked up and our eyes met. "Because of *me*," she admitted in a low voice, tapping an index finger against her chest. "I'm not a big 'girl talk' kinda girl. With anyone," she added for my clarification.

"Even your friends back home?"

She shook her head, her braids swishing against her shoulders. "Especially them. Keyla and Joy, boys are all they think about." She absently fiddled with the corner of the pillowcase. "That's part of why I wanted to get away, go someplace where there's more to talk about, more to see."

I nodded, understanding completely. "And yet," I said, pointing a french fry at her. "Here we are, talking about a boy."

She laughed at the irony, then fanned herself. "I'm telling you, Finley, he is *fine*."

Now I laughed.

I hadn't really known her when she was the girlfriend of our mutual ex, Brody, back home in Oklahoma, but I couldn't imagine her acting so openly girly about him. She had always felt like a fully formed adult in comparison to him. Though, most people did when compared to Brody. And frankly, she seemed like an adult next to most kids. But there was something about this Scotty guy that turned the normally stoic Ayisha almost starry-eyed. Which, now having seen his photo, I got.

There was more.

"He's having a party tonight," she said casually. "At the cabin. We could go . . ." Her eyebrows rose questioningly, a hint of hopefulness.

An uncomfortable tightness came over my chest, which was pretty standard whenever I thought about going to a party, especially when I didn't know the people who'd be there. It was why I'd downed one of my old roommate's tiny bottles of wine before venturing out to Bronwyn's Halloween party last year.

Ayisha sensed my hesitation, or maybe it was that obvious. Probably the latter.

"If you hate it, we'll leave," she promised. "It's just . . ." She sighed. "I want to see if there's something there. Or if I'm just imagining it."

"Because of the hotness?" I teased lightly.

A cheeky grin blossomed across her face. "Well, that doesn't exactly *hurt*."

We both giggled.

Ayisha had stepped up at several points last Christmas when I was trying to figure out how to go out into a raging blizzard to find Arthur as part of an ill-conceived grand gesture. I couldn't have done it without her, and while I didn't think she'd use the "you owe me" card, I *did* owe her.

I also wanted her to meet a guy who could maybe be *her* guy. She had done so much for her mother and her sisters, to the point she almost lost her own dream. She deserved to have something, or in this case some*one*, she wanted.

There was also my own vow to push myself out of my comfort zone, for which this definitely qualified. Besides, what else was I going to do tonight? Stay in and think about what Arthur would have said if he hadn't been taken out midsentence?

All these reasons swirled around my head, and I found myself nodding even before I said, "Sure. Let's go."

Then I sent up a silent prayer.

Seventeen

The Bu family cabin wasn't part of the Lancaster lodge cabins and was considerably nicer.

It was off a dark, winding road thankfully cleared of snow and looked like it should be on the cover of *Architectural Digest*. All windows and logs and artfully arranged lighting to help create an effect.

A cab dropped me and Ayisha to the start of the driveway, the driver refusing to tackle the steep angle. I couldn't blame him. It was daunting. Thankfully, it was also cleared, otherwise there was no way Ayisha and I would've been able to make the climb in our fashionable boots.

But make it we did, and made our way up the front path as well.

Thundering music from within greeted us before Ayisha reached for the handle and opened the unlocked front door.

The entry led straight into a massive living room with high pine-log ceilings and sleek furniture, more modern than expected and likely custom-made.

Heavy linen drapes covered the windows on the far side of the room, and there was a group of sweater-clad guys playing a video game about skiing on the enormous flat screen. (Because why not fake ski when you've probably spent all day real skiing?) I recognized Nolan Zhào and Eadrich Pinto from school in that group and fleetingly wondered if they were together.

The sounds of the gamer activity were drowned out by the resounding thump of a top-of-the-line sound system that made the songs feel like they were coming at us from every direction.

"You came!" The deep voice managed to rise above the din.

Ayisha and I turned to see an Adonis I instantly recognized as Scotty Bu weaving through a few clusters of partygoers on his approach to us. His smile split his perfect face. He wore expensive jeans and a solid sapphire-blue sweater that really did him justice.

I could tell by the way she straightened up beside me that Ayisha thought so, too, but her voice was the epitome of nonchalant. "I told you we'd consider coming by."

He stopped before us, grinning. "That's awesome." He then— politely—turned his attention to me, and I felt the power of his smile. "You must be Finley. I'm Scotty."

I gave a little wave. "Hi."

As expected, his focus remained mostly on Ayisha. "Can I get you ladies something to drink?" he offered as he smoothly guided us farther into the room semi-full of teenagers around our age.

A couple of clusters of kids moved, and we got our first glimpse of what had to be the most elaborate food and beverage table I'd seen not at a wedding. At the center there was a sizable pyramid of colorful Jell-O shot cups that I felt confident were spiked. There was also a three-tier party punch bowl with a red beverage of some nature cascading over the sides, a chocolate fondue fountain, trays of sandwiches, cheese plates, and a side table for bottles of wine.

Ayisha's wide eyes reflected how I felt. "Wow."

Scotty puffed up his already impressive chest. "I like to do things right," he said with no effort at being humble.

Ayisha's lips twitched. "You paid to have it catered."

"Impressed?" he said with a charming grin straight out of a toothpaste commercial.

"We'll see how the night goes." She looked up at where the speakers were probably embedded. "Music's kinda lame."

"You don't like Kanye?"

"Is it 2005?" she retorted.

He made a motion with his hand as if it were on fire. "Damn. Tough crowd." But it was clear he liked her comeback. And everything else about her. "How 'bout you help me pick out some bangin' tunes?"

He offered her his elbow.

Which she took, telling him, "Somebody's gotta do it up right."

She glanced back at me, checking, but sometimes the best thing a "wing-woman" could do was know when to step back, so I shook my head. She got it, and I watched them walk off together.

Leaving me with the three-tier punch bowl. Bookending it were two large candles decoratively ensconced in glass holders with open tops, a surprising attempt at "classy," I suppose. All I could think was: *If someone bumps into that . . .*

Maybe that said more about me.

Then again, if Arthur were here, I knew he wouldn't approve either. Especially situated above a fancy rug that screamed "expensive!" Which was a roundabout way to get me back to thinking about Arthur. And the text I'd sent him earlier, while I sat on my bed as Ayisha finished getting ready in our shared bathroom.

It had been quick and friendly: **Hope you're feeling better! Let me know if you need anything.**

That was something friends would send, right? Showing concern about a recent injury and offering assistance, though I knew he'd have every convenience at his disposal.

Still, it was the thought that counted.

The friendly thought. Totally friendly.

Because that was what we were. Friends.

Though I didn't want to.

Then again, there was that. He'd said *that*. And I was pretty sure friends *didn't* say that. Or look at your mouth through half-hooded eyes as they lean in to almost kiss you . . .

I swallowed and my heart started to flutter again as that particular memory made its approximately one billionth appearance across my mind.

Despite the *Read 7:14 p.m.* below my text, he had yet to reply.

I was trying very, very hard not to take that personally.

"Fin!" a boy's voice called.

American. Not British.

Surprised to hear my name, I turned to see Gaines Alder approaching, arms thrown open wide, his eyes slightly glassy. His hair was gelled and his black turtleneck sweater reminded me of a Calvin Klein winter catalog. He was handsome, no doubt.

Just not my kind of handsome.

"What are you doing here?" I asked as his arms came around me. He smelled like rum.

"It's a party." He leaned back, his grin goofy. "And I do likes myself a party."

There was something about how he said it that made me laugh. Moving back out of his embrace, I glanced around the room.

I recognized several of the faces. Pouty Pashley from the Valentine's Day Committee was here, talking with two other girls who I knew by sight were also from our school.

Caldwell Harrington was with some friends I didn't recognize.

He'd noticed Ayisha's arrival, and the fact she'd gone off with Scotty. I felt for the poor guy, but another part of me wanted to tell him, *Get in line.*

"There's a lot of Barrington people here," I noted to Gaines. "I didn't expect that."

"Scotty throws some of the best parties. His mom owns a catering biz, which he liberally utilizes." He randomly booped the top of my head with his index finger, then took a long pull from the clear glass bottle. I didn't recognize the label. "And Mr. Scotty B. went to Barrington our freshman year before transferring, so these people"—he waved his arm toward the crowd—"know him."

"Why did he leave?"

Gaines rolled his eyes. "Girls."

My back went up. "That feels misogynistic."

He pursed his lips mischievously. "Would it be better if I said 'relationships' but with the same eye-roll effect?" He demonstrated. "Thus taking gender out of the equation?" He pressed his palm flat against his chest and said dramatically, "For we have all struggled with matters of the heart."

Despite myself, I laughed at his silliness. "Yeah? What are your struggles?"

He sighed, and I felt a hint of actual pathos behind the façade. "Invisibility."

It was such an odd answer it caught me by surprise. "You don't seem invisible," I said. With his good looks and impressive attire, that seemed almost impossible.

He liked that, standing straighter before he bowed. "Why, thank you. You're looking mighty visible yourself." He touched the end of a lock of my hair in a way that should have annoyed me, but his energy wasn't predatory. More boyish, despite his height and clear trajectory toward manhood. "Were you always this blonde?" he asked, puzzled.

"Yep." I nodded. "It's natural."

His eyes narrowed thoughtfully. "I've heard of such creatures, the genuine blonde. A rare breed."

I nodded to the bottle in his hand. "How many of those have you had?"

"This?" He waggled the bottle. "This is my first. But what I'm holding contains hops alone, no alcohol. I have, however, had three green Jell-O shots in the past half hour, and it's entirely possible they may be having an effect."

He pointed over his shoulder at the pyramid.

"I think that's a good bet," I agreed, biting back a chuckle.

He narrowed one eye. "And what, pray tell, brings you to this fine gathering of humanity, Miss Finley Brown with the authentic blonde hair?"

"I came with Ayisha."

"Ah." He nodded, and I was concerned it might make him dizzy. "The lovely Ayisha. Our fearless Valentine's Day Committee co-leader." He glanced around. "Where is she?"

"There." I turned to point across the room, where she and Scotty were talking next to the sound system in the corner. He said something and she laughed, her hand touching his shoulder. Flirtation was clearly afoot. "Talking with Scotty."

To my surprise, Gaines's goofy demeanor slipped at the sight. "So she is." He appeared to quickly sober up. "They seem friendly." He frowned as if concerned. "*Are* they friendly?"

I cocked an eyebrow at the odd question. "Should they be fighting?"

His voice was low as he muttered, "It might turn out better for everyone if they were . . ."

Now I was just confused. "What?"

He ignored me. Instead, he set down his bottle. "I'm probably too late," he said to himself as he grabbed his phone from his back pocket. "But I have to try to . . ." He didn't finish his sentence, tapping on the screen. "Excuse . . ." He didn't finish that sentence either as he moved away from me, headed toward the front foyer with purpose.

It was baffling. As far I knew, Gaines was not one of the many guys to fall for Ayisha at first sight, then why—

"He's gone to call her," a familiar girl's voice said from behind me, and I turned to see the last person on earth I expected standing beside the red punch fountain.

Petra Bergerac.

I jumped back in shock. "Holy shi—" I blinked rapidly trying to process the fact that, "You're . . . not in our room!"

No, she was not.

She was watching me as if I was a weirdo, which, to be fair, I deserved, given how I'd just reacted.

But I had never seen my new roommate anywhere other than our room. I also hadn't seen her in jeans or a purple sweater. It was disorienting. At least she still had her red hair pulled up in that mega-tight ponytail. I might not have recognized her if she didn't.

"What?" she asked, pushing her glasses up the bridge of her nose. "Did you think I was a ghost of a former student who haunts that dorm room?"

"No," I said with a laugh, "but in hindsight I'm a little disappointed in myself that that possibility didn't occur to me."

"It *would* be cool," she agreed without a hint of a smile. "But I'm not a ghost."

I waved a hand over my brow. "Whew." Then I remembered, "Weren't you were going to stay at school for the weekend?"

Her hazel-green eyes grew annoyed, though you would have to look closely to notice. Micro-expressions were her method of choice.

"That had been the plan. Then Scotty promised to pay for all of my books for the next two years if I agreed to be here, otherwise our parents wouldn't let him come up here."

I blinked rapidly as my brain processed the realization that, "*You're* Scotty's stepsister?"

The tiny flash of annoyance grew ever so slightly brighter. "We are each other's stepsiblings." She arched a single red eyebrow. "It's equal."

Being an only child, I wasn't familiar with sibling dynamics in general or stepsiblings in any capacity. Brody used to complain all the time about his older brothers, and Mia's relationship with her sister, who was only a year younger, was a constant source of aggravation for her. Even what little Arthur had mentioned about his older sister, Polly, wasn't the strongest bond. To put it mildly.

"Noted," I said, my mind still abuzz. "When did you get here? I thought you were in our room when I left."

"Yes, and you were loud."

"Sorry."

Her nod was perfunctory. Apology accepted? "Scotty picked me up later this morning after you'd left."

That made sense. Also, I wish I'd known anything about their relationship. I'd have asked to catch a ride so I didn't have to deal with the bus.

Then I remembered another thing.

"What did you say a second ago? About Gaines?"

At the mention of his name, the tiny light in her eyes shifted to something else I couldn't identify. Something personal. "He's gone off to call his keeper. But I already saw her coming up the driveway. That's why I came out of my room, to record the fireworks."

She held up her iPhone.

"Who's his 'keeper'?"

Petra didn't answer. Instead, she hit the "video" button to start recording as she turned to face the front foyer.

I glanced over in time to see a rage-filled Bronwyn stomp through the front doors as if she were about to storm the US Capitol, with a concerned Gaines and Josie behind her, hurrying to keep up.

"Her," Petra finally said, nodding at Bronwyn as she blazed her way across the central room.

What was most surprising, though, was who she was laser-focused on.

Ayisha and Scotty.

Or, more specifically, Ayisha.

Bronwyn shouted "You *bitch*!" loud enough to be heard above the music, and though it was entirely digital, that was a total "re-cord scratch" moment.

Ayisha's eyes flashed. "*Excuse* me?" she shot back at Bronwyn, her back up.

Scotty turned to see her. His eyes widened in the definition of "Oh, shit!"

Petra kept her phone trained on the unfolding scene.

I quickly moved around her and got closer to the situation as Bronwyn jabbed her index finger at Ayisha. "*Get* away from him. Right. Fucking. Now!"

Kids turned to watch the spectacle.

"What is your deal?" Ayisha was not about to back down.

Scotty's focus swished between them. "Bron—"

"Shut up!" she shouted.

He frowned. "Hey, now." He reached a hand in front of Bronwyn to block her advance.

"Do not *touch* me!" She hip-checked him backward and he bumped the table. Things shimmied.

Scotty jumped away. "Careful! My dad just had this place renovated!"

I reached Ayisha's side and whispered, "What's happening?"

"I don't know, but"—her jaw jutted out—"nobody talks to me like that!"

Bronwyn clenched her fists. "Then you *need* to keep your hands off other people's person!"

Ayisha shook her head in frustrated confusion. "What are you talking about?"

"I'm talking about *you* touching my boyfriend, Prescott Bu." Bronwyn pointed at Scotty and—

Oh!

Well, now I knew where Prescott had gone. Not far, as it turned out.

Ayisha shot him a sharp look. "Boyfriend?"

Scotty held up both hands in surrender. "We broke up!" Then to Bronwyn, "We broke up!"

Bronwyn wasn't having it. "We've broken *up* three times a year since we were fourteen! It never sticks!" She narrowed her gaze at Ayisha. "Ne-*ver*." Then she looked back at Scotty/Prescott in accusation. "This is why you tried to get me not to come skiing this year!"

Scotty looked guilty, which he quickly deflected into anger. He glared at Gaines. "Why the fuck didn't you tell me she was here? I thought she was in New York!"

"Bron wanted it to be a surprise," Gaines said in his defense. "I didn't know you were trying to get into some other girl's pants, Scotty."

Ayisha waved her hand at them. "Okay, this is way more drama than I bargained for." She turned to me. "You ready?"

I nodded. "Yep." *So ready.*

Ayisha and I got halfway back across the living room before

Scotty caught up with us, scooting around to block our exit. By this point, even the gamers had stopped to pay attention.

Petra wasn't the only one with her phone out.

"Please don't go," Scotty begged to Ayisha, his hands on her shoulders to stop her.

Bronwyn joined us, with Gaines and Josie in her wake.

"You're touching her?" Bronwyn scoffed disbelievingly. "In *front* of me?"

Ayisha kept her focus on Scotty. "Let go of me." Her tone was low and icy.

He instantly dropped his hands. Which somehow further pissed off Bronwyn.

"*Don't* tell him what to do," she snapped.

Ayisha leveled her an incredulous look. "You are seriously mental."

I snickered because, well, the whole situation was bordering on ridiculous. Suddenly the piercing anger in her blue eyes was directed at me.

"And *you!*" she seethed, moving closer to me. "You think you're going to land someone like Arthur Watercress? Ha! You don't have a chance! I know that for a *fact!*"

My mouth dropped open. *Whoa.* I was not prepared for this turn. I felt her words as if she'd struck me.

Blinking rapidly, I took a step back, my hip coming in contact with an edge of the food table. It shook.

"Careful!" Scotty said, his voice tight with panic.

Bronwyn kept going, though. "His father won't *ever* allow it. So now you can kiss all your dreams about being his little girlfriend and being *a lady* in London bye-bye." She added a finger wave to up the taunting factor.

I felt the prick of tears threatening at the back of my eyes. It was mortifying. I wished I could have come up with something smart or quick as a comeback, but my mind went completely blank. Like, words? What are you? Where did you go? Come back!

To my surprise, Gaines stepped forward. "Hey, not cool, Bron," he told her.

If the flash in Bronwyn's blue eyes was any indication, she wasn't expecting that either. She recovered fast to snip at him, "Shut up, Gaines. You're drunk. And I'm the one who told you to be nice to her"—she pointed at me—"in the first place."

Petra said, "You can't trust him."

Gaines frowned at her, and Bronwyn snapped, "You're such a weasel, Petra."

My heart was beating about a million miles an hour. A glance around the room revealed several people were recording this, and I realized they had captured everything Bronwyn had said about me and Arthur and I felt lightheaded, like that woozy moment when a roller coaster drops its first sharp drop and your body thinks it's plummeting to its death.

Scotty's attention was still on the table. "Could we all just move away—"

Ayisha stepped around him. "I'm so over with this *Real Housewives* wannabe crap."

Then I saw a raw anger in Bronwyn's eyes that made the hairs on the back of my neck go up as she shouted, "You hold on! I'm not *done* talking," while simultaneously lunging toward Ay, reaching out to grab at her—

And I can't really explain it.

Maybe it was because of how many different emotions were already churning inside me—fear, anger, a strong protective instinct, embarrassment at having the end of my fledgling relationship with Arthur made unexpectedly public, confusion over the as yet unknown backstory between all of these people, and a very clear sense of burning resentment—but seeing her go after Ayisha like that had me react without thinking.

"Yes, you are!" I shouted as I moved to intercept Bronwyn.

Now, to be clear, my intent was to put my arm in front of her, blocking her from touching Ayisha.

However, that didn't happen.

My move to "block" her advance inadvertently wound up with my hand connecting hard with her upper chest, knocking her sideways and backward.

And straight into the food table.

Which was not planned.

None of it was planned. It was all pure impulse: *Stop her!*

But the way Bronwyn landed across the table, dead center, breaking it in half so she was immediately covered in red punch and gooey chocolate and plastic cups of Jell-O?

Yeah, *absolutely* not planned.

I heard several partygoers go "Oh!!!" like when a crowd watches the replay of a football player knocked on his ass by a perfect tackle and my breath caught in shock.

Oh. My. God . . .

What had I done?!

Scotty looked like he might faint. Particularly when one of the large candles hit the floor, shattered its glass container, and rolled up against the curtains—

Let's just say I was right about that particular open-flame-at-a-teenager-party miscalculation.

Scotty yelled and ran into the other room as fire started to take hold of the thick linen fabric.

Red punch spilled out in every direction, leaving its stain on the fancy rug like the aftermath of a murder scene. Someone somewhere was screaming, and I watched Josie try to help a struggling

Bronwyn get to her feet only to lose her own balance and fall into the spontaneous chocolate/punch/Jell-O concoction as Gaines merely watched and Kanye blathered loudly over the speakers.

I felt a hand clamp down on my wrist. "Now," Ayisha commanded, and pulled me after her without waiting for my reply.

Believe me, I went willingly.

It was only when we reached the threshold of the front door that I paused to glance over my shoulder in time to see Scotty frantically unpinning the fire extinguisher to tackle the drapes that were now half-engulfed in flames as a stunned Bronwyn stood covered in the contents of the food table while Petra and a dozen other kids steadfastly recorded the whole darned thing.

Eighteen

JANUARY 18

"I'm going to get kicked out of Barrington," I said for the thousandth time since the events of the night before, my stomach cramping with anxiety.

It made sense. I'd "pulled an Arthur," and that had been what had gotten him banned from darned near every major private school in England. Granted, I only took out my intended target, whereas he had inadvertently caused harm to that backstabbing Astrid girl when the boy he'd struck had fallen back like a domino and hit her in the face.

But the ultimate outcome was sure to be the same: expulsion.

What else could be the result? I mean, that's the punishment I'd give myself if I had been an adult hearing about what had taken place at the Bu family cabin. It was totally justified.

The only thing was nothing had happened yet.

It was nine the next morning and I knew, with that many people at the party and that many phones recording, there was no way it hadn't gotten out and spread like wildfire.

And yet . . .

Nothing.

Not a single TikTok. Or Insta Story. Or tweet. Or Snapchat.

It was radio silence on all fronts. Including Bronwyn's, with her thousands of followers. Her last Instagram post had been a smiling photo of her and Josie in their ski suits atop one of the slopes.

Ayisha and I had been checking since the moment we'd arrived back in our lodge room, but twelve hours later there wasn't even a peep from any of the socials from a Barrington student. Neither one of us could make sense of it.

That didn't mean I wasn't still entirely convinced that my doom was imminent. How could it not be? There was no way someone like Bronwyn Campbell would allow this transgression to go unavenged.

Dramatic? Yes. But this was Bronwyn. Drama was her nectar. (See last night for examples.)

There was also our chaperone teachers to consider. While, yes, The Shove—as Ayisha and I were now calling what I'd done—was technically off school property and away from the official lodge designated by our school-sponsored trip, it was still going to be considered under the umbrella of Barrington's rules. Rules that stated very clearly violence of any nature was grounds for immediate removal. They had to have heard about it by now. Right?

I knew nothing.

Hence my anxiety-induced pacing back and forth in our room as Ayisha sat on her bed, watching me wear down the flooring so it'd soon rival the lodge's front lobby.

Scotty had texted her about an hour after we'd left his place to tell her they'd gotten the fire out before too much damage was done. The custom-made rug from Morocco, however, was a goner.

So was the enormous TV screen. That part hadn't been my fault, happily. One of the gamers had gotten frustrated and tossed the wireless remote at the screen, shattering it.

We didn't get many more details about the events. Turned out, the romance between Ayisha and Scotty—aka *Prescott*—Bu was shorter than the one between me and Arthur.

Who had at least replied to my text later last night with: Thank you. I'm well and healing. No need for assistance, but your offer is greatly appreciated.

Seriously, who texted like that? I was surprised he didn't sign off, *Sincerely, Arthur. The idiot.* So why did it make me like him, and miss him, even more?

Clearly, *I* was the real idiot.

Especially given everything Bronwyn had said the night before. *His father won't* ever *allow it.*

The memory sent a chill through me. How did she know that? (*"For a fact!"*)

A swarm of questions buzzed around my brain like a plague of locusts. I hadn't been able to sit down for the past hour, or sleep all night, either, except for a couple of moments when my exhausted body had finally given in, only to have me wake up in a gasping, shouting panic not long after. Ayisha had loved that since I'd also woken her up in the process. (She would never be my roommate now, imminent expulsion aside.)

As if reading my mind, she swiped my phone off the end table jutting out of the wall between our beds and held it up to me.

"Ask Arthur questions," she said. "At least it'll take your mind off The Shove."

I hesitated, biting my lip. Then, feeling she might be right, I took the phone and stared down at his last dorky message. "What do I say?" I wondered helplessly.

"I don't know. But at least you're not pacing anymore. I was getting dizzy."

"Sorry," I mumbled, and resumed staring at my screen, feeling out of my depth.

Ayisha sighed and rubbed her eyes and I was reminded that I wasn't the only one going through something. I moved to sit on my bed opposite her, setting my phone aside atop the pine-green bedspread.

"How are *you* doing?"

"Peachy," she responded dryly.

"C'mon." I reached out my foot to lightly tap the top of hers. "Share."

Her lips twitched. "Are we going to talk about a boy again?"

I shrugged. "Unless you want to talk about the different types of love the ancient Greeks had."

"That was a good idea!" she pronounced in her own defense.

"It was," I agreed. "Are you and Scotty done-done?"

Her eyes hardened. "Oh, yeah. I don't need that kinda of whatever *that* was in my life." She shook her head, determined, and I could see they were definitely done-done.

"It wasn't his fault," I said, playing devil's advocate. "He said they were broken up."

She fixed me with a look. "Finley, he cared more about that damn table than he cared about how his spoiled-rotten on-again, off-again, whatever-again girlfriend was acting out, toward me *and* you. Uh-uh. I don't need someone like that in my life." She sighed. "No matter how hot he is."

"He really is."

"I know! *Ugh!*" She flopped back across her bed in frustration, crushing the pillow over her face with both arms. Then she tossed it aside and shifted to look over at me.

"Thanks, by the way," she said sincerely.

I frowned, confused. "For what?"

"For having my back when Bronwyn was coming at me like a vampire." She grinned.

I felt a blush of happy embarrassment at her gratitude; it didn't come easily. "Of course."

Her eyes sparkled. "Though we're gonna have to work on your defensive technique for next time."

I scoffed, "I seriously doubt there'll be a next time." *For so many reasons.*

Ayisha shrugged one shoulder. "With girls like her, there's always something. They aren't used to hearing 'no'."

She was right.

My phone buzzed from the bed.

I glanced down and sucked in a breath of surprise when I saw the texter's name and read the message.

Ayisha heard and sat up. "What?"

I held up the phone to show her the text.

It was from Arthur: Would you be able to come by the Franz Klammer Cabin within a half hour? My father will be away at a brunch and I do believe we should talk.

Nineteen

This was weird.

I stood on the cabin's front porch, shifting my weight from one foot to the other, clenching and unclenching my hands, not so much against the cold as against the nervousness that had me sweating beneath my layers of clothes and black peacoat.

Oh, great. I was sweating. In freezing temperatures. Always a fun combination. Especially on the cusp of seeing Arthur in a non-life-or-death-or-medical-clinic setting.

And talking. We would—thank you, God!—at long last be talking.

Which was what had me sweating. Also not knocking on the door. But when I did knock on the door, would a butler open it?

The Franz Klammer Cabin looked like any other of the cabins sprinkled around the Lancaster lodge's grounds—very nice, though the Bu family clearly won in the fancy-cabin contest. Then again, according to Ayisha they owned their cabin, while the Watercress family was probably renting this one and—

And boy, was I dragging this out.

I knocked on the door.

Really, though. *Would* they have a butler? A Jost? No, wait. Jost was their chef. Former chef. Who was retired now and no longer making delicious waffles and—why was I focusing on this?

Because as much as I wanted answers, I also dreaded them.

Because deep down I didn't think the answers would change our situation.

Because that was what I truly wanted: a change.

Arthur opened the door.

My heart leapt into my throat and it was possible I gulped.

He only had a single crutch and barely leaned against it, which was nonetheless closer to legitimate slouching than I could recall seeing from him.

He wasn't in lounge attire. Despite his knee being in discomfort, he wore pressed black slacks (the brace visible beneath) and a soft light gray sweater. The top of a starched white button-down peeked out from the crewneck collar. No Wranglers or vomiting-reindeer sweater anywhere in sight.

At least he wore the same slippers I remembered from his stay at Grandma Jo's inn, so there was some effort at comfort. Overall, though, he seemed like the boy whose chair I'd inadvertently stolen on our first day of classes back in the fall, not the one who roasted chestnuts by the inn's firepit.

And kissed me senseless.

Except for his eyes. There was a softness to their depths now as he looked at me that had been absent all those months ago, and for the past week.

I reminded myself to breathe.

"Please come in," he said, and opened the door wider for me to enter.

I did, passing closer to him than necessary. Sue me.

He closed the door as I stole a quick look around. The foyer was smaller than at the Bu's, with a staircase leading up to a second floor not visible from here. It was nice but gave off the aura of a rental: Neutral colors. Obligatory pine. A generic print of a snow-covered mountain.

"Would you like to hang your coat?" Arthur asked, nodding to the mahogany coat rack and umbrella stand in the corner to my left. It also held Arthur's puffy green jacket.

"Sure." I shrugged off my coat and hung it up.

I rubbed my sweaty palms against my jean-clad thighs as covertly as possible, then turned to face him. Plastering on a big smile, lips pressed together, totally fake.

"How's your knee?" I asked. Pointing, as if he didn't know how to locate his own knee.

"Much improved. I only need one of these now." He toggled the crutch.

I nodded and kept smiling. "Great!"

He cleared his throat and pointed farther into the house. "Shall we go to the living room? There's a fire going."

I followed him around a corner into said living room. Where there was indeed a log fire burning in the stone-faced fireplace.

This room was large and cavernous, though an effort at comfort had been made. A cluster of evergreens in front of the windows cultivated a rustic atmosphere and obscured any view. The furniture wasn't modern like it had been at the Bu's. This was dark brown leather mixed with heavy wood and more in keeping with what I would imagine for a cabin.

Arthur waved his free hand at the sofa, and I took a seat. To my disappointment, he sat on one of the two chairs flanking the central coffee table. I noticed a book on the end table beside his chair. Bookmark in place. *The Amazing Adventures of Kavalier & Clay.* My dad had that novel too. It was one of his favorites.

"Would you like something to drink?" he asked. "I could make some tea."

He started to rise again, but I waved a hand.

"No, that's okay."

He sat back down.

And said nothing. So, I said nothing. I wasn't the one who'd called this meeting. Or started our rift. (That I knew of.) *He* could be the one to get the ball rolling.

That turned out to be a terrible strategy. Moments of silence piled on top of moments of silence. Only thing missing was a grandfather clock ticking loudly to make the awkwardness complete.

He and I had had our uncomfortable moments before. Mostly either fighting or ignoring each other. Here we were doing neither.

And it was excruciating.

For a moment I considered breaking the ice with: *Guess what I did last night.*

I refrained. It would derail the non-conversation we were having from the one we needed to have, and that was more important to me than a chocolate-covered Bronwyn disaster.

Finally, I channeled my inner Midwestern politeness—which, like nature, hated a vacuum—and forced a smile. "Franz Klammer's a nice cabin," I said. Then, to make matters worse, I attempted a joke. "I hear he's a good skier, too."

Did I wiggle my eyebrows? Maybe.

Would my dad have said something like that? One hundred percent.

Was it awful? Beyond.

The worst part was Arthur chuckled. Not genuinely, of course. No one would. His was the chuckle one gave to be polite.

And that sucked.

Then the imaginary clock ticked off several more ticks, and all I wanted to was to go back to the lodge, where I could continue my anxious pacing as I waited for my inevitable ruin. Suddenly that felt preferable to this.

What I wanted to do was tell him, *I miss you.*

I didn't. I did sneak a peek at him and saw his fingers were toying with the arm of his chair, tugging on a stray piece of fabric that had escaped its bolting. This made me feel the tiniest bit better. I wasn't the only nervous person in the room.

A burning log in the fireplace popped loudly like a firecracker and we both jumped.

Our eyes met.

And I asked, "How long is your father going to be out?" Subtext being: *How much longer can this possibly go on?*

The answer was, "He should be home by noon, so about an hour. He's having a business brunch with Hatcher Campbell."

It took a second—Hatcher Campbell sounds like an aeronautics corporation—but then I realized with a frown, "Bronwyn's dad?" Arthur nodded. I remember something she'd said during that brief moment when she was being nice to me. "They have a deal going together . . . ?"

"That's right. It's what brought him to the States. Don't ask me the specifics."

Okay. Well. The mystery of Lord Watercress's unexpected presence was now solved. Check.

"I thought you liked finance," I said in an effort to keep the conversation going.

"I do. To a degree. Mostly because I'm good at it."

For some reason, my focus went back to the book beside him. I pointed. "Dad says that's in his top-ten reads."

A light sparked in Arthur's eyes then. He sat up straighter. "It's excellent! Mr. Brown recommended it to me over Christmas. I'm only halfway through, but it's absolutely brilliant!"

I smiled then. Arthur and my dad had bonded almost immediately over books once they found they had similar tastes. If it had been any other boy talking to Dad like that, I would've thought he was kissing up. But that wasn't Arthur's style. Plus, he and I had barely been cordial then, so he had no reason to kiss up to my father.

"Dad'll be happy to hear that," I said.

"Please tell him for me . . ."

Our eyes connected. My heart fluttered. *Stupid heart.*

"Sure."

What I wanted was for them to be in communication with each other directly because there was no more weirdness. And maybe because Arthur was my boyfriend.

His father won't ever allow it.

My stupid heart lurched.

It still stung.

And it brought up an important question: "What does your dad know about me?" I asked, doing a reasonable job of keeping my resentment out of my voice. "Did you tell him anything? Because I got the impression he didn't like me from the moment he met me." *Also what Bronwyn said.*

"Most people have that impression of Papa," he said drolly.

I believed that. Still, "But is it true for me?" I pressed.

Arthur sighed. "My father doesn't dislike you, Finley. He doesn't *know* you. Only . . ." His voice dropped into a softer register as he shyly admitted, "only that *I* like you. Very much." A blush darkened his cheeks. He glanced up at me then, and I saw his vulnerability. It would've melted my heart if I wasn't so on edge.

"You do?" I said in surprise. My cheeks grew warmer.

He nodded. "Isn't it obvious?"

I let out a strangled sound of frustration, and I stood abruptly. "No, Arthur! It basically the *opposite* of obvious!" I started pacing. "It's obtuse. Obscure. Unclear. Confusing. Vague. Ambiguous—"

"You're a veritable thesaurus," he murmured.

I stopped and locked eyes with him. "What happened after you left Christmas?" I fought back against the wave of emotions, my voice barely above a whisper. "Why aren't we together?"

He let out another sigh, which seemed to bounce all around the room. "It's a longer story."

"Well, we've got until noon. And that's why I'm here, right? To talk?"

"Yes. All quite right." He rubbed the back of his neck, a ripple of something that could be anguish darting across his face. "And—and I'm sorry, Finley. For having let my . . . pride and my fears get to me. For mucking up an important moment. Which caused you pain. It's unforgivable." His jaw clenched hard and his grip tightened on the chair. "Though I do hope you *will* forgive me."

Now I did melt for him. His regret was genuine. I could feel it, regardless of still not knowing the cause. It wasn't easy for him to lower his guard like that.

Uncertain how to respond, I moved back to the sofa and sat in the same spot. I reached out and patted the bulky leather cushion.

An insistence.

To his credit, he understood. Using his crutch, he rose to his feet, moving from his chair to the sofa. He leaned the crutch against an end table.

"Now," I said when he was settled. "Tell me what changed."

"My father overheard one of our conversations. Sometime after New Year's, I'm not certain when, exactly. He sensed you were . . . important to me."

"Did you tell him about us?"

"Not at first." Arthur crossed his arms, his gaze dropping to the fire. "He asked Aunt Esha about our time in Christmas. Naturally, she told him of our experiences. Though she said she didn't tell him about you and me . . ." He nodded and I nodded, and he continued. "She knows better."

"Knows better why?"

His eyes hardened. "Papa has a plan for me. Quite specific." He looked back at me, his tone wry. "And it does not involve dating an American."

I balked. "Then he shouldn't have sent you to school in America."

Arthur laughed then. Genuinely. "A salient flaw. Though at the time we were in the position of 'beggars, not choosers.'"

"He can't expect you to not get together with anyone in high school."

"Oh, but he can," he said dryly.

I scoffed, "That's ridiculous. You're a teenager, Arthur. Even though you don't act like it half the time." He cocked a single brow, and it was so crazy adorable, I wanted to launch myself at him and hug him around the neck. I didn't. But the desire was intense. "You know it's true."

He capitulated with a half shrug. "That is also part of the problem."

"You being an old man trapped in a teenager's body?" I teased. Testing the waters. Or maybe indulging myself. Who knew if I'd get to tease him in the future?

"Me being a teenager." Then he added, "Specifically, I'm turning eighteen soon." By the way he said the last part, I could tell it was important to him.

I nodded. "On Valentine's Day, I know."

His eyes widened in surprise. "You do?"

"Was it a secret?"

"No," he said hesitantly.

"Then why do you look like that?" I made a circle in the air around his face with my index finger.

He scowled. "It's silly."

I scooted closer. "That's okay, you can tell me."

"No, the fact I was born on Valentine's Day is silly." He practically huffed in indignation. "It's a ridiculous holiday that was manufactured by the greeting-card industry as a way to drive their profits. It has absolutely nothing to do with love, and frankly, I resent having to inevitably be associated with something so disingenuous and trivial for the entirety of my life."

Another log crackled in the ensuing silence.

"Well," I said after a moment, not bothering to hide my amusement at his glowering expression, "it's a good thing we broke up before then, since you *clearly* would've resented the idea of getting me anything."

He held up a finger to make a point. "I would have gotten you something."

"Under duress," I countered.

"But I would have."

I rested my head on my hand and rolled my eyes at him. "You really are a romantic, Arthur," I murmured wryly.

He shifted his position to face me. "I very well can be," he said seriously. "I simply prefer it not to be forced." He nodded, maintaining, "It should be authentic or not at all."

"Fair enough," I agreed, because, in a way, his purist outlook was more romantic than any box of chocolates or last-minute purchase of grocery store flowers ever would be. Not that I'd tell him that, of course. Instead I asked, "What does you turning eighteen—regardless of the day it happens to be on—have to do with anything?"

"Because I'll be graduating in a couple months. And when I do . . ." His gaze was steady. "I'll be returning to England to attend Oxford University."

Oh.

I hadn't considered that.

Which was foolish now that I actually did.

I had been so busy my first (*putrid!*) semester at Barrington that I'd only paid glancing attention to anyone else's station at school. Yes, classmates were freshmen, sophomores, juniors (like me), or seniors. *Big whoop!* I didn't care about that because I was struggling to survive and other people's grades didn't impact me.

Now they did.

Or one person's did.

Thanks to having skipped a grade in elementary school, I was a sixteen-year-old junior, and, sure, I'd given some thought to placement tests. But those were in my future. My "right now" had been all-consuming since arriving at Barrington.

And when it came to Arthur . . . well, our time together had turned out to be so short—nineteen days!—and tangled with things like being emotionally blackmailed into helping him and Esha have a great Christmas, or driving through a blizzard and, oh, by the way, my grandmother wanted to be with his aunt, that I hadn't had time to indulge in simply thinking about our future.

Only to find out, too late, that we didn't have any.

"Oxford. Th-that's . . ." I stumbled with what to say, landing on, "A really good school."

Nice job, Finley.

But I was still processing the blow.

He was going away in a matter of months.

Back to England.

An entire ocean away from me.

What was interesting, though, was his reaction when I said "Oxford": he averted his gaze and gave another shrug.

While my knowledge of Oxford University was passing at best—lots of famous British people went there; don't ask me to name any—I knew that it deserved more than a half-hearted shrug. And that was before adding the extra layer of his mother teaching there.

"Don't you like it?" I pressed.

"It's brilliant," he said in the same bored tone. "I've always enjoyed visiting Mummy there. And I've already completed my admission interviews early last month." He made a face. "That was a process."

I studied him a moment, trying to gauge his feelings on the matter. "Are you excited to go?"

He picked an invisible piece of lint off his slacks. "I'm sure I will be. Frankly, it's been planned for me for so long that it feels as if I've already experienced it. Go to Oxford. Get a MSc in financial economics." His gaze drifted to the side. "Move to a job at the ground floor of Watercress Industries, where I will then work without preferential treatment until such time as I am legitimately promoted." He rolled his hand. "And so on, and so on."

I frowned at his jaundiced attitude, so different from the flash of excitement from moments ago, when he talked about the novel. "You keep saying it's planned."

"It is." He clenched his jaw. He may be prepared to go, but it was evident that he wasn't happy about the idea.

"Is this what you want?"

He shook his head. "It doesn't matter what I want."

I recoiled. "Of course it does. If you don't want to go there, go someplace else. You have great grades."

His expression was indulgent but weary. "You don't understand,

Finley. Either I attend Oxford, one of the world's premiere universities, or I go elsewhere and pay for education with money I assure you I do not have. That has always been the understanding." His voice lowered. "It simply has never before been a concern."

The tacit "until now" was not lost on me and gave me a muted thrill.

Unfortunately, it failed to alter the situation. Arthur may want to be with me as much as I wanted to be with him, but he was clearly unwilling to go against his father's "plan," which didn't include me.

The American.

I was insulted.

Then again . . .

I smiled to myself, which he noticed. "What?"

"Nothing, it's just. If you're 'forbidden'"—I made air quotes around the word—"from dating an American, that means Bronwyn is out of the picture, too."

He made a face. "Bronwyn was never in the picture, at any time. Ever."

"Did she know that?"

"It doesn't matter. *I* know that."

I nodded. Believing him. Trusting him. Again, I thought about telling him what happened the night before. But honestly, I'd given her enough of my time.

A hint of intrigue gleamed in his eyes. "Were you jealous?"

Suddenly the energy that was always low-key around us now came to the forefront. It crackled and popped like one of those logs.

"Depends," I said, lacing my words with a flirtation that was unadvised and impossible to stop. "Were you jealous of Gaines Alder?"

He frowned. "Why on earth would I be jealous of Gaines Alder?"

"When we were talking that day. It seemed like you were maybe a little jealous." Yes, I was pushing. And, yes, my heartbeat was starting to shoot up again.

He balked. "Hardly."

"No?"

He shifted his position, bringing us closer. "If you were going to date someone else—which you threatened to do at the time, as I recall—I would certainly hope you would choose someone far more worthy of your time than Gaines Alder." He dropped his arm across the back of the sofa, his hand near mine.

"Like who?" I said softly. I was blushing.

"No one comes to mind," he murmured, and I knew then he was feeling the pull right along with me.

"Do *you* want me to be together with someone else?" I asked, letting my hand rest upon his. He felt warm.

His thumb lightly brushed along my fingers. "I have no right to tell you not to." A zing of electricity went from his touch straight up my arm, and I had to tamp down a shiver.

Neither of us let go. I forced myself not to stare at his mouth or remember what it was like to kiss him. How soft his lips were and how it felt to be in his arms . . .

It was a relief to be this close again. At the same time, I was also fighting my crushing disappointment at our predicament. *This* was what I wanted. Being with him.

This was also what I couldn't have. Not without completely upending all of the plans that had been in place for Arthur long before I came into the picture due to some altered website for my hometown and a perfectly imperfect Christmas.

We'd only had nineteen days together. That wasn't enough to blow up eighteen *years* of a lifetime. Even I knew that much.

"What do we do?" I asked, helpless. "I don't want this to be the end for us."

My chest tightened at the thought.

"I'm not sure you'll like my suggestion," he said cautiously. "I don't, though the option of avoiding each other completely—"

"Sucks."

His lips pulled up in amusement. "Sucks." Then he again grew serious, his eyes hooded as he mustered the courage to ask, "Do you think it's at all possible we could become . . . friends?" He said it with such trepidation, I felt a pain in my chest. "I haven't many, you see. Most people annoy me." I laughed despite my rising emotions. "It's true," he insisted, wiggling our joined hands.

"I know it is," I said warmly. "That's why it's funny. You're such a misanthrope."

"Not as much when you're around. I like talking with you, hearing what you have to say. I like you." He held my eyes, his voice barely above a whisper. "And I've missed you."

Warmth seeped through my chest, wrapping itself around me like a long-needed embrace. "I've missed you too," I whispered back.

So much.

"So, what do we do? Is my suggestion even a possibility?"

Taking a long moment, I considered if what he was proposing was something I could do. Sincerely. With no ulterior motives.

And the answer was . . . no.

At least I didn't think so.

A part of me would want more.

Maybe, over time, that would go away. Maybe we could be friends and friends only. Was I supposed to have no contact with him until then? That wasn't what I wanted, either.

I liked Arthur. I liked talking with him. I wanted to find a way to keep talking with him.

And as far as I could tell, he was right: friendship was the only way.

It wasn't ideal, but not being around him at all was so much worse.

Besides, "It's funny," I said. "We went from being annoyed with each other to liking each other so fast, we did kinda skip over the whole 'friends' part. Which is important." I reached over to place my other hand around the one of his I was already holding, and, pressing, I looked him in his beautiful dark brown eyes. "Yes, Arthur Chakrabarti Watercress," I said. "I would love the chance to be your friend."

Just don't ask me how it's gonna work.

Twenty

The walk back from Franz Klammer to the main lodge was about twenty minutes. I'd already managed to drag it out to thirty, and I still had a distance to go. Too many thoughts, too many emotions were zinging through me, slowing me down.

Not so many that I didn't notice the black Cadillac SUV with darkened rear windows pass by me before it turned down the short road that led to Arthur's cabin. There was a driver in the front I didn't recognize, but I sensed without evidence the identity of his passenger.

Lord Watercress.

It had to be. I felt his eyes on me as the car passed. It was all I could do not to stare daggers at the back window. I was proud of my restraint.

Luckily I got a text from Ayisha: When you get back, meet me at Embers. First floor. Updates to The Shove.

I was pretty sure Embers was the lodge's casual restaurant.

I texted back: On my way!!

She sent back a thumbs-up emoji. Followed by a smile emoji.

My curiosity was instantly piqued. I wonder what she meant

by "updates"? Particularly with the smile emoji that had big teeth. That was *super* happy. You didn't send that if things were about to totally tank, right? That would be like creating false hope. And I didn't want that, not after the still-new truce with Arthur. A truce paving the way to . . . friendship? Yeah, still not sure what that would look like. We'd have to figure that out as we went along.

But, hey, we were going along! I'd take it.

I was about to put my phone in my coat pocket when I felt it buzz again. To my surprise, it was a FaceTime call.

From my parents.

I was on alert. They knew where I was this weekend, and we'd agreed to have our weekly call once I returned to Barrington. So seeing them on my phone screen was unsettling.

Unless this was about what happened with Bronwyn.

I felt sick.

What if her father had already contacted an attorney and that attorney had already contacted Mom and Dad?

No, wait. It was still a federal holiday weekend. No attorney worked then. That would have to wait until Tuesday at the earliest.

Maybe it was the school! Had they contacted my parents? Was I being disciplined? Was this a call about me getting kicked out? Wouldn't they want to talk to me first? Get my side of the story? I think I deserved my day in court! (Though, hopefully not an *actual* court.)

The call was on its fifth ring and about to tip over into voicemail when I answered, holding up the phone so I could see them despite the bright light of the cloudless sky.

"Hi . . . ?" I asked, doing my best to keep the kaleidoscope of concern out of my voice. I wound up sounding squeaky.

Mom and Dad were seated close together on the sofa in the TV den of our house. Dad had moved back after Christmas Eve. Both were smiling happily in a way that put to rest any fears about this being related to what happened at the Bu cabin.

Both waved in that parents' way. "Hi!" they said in unison. I could tell by the angle that they were using the camera on Mom's laptop, propped up on a stack of coffee table books.

Dad said, "Hi, sport!"

Mom said, "How are you?"

A loaded question right at the top. Though I saw in their expressions they didn't know that, which was somewhat encouraging.

I plastered on a huge smile and said, "Aces!" Then deliberately didn't think about how we'd made a family pledge about this exact sort of thing only a few weeks ago.

Dad asked, "How's the skiing?"

Well, Dad, yesterday I defied death on a mountain with the help of my ex-boyfriend, who still likes me and who I still really like, but we can't be together because his father holds his future in an iron grip, so we're going to try to be "friends only," and, oh, yeah, I sort of knocked the school bully into a pot of red punch and a fountain of melted chocolate and now I'm waiting to hear if I'm getting kicked out.

"Good," I said instead.

Dad's smile widened. "Seems like you're in one piece after the first day!"

"Mm-huh," I replied, while thinking: *TBD, Dad. TBD.*

Mom leaned in. "It looks really pretty where you are." She pointed to the edges of the screen. I assumed she meant my surroundings, which, yes, were pretty. Pine trees and blue skies and skiers in colorful outfits all around. "Are you headed back out onto the slopes today?" she asked in a chipper tone.

Almost too chipper.

"Um, no," I answered. "I'm going to meet up with Ayisha.

For lunch. I'm not sure what happens next." Which might be the understatement of the year, and we were still in January.

"Maybe you could go for a hike," Dad suggested. There was a little too much . . . exuberance in his tone, too.

Things felt off.

Which shifted "suspicious" to "high alert." They were clearly not calling me about anything that would have me in trouble. They would have led with that. But something was going on, I knew it.

"Is everything okay?" I blurted out. "With you two?" When they exchanged glances, I felt a quiver of concern. "Something's up, isn't it? Oh, no."

How many things could go batshit in one stupid weekend?!

I moved to sit at a nearby empty picnic table, resting my elbows on its top because my hands were starting to shake and I needed to stabilize their image.

"Whoa there, sport."

"Take a deep breath, Finley." Mom used both hands to signal for me to calm down. "Everything's fine."

"Really? Or are you saying 'fine' because that's what people say when things aren't fine but they don't want to talk about it?" I frowned. "Although, you're calling me, which means you *do* want to talk about whatever's going on, so now I'm just confused." I sighed, my breath crystalizing in the cold air.

Dad grinned. "Things are good, Finley."

I felt my eyebrows go up hopefully. "They are?"

Mom nodded and said, "Yes."

But then she and Dad exchanged another glance, and I got irrationally concerned again. Whatever it was, they were on the same page. Which could be good. Maybe they were planning a family vacation to somewhere fantastic.

Or it could be they'd both agreed to something awful. Like:

"Are you two getting a div—" I started to ask the same time they announced:

"We're pregnant."

I did a double take. "I'm sorry?"

They couldn't possibly mean—?

Dad sat up straighter. "You heard right." His smile couldn't get any bigger.

Mom's smile was mostly calm but also slightly apprehensive as she stared into the monitor. At me. Watching closely. "We're a little past three months—"

"Three months!" I exclaimed in a high-pitched voice of utter disbelief.

"Finley—"

Then I realized, "Hold up! That's *before* you left to go to Missouri!"

Dad looked over at Mom. "She was always fast with math."

Mom patted his knee indulgently but addressed me. "Yes, it's before I left for Missouri. Actually," she said, leaving her hand to rest on Dad's knee, "that was part of why I left. I thought I was pregnant—"

"You just said you *were*!" I interjected.

"Sport, let your mom tell the story."

"Sorry," I mumbled.

Mom continued. "I'd taken a test when I first suspected and it came up positive, which is part of what got me . . ." She hesitated, frowning slightly.

Dad covered Mom's hand with his own. "Reconsidering things," he supplied, tactfully glossing over their weeks-long separation over the holidays when she went to stay with her sister, Aunt Jennifer, up near Branson.

Mom nodded, her energy now more serious. "Yes." She refocused on me. "But then I took a second test—"

"One of those over-the-counter ones."

"—and it came back negative."

"They're unreliable."

Mom gave Dad a wry look. "Skip . . ."

He grinned, contrite. "Right." Then he pressed his lips closed.

"So, over Christmas, I didn't think I was. Which is why I didn't mention it. Plus, there was so much going on. But then after you left, I started feeling off again and my period was very light and spotty. This time I decided to go to the doctor, and he confirmed it."

"We're pregnant!" Dad was beaming.

I was so stunned that "Holy shit" just slipped right out before I could stop myself.

I slapped a hand over my mouth.

Mom frowned. "Language, Finley."

I dropped my hand to whisper, "Sorry," contritely.

Dad laughed. "I said the same thing." Mom shot him a look and it was his turn to be contrite again. "But yes. Language." Then he leaned back and mouthed "Holy shit!" and I laughed.

Mom let out a frustrated huff at my dad. "You know I can see you, too," she said, pointing to their smaller image in their screen's corner.

He kissed her cheek and she lost her bluster.

And I knew then they really were okay.

My heart felt warm and I relaxed. "Does Grandma Jo know?"

Dad nodded. "We told Mom a couple days ago."

"We were going to tell you when you got back from your ski trip, but she hinted you were worried about how we were doing.

And she said something about you maybe needing good news."
Mom leaned forward. "Is everything okay, honey?"

That same loaded question again.

For a moment, I considered telling them everything. Soup to nuts, as GGB used to say. But all I could think was: *They are so happy*. Probably the happiest I'd seen them in ages. I didn't want to be the one to take that away from them by making them worry needlessly. Or worry too soon.

I had no idea no idea how I could possibly emerge from my present predicament without repercussions, but Ayisha's smiley-face emoji gave me a glimmer of hope.

I clung to it.

"Everything's fine," I told my parents, and prayed that turned out to be true.

We talked for a little longer. Mom asked how I was feeling about the news and I told her I was excited, because I really was. Mainly because of the glow I saw in both of them. They probably had had a very different reaction when they found out they were pregnant with me. I couldn't recall details about how they initially took the news, but they were both eighteen when it happened, so I had a solid idea. The expectations for their lives were suddenly upended. It had to have been a shock, and not a good one.

Now, though, all these years later, they were in a completely different place for something like this. To bring a new person into the world. This time they were ready.

My heart swelled with happiness and love for them. For our little family, about to grow.

My shivering from being stationary in freezing temperatures, regardless of the overhead sun, had Mom telling me to go get myself inside ASAP. Which I agreed to do.

After the call was over, I sat at the table a minute longer to process their amazing news.

It was a lot to take in. Especially on top of everything else going on. Which was why it didn't fully hit me until I was making my way back to the lodge that, after sixteen years of being an only child, I was going to be someone's big sister.

I couldn't wait!

Twenty-One

Ayisha knew something. I saw it twinkling in her deep brown eyes the moment I spotted her seated at a corner table on the far side of Embers's dining area. It intrigued me.

But not as much as the two people seated opposite her.

Petra and Gaines.

Unexpected.

My heart started its pitter-patter again. Though I wasn't as anxious as I maybe would have been before my parents' news. Residual happiness for them lingered and tamped down my natural instinct to panic.

Still. What were they doing here?

Ayisha read my wariness and her smile bloomed. "Oh. Just wait."

Then both Petra and Gaines noticed my arrival. She was in dark denim again with a lavender sweater this time. Gaines wore baggy jeans and an oversized sage-green hoodie that probably cost as much the last five items of clothing I'd bought for myself combined.

I looked between them. "Is this like some sort of summit?" Pointing to Petra. "Where you're representing the Bu family."

Pointing to Gaines. "And you're here in Bronwyn's interest?" A thought occurred. "Do I need a lawyer?!"

Yep. Still had the capacity for leaping to conclusions.

There was no evidence of any of them having eaten, so why else were they gathered here? Ayisha only had a cup of coffee, almost gone, and Petra had a white ceramic pot of tea beside her. Gaines casually rolled a bottle of Mountain Dew between the palms of his hands.

Petra raised a single dark red eyebrow. "I don't represent the Bu family," she said evenly. "My father is Percy Bergerac."

Gaines gestured flippantly. "And I am on the Bron's shit list. Cast to the side."

"Because you defended me?" I asked as I sat on the wooden chair beside Ayisha's.

He shrugged. "It's not my first time residing there. We'll see how long this one lasts." That felt like bravado. He was more bothered than he wanted to admit.

Ayisha waved her hand at Petra and Gaines. "They've all known each other since elementary school."

"'They' being . . . ?"

Petra clarified, "Gaines, Bronwyn, Josie, me, and Scotty."

Ayisha explained, "They're all from Edge Hill."

I recognized the name. "That's the town where La Belle's is."

"That's right," Ayisha said.

Gaines noted, "There's more Edgies at Barrington."

Petra frowned. "That's not relevant to this discussion."

He lolled his head to look at her in a way that spoke to their familiarity. "I was being *thorough*, Pets." She glared at him and he rolled his eyes, amending, "Petra Louise Bergerac."

That didn't cease her glare. Was it an "I hate you, you're an ass" glare or "How dare you speak to me like that, peasant" glare?

Hard to tell.

I interrupted their silent duel with a raised hand. "I'm guessing this meeting is about, you know . . ."

"The Shove." Gaines grinned as he looked back at me.

"I didn't shove her!" I protested. "Does she think that? Because I didn't. I was trying to block her from going after Ayisha and may have inadvertently shoved. *May.*" I added a point by way of emphasis. "But I didn't *mean* to do that, either! That has to count for something. Is she suing me?"

"Nope." He shook his head, his sandy hair almost wobbling despite the gel.

"Bronwyn isn't going to do anything." Petra seemed certain.

I wasn't. "How can you be so sure?"

Ayisha grinned and rubbed her hands together. "This is the good part."

"Because Petra is blackmailing her," Gaines said matter-of-factly, then took a sip of his fluorescent-green soda.

Petra shrugged the shrug of "basically."

I blanched. "Blackmailing?! Does Barrington teach a course on that?"

Gaines's eyes brightened. "Ooooh! That's going in the suggestion box!"

Petra held up her phone. "I recorded her ranting and the part where she—"

"Hit the food table like a pro wrestler," Ayisha finished, not bothering to hide the lilt of satisfaction in her voice.

"Yes, but a lot of people at the party had their phones out," I pointed out.

"Their phones were confiscated before they could upload anything," Petra said.

"Confiscated?"

Gaines nodded. "Scotty's a big guy with big-guy friends. He made sure everyone who recorded it deleted it from their phones before he let them leave."

"*Almost* everyone." Petra's smile was subtle.

"Right," he agreed. "Petra Louise here has the advantage of being automatically connected to the Bu family's server."

Ayisha said, "She uploaded the clip to the cloud before Scotty got to her."

"And when he deleted it off my phone—"

"It wasn't gone."

I leaned back in my chair. "So that's why no video got out."

Gaines snapped his fingers and pointed at me. "Yeppers. Though some people are using the hashtag 'PunchBowl' to talk about it."

Ayisha snickered. "I like that."

Gaines brightened.

The weight that had been with me since last night lifted. My shoulders dropped in relief.

Amazing.

However, I still had questions. Like, "Why did Scotty go to all that trouble to delete the video? He and Bronwyn aren't together. He made a big point about that."

Ayisha's smile now dimmed and Gaines grew quiet, leaving Petra to explain, "Bronwyn was right. Scotty is her person. And they do break up three times a year."

"I happened to be one of the reasons this year," Ayisha said sardonically. Her finger lightly tapped against the edge of her coffee cup. She was annoyed.

"In the end, Bronwyn tells Scotty what to do. And he does it." Petra's look at Gaines was piercing. "Like so many people."

Gaines frowned at her. "What do you want from me, Petra? She's been my friend. She used to be *your* friend, too."

"Not for a long time." Petra pushed her glasses back in place. Sat up straighter.

"Don't blame me for that." His grip around the plastic bottle tightened.

"I don't. I blame Bronwyn. I blame *you* for enabling her crappy behavior ever since—" She stopped abruptly and didn't continue.

"Whatever." Gaines crossed his arms and pouted.

I glanced at Ayisha. "Did you take notes on all that?"

She tapped a perfectly manicured finger against her temple.

"Bottom line, Fin," Gaines continued, "you don't have to worry about Bronwyn going to the teachers. The moment she does—"

"I release the video of her looking like she swam through a lake of shit and blood." Petra's smile was pleased.

"She may be angry at the two of you." Gaines nodded to me and Ayisha. "But her vanity is stronger."

Ayisha swiped her braids over her shoulder, her mood lightening. "Who knew that'd come in handy?"

I raised both hands. "Then . . . I'm not being expelled?"

"Not because of hashtag PunchBowl, no," Gaines assured me.

Petra was serious as she warned, "You'll still need to watch out for her."

Gaines agreed. "She'll find a way to get back at you somehow. That's her MO."

"Speaking of MO." I leaned forward to zero in on Gaines. "What did she mean when she said she told you to be nice to me?"

His cheeks grew red. He was embarrassed. It took him a second to admit, "She heard that you and Arthur had hooked up over Christmas and she wanted to know if it was true. So she asked me to get to know you and see if it was."

My eyes widened. "Who told her that about me and Arthur?!"

"I'm not sure, exactly." He picked at the corner of the Mountain Dew label. "Her dad, maybe?"

Ayisha's eyes narrowed. "Why did she care, though?"

Petra removed a packet of stevia from the selection of sweeteners.

Gaines explained, "She liked CW at one point. At least around her Halloween party." He looked at me. "She was pissed that he was talking to you and not her."

I cocked my head in irritation. "What about Prescott?"

Petra stirred her tea. "One thing you should know about Bronwyn—she's basically Veruca Salt." She raised an eyebrow. "She wants it all. Now. Fuck anyone else."

It was a disconcerting to hear "fuck" come out the mouth of someone who looked like a librarian. I got the impression Bronwyn brought out Petra's harsher side.

Ergo, the blackmail.

The much-appreciated blackmail.

Ayisha regarded Gaines in curiosity. "Why are *you* friends with her?"

He ducked his head down, covering his discomfort. "I don't know. Always have been?" His cheeks were still fiery.

"I had a friend like that back home," I told him. "She wasn't the Queen Bee monster that Bronwyn seems like. But she had her moments."

His eyes focused on mine and I saw his uncertainty, but it was Petra who asked, "What happened?"

I considered the answer a moment. "Maybe I grew up? At least a little. All I knew was, I didn't want to be her friend anymore. And I walked away."

"Was it hard?" Gaines asked. As if searching for a blueprint: "How to Leave a Toxic Friend." Who knows if he was serious about it, if he wouldn't turn around the second she asked him to do something else; some habits of friendships were hard to break.

Ayisha grinned mischievously. "It helped that the ex-friend was with Finley's ex-boyfriend."

"*Your* ex-boyfriend, too," I volleyed back.

She languidly shrugged one shoulder and took a sip of her coffee.

Gaines sat up in his chair, relieved not to be the center of attention anymore. "Well, well. Now we're all learning a little sumptin' about each other." He pointed at us. "Turnabout's fair play, ladies. I want full scoopage. But first? Food. I'm starving!"

"It's the mountain air," Ayisha said, handing him a sizable laminated menu from where they were tucked against the wall next to the condiments.

He wiggled in his chair. "I know!"

As Gaines perused the options, I looked across the table at Petra, who seemed lost in thought. Maybe planning her escape. Which I suddenly realized I didn't want to happen. "Are you going to stay for lunch, too?" I asked her.

Gaines heard the question and glanced over at Petra, too. Then handed her his menu. "I already know what I want."

It was a peace offering.

She stared at it for a long moment. Then slowly took the menu from him and admitted, "I am kind of hungry."

Later Ayisha and I filled Petra and Gaines in on the long and winding road that we took to go from enemies to friends, and gave them some fine tidbits about the events of last Christmas. And I couldn't help think, if you were an outsider who didn't know any better, you'd swear we were all friends. Which, who knew? Maybe we were on our way.

Wouldn't that be something . . .

Twenty-Two

The rest of the day at Lancaster had been spent hanging out with Ayisha and Petra. After lunch, Gaines had gone back to hang out with "the guys" (which didn't include Scotty Bu, who apparently was back to spending time with Bronwyn).

He invited us to join, but we declined.

Petra had lingered after we'd paid the Embers' bill. She didn't say it outright, but it was obvious she didn't want to go back to the Bu cabin. Understandable.

Ayisha took charge. She looped her arm around the other girl's shoulders and told her she was going to hang out with us the rest of the day. Petra hadn't protested, which we took as an agreement.

We stayed around the lodge, where they were having a mini outdoor arts festival showcasing local artists. Much more our speed. It wasn't what we expected from our ski trip, but it was nice. No near-death moments or boys who couldn't make up their minds. Not much talking, but zero drama.

God, was that appreciated!

When it got late, we said our good-byes to Petra, who returned to her "not family's" cabin. To my surprise, I found I was looking forward to seeing her back in our dorm. She was cooler than I realized. Her humor was exceedingly dry, but I was starting to pick up on her rhythms.

What was funny, though, were the looks I got all day anytime I passed any other kids from Barrington.

First of all, that there were looks at all. I'd grown accustomed to being ignored by this point in my time in the Barrington world. Or, if someone did notice me lately, it was as the person standing next to Ayisha.

These looks on Sunday, though, were for *me*.

Being noticed threw me off. I wasn't sure how I felt about it.

There were also secret smiles of approval and passing whispers of "punch bowl." Two guys I knew to be sophomores at Barrington had added fist bumps.

It seemed that everyone knew what happened, but there was also a tacit understanding to keep it on the q.t.

No adults.

I wanted to talk with Arthur about everything. Partly before he heard about it from someone else. Mainly as an excuse to reach out to him.

When Ayisha and I got back to our room, I texted him to see if he could talk. He'd texted back that he was having an early dinner with his father.

I could wait.

That night, as I went to sleep, thinking about Arthur didn't hurt. We had Dr. Oswald's Astronomy class together on Tuesday, and for the first time since the first day, I was excited about going.

Arthur would be there.

We would see each other and not look away. We would sit near each other and not recoil. We would talk and it wouldn't be angry or sad or evasive.

Thinking about it made me eager to talk to him now. Since we couldn't, I did the next-best thing.

I texted: Remind me to tell you a funny Bronwyn story tomorrow.

He texted: Are there such things?

I snort-laughed.

I texted: Good point! This one started as not funny AT ALL!! It got funnier. But now that I think about it, maybe it isn't funny?

He texted: I'm curious.

I texted: Let's just say I'm never going to look at chocolate fondue the same way again. Or fruit punch. 😵

He texted: That sounds like an unfortunate combination.

I texted: It worked out for me!! 😊 😊 😊

He texted: I look forward to hearing about it.

I sat there a moment. Smiling at how everything had turned out today. Totally not like I thought when I woke up this morning.

Expulsion was looking less likely. The expressions from Ms. Martinez, Dr. Oswald, and Mr. Poisson made me confident, whenever we passed, that they hadn't heard anything. It probably helped that Hawley Chen had gotten caught late Saturday by Oswald and Poisson making out with one of the resort's crew members in a hot tub so they were distracted.

Then there was the fact I was also going to be a big sister.

When I was younger, I'd desperately wanted to have a sibling. My parents had smiled and moved on to other subjects when I'd brought it up. At the time I'd figured it was because they were content with just me. Conceited, I know. Them wanting another child but unable to have one hadn't occurred to me. I was older now and I wondered if this was a bigger miracle for them than I realized.

Maybe Grandma Jo could fill me in on this subject.

My phone pinged. I looked at the screen.

It was another text from Arthur.

He texted: I'm glad we can text/talk about things once more.

I texted: Me too!!

He texted: 😊

My eyes flew wide. The emoji just about knocked me out! It was not like him. At all.

I grinned for the rest of the night.

Twenty-Three

JANUARY 19

Ithought I was happy to leave Barrington, but I was *much* happier to return. By the time the bus pulled into the parking lot near the Taft Rec Center, it was the end of Monday and I was exhausted.

The winter sun had already set though it wasn't yet five p.m. One of my least-favorite parts of the season was the short days. (Who still thought daylight savings was a good idea? No one! Not even farmers.)

Despite our texts the night before, Arthur and I didn't get a chance to talk. Apparently, his father wanted to actually spend a day with his son. I gathered from Arthur's text this was not a common occurrence.

I wondered at the impetus. Was he using their time together to prevent the two of us from talking? Or was that me being hella paranoid? Whatever it was, I didn't tell Arthur about my ski weekend adventures just yet. We'd catch up on Tuesday morning when we met at the café in Quinten Hall for coffee.

Our inaugural "friend date."

It was within the bounds of friendship, right? I'd gone there with Ayisha several times and *we* were friends. Totally the same thing.

Not totally the same thing, said another part of my brain.

Shut up, brain.

My *body* was eager to collapse across my dorm bed. Arthur had been completely right about the "jelly legs." Lord . . .

Ayisha was in slightly better shape, but she still bid me adieu with a weary salute then headed down the hall to her room.

I had my room to myself tonight. Petra was staying at the Bu cabin one more evening. Scotty would drive her home in the early morning before going on his way to Mayo Prep.

Which meant I could lie at an angle across my bed for as long as I wanted without worrying what anyone else thought.

And I did.

The last thing I expected was a knock on my door. It pulled me out of my spontaneous catnap. My brain was foggy and doing its best to coax me back to slumber time.

Knock! Knock! Knock!

Ooof.

I half sat up again. Rubbed my eyes. "Who is it?" I croaked loudly.

The voice on the other side was muffled but it sounded like Farris Roswell, the proctor for our floor.

"You have a guest downstairs," she shouted. Followed by the sound of her footsteps heading away from my door.

Guess I wasn't going to get any further info.

I frowned, confused. The clock read 5:23 p.m. *Dammit.* Barely a power nap.

A quick look at my phone screen showed no new texts. Anyone I knew would've messaged me first before coming over (*No! I'm sleeping!*).

Even Arthur. Who I knew was being driven home with his father. I doubted it was him downstairs, but you never knew.

I hit the floor, slipped on my cruelty-free Ugg knockoffs, and checked my reflection. Grimaced. Ran a brush through my hair. Quick hand-swipe of my mostly flat chest and I knew I still had my bra on. Then I headed down the stairs that led to the common room.

Several people were already hanging out. I didn't see anyone who looked like they were waiting for me.

A girl with short hair was perched on one of the sofas, a cozy blanket covering the lower half of her body as she read a textbook noticed me looking around in confusion.

"I think your dad went outside to wait for you," she said, pointing to the heavy, double glass front doors.

I knew that wasn't true. Dad and I had texted earlier this morning when he detailed the homeopathic remedy he'd concocted for Mom to help her through a rough bout of morning sickness. I didn't really want to know any of that, but he'd been so proud of himself, I didn't have the heart to cut him off.

At the same time, if I *did* have an actual guest, they weren't here.

I smiled my thanks to Cozy Blanket Girl and moved to exit the dorm's front doors, wishing I'd grabbed a coat along the way. My heather gray wool sweater with a T-shirt base and jeans would have to do.

Outside was cold but in a doable way. Maybe it was the contrast to the recent mountain air. Not that I planned to stay out here long.

There was a wide pool of bright light at the entrance. Beyond that it was darker. Tall lamps illuminated the pathways, and in the one closest to the dorm was where I saw the figure of a man in a long, dark coat with a dark fedora.

WTF? Am I suddenly in a spy movie?

He had his back to me but must have heard the door slam closed behind me because he turned. Despite the shadows and only having met him one time, I recognized him instantly.

Lord Watercress.

The shock hit me like a bucket of ice water. I sucked in my breath.

"Ms. Brown," he said. Perfectly formal. In control.

He stepped closer.

I stammered, "Sir . . . Lord . . . Sir . . ." Okay, not great. I took a breath and tried again. "I'm sorry. I don't know what's correct."

He stopped in front of me and the shadows from the different angles of light moved when he did. I caught his polite smile.

"Mr. Watercress will do."

"Got it. Sir." A huff of self-directed frustration. "Sorry, you just seem like a 'sir.'"

"That was my grandfather."

"Oh." My brain struggled with what to do with that. "Cool." And failed.

He regarded me for a moment. His expression was inscrutable. The light and shadow playing across the sharp planes of his pale face weren't helpful.

"I wanted to apologize to you," he said.

I blinked, not sure I heard right.

"I've just dropped off Arthur at his dorm, you see. And on our ride back, he informed me that you helped him get to his medical assistance after the collision. I had been unaware when we met at the clinic, otherwise I would have thanked you there."

"Oh. Um, yeah. Well, I mean . . ." *Stop it, Finley!* I linked my fingers in front of me and mentally counted back from three. Subtly clearing my throat, I asked, "Did he tell you the part about how he rescued me from the mountain?"

"He didn't put it in those terms, but yes. He explained what preceded the accident."

I nodded. Good. "I was really scared. He helped me," I said. I knew Arthur would never highlight his own bravery. "I'm just glad he's okay."

"Yes. He is. Thank you for assisting my son."

"You're welcome."

I expected him to smile and leave.

He didn't.

He tipped his head to one side, taking stock of me. "It's also my understanding that the two of you spent time together this past Christmas."

My defenses went back up. Of course the apology on its own was too good to be true.

"We did. Ms. Chakrabarti and Arthur stayed at my grandmother's inn over the holidays."

"Yes. It sounds as if it was a wonderful time. Esha and your grandmother have grown close." The question was implied. I chose not to respond. He watched me another moment. "To be clear, I'm quite happy for them. Esha is a wonderful sister-in-law. Bishakha and I wish nothing but the best for her."

I nodded but remained silent. It seemed easiest. No lie, he was pretty intimidating even without the "dark coat and fedora at night, backlit by a lamp" vibe he had going on.

"I also wish the best for Arthur," he continued smoothly. "He is my only son." I nodded when it seemed as if he wanted to see if I was aware of that fact. "His well-being is my utmost concern."

"Uh-huh." Something verbal this time. *Progress!*

"Forgive me for being presumptuous"—no good sentence ever started with those words—"but I'm aware that Arthur has feelings for you."

I swallowed hard, stuffing my chilled hands into the front jeans of my pockets. *Guess we were done with the warm-up part of this conversation.*

"This is no small feat for him," Lord Watercress continued. "He does not give away his heart easily. Or lightly."

"No one should," I managed to answer. My mouth was dry. *Did this man blink?*

"I quite agree. Are you aware of a girl by the name of Astrid?" I nodded.

That surprised him. "He told you about her?" he asked skeptically. "About what happened?"

"He did." I met his eyes then and somehow managed to hold them. "All of it." I rocked back a little on my heels. "It's why he's here, in America." The cold was starting to set in.

"Though, not for much longer."

"Oxford is a great school," I offered before he could ask if Arthur had told me that part, too, because I knew it was coming. By the look of his expression, I'd been right.

"It is. It's my alma mater. And my father's. And his father's. And so on, for at least four hundred and fifty years."

My eyes widened. "Wow." Because when you can trace your family's scholastic history at one university further back than the United States had been in existence, that deserved a wow.

He pursed his lips in amusement. "Well said," he murmured. "It is the world's second-oldest university in continuous operation. Did you know that?" I shook my head. "The sons of the Watercress family have been an integral part of that illustrious history for nearly half of Oxford's existence."

"Congratulations." *What else was there to say?* I was starting to get annoyed. And really, really cold! The last thing I wanted was to have a runny nose in front of Lord Watercress.

"Sentimentally, it's also where I met Bishakha. It means a great deal to our family."

"Yep. Got that," I said, upping my rocking back and forth. *Please don't let my teeth start chattering.*

His blue eyes pinned me. "It is important for Arthur to take his place there when his time comes. Which is in a matter of months."

"I don't mean to be rude, sir. But I know all this." I blamed the rapidly dropping temperature for my abruptness. I wasn't going to be able to stay out here much longer.

He nodded once to himself. "Ms. Brown, you seem to be an intelligent sixteen-year-old young woman." He placed special emphasis on *sixteen*. "Arthur mentioned you earned your right to be at Barrington through hard work and accomplishment. That's wonderful. Your parents must be proud."

"They are."

"Good." He smiled and I looked for any trace of Arthur in his face but found none. "I don't want you to be under the impression that I harbor any ill will for you. I don't. I simply want to impart to you the importance for Arthur to continue his chosen course."

My eyebrows dipped. "Chosen?" *More like imposed.*

"Yes. This is a tremendous opportunity for him, one that is offered to only a handful of people. He must not be swayed from this by the fleeting illusion of young love. Such as it is."

Anger began to stir in the pit of my stomach. I knew what the purpose of his coming to me like this was—to warn me off from his son. That didn't mean I had to be happy about it or let him toss out veiled insults without some sort of response.

"Mr. Watercress, I'm not trying to *sway* Arthur to do anything."

"You don't need to. Your mere existence and his emotional attachment to you are enough." He briefly dropped his gaze before bringing it back to meet mine. "Did he tell you about my first wife?"

I blinked in surprise. "Uh, no." This was a left turn I hadn't figured for.

"It was very brief." He let out a small sigh. "We'd known each other through secondary school, and we considered ourselves madly in love. Certain we knew better than anyone who said otherwise. Juliette was from Paris, only in London because of some business of her father's, it's incidental." He brushed it aside. "When it was time to go to university, I shocked my family by marrying her and enrolling in the Sorbonne behind their backs."

My eyes bugged. That did *not* fit with the man standing before me.

"Six months later, we filed for divorce, and I came slinking back to my father to beg forgiveness. And to see if there was a way to undo the harm I'd created, for others and for my own future. After a considerable amount of effort, I was able to enter Oxford, where I later met Bishakha, and my life was significantly better for the experience. As you can imagine."

"Sir, honestly, Arthur and I aren't together like that. We both agreed on that." He watched me closely, gauging my honesty. "He's my friend," I continued. "I want him to have what's best for him, just like you do."

"Oxford is what's best."

"Then I'm sure he'll wind up at Oxford. With no interference from me. But, sir? I'm not going to tell Arthur *what* to do, one way or the other. It's not my place. I personally don't think it's anybody's place." The part of my lips I could still feel perked up in amusement. "I'm kind of American like that." I couldn't resist the jab.

For the longest time he didn't speak. The wind was starting to pick up, and I knew I had to get back inside soon.

Fortunately, Lord Watercress seemed to finally notice I didn't have a coat and was on the verge of becoming a human Popsicle.

"I won't keep you out here any longer," he said. "I appreciate you giving me your time, Ms. Brown." He took a step back then hesitated, searching for the right words. "I know I may come across as . . . harsh at times. And while I've not always been as thoughtful about communicating it, I truly love my son. On his shoulders the Watercress legacy will be carried into the next generation." A tiny smile hovered over his thin lips. "As it was, it shall always be." He caught himself and, for a moment, looked bashful. "That was something my father used to say to me. I hope to instill the same resolution to my son. Now, please, Ms. Brown." He waved a gloved hand in the direction of the front doors. "Do go inside at once. It's getting quite chilly and I believe you have class in the morning."

I slowly walked backward a few steps toward the front doors. Kept watching him. As he kept watching me. When I gripped the handle, he briefly lifted his fedora, tipped his head, and smiled.

Twenty-Four

It was 7:20 a.m. and the café at the bottom of Quinten Hall was packed. The place smelled like roasted coffee, with the sounds of student chatter intermingling with a foam machine in action bouncing off the concrete floors to create a cacophony.

But Arthur's gasp was loud and clear.

"Good God." His mouth hung slightly agape. "Have you seen her since?"

We sat at a small table at the back of the café, his crutch propped up against the wall. He now had the full story of Bronwyn and #PunchBowl and he was as gobsmacked as I'd been when I'd been in the middle of the melee.

"Once," I said. "Monday in the lodge."

She'd been dressed in her ski attire, looking *much* different from the last time I set eyes on her. Scotty was by her side. I was alone, having popped down to the convenience store to get two cups of hot chocolate for me and Ayisha. Petra remained at the family cabin. An introvert by nature, the weekend had already drained her.

Bronwyn and Scotty had been exiting the lodge's minimart on

the first floor. He had been talking with someone on his phone and oblivious.

Bronwyn was not.

Our eyes met and held for a long moment in a way that had sent an honest-to-God chill through me, before she looked away and guided a yammering Scotty out the front doors.

This is not over.

That's what her vivid blue eyes said.

I didn't doubt that for a second.

Dammit. Couldn't we go back to that bizzarro place when she was pretending to like me? It was awkward and weird, but I didn't have to worry she was going to leap out of a darkened corner when I was least prepared and murder me.

Not that she would . . .

Would she?

No! Gah! I shook my head at myself.

I noticed the divot between Arthur's eyebrows as he pondered. "How is this going to affect your interaction with her? In class but also on the Valentine's Day Dance Committee?"

A very good question. One I hadn't considered fully until this morning as I was getting ready for the day while thinking about the week, a part of which was the committee's meeting today after classes. Alarm had seized me then. Being at the ski lodge, away from school, had made things feel removed. Protected.

But we were back now. I was going to have to interact with her. Soon.

That wave of fear started to make its way back when Arthur's hand came to rest over mine atop the small tabletop. It was warm and soft and calmed me.

"It'll be all right," he said simply, his voice low, for just us two. The surrounding noise was like a bubble.

I stared into his dark eyes, where I saw a quiet assurance gazing back. "How can you be so sure?"

"Because we're friends now."

I made a face. "How does us being friends protect me from her?"

"Well, you see, our fathers are in business together, as you know. And as a gesture . . ." He blushed. "My parents are having my eighteenth birthday party at her parents' restaurant in Edge Hill. That was what Bronwyn and I were discussing that time you accused us of 'high-octane flirtation.'" A smile danced across his eyes at the memory, and I was embarrassed to have been wrong— at least about his side; Bronwyn's was still a little murky.

But my main takeaway from his reasoning was, "You're having a party?" *Without inviting me?* was left unsaid, but not unthought. Or unfelt.

He hurried to add, "You and I weren't talking when the plans were being finalized, otherwise I would have absolutely had your name on the invitation list."

"There are invitations?"

"In my family, there are always invitations."

I could just picture it. Fancy because everything he told me about his upbringing was fancy. Cream stationary with names and addresses in hand-drawn calligraphy on the front of the envelopes. This family didn't strike me as one for e-vites.

I leaned back in my chair, though not enough to disconnect the way our hands were still touching. "Is this a big party?"

"Compared to what my family has thrown in the past, no."

"For normal people . . . ?"

"Three hundred."

My eyes popped. "Holy—!"

"That many people won't show up," he assured, laughing. Then considered. "At least, I hope not. Most are ceremonial invitations.

The Queen, obviously." Off my open-mouth astonishment he off-handedly explained, "One always invites the Queen. She sends a lovely letter explaining why she cannot attend and we all move on. It's standard."

Boy, did we have different standards.

"Then Papa invited everyone from his company and Mummy invited all of her colleagues, but since we'll be having the party here in the States, they shan't attend, either."

The half-shadowy image of his father's face from the night flashed across my mind.

He must have seen a change in my bearing, because he frowned. "What is it?" His hold on my hands tightened slightly.

I bit my lip, suddenly uneasy, despite having done nothing wrong.

"It's about your father," I said.

His frown deepened. "What about Papa?"

I explained then about how Lord Watercress came to see me last night, and Arthur's expression shuttered, but not before I caught a glimpse of his anger and a trace of embarrassment. He sat back in his chair, his shoulders rigid.

"I'm sorry you were put on the spot like that," he said stiffly.

For some reason I felt the need to defend his father. "It was okay." Arthur's eyes met mine. I couldn't get a read on what he was thinking. "He just wanted me to know how important it was for you to go to the same school his family has gone to."

"He was very deliberately putting you in an uncomfortable position," Arthur countered. "Which is unacceptable." His expression darkened further.

"Please don't be mad at him," I said to his and my surprise. "I think . . ." I hesitated. How to put this? Lord Watercress hadn't done or said anything wrong, and honestly, whatever intimidation

I might have felt could easily have been about me being alone for the first time with my (sorta) ex-boyfriend's father. Who was a lord. Plus, the gulf in both years and experiences between us. He had emphasized wanting what was best for his son, which was understandable. "I think he means well," I said.

"I know that he does," Arthur agreed. "In his way. My father is not a villain. He simply has his . . . perspective on how things should go and a lifetime track record of making certain they become reality."

"Oxford. Finance. Take over the company," I recited, remembering his lack of enthusiasm when he told me. It remained.

"Yes." The weightiness in his tone made me want to hold him and play with his hair and tell him it would be all right, just like he'd said to me a moment ago.

Was what he truly wanted for himself?

Didn't feel like it. Then again, if someone asked me right now what I wanted to be "when I grow up," I wouldn't have a definitive answer. I knew things I liked, things I was good at, but don't ask me to choose my life's path yet. I needed a bigger sample size first.

He lightly squeezed my fingers. "Anyhow, I'm sorry you had to deal with Papa the first time without a buffer. I know from experience it isn't easy."

"It wasn't so bad," I pretended. He raised an eyebrow, clearly doubtful. "He did say nice things."

"Did he?" Arthur asked in tentative surprise. "Such as?"

I moved my hands so our fingers were interlinked. "He said that you cared about me," I told him, walking right up to that line we'd set for ourselves only a couple days earlier with more bravery than I truly possessed.

Our gazes met and held and I felt a shiver run through me.

"I should think by now you know that I do," he said quietly.

I did. That was the problem.

Both our gazes then dropped to our hands atop the table. Still linked. He slowly withdrew his and I followed.

I missed him instantly.

Friends held each other's hands, right?

Yes. They did.

What they didn't do was blush furiously afterward.

Like Arthur and I were both doing.

Or think about how much they liked kissing each other, once upon a time.

Like my brain had just done.

I sighed to myself.

This whole "friends only" transition was going to be a process.

Twenty-Five

Arthur filled me in more about his party. And invited me. Though not via the fancy card stock and fancy calligraphy.

Of course, I said yes.

However, it was going to be tricky since it was being held at the same time as the Valentine's Day Dance. If it was merely a question of which one I preferred going to, obviously it was Arthur's birthday party. Despite the terrifying notion of being surrounded by his whole family.

Thankfully, it also included Esha Chakrabarti. I was excited to see Arthur's aunt again. She had a calming presence, one of the many reasons I was happy for my grandmother.

My other hesitation about attending the birthday soiree was I didn't want to let Ayisha down. She took her role as co-leader very seriously, even before the Scotty Bu complication, and I was going to have her back.

I just wasn't sure how I was going to be able to be at both at the same time.

When I asked him if Bronwyn would be at his party, Arthur reluctantly admitted she and her family were invited. After all,

Hatcher Campbell was the reason the party was being held at La Belle's in the first place, to curry favor with him and improve the deal with Watercress Industries, which I learned had something to do with Mr. Campbell's real estate development company buying an impressive quantity of Watercress Industries' building equipment. Getting a stronger foothold in the US had been a longtime goal of Lord Watercress's. It seemed that while he may not have been keen on his son being with an American, when it came to accepting American money, there were no such restrictions.

What that meant was, Bronwyn had the same dilemma as me: the Valentine's Day Dance or Arthur's birthday party. Not that I could ask her what she intended to do.

For obvious reasons.

I'd spent the whole of Tuesday classes dreading the moment we ran into each other.

I'd assumed it would be in Dr. Oswald's Astronomy class. My stomach had been clenched for two hours ahead of time, yet when I arrived, Bronwyn's desk was empty. And remained empty through the rest of the hour.

Arthur had shrugged once when I'd sent him a questioning look. She hadn't been in Mr. Mehdi's Contemporary History class the next hour, either.

A part of me was hoping that the #PunchBowl controversy—which had definitely migrated back to Barrington if the number of nods and smiles I'd received all day was any indication—had gotten to her and she decided to pack it up and move away to someplace like Tasmania. (Before you think I'm being mean, go look it up. It's very pretty.)

I knew I wouldn't be that lucky.

My luck *did* manage to hold on through the end of the day.

When I arrived in Mr. Poisson's classroom after classes were over for the first meeting since the ski trip of the Valentine's Day

Dance Committee, I half expected her to be there despite having been absent the full day.

She wasn't.

Neither was Josie.

Or Gaines.

It felt . . . ominous? Also, like a relief. I wasn't sure which was greater.

Nolan and Eadrich were both already in the room, chatting. They stopped to greet me with knowing grins, which made me blush. Both had been there at the time of The Shove and saw the whole thing. For some reason that made me more self-conscious.

I nodded briefly to them then went straight to the same desk I took last time.

A minute later, Caldwell's eyes lit up when Ayisha entered.

She gave him a cursory smile then her glance darted to the empty seats where Bronwyn and Josie typically sat.

"Where's the princess and her handmaiden?" she asked, hooking one strap of her book bag over the corner of her backrest, before taking the seat beside mine.

"I haven't seen either all day."

"I wonder if they caught a ride back with Scotty," she mused, setting her notebook and pen out in front of her, ready to get to work.

I glanced over to see if the idea of Bronwyn being with Scotty bothered her, but I couldn't tell. I was pretty sure she wasn't too upset over Scotty, despite her interest in his obvious physical appeal. Not enough that it showed, anyhow. Other than flashes of annoyance if his name came up.

Ms. Martinez entered the classroom.

"Okay, everyone," she said. "Settle down." She waited until everyone did though she remained standing. "Now, there are some changes to the committee. First up, Bronwyn and Josie have both decided they can no longer participate in the committee's activities." Ayisha and I exchanged looks. "It's taking too much time from their studies." No one believed that for a second. Ms. Martinez continued, "Which means their responsibilities will be redistributed among the group. Since Bronwyn was co-leader with Ayisha, that means her position is now empty. Is there anyone who would be interested in stepping into that role? If not, Ayisha will assume full leadership. Unless, Ayisha, you would prefer otherwise?"

Ayisha leaned back in her desk. "No, I'm good with it."

Ms. Martinez returned to address the full group. "Does anyone else want to be co-leader?"

No hands went up.

Ayisha looked at me and reconsidered. "You should do it." She grinned. "I'm going to make you do everything with me anyhow so you might as well get the credit."

I laughed. Because we all knew it was true. And raised my hand.

Ms. Martinez acknowledged, "Finley. Anyone else wish to toss their hat in the ring?" No one did. She turned back to me with a smile. "Okay. Ayisha and Finley, you're now in charge."

So, not how I thought this meeting was going to go.

Ayisha leaned in closer to me. "You realize the 'co' part is ceremonial, right? I'm gonna be bossy."

"Yeah, I've met you," I replied dryly.

Ms. Martinez handed Ayisha a quarter-inch pink binder. "Here you go. Bronwyn gave me this when she withdrew." We glanced at the front, which had a large red heart with smaller hearts around the edges. Ms. Martinez tapped the part that read *VDDC*. "It's all of the preparation she'd already completed."

Ayisha opened it and I leaned in to peer over her shoulder.

There were colorful tabs and a printed table of contents, which felt excessive. I appreciated it.

Ayisha went straight to the section designated *VENUE*.

Ms. Martinez noticed. "She booked Nostos for the location."

I frowned. "What's that?"

"It's a restaurant in Edge Hill," Caldwell supplied helpfully. "Very nice. Great for dates."

Ayisha frowned. "I would've thought she'd have wanted to use her parents' place."

Before I could stop myself, I said, "That's reserved for Arthur's birthday party."

Dark brown eyes zeroed in on me. "Arthur's having a birthday party the same night as the Valentine's Day Dance?" Ayisha asked, spotting the conflict with impressive speed.

I rolled my lips in on each other and bit down, wishing I hadn't let that slip. I'd have told her eventually, of course, but only after I had determined what I was going to do.

Too late now, genius.

I nodded.

She shifted in her seat to nail me with a piercing look. "Finley, you'd better still be going to our dance. Which you are now co-head of."

"I know, it's just—"

"Finley." Her tone was so firm I felt like I was back in preschool, when Ms. Cleveland caught me mixing all the Play-Doh colors together. "You're planning to be there, right?"

I swallowed hard. What else could I say but "Right."

"I have no idea how I'm going to be there *and* Arthur's birthday party," I whined, chewing on my left thumbnail as my right knee bobbed incessantly. I was seated on the edge of my dorm bed.

Petra didn't bother to glance up from her latest novel. She'd gotten back to Barrington in the late afternoon, right before it got dark, and was seated in her favorite spot on her own bed.

"Who's more important to you?" she asked plainly.

"They're *both* important to me," I insisted, briefly pausing from my disgusting anxiety chew to gesture. "Ayisha is my friend and has helped me *so* much, while Arthur is my—" I cut myself off. Then went back to chewing.

Now Petra glanced over the top of her book at me. "Friend?" she suggested in a way that said she clearly knew he was more. Or that I wanted him to be.

"Yes. Friend." I tucked my left hand under my butt to stop myself. "I can't choose between them. Ayisha's going to need help to pull off the dance and I'm the one person here she can trust. We've already divided up the new stuff we have to do." I wasn't happy about having to go to do an on-site inspection of Nostos later this week. Mr. Mehdi had gone crazy with the homework! And I had yet to crack open *On Love* for Mr. Poisson's class. I was doing better so far since I'd been back, and I wanted that to continue.

Still, I needed to pull my weight with the planning.

"It was her decision to take on that responsibility," Petra said. "You didn't want to be a part of that committee."

"But I am."

"Then go to the dance."

"But it's Arthur's eighteenth birthday! And his family is coming in from out of the country, including his aunt Esha, who I really like."

"Then go to Arthur's birthday."

"Ayisha will kill me!"

"This is why I stay away from people." Petra turned a page in her book so she missed the look I gave her.

"Not helpful, Petra."

"Maybe not for you, but it's a *great* reminder for me," she said, her eyes never leaving the page.

I reached across the divide between our two beds and laid an index finger in the interior spine of her book.

She looked up at me.

"Don't think you can just go back to being my ghost roommate," I told her. "You broke that barrier, so now we're *real* roommates who talk to each other."

She stared at me a long moment then she put a marker in her place and closed her book to pay direct attention to me with a patient sigh.

"What do you want me to say, Finley?"

"I don't know. Maybe help me figure out a solution?"

"Don't do either event. There. You have a solution. That's what I would do."

She started to reach for her book, but I put my hand over the cover.

"Okay," I persisted. "Pretend for a moment that you like people. Or at least two people. And they're both doing something important on the same day, and both want you there. What would you do?" She started to speak. "And don't say you don't like two people. This is pretend. In pretend, you do."

She sighed.

After a moment's consideration she said, "Start with one then go to another."

"Which one first?"

"The dance. Once it gets going you won't be needed as much."

It was a logical option. Except, "I have to supervise cleanup."

"Can you delegate that?"

I bit my lip. "I *could* ask Gaines . . ."

"Is he still part of the committee?" she asked in surprise.

"Possibly. He wasn't at the meeting, but Ms. Martinez didn't say he'd left with Bronwyn and Josie."

Petra tipped her head to one side. Faintly, because this was Petra. But the look said she found this interesting. "Then ask him."

That was a good idea.

I didn't have his contact info.

Fortunately, I knew where he would be this evening: The same place as me. And Arthur.

Twenty-Six

Part of our coursework in Dr. Oswald's Astronomy class was a night class trip to Barrington's planetarium.

Having a campus as big as Barrington, which was close to a state park near Avon, meant there was less light pollution here.

This was also the only spot on the campus opened to the public from time to time.

Or it had been until Oswald had them close it down. As the head teacher of Astronomy for the school, part of her responsibilities included supervision of the planetarium.

The previous teachers had all opened the building up to outside visitors for special events. Oswald thought it was too much of a hassle.

That meant no more public visits, other than school-recruitment private tours.

The private class visits, however, were one of the opportunities that had most appealed to me when I first read the brochure on the school. There had been a four-page photo spread with the space for pics dedicated to the telescope and main dome room for 360-degree viewing.

I'd been entranced.

While I may not have the gift of knowing exactly what I wanted to do with my life by the age of sixteen, I did know that I loved astronomy.

It was something Dad and I used to do together when I was younger. Go outside town where it could be unbelievably dark and set up his telescope to gaze up at the heavens above. His scope was pretty basic six-inch aperture, so we looked at the nearest planets or the moon or the occasional fuzzy gray shape of a nebula.

I loved it.

We hadn't done it in a while. Not for a couple years, maybe longer. I'd gotten busy and he stopped asking. Now, though, he would have the chance to do it again with the new baby, once they weren't a baby anymore, of course. It made me happy for him. I also wished I could bring Dad here to the planetarium. Maybe I could convince Oswald to open it up when he and Mom came to get me at the end of the semester.

It's a testament to how much stuff was going on in my life that I'd forgotten about this night visit. When Oswald had announced the reminder earlier today in class, I'd felt a surge of excitement that caught Arthur's eye. He laughed at my little jump.

"I gather you're pleased?" he'd said to me in a low voice from across the aisle.

I nodded enthusiastically and whispered back, "My calendar is marked!"

He grinned at me. "Shall we meet there?"

The sarcastic part of me would have replied, *Well, duh. We're both going.* But my heart wouldn't allow me to be snarky to Arthur. Not now, when we were still tentatively trying to find our way together, and his voice held the slightest tremor of uncertainty that melted me.

I smiled and nodded. "Front doors by seven forty-five?"

He drew in a breath to respond when Oswald's sharp voice stopped him:

"Mr. Chakrabarti Watercress and Ms. Brown."

We both quickly turned to find Oswald only a few steps away in the desk aisle, staring sternly at us through her thick glasses. While some teachers couldn't intimidate a kitten (I pictured Mr. Poisson), I was certain Oswald could make a charging cougar reconsider.

"This is a classroom, not a dating app!" she reminded, earning giggles from the other students.

A chastened Arthur and I spun to face forward.

"Socialize on your own time," she added for good measure before pivoting to walk back to the long table at the front of the room.

My cheeks were on fire. A quick glance told me Arthur's were too.

But a part of me was also giddy. We were going to meet up!

As *friends*, of course.

Whatever.

It was a good thing. It meant we were seeing each other again, albeit with the *shhhh*-ing Dr. Oswald supervising, and the rest of our classmates.

But I would get to be with him.

I'd spent the hours after my last class counting down to when I could leave for the tour without being embarrassingly early. Also changing my clothes three times—searching for the balance between looking like I'd put in an effort and not looking like I put in any effort—until an annoyed Petra rolled her eyes and told me to "just *go* already."

It was one of our more authentically roommate-ish exchanges.

A part of me hoped to run into Arthur as I exited Charity

House to start the walk along the concrete pathway that wound across the campus from the dorms to the planetarium itself. However, when I spotted two figures ahead of me on the path, neither was Arthur.

They were Bronwyn and Gaines.

Having a pretty heated argument, by the looks of it. Though as I neared, I realized it was more Bronwyn berating him, complete with jabbing finger and a wicked scowl, while Gaines appeared to be taking it.

Guess she hadn't dropped out of school after all.

Too bad.

I was surprised to see them together again after our lunch at Embers. Then for a moment I had an uncomfortable thought: what if the *only* reason Gaines had been acting as my friend was because of Bronwyn's orders, like he was a spy for her. That had been what she said at the Bu cabin, after all, when she'd been in her fiery snit.

Yet, deep down, I found that hard to believe. It was so . . . extra, of her and him. And while both had shown they knew how to play with drama—and for Bronwyn it was a comfortable headspace—Gaines didn't feel the same. I'd seen the conflict in him. At Embers he'd been genuine, I'd bet on it.

They heard my footsteps and turned and despite the poor lighting of the spot where they were standing, the loathing in Bronwyn's blue eyes was breathtaking.

I almost rocked back, but recovered swiftly, and did my best to be cool. Still, it wasn't easy to be on the receiving end of that much venom.

Luckily, she didn't come after me.

Much like she had when our paths crossed at the ski lodge, Bronwyn spun away from Gaines—and me—and stalked away in the opposite direction without a word.

Huh. Not what I expected when I imagined the moment of our first post—ski trip encounter.

"Hey," Gaines said, having waited for me, his hands jammed in his long coat's pockets, his breath visible. His energy was more mellow than usual.

"Sorry to interrupt," I told him, nodding after Bronwyn's retreating figure, already enveloped by shadows.

"It's fine." He scratched the stubble on his square chin. "She was just giving me more shit because she found out that I had lunch with 'the Christmas Girls' and Petra back at Lancaster."

I grinned. "I'm guessing Ayisha and I are the Christmas Girls."

He smiled in return. "It's my own personal nickname. What do you think?" His eyes twinkled then.

"Not bad."

We fell in step. Hopefully Bronwyn would already be inside by the time we reached the planetarium, and, if I was going to make impossible wishes, that she would stay away from me for the whole field trip. Or forever.

"Are you the one who came up with hashtag 'PunchBowl'?" I asked, pulling the ends of my red beanie down around my already freezing ears.

He lowered his voice to be safe. "Not if the Bron is the one asking. She's not keen on it, so let's keep that origin story on the down-low."

I raised my gloved hand. "I promise not to tell her."

"Much appreciated."

We walked a little farther in silence until I remembered to ask him to help out at the end of the dance and he agreed with a self-deprecating smile.

"It's not like I'll be going with a girl," he added.

That surprised me. He was cute and could be personable when he wanted, though sometimes he was goofy or foolish. I assumed girls would have lined up for him. And now that I thought about it, I recalled seeing him chatting with a variety of girls. I'd viewed it as flirtation, but now I wasn't so sure.

To test the waters I suggested, "Why don't you ask Petra to go with you?"

His eyes became hooded and he shook his head. "Bron-Bron would have me eviscerated."

I frowned, not expecting that. "Why?"

"You may be resting comfortably in the number one position on her Enemies List for now," he said, raising his hand over his head, "but Petra had held the spot for a *lot* longer."

That startled me. "Really? Why?" I hadn't even been aware the two knew each other until Scotty's party when Bronwyn had snapped at Petra in a way that spoke to familiarity.

His lips pursed. "That's high drama from our younger years."

"I'm listening."

"You already know we all grew up together out in Edge Hill. It's a super-tight community, not just the kids but our parents too. Sometimes it gets a little too tight, if you know what I mean."

"Oh, I grew up in a town about half that size."

"Right. Then you get it. Everybody grows up with each other. In the case of Petra and Bronwyn, their moms were super close. BFFs since they were little. Petra and Bronwyn grew up together since they were babies."

"I can't think of two people less likely to interact. Except maybe *me* and Bronwyn."

"They were practically sisters. Then Petra's parents got divorced about five years ago, and that's when everything started changing, not just with the adults, but with all of us too."

"Just because someone's parents got divorced?" I queried, perplexed.

"It's *why* they got divorced," he clarified. "Petra's mom had an affair with Bronwyn's dad."

"Ohhhhh . . ." I cringed. *Yikes.* I may not like Bronwyn—at *all*—but that sounded brutal. Heck, just having my parents separate over the holidays had been enough to throw me off, and that was without any infidelity! But to have it be with someone close to the family?

Yeah. That sucked. For her *and* for Petra.

Gaines continued, "Bron took it way hard. She'd always acted like her dad was a god."

I was tempted to point out that Petra had gone through the same thing with her mother and that couldn't have been easy for her, either.

"What happened?" I asked.

"The Bergeracs split up. The Campbells didn't. Though I personally think they should have. The tension's so bad, I don't go over there anymore." He shuddered and grimaced. "Mr. Bergerac moved to Boston and a couple years later, Mrs. Bergerac married Scotty's dad."

"That's intense. But what does that have to do with you and Petra?"

I was surprised when I saw a blush creeping up his neck when we passed under a pool of lamplight along the path. "Bronwyn basically took out all of her mom's anger on Petra and made it so no one in her circle would talk with her."

"Including you?" I guessed, feeling a surge of hurt on my room-mate's behalf.

He nodded. "Look, I'm not proud of it," he said, not meeting my eyes. "But she basically said we all had to choose."

"And you chose Bronwyn."

"Petra's not the easiest person," he said.

My look was incredulous. "Compared to Bronwyn?"

"Yeah, I get it." He ducked his head, embarrassed. "But you're seeing everyone now, not then. The Bron can be a lotta fun when she wants to be." He paused as if many other moments danced across his memory. He shook his head. "Anyway, Petra retreated into her room and books and became harder and harder to talk to. Last year at Barrington, she didn't even have a roommate the whole time. And she took most of her classes online."

"Wait, she takes online classes *at* a prep school?"

"Her mom and dad travel all the time. They worked out some kind of deal with Barrington. I'm pretty sure it involved a major donation."

"That's so wild . . ." Then a thought occurred to me. "I wonder why she got a roommate this semester."

"That, young Fin, I do not know. We haven't talked in a long time. I used to like her better than the Bron. But . . ."

"Are you going to be friends now?"

I wasn't sure that was even possible, given Petra's reactions whenever Gaines's name was brought up in conversation.

He lifted his shoulders. "Another thing I have no idea about."

"Do you want to be?" I pressed.

I wished I could've seen his expression but we were in one of the shadowy parts of the walk. "Honestly, I don't know." His voice was tighter than usual for him. "Maybe. It was cool hanging out with her at Embers. But I think she only accepted me because I was with you and Ayisha. I'm not sure she'd let me hang out with her if you two weren't there. Plus, there's the Bron to consider."

"She wouldn't like it."

His laugh was short. "My status on her shit list would become permanent."

"What would that look like . . . ?"

"Ostracization. She's beyond cold when she wants to cut someone out of her life."

Yeah, made sense. Bronwyn wasn't someone who took getting crossed lightly. "Would that be such a bad thing?" I asked. "If it meant not having to deal with her?" *Sounds like heaven to me.*

He frowned. "I've known her a long time, Fin." His expression grew serious in a way I hadn't seen from him before. "But I'm not gonna lie. Lately, I've been wondering . . ."

Before I could think of anything else to say, we rounded a tree-lined corner on the path and the planetarium came into view. It was a two-story structure; the dome jutting from the center was standard, but still set it apart from the other buildings on the Barrington campus.

There was also a roof deck for people to use their own telescope, if they had one. Even though mine was at home, I'd always wanted to go up there to simply gaze up at the dots of light in the night sky and think about all they represented.

Seeing the planetarium always gave me a tiny thrill.

It was too bad it was on the far edge of the campus, near the trees, and out of the way. Partly because of that, I'd only been here one other time, when Mom and I came to visit the campus last spring.

We'd gotten a tour, but it hadn't gone beyond the lobby and a couple of minutes in the dome room. It had also been during the day and the building wasn't illuminated with cool blue LED lighting under the roof's edge.

A few other people either lingered around the front, talking and waiting to enter, or were approaching, like me and Gaines.

One of those waiting was Arthur.

In his green jacket, a black knit cap was perched on the back of his head and, if my eyes didn't deceive me, he was wearing jeans! I did so love it when he wore one of the pairs of Wranglers we'd bought. Tucked under the arm without the crutch were two rolled-up throw blankets we'd agreed to bring for when we watched the movie in the dome room.

Then I noticed he also had an oddly closed-off expression and his body was tense as he watched me approach with—

Oh. Right.

I'd been so preoccupied with hearing the story about Petra and Bronwyn and Gaines that I didn't process how it would look if Gaines and I arrived together.

"Hey!" I waved with more enthusiasm than was probably needed as we headed over. I pointed to the blankets. "Is one of those for me?"

Arthur's gaze darted between me and Gaines. "Yes." His tone was clipped as he handed me a gray-and-cream cotton blanket with tassels.

Gaines gave a cheeky grin. "One for me?"

Arthur didn't miss a beat. "No."

Gaines cocked his head, but with a teasing gleam in his eyes. "Why you gotta be like that?"

Arthur adjusted his hold on the blanket he kept for himself. "I only brought the two and they're both spoken for." He gripped the padded handle on his single crutch.

"It was a rhetorical question, man," Gaines said, rolling his eyes.

Arthur nodded. "Yes, I recognized your intent."

Gaines half snorted. "Always an adventure with you." Then he took out his phone and tapped an app, turning to me. "There you go, Fin." I heard a soft noise from where my own phone was tucked inside my coat. "Now you have my info. We can talk dance details later." He returned his phone to the back pocket of his jeans and saluted Arthur. "See ya, CW."

Gaines walked into the planetarium.

Arthur clenched his teeth then schooled his expression to be more neutral. "Dance details?" he said to me. "The two of you are attending the dance . . . together?"

"No. I—"

He held up his right hand. "Not that it's any of my business, I'm quite aware. I've no right to ask. Shall we go inside?" He swept his hand toward the front doors. But he couldn't help himself and stopped. "It's just, you had implied you weren't interested in him—"

"I'm not."

"—so it takes me a bit by surprise that you're—" He stopped. "You're not what?"

"Interested in Gaines like that."

"You're not?"

"No. I ran into Gaines on the way over here and I asked him to help out with the Valentine's Day Dance."

"Ah." He processed swiftly. "The one Ayisha roped you into organizing?"

"Yeah. I'm co-leader now. Bronwyn left the group," I explained as we made our way to the building's front doors.

"That must be a bit of a relief," he said.

"Totally."

"Then, how does Gaines figure into your situation?" He opened the front doors for me to pass through. It was warmer inside, but not as much as you'd think. Fortunately, Oswald had warned us well in advance that she liked to keep it cool, hence the blankets.

"Gaines is going to take over the post-dance supervision so I can go to your birthday party."

We walked farther into the lobby. The high ceilings combined with white marble floors and walls made the space feel larger than it was. It was impressive, like a museum, and newer than the other parts of Barrington.

The rest of our class was spread out in all directions, talking in pairs or small groups, like Gaines and Eadrich. Bronwyn leaned against a wall, typing on her phone, while Josie stood beside her, chatting with Landon. A few other classmates read informational paragraphs beside the mounted photos of famous nebulas or Saturn's moons or a painting of Galileo. Dr. Oswald was off to the side, with Mr. Poisson, who was gesturing about something.

Wait, was she smiling? And did she just giggle? And did he laugh?

So weird. It was like they were people.

Oswald had told us earlier in class that we would be able to wander around the planetarium before we gathered in the dome room for a screening of a video. Her goal was to get us familiar with the place for future papers, and to foster in us a love for the subject.

Arthur and I stopped in front of a photo of Neil Armstrong on the Moon.

I noticed Arthur fidgeting. "What?"

"Are you certain you want to come?" he said, then realizing his omission, "To the party? It'll be deadly dull. Everyone over thirty. Talking business and deals and which island in Greece to go to next Christmas. The only part I'm moderately looking forward to is when my great-uncle Hubert on my father's side gets sloshed and tries to hit on Auntie Esha." My eyes widened and he explained, "It's more about how she dispatches him. You needn't worry for Auntie, I know of no one more capable of handling herself."

"I want to come to your party," I insisted, and when I saw lingering doubt, I bumped my shoulder against him. "How else am I going to know which Greek island is the next holiday destination?"

He relaxed into a smile. "Very well. You've been warned."

"I have." We smiled at each other and I felt that familiar feeling in the area slightly left of center in my chest. Which reminded me. "Does your dad know I'm coming?" The idea had me nervous. But not enough to not go.

"I haven't told him yet, but I shall." He grew slightly defensive. "I should be allowed to have at least one person my age at my own party, especially since I would much prefer not to be having a party at all."

I cocked my head at him. "You don't want a birthday party?"

"Is there anything about me that leads you to believe I would?" he retorted.

I narrowed my eyes. "Now that I think about it, no. So why are you?"

"Because that is how things are done." He sounded resigned. As he so often did when talking about his family and the expectations that came with them. Every family had expectations, there was no way around that, even if they were good.

Most people's were probably good. But I wasn't sure they were always correct.

"What if you told them you don't want a birthday party?" I asked.

"They would then rightly point out that it's a bit late in the game to make such a declaration."

"Well, what if you invited more classmates?" I glanced around and lowered my voice. "Other than Bronwyn."

"Such as?"

"There's Ayisha," I pointed out.

He suddenly looked stricken. "You're right. How remiss of me, I should have invited her! I'll remedy that tomorrow, straightaway. And I'll understand if she would prefer to stay at the dance, given that she's put in so much effort organizing the event."

I cocked an eyebrow, not proud of that stab of jealousy I was feeling, particularly since it was aimed at my one good friend, but, "You don't have to get slobbery over her."

"It's not slobbery, it's manners. She was instrumental in helping us during the blizzard, and I rather like her company." He quickly added, "In a strictly platonic capacity."

"You don't have to explain it to me." I waved him off like I didn't just snip at him.

"I want to make sure you know." I met his dark brown eyes and they sparkled with a hint of humor as he murmured, "If I *were* to be free to date one of you American lot, it would only be one person." Though his tone was teasing, there was an underlying certainty there, too.

One we both felt. I was sure of it.

"I'll make sure Ayisha knows," I whispered, deciding to keep up the pretense of playfulness and tamp down the disappointment of his reminder.

He rolled his eyes. Then looked at me. Our stares held and those earlier flutters morphed into a flush of warmth that had nothing to do with us being inside away from the cold. I swallowed and felt a change of subject was definitely needed.

I pointed around at the walls with hung images and the glass display cases interspersed.

"This must be old hat to you," I said, unbuttoning my coat. *Whew, it did get hot in here!*

He tore his eyes away from me with a soft sigh. "How so?"

"Because your mom is an astronomy professor."

"Ah. Yes. That she is."

We continued to stroll, side by side. Not paying much attention to the rest of our classmates. Some were clustered and joking around, shoving and getting shushed by Oswald.

It felt like Arthur and I were our own island.

I said, "You mentioned visiting her at her work. Did she take you there often?"

"Not often, no. There were a couple of her colleagues who weren't keen on children's presence, especially young children. She was mindful of that." He stopped before an image hung on the wall. It was a recreation of the famous first black-and-white photo of the Andromeda Galaxy, taken in 1888, when people mistakenly thought it was a nebula. "She did like to tell me about her work from time to time. When I was very little, I didn't much understand it." He chuckled. "I don't much understand it now, if we're being honest. But it was enough to spark my imagination. I used to write all sorts of space adventure stories when I was younger—"

I stopped in my tracks. "Arthur Chakrabarti Watercress!"

"What?" He was genuinely puzzled.

"You've never told me that before!"

"Told you . . . ?"

"That you write!"

He looked around us, embarrassed. No one was paying attention. "They're not very good, it's merely a hobby," he said, barely above a whisper.

"I want to read some."

He shook his head vehemently. "Absolutely not."

"Please . . ."

"Oh, well, since you said please." He rolled his hand.

My eyes brightened. "Really?"

"No!" he laughed, earning a reproving look from Oswald. He lowered his voice again. "It's private."

"Have you ever shown anyone what you've written?"

"No."

"Not even Esha?"

"Not even Auntie, no."

"Then how do you know they're not any good?"

"Because *I've* read them and I know what's good, and they're not. They're silly space stories of the sci-fi sort."

"Like the novels you and my dad read."

"Precisely."

"Including the one you were reading back at your rental cabin, which, as Dad reminds me when he's trying to get me to read something he likes, won a huge award?"

Arthur cleared his throat. "The Pulitzer, yes. Though that one is not *technically* science fiction."

"But that author writes science-fiction-type stories," I lobbed back. "I know he does because Dad told me so."

By his perturbed expression, I could tell I'd landed that point.

"Yes," he conceded. "Michael Chabon does indeed write science-fiction- and fantasy-type stories." He held up a finger. "Among *other* genres."

"Guess the silly stories are working out pretty nicely for him," I said smugly.

"They are. But I am nowhere near Michael Chabon in terms of talent."

"I'll bet almost-eighteen-year-old Michael Chabon wasn't anywhere near the talent of grown-up Michael Chabon either." I poked my index finger into his shoulder. "And I'll bet he needed to let someone read what he wrote to get better."

A ghost of a smile danced around the edges of his mouth. "Have you considered becoming a barrister? You're awfully dogged when you want to convince someone of something."

I grinned. "You inspire it in me."

"Lucky me."

"So, are you—"

"No."

I shoved him and he laughed, but he didn't give in.

Right then I felt like I was being watched. I glanced over my shoulder and straight into Bronwyn's icy glare. She'd been watching me and Arthur for a while, I could tell.

I dropped my gaze and looked back at a photo of a Martian meteorite found in the Sahara. Which was where I wished Bronwyn was at this very moment—the Sahara. Or Mars; I wasn't choosy.

I felt a tingle of paranoia. Maybe that whole "jumping out of the dark to murder me" thing wasn't hyperbole? But I also noticed interwoven in all that hatred she was directing at me was a bright-green thread of jealousy. Of Arthur? I wasn't sure. I totally believed she liked him, at least around the time of the Halloween party. I'd seen her lay on some serious flirt. Sorta like she'd done that time by the lockers with him.

She had Scotty back now, unless they'd broken up in the under thirty-six hours since the last time I saw them . . . which, honestly, was possible. I'd only met him once, but those two as a couple didn't strike me as the model of stability.

I didn't know why she would be jealous of me and Arthur being together, though. She'd made her choice. Not that she ever had a chance with Arthur. That much I *did* know was true, because I knew him. Or knew enough.

I remembered back to when Grandma Jo had been cleaning the reindeer poop off my favorite boots in the too-gorgeous bathroom at the reindeer ranch. She'd told me then when someone bullied you, it was "*never* about you. It's *always* about them and whatever deficiency *they* harbor."

It hadn't really registered then. It did now. A little bit. I couldn't control whatever it was she was thinking or going through, but I also knew it went way beyond me.

About ten minutes later, Oswald announced that it was time to go into the dome room, and we all migrated in that direction. I had a moment of heightened anxiety when it looked like I would enter the room behind Bronwyn, bringing me the closest to her since last Saturday, but at the last minute Gaines swooped in and stepped between us. He glanced back at me and winked conspiratorially.

Arthur's jaw clenched.

I surreptitiously squeezed his forearm through his jacket.

"It's okay," I whispered.

Arthur relaxed.

The lights in the dome room were already dimmed, with the only source being a blue glow coming from the circular center beneath the dome itself. There were rows of cushioned theater seats surrounding the central carpeted open space.

Some of us chose to sit in the seats, clusters of cliques.

Bronwyn and Josie were in a bunch in the chairs. Gaines had moved to a different group, close to hers. I caught him looking in Bronwyn's direction a couple times. She kept her back to him. When he didn't know anyone was watching, he seemed dejected.

"Let's sit on the floor," I said to Arthur.

He nodded.

Arthur and I went for the middle and wound up with other students all around us, pushing him closer to me until we were seated practically shoulder to shoulder.

I knew I shouldn't be having these thoughts because this wasn't romantic. Arthur and I were working on being friends only, which was as much for my benefit as it was for his. *I* would be the one left behind when he graduated in a few months and returned to England, and *I* would be the one who had another year at Barrington while he was getting his bearings at Oxford, and I *was* the one who was newly sixteen, so there was that to consider, too.

I knew all of this.

Didn't help, not really.

I held my blanket close to my chest.

"Is this okay with you?" he asked, nodding to how close we were to each other.

I nodded. *More than okay.*

Everyone around us was chatting, albeit in hushed tones.

I let my gaze wander around the room. The place smelled new and the carpet we were sitting on did, too. Like paint and plastic. There were yoga-type mats for us. We sat on ours. Those who brought blankets used them now. By accident, I caught Bronwyn's gaze lingering on Arthur. This time I knew for certain there was a trace of wistfulness in her gaze and I knew then that if Arthur had given her even the slightest hint of interest, she would've been "Prescott *who?*"

But he didn't.

Arthur unzipped his jacket, which was when I saw his sweater.

It was the vomiting reindeer one he'd bought from our visit to the reindeer farm. When he saw where my gaze was he gave a single shrug but there was a smile in his eyes.

And, *ugh*! Who'd have ever thought a reindeer sweater would be romantic?

Then the room went dark and the half-hour planetarium documentary started.

We both lay there, close to each other, staring up at the 360 dome as a depiction of the Milky Way and the Hubble Ultra Deep Field and the moon and stars played out above us. I could smell his sandalwood soap and feel the heat from his body.

I turned my head and saw the light of the overhead digital projection playing out across his features. He turned to meet my eyes and I wanted nothing more than to roll over onto my side so I could press against him and kiss him as the images of the heavens unfolded above us. The way he stared back at me, I knew he was thinking something similar. Maybe because we were in a place where we couldn't act on what we were feeling it somehow made it safe to show it to each other.

Though nothing had changed.

He would still be leaving.

He's here now, a voice inside my mind whispered.

I swallowed, my throat dry. Then returned to watching the cosmos above.

The images were crystal clear and breathtaking. One of my favorite things to do was go to the NASA-co-run Astronomy Picture of the Day (APOD, for the in crowd) website and see any new fantastic images of the universe. The best of the best were all here, in glorious detail.

I could barely focus.

Later, when it was over and Oswald released us to go to our dorms, we gathered up our blankets, and Arthur hesitantly asked, "Is Gaines walking you back?"

"No, we only ran into each other."

"May I walk you back? It's dark and . . ." He didn't finish. We both knew it was an excuse.

I nodded and he smiled, handing me his blanket as he rolled up both of our yoga mats to return them to the bin that lined the side of the far wall. As I waited for him to return, my mind was thinking about if the chance to kiss him arose, would I go for it? It would be against our agreement. For both our sakes.

As I let my imagination wander while watching Arthur's back as he crossed the breadth of the room, I wasn't paying attention to my surroundings.

"You won't *even* see it coming."

The low voice was by my right ear.

Startled, I turned quickly to see Bronwyn only a few feet away, staring straight at me, her eyes piercing and full of spite. The part that freaked me the most, though, was the small, confident smile tugging at her full lips that said she had a plan to get back at me.

And I couldn't do a damn thing about it.

Twenty-Seven

It's like she was Cersei Lannister!" I threw up my hands and paced my dorm room as Petra sat on her bed and Ayisha sat on mine, doing her nails. Deep pink.

It was the next afternoon after the planetarium. Bronwyn and Josie had both returned to class, but in the ones we all shared, they moved to different desks and made a point of icing me out.

"Or Maleficent!" I continued, having told them about the encounter.

"Maleficent was actually a good fairy," Petra noted.

I managed not to roll my eyes. "Fine, okay, but who really talks like that?!" I mocked her voice, "'You won't *even* see it coming.'" Now an eye roll, followed by chewing on the side of my thumbnail. "Should I be worried?"

Because I'm worried.

Petra propped her chin on her palm. "With Bronwyn, it's always a good idea to be at least a little worried."

Awesome.

Ayisha snorted, not looking up from her task. "It's not like she's going to jump Finley in the halls and kill her."

Okay, I felt mildly better that I wasn't the only one to come up with that ludicrous scenario yesterday.

"Metaphorically, she might," Petra said casually, leaning back on one elbow.

Feeling better is now over.

"Have you heard anything?" I asked, making a meal out of my thumb.

Petra raised a single eyebrow. "Who would tell me anything?"

"Other Edgies? Maybe your—" I slammed my mouth shut and stopped pacing. And chewing my nail.

"Stepbrother," Ayisha finished without missing a beat.

"Scotty would never tell me anything," Petra said. "He's back to being wrapped around the Wicked Witch's finger." She held up her middle finger for a visual.

"So unhealthy." I leaned against the side of my well-worn wooden desk, permanently fixed to the concrete wall, and nervously twisted the hem of my Barrington sweater.

Ayisha said matter-of-factly, "It's mania."

Petra and I looked over at her as she deftly managed to screw on the top of the polish bottle without smearing a single nail. *(How?!)* She set it aside and met both of our questioning eyes as if she hadn't just casually thrown out a random word like it was a string of beads at Mardi Gras.

"One of the ancient Greek love words I found," she said. "Mania is the jealous, obsessive kind."

"That's it," Petra nodded.

"What do the other words mean?" I asked.

Ayisha leaned her back against my wall. "Eros is obvious: it's the sexy, passionate love where you want to hump the other person *all* the time."

I blushed and nodded to myself internally. *Yep. That's familiar.*

Or was . . .

"Pragma is more about duty and responsibility than romance. Like, some couples start with eros and over time wind up in pragma, which is a lot deeper but also pragmatic."

"Hence the word," Petra noted.

Ayisha pointed at her. "Bingo. Storge is like family love. Ludus is being all flirty, kinda like the early phase when you're all playful and ooey-gooey with each other but you haven't fully committed."

Also a familiar feeling.

At least for nineteen days.

Ayisha pushed on. "Philautia is self-love. That's more like 'to thine own self be true.' But you gotta keep it in balance or else you end up acting like an asshole. That's 'hubris.'" She shrugged. "Philia is friendship love, and agape is the highest form of love."

"Unconditional," Petra chimed in, adding, "My dad goes to an agape church now."

That reminded me about what Gaines had told me last night. I wanted to talk with Petra about it, but it felt deeply personal, so I'd held back.

"So, I think we can all agree they're both maniacs," I said. "At least when it comes to each other."

"I'm thinking she's pretty messed up all on her own." Ayisha cocked her head at me, done talking about the boy she'd liked for a millisecond. "Now, are you ready to divide up responsibilities for the dance? We're down to less than three weeks before Valentine's Day and I have an AP Calc test on Friday to study for."

Managing to keep her nail polish pristine, she held out a sheet of paper.

At the top read *Finley's Responsibilities*.

Two columns followed with my future tasks:

- *Visit Nostos Restaurant. Get photos for layout.
  (No later than 1/25)*
- *Order customized name badges (Love Is . . .).
  (No later than 1/25)*

Ayisha already had three possible stationers we could use. With phone numbers. And contact names. I'd say she had control issues, but since it was working in my favor, I was cool with it.

I kept reading.

- *Pick up the printed flyers from Caldwell and have
  the committee post them around school/email
  them to each junior-/senior-year student. (By 1/29)*
- *Pick up the printed tickets, available at the door.
  (By 2/2)*
- *Purchase twenty boxes of white twinkle lights
  (<u>NOT BLINKING!</u>). (By 2/3)*
- *Projector, and confirm digital downloads of
  Valentine's Day/romance movies (from
  preapproved list vetted by Ms. Martinez). (By 2/3)*
- *Confirm Nolan has ordered the correct number of
  boxes of candy hearts (he might go over). We are
  going to put them in crystal bowls as part of the
  table centerpieces. (By 2/10)*

"You should see my list," Ayisha said.

"No thanks." I held up the paper. "This is freaking me out enough."

How much of these had once belonged to Bronwyn and Josie? Had they bailed on the committee as a way to get even with Ayisha and me?

Probably.

I could hear Bronwyn say something like, *If they want to lead it so bad, let them.*

Which, in the interest of fairness, would be something I might do. If I was spoiled, petty, and vengeful. I liked to think I wasn't. *(Though maybe a little judgy . . . ?)*

"I emailed you a copy, too," Ayisha said, pointing at the paper, then blew on the drying polish.

"No wonder you and Grandma Jo get along so well," I muttered under my breath. Grandma Jo had lists for her lists.

"Your grandmama knows how to throw a good event," Ayisha said. "That's what I wanna do."

"Be an event planner?" Petra asked.

Ay nodded. "Yeah. I think I'd be good at making things happen. Parties, dance, weddings."

Petra shuddered. "That's my total nightmare."

I looked over at her. "You're going to our dance, though, right?"

Petra lightly furrowed her brow. "Why would I do that? I barely leave this room."

"But, I mean, that was before the ski trip. And before, you know." I shrugged. "We all started hanging out . . ."

"You're having a mini dance meeting in our shared room. I don't have a choice."

My shoulders slumped in disappointment. I'd thought we were making friend progress, but maybe not.

She didn't know all the things Gaines had told me, that I knew part of her history now. It had made me feel closer to her, but it hadn't come *from* her, so it wasn't mutual.

Petra picked up her book.

Ayisha said, "You're going to need to go into Edge Hill for most of these. Do you think you can catch a ride with someone?"

Neither one of us had a car at school. Ayisha would get one next semester, if her grades met her mother's approval. I, on the other hand, had yet to get a driver's license, despite my blizzard escapade a few weeks ago, so borrowing a car was out of the question.

I glanced at Petra who shook her head. "I don't have a car either," she said.

These East Coast people and their love of public transportation, so annoying.

Ayisha's grin turned playful then. "I bet I know one person who could drive you into town . . ."

Oh . . .

Twenty-Eight

Arthur rented a Mercedes this time instead of a Hummer. An EQE SUV. The white faux-leather interior glowed with soft blue lights and everything was controlled by a twelve-inch touch screen. If Swedish minimalism and a spaceship had a baby, it would be this car.

I couldn't figure out how to control the radio to save my life but I'd somehow turned on the heated seats so I called it even. Plus, it practically drove itself, which helped Arthur with his knee. Which was mostly healed by this point. He didn't need the crutch anymore; a soft brace was enough.

The Watercresses had an open account at a local car rental so Arthur could have a car at his disposal within an hour whenever he so desired, and I wasn't even impressed at this point, because these rich people were ridic. Meanwhile I was hoping Dad would get a new car and I could get his old Jeep on its second transmission. Whenever I got around to studying for my driver's test.

Once he secured the rental, Arthur regaled me with its many features ("Comfort doors!") on our Sunday afternoon drive from

Barrington to Edge Hill, specifically Sheridan Boulevard, the swanky epicenter of the shopping district.

His enthusiasm was freakin' adorable and it made my heart hurt looking at him.

Then stop noticing those things! I yelled at myself.

I can't! I yelled back.

(I'd had healthier exchanges.)

We'd been good about the "friends" thing, seeing each other every day since the planetarium. In class, but also after, for studying, where studying genuinely did take place.

Turns out, among his many talents, Arthur was a wizard of a study partner. It helped that he was in a grade above me though I tried not to dwell on that part.

It brought reminders.

And while I'd prefer if our studying and talking also came with kisses and cuddling, I found that I enjoyed his company even without these benefits.

I liked him. I liked Arthur.

Not a news flash, obviously, but it felt different.

Deeper.

He was funnier than I remembered, maybe because he was looser around me these days. It reminded me of when he'd put on that red reindeer nose in the gift shop and how he'd smiled . . .

There were still moments when I'd catch him looking at me a certain way or he caught me doing the same. We'd blush and go back to studying or whatever, but we were both doing our best with our agreed compromise.

It was going to hurt when he left for England, no matter what, but it had to be easier than if we were still together the whole time, right? While getting to be with him in the here and now.

Not ideal, but not the free fall disaster we had there for a while.

Anything to avoid *that*.

He'd also been a good sounding board when I needed to vent or process, like when he walked me home from the planetarium after Bronwyn's warning.

"There's nothing she can do to you," he'd noted logically.

I hoped he was right, but I wasn't sure "logic" and "Bronwyn" belonged in the same hemisphere.

We parked in front of Nostos, the restaurant that would be the dance's venue.

It was the last part of January and the whole boulevard was decorated for Valentine's Day. I wasn't sure if that was too early or normal.

One of the quirks about growing up in a town called Christmas was that you never decorated for any other holiday. It went against the official theme that drew in the tourists. None of the businesses back home wanted to be the one that had Halloween or Thanksgiving decorations up in the background for the tourists coming there for the King of All Holidays.

So seeing Valentine decor along a main shopping street and in storefront windows was novel for me.

There was a lot of red and white and pink hearts, with the occasional lavender or royal purple. Paper roses in windows and around doorways.

"It's pretty," I noted, snapping a few shots with my phone. I'd send them to Grandma Jo.

"Very," Arthur agreed, standing beside me as we both peered down the length of the wide, immaculate street with its angled parking spaces and redbrick sidewalks. "Though it's no Christmas."

Our eyes met and he winked.

I flushed furiously but couldn't help but smile.

Making a mental note that I still needed to get a dress for

the dance—not that I could afford anything on *this* street—I led Arthur up the steps to the front of Nostos Restaurant. Which was quite nice on the outside, but even nicer inside. It was deceptively large, going much farther back than I initially imagined. Once all the tables and chairs were removed, it would be a good space.

We were early for our four p.m. appointment with Mr. Tucker, the Nostos manager.

He was a doughy-looking man with a distracting section of fresh hair plugs on the left side of his skull. At least his dark blue suit was nice.

Regarding me with open puzzlement and a hint of suspicion, his eyes darting over to where Arthur stood by the restaurant's front windows. Arthur had insisted on hanging back so it was clear that I was the person Mr. Tucker should address, not the guy.

Within seconds of our meeting, I knew he was right.

"Where's Bronwyn?" Mr. Tucker asked, frowning. "She's the point person I've been dealing with."

"She's no longer on the committee," I said with a cheerful, Midwestern smile. "I'll be your point person now. Or Ayisha Lewis."

His eyes narrowed. "I see."

Hmmm . . .

I dug my short nails into the palms of my hands, both in the pockets of my coat, hidden from view. I didn't want him to know how out of my depth I was feeling.

It had been a while since I had helped plan any school events and those had all been back home, where I knew everyone or they knew me. ("Tell your grandma howdy for me," someone would say with a smile as I bought supplies for the school carnival or movie night in the junior high school gym.)

This wasn't going to go like that.

I cleared my throat. "Barrington is still having the dance here on Valentine's Day," I made sure he knew, adding extra enthusiasm, hoping that would mollify him.

It didn't.

"And you're the new person I'll be dealing with?" He didn't openly sneer, but he might as well have.

"Yes." I stopped myself from adding "sir" because I already felt at a disadvantage. I knew I looked every bit of sixteen. "Well, me and Ayisha. And our advisor, Ms. Martinez."

"Do you have Ms. Martinez's contact number?"

The underlying—*I'll talk with her instead of the teen*—was difficult to miss.

"Um, sure." I retrieved my iPhone and pulled up Ms. Martinez's office phone number, texting it to him.

Mr. Tucker glanced at his phone screen but didn't say anything. The way he assessed me reminded me a little of Lord Watercress, and it grated.

"Nothing's changed, other than Bronwyn leaving," I assured him. "We still want to have the dance here. We're not breaking our contract."

"Wonderful," he said with a distinct lack of wonder.

"Do you, uh, is it all right if I take some pictures?" I held up my phone and waggled it. "I'm scoping the layout for decorations."

He checked his watch then leveled me with a wan smile. "We don't get our dinner rush for another half hour."

"We'll be gone by then," I promised him.

"Wonderful," he repeated flatly.

With that, Mr. Tucker spun on the heel of his shiny loafers, walked back to the back of the restaurant, through the doors to the kitchen, and out of sight.

When he was gone, I moved over to stand beside Arthur, who was still near the front windows overlooking Sheridan Boulevard.

"Did you hear that? It was weird," I whispered. "Did you think it's weird?"

"He appeared thrown by you not being Bronwyn."

I rubbed the back of my neck, which was warm. "Why should that matter? She's a teenager just like me."

"I wouldn't go that far. Perhaps he's familiar with the Campbells." He pointed out the window. "La Belle's is directly across the street."

Sure enough, across the street I saw the refined white wood exterior of a restaurant with a sign that read LA BELLE's in elegant gold script against a black backdrop. Owned by the Campbell family. The site of Josie Sutton's birthday I wasn't invited to last month. And where Arthur's birthday would be held.

It was beautiful and I hated it on sight.

"I didn't realize they were that close to each other," I said neutrally.

"It's possible there's some cross-pollination, so to speak. I would hazard a guess that's why Bronwyn selected Nostos, given La Belle's is unavailable. They probably knew each other already."

A thought popped into my brain. "Do you realize what this means?" I asked, feeling better than I had a moment ago.

"I do not. What does it mean?"

"I can go back and forth between your party and the dance! I don't have to choose after all." *Proximity eclipsed resentment.*

"How convenient."

"Right?" I smiled. "Come on, let's take the pictures before Mr. Hair Plugs comes back." Arthur chortled. "Then you can buy me ice cream. I noticed there was a store down the street."

This appalled him. "Ice cream? It's bloody cold outside!"

I nudged his arm with my elbow as I opened my photo app. "That's why you'll also order hot fudge topping!"

"Done."

I set my spoon down and leaned back. Arthur and I were seated at a counter set up against the front window overlooking Sheridan.

It was almost dark out now, despite being still early, and the fairy lights threaded through the bare branches of the trees along the street created a romantic atmosphere outside. Inside, the shop played light jazz music. Arthur had his jacket off and that red sweater he was wearing with a white button-down underneath looked preppy hot on him. Like he'd taken some extra time getting ready. Adding spicy aftershave and my favorite soap, which I could still smell when I innocently leaned in.

If I wasn't careful, this was going to start to feel real.

It already does . . .

The ice cream shop had been covered in hearts, on the walls and hanging from the ceiling. Impulsively, I snapped a couple of quick photos of them, for inspiration later. Then, just as impulsively, I snapped one of Arthur seated on the backless stool beside me as he licked the spoon.

He shot me a look. "A little warning would be appreciated," he muttered, but the curve to his beautiful lips—that I knew from experience were kissably soft—told me he wasn't upset.

I really wish this was a date . . .

But it wasn't.

It was a fun time, though. That was good enough.

I finally remembered to tell him about my parents' having

another baby. You'd think that would've come up earlier, but Bronwyn's impersonation of Hela from *Thor: Ragnarok* had been distracting.

"Another oopsie," he commented.

"We'll have to add him or her or them to our club."

He set his spoon down. "You'll be close to the same age differential as is between me and Polly." Though he'd kept his tone light, I knew the subtext.

"I promise not to have any other similarity between me and the Bean." Off his questioning look, "That's what I'm calling it instead of 'it.' 'Him slash her slash they' gets wordy."

He nodded. "Be good to the Bean."

"I'll be the best," I promised.

He smiled. And my heart did that little clench thing it did sometimes when I was around him.

Arthur's phone buzzed once. He glanced at the screen with its new banner notification and frowned. Then picked it up. "My mother. She rarely emails. I wonder if her ears were burning." He quickly checked the message.

When his brows knitted again, I couldn't resist. "Why the face?"

He blinked in confusion. "What?"

Pointing at him, I clarified, "You're frowning. What's up?"

"Apparently there are two hundred and fifty people who've accepted the invitation to my party."

Damn! That was a lot of people.

"Even the Queen?" I asked, joking.

"No."

Before I could ask him how many of those 250 he *wanted* to come, I saw him react to something he saw out the window.

Following his gaze, I noticed two figures walking on the other side of the street, arm in arm, clearly together. The short man had curly black hair that looked as if he ran his hands through it too much and was gesturing wildly about something. The woman's honey-blonde hair was piled high, like a beehive, and she towered over him.

Holy—

Arthur leaned forward, squinting. "Is that—?"

"Uh-huh."

Dr. Oswald and Mr. Poisson. Together.

"Are they—?"

Oswald giggled at something he said. Like she had back at the planetarium.

"Looks like it," I murmured in amazement.

It was always weird to see teachers out of the school environment, even back home. But at Barrington it felt so insular, as if nothing existed beyond the property. Certainly not two teachers who, by all appearances, were an item.

Arthur shook his head. "I can't fathom a less likely couple."

"Pete Davidson and Kim Kardashian."

His lips twitched. "You came up with that remarkably fast."

I threw my hands up. "I mean, why?"

Look, I know some pop culture. Maybe I should mention them to Ayisha, score some cool points.

He tipped his head to one side. "Is that proper? With the school and all?"

"Pete Davidson and Kim Kardashian?"

"No." He nodded out the window at the retreating figures. "Dr. Oswald and Mr. Poisson."

Thinking about it for a moment, I shrugged. "I don't see why not. I suppose Barrington *is* their workplace." Where else were they supposed to meet someone?

It's where I met you.

Stop that right now, brain!

Or was it my heart?

Either way? Stop!

We both stared at them as they ducked into a small bistro.

"Right." Arthur stood, taking the tray with the remnants of our sundaes, and crossed to deposit them with the clerk at the counter. When he came back, he changed the subject. "I forgot to mention, my auntie is coming by later this this week. We're going to lunch."

I perked up. Not including the period of my spectacularly erroneous assumption that Esha Chakrabarti was flirting with my dad over the holidays, I'd liked her from the beginning. She had a calming presence about her that I would someday love to emulate.

"I thought she was coming to the States for your birthday," I said.

"She is. But I suspect your grandmother is something of a draw this time." Slipping on his gloves. "Anyhow, she asked if she could see you for a bit before she heads off."

Standing, I slipped my purse strap over my shoulder. "Sure."

He held open the door for me as we exited onto the sidewalk. The temperature had dropped a good twenty degrees since we'd arrived at Edge Hill and the cold took my breath away.

For a moment it seemed like he was contemplating putting his arm around my shoulders, to keep me warm, of course, when we heard someone say:

"Arthur!"

We both turned to see a tall man in a gray wool coat.

He was a little older than my dad, had a full head of sandy-blond hair, stylishly cut, and lines around his eyes when he smiled.

The diamond earring in his left ear twinkled in the light from the street lamps.

Arthur recognized him and brightened. "Mr. Novak! Hello!"

The man smiled genially as he and Arthur shook hands. "I thought I recognized you."

Arthur turned to me to make introductions. "Mr. Vaughn Novak, this is my friend, Finley Brown. Finley, this is Mr. Vaughn Novak. He's a senior lecturer of English and creative writing at Yale."

Mr. Novak grinned, making himself seem even younger. "It's a little school about an hour down the I-91."

"Never heard of it," I joked. *I mean, hello?*

He chuckled and looked to Arthur. "She's quick."

The tips of Arthur's ears grew red. He explained to me, "I met Mr. Novak when he came by Barrington last spring."

Mr. Novak nodded. "I'm an alumnus there. Class of '95." He pointed to Arthur. "I saw this young man on a bench outside the library, reading *Solaris*, and I had to chat with him. I don't see many young people reading that."

"*Solaris* was a good book," I said.

Arthur's brows rose in surprise. "You've read it?" When I nodded, he said, "I thought you didn't care for science fiction."

"No, I don't like the jokey fantasy stuff that you and Dad talk about. But I like reading about 'what if' science possibilities. Like the Nick Bostrom paper," I added knowingly to Arthur, who bit back a smile.

Mr. Novak's expression lit up. "Nick Bostrom and *Solaris*. I'm impressed. And I'm guessing by your uniform you go to Barrington, too?"

I nodded. "Yes, sir. I'm a junior."

"That means you'll soon be taking your SATs. Have you begun studying?"

"Not yet. I planned to take them in June."

"Then you still have some time, but it comes faster than you'd think. When did you take yours, Arthur?"

"Last May."

Mr. Novak looked back to me. "He almost didn't study, he's so certain he's going to Oxford."

"Well, he does have connections," I noted.

"True! And the grades." Mr. Novak smiled, then said to Arthur, "If you ever do change your mind, remember, you have options. Yale isn't such a bad choice." Then to my surprise he looked back at me. "Keep that in mind, too, Ms. Brown."

Happily, I didn't let my eyes bug too far out of my head and answered, "Yes, sir."

"Sir." He took that in. "You don't sound like you're from the East Coast."

"Do I have an accent?" I couldn't really hear one in myself.

Mr. Novak held his thumb and forefinger close together. "A little bit." Then he winked.

Arthur shrugged. "All Yanks sound the same to me," he teased. "Finley is from a town called Christmas in Oklahoma."

"I'll bet that's an interesting place," the older man commented.

I bit the inside of my cheek. Arthur said cryptically, "In many ways."

Mr. Novak crossed his arms, thinking. "That could be a good subject for your essay when you apply to Yale, Ms. Brown."

I blinked but didn't know what to say to that. His assumption about my application to Yale kind of blew my mind. I've been working to get my bearings at Barrington, which was a big enough undertaking. Applying to any of the Ivy League schools for college seemed very far away. But Mr. Novak was right. It would get here faster than I realized.

Then what? Arthur would be at Oxford.

Where will I be next?

Giving Arthur's upper arm an affectionate pat, Mr. Novak said with a good-natured formality, "It's good to see you again, Mr. Chakrabarti Watercress." Then he nodded once to me. "Nice to meet you, Ms. Brown."

I waved. "Nice to meet you, sir."

"Good night, Mr. Novak," Arthur said.

Mr. Novak continued on to where his sedan was parked farther down the street while Arthur and I turned in the opposite direction.

"What do you think?" Arthur asked me as we slowly strolled. "About applying to Yale?"

"I hadn't really thought about it," I admitted. Not in the concrete, actually doing it sort of way.

"Really? It's only an hour's drive away."

"I know, but it feels a lot farther." I exhaled and watched my breath fog up the crisp night air. "It's not as if I'd get in."

We arrived at the rental car.

"I thought your grades had improved."

Arthur deactivated the alarm.

I nodded. "They have so far. It's early, though. Anything can happen."

"You'll do it," he said with more certainty than I felt. He opened the front passenger door for me. "Should you want assistance studying for the SATs or filling out the application, I could help you, if you're interested. I've already done one for Yale."

"You did? Why?" I leaned against the car, not yet entering, the door between us.

"To appease Mr. Novak, who asked me to when he was here as a guest lecturer. I'd be happy to read over your Common App essay when it's time."

"That depends," I grinned at him, poking him in the shoulder. "Did you get in? Because I only want help from the best."

He straightened himself, affecting a haughty air. "I already got in to all the schools to which I applied, thank you very much."

"How many schools did you apply to?" I asked.

"Fifteen."

My eyes widened in surprise. "Fifteen? Jesus, Arthur, that sounds exhausting! And sort of pointless since you've known where you're going to since birth."

"Oddly, I rather like the process of applying. It was an intellectual challenge of sorts, particularly the essays. I enjoyed crafting them. I'm rather good at them, if I may say."

Smiling, I said, "I'll bet you are." My gaze lingered over his face, noting the tiny darker spot dusting his skin on his cheek beneath his left eye. I remember kissing it once when we were fooling around in the snow on Christmas Day.

I sighed and shook myself a little, pulling back from going "there." "Sure, I will absolutely lean on your weird love of applying to colleges when it's my turn." I moved to sit in the passenger seat. "Even if that feels like forever from now."

Arthur remained leaning on the open car door a moment longer, gazing down at me, though he seemed lost in his own thoughts. "It does. But Mr. Novak was quite right. It arrives faster than you can possibly imagine . . ."

He shut the door.

Twenty-Nine

JANUARY 29

Arthur explained what GCSEs were to me, and I had a new appreciation for not having to go to school in the British scholastic system. General Certificate of Secondary Education. That basically meant each student had to take a bonkers number of tests on all the subjects over a six-week period, and honestly, the whole thing sounded draining. And beyond stressful. It also gave me a new appreciation for the papers, tests, and pop quizzes I had to slog through.

The good news was the studying with Arthur was starting to pay off. My grades were up across the board. Not at the same "A+" level I was used to back home, but I was now solidly in the "B+/A-" side of things.

It was a start, and a better one than I'd had in my first semester.

I told Arthur that he should consider being a tutor if the whole "running an international construction equipment family business" thing didn't work out.

He was less amused than I would've thought. I'd noticed he would get like that every time I mentioned anything about his future. He'd wilt a little, then switch the subject. Naturally I wanted to press him on it. But it felt naggy. And very "American."

So I didn't.

Instead, we confirmed that I'd meet up with Esha when they came back from Saturday brunch. I was looking forward to seeing her and learning if there was any good gossip that Grandma Jo didn't feel was appropriate to tell her granddaughter.

I also did a deep dive into possible presents for Arthur's birthday. It couldn't be just anything, either. That part was important. I wanted it to be something that resonated with him, something he'd remember me by when he was old and married to a brittle British woman who would never understand him like I did but who fit the expectations of Lord and Lady Watercress.

This was a tall order for someone on a limited budget already stretched thin by a ski weekend. In hindsight, I should've planned better. In reality, I hadn't known Valentine's Day was his birthday, so it hadn't occurred to me to plan at all.

An idea came to me one afternoon when I was studying alone in the library.

Eadrich had been at a table near me with a copy of a graphic novel hidden behind his textbook, and an hour later I'd searched for and found Mr. Novak's contact information at Yale. Arthur had said he was a senior lecturer of English and creative writing. My hope was that he'd have connections I couldn't possibly have.

When I told Mr. Novak what I was looking for—and why—not only did he think he could find it, but he knew how to get an even better version of it directly from the source. Putting a lot of faith into a man I'd only met in passing, I agreed and gave him my address.

Now all I could do was hope that Mr. Novak came through and that the gift in question arrived before Valentine's Day.

Too much effort for a friend?

I chose not to answer that rhetorical question.

Especially when things were going well.

We'd been texting a lot. Totally nothing to read into that. Sure, sometimes those text exchanges went deep into the night and I had to pull the comforter over my head so the light wouldn't bother Petra, but that happens.

When we'd play each other on a chess app, it would happen quite a lot.

Arthur was teaching me certain moves, which sounds sexy but really involved things like learning the "en passant capture," which, okay, I still don't understand. Arthur got so excited as he was explaining, his eyes widening on the screen as he said things like ". . . and the white pawn of the fifth rank or the black pawn of the fourth rank to capture another pawn that has passed it!" I interpreted it to mean that a special pawn could double back if it needed to so it could take care of business before going forward. Arthur told me, "Close enough." Then never tried that move again because it "might be a bit advanced." I tried not to be insulted.

Mostly I just enjoyed his company.

His friend company.

And yet . . .

Be careful, that voice in my brain warned.

I was being careful . . . wasn't I?

Am I?

On Friday after classes, I wanted to ask Arthur what else he was up to over the weekend. Like, maybe we could go see a movie, or watch something streaming in the common rooms, either at his dorm or mine.

We could've gone to each other's room, which happened all the time (within established hours), but it felt rude to Petra—who was as camped out as ever in ours—and Arthur said Landon had taken things to a new level of unbearable since he'd started "snogging" Josie. (No one wanted to risk an encounter like *that*.) Plus, Landon's side of their room was "a rubbish heap."

Ultimately, I didn't ask Arthur about his plans.

Despite every part of me wanting nothing less than to blow right past the promise we'd made to each other about not being boyfriend/girlfriend, and being reasonably sure Arthur wanted that too, I knew we shouldn't.

Hanging out in each other's dorm rooms or going to a movie or sharing another ice cream sundae was too tempting.

The line we were walking was already close enough.

Which meant as Friday started to settle into its too-early twilight, I parted company with Arthur at our fateful bridge and went straight to my own dorm. I didn't even pause when I passed Caldwell and Pashley making out like clumsy penguins against the north wall of Charity House (though I did go wide-eyed at the sight—briefly, not like a weirdo gawker).

I wondered if that meant he was over his crush on Ayisha.

Doubtful.

I was proud of myself for knowing both parties involved, which wouldn't have been the case last semester, and was going to share the gossip like a normal person with my not-exactly-normal roommate, who would then ask me, "Who are Caldwell and Pashley?" since she never went *anywhere* and I was pretty sure neither were Edgies.

Except when I opened the door to our dormer, I was faced with an improbable sight: Petra wasn't there!

I froze. Full-on, in the doorway, one hand still on the knob.

My gaze swept the standard 185 square feet of space with its two twin beds, both bolted to the wall and floor, with two sliding drawers beneath them for storage. The two narrow wind-out windows flanking the central larger pane of glass were both closed. Not that jumping was a possibility with that setup.

She wouldn't jump.

Would she?

No.

Okay.

The door to our bathroom was open but the light was off. Which usually meant it was clear. Not that I ever had to wonder about such things with her before since I'd always know whenever she went in while I was in the room.

However, in case she *was* in there, in the dark, for whatever reason, I called out, "Petra?"

Loudly.

No response.

Maybe she had slipped and fallen in there and was unconscious and couldn't hear me . . .

Did she also turn off the lights as she was falling to the floor?

Was it possible to roll your eyes at your own inner voice? Because I just did.

Then I turned on the bathroom lights.

Nope. She wasn't lying there. Which was a relief. The potential amount of germs on the tile floor alone was terrifying.

Then, where was she?

Another glance. Her bed was neatly made, but I noted the familiar impression on her comforter where she normally sat. A paperback book was there, facedown, bookmark in place. Like it would be if she had been sitting there.

Now, I admit to watching far too many murder shows, both the *Dateline/Making a Murderer* variety and the British/Nordic/French programs with the weary detective who never smiles struggling to find out who's killing young people in a small, poorly lit village.

Which was why my mind avoided the many obvious potential answers and went directly to, "Kidnapped!"

I whipped out my phone from my coat pocket and started taking photos of the room in case there was a potential clue that could be useful in a future investigation.

On the eighth snap, the dorm door opened and Petra entered.

I jumped and: "AHHHHH!" (It was dramatic.)

She paused a moment before asking, "Are you okay?" adding the universal "you're acting like a giant weirdo" look for good measure.

My hand was on my chest. "You scared me!"

"Clearly."

She kicked the door closed behind her. That was when I noticed she was holding a cardboard box, the kind that came with reams of eight-and-a-half-by-eleven paper.

She set it on my desk.

"What's that?" I asked.

"Ayisha came by earlier and said Caldwell had dropped off the flyers for the Valentine's Day Dance. I picked them up." She brushed some stray bits of cardboard from her sweater sleeves. "These are for you to distribute."

"Oh."

I was still standing in the doorway to the bathroom when she stepped in that direction. It took a second before it clicked and I moved out of the way.

"Sorry."

She turned on the lights as she entered and I heard the sound of her turning on the tap water.

I opened the box's cross-folded top and took out a single glossy sheet to look at the flyers' design.

It was basic but competent: Red hearts of varying shades in the background with a central white negative space also in the shape of a heart where the information about the dance was printed out:

Valentine's Day Dance

When: February 14
Time: 7:00 p.m.–10:00 p.m.
Where: Nostos Restaurant
2235 North Sheridan Blvd.
Edge Hill, CT 06001
Theme: Love Is . . .
Dress: Semiformal
Tickets: $10 presale
$20 at door
Photo booth! Live DJ! Nonalcoholic drinks!

"Why did you scream when I came in?" Petra asked as she reentered from the bathroom, shaking her hands dry.

I covered my second startled jump and set the flyer back in the box. "I wouldn't say it was a scream—"

"It was."

"Fine, whatever. You startled me." She continued to regard me in a way that, frankly, rivaled Lord Watercress for her ability to not blink, waiting for me to elaborate. "You weren't here." Turning away from her, I unbuttoned my coat.

Petra sat on her bed. "Why were you taking pictures of the room?" she asked. "Don't pretend you weren't; I saw you."

Shrugging out of my coat, I replied, "In case you were murdered."

"Are you planning to murder me?"

I looked over my shoulder with a frown. "No! In case you *had* been murdered," I clarified, feeling dumber the longer this went on. "By someone else who is *definitely* not me. I wanted to have fresh evidence for the detectives."

Yes, I knew how that sounded.

I shut the door to my small closet and turned to find her watching me with curiosity.

"Were you worried about me?" she asked in a measured tone, but there was a gleam in her eyes I couldn't quite define. Cautious? Seeking?

"Worried?" She nodded. I considered it a moment then shrugged. "I mean, I guess, kinda? Probably more in a 'freaked out' phase still." In my defense I added, "You never leave, Petra!"

"That's not true. I was at Lancaster Mountain. You were there too."

"You know what I mean. You're always here, in our dorm room." I decided now was as good a time as any to ask what I really wanted to know: "Why is that?"

"My mother wants me to go to Barrington, I don't. This is our compromise." She shrugged and drew her legs up, back against the wall, and grabbed her book.

Unfortunately for her, I wanted to know more.

Deep breath. I decided to go for it. "Is it because of Bronwyn that you don't want to be here?"

She stilled, her eyes narrowed. She set the paperback book aside without opening it. "Why would you ask that?" Her tone was the closest I'd heard her come to angry.

I swallowed. "Gaines told me about everything. With, um, your mom and Bronwyn's mom and, well, everything." I spewed some of the highlights: moms are BFF; raised with Bronwyn; the affair; Bronwyn made people choose.

Her jaw clenched before she murmured something under her breath. Then fixed me with a piercing look. "Did he tell you about the hashtag?" I shook my head. "After it all happened, a rumor started at school. About me. And how I had sex with a bunch of boys. I got a hashtag: hashtag PoundPetra."

I gasped! "No!"

A protective surge came over me for her. *Who would do such a thing?*

Though the instant I thought that, I had a good idea who the culprit was.

"I thought it would be over quickly but it wasn't."

"Oh my God, Petra. That must've been—"

"Shitty? It was."

Yet she seemed so nonchalant, as if she was describing a bad meal or boring movie. It didn't make sense to me, unless it was a self-protection technique.

Like locking herself away from everyone . . .

Right. That.

My heart hurt for her. She wasn't the warmest person I'd ever met, but who would be after something so awful?

"I'm sorry," I said softly.

She looked puzzled. "Why? You didn't have anything to do with it."

"I shouldn't have brought it up. And I should've stopped Gaines from telling me."

A shoulder shrug. "It is what it is." She continued to regard me. "You're lucky your parents are still together."

I moved to sit on my bed, opposite her. "Actually, they almost weren't," I said, gripping the edge of my mattress, feeling an echo of the anxiety I'd gone through. "I found out they were separated when I went home for Christmas." I tucked a loose strand of my hair over my ear. "They worked it out, and they're okay now."

"I'd hope so," she said.

A few days ago, I'd told her about Mom being pregnant, before I knew about her issues with her own mother. She'd noticed me doing online shopping for infant clothes and I wanted to stop any potential misconception about whose baby it was tout de suite!

Petra pushed her glasses up her nose. She seemed to be considering something before she launched straight to it with, "My parents hated each other for as long as I could remember. There's about twenty years between them. Mom married Dad for his money. He's not handsome. Or interesting. Or kind. She was the runner-up to Miss Connecticut back in her heyday. Men still flock to her, and she likes the attention. I think my father was relieved when my mother got caught cheating. It gave him an out. From her, and from me."

Harsh. But I wasn't going to call her on that. She knew the truth of her situation better than I ever could since hers was a front-row seat and I was just reading old reviews.

"I don't see him much lately," she said. "He has five other children from his previous marriages. I'm the least interesting of the bunch so he doesn't bother."

"I'm sure that's not true."

Her green eyes were hard. "Finley, we both know I'm excruciatingly dull. You said it yourself."

"No." I held up a single finger, realizing I was mimicking one of Ayisha's patented gestures, but it worked. "I said you never leave this room, I never said you were dull. You're totally not. You're weird." I shrugged both shoulders. "But so am I; so is Arthur."

"Ayisha's not weird."

I laughed. "That's true. But she appreciates the weird, otherwise she wouldn't hang out with me. And I know she likes you, too. She wouldn't have asked you to hang out at the ski place if she didn't."

This appeared to resonate.

She was quiet for a long moment in contemplation. Her voice was lower when she said, "I asked for you to be my roommate."

I blinked. Several times. Then stared.

Honestly, I was so astonished, it was like she'd just spoken to me in Aramaic.

"What do you mean?" I managed. "We never met before I got moved here."

Petra's fingers fidgeted with the fabric of her black sweatpants. "I don't expect you to remember . . ." She bit her lip. "It was last summer when you were moving in. I was already here, at the dorms, because Mom and my stepdad were going to be gone all summer in South Korea to do whatever diplomatic stuff it is that he does." She gave a dismissive wave of her hand. "You were coming out of the elevator at the bottom of Charity, and I was coming in, and you were super excited . . ."

That much I remembered: on my move-in day, I was practically golden retriever level of giddy about finally being at Barrington.

She continued. "You came out of the elevator in a rush and almost ran into me. You were apologetic and smiling and happy. You held the doors for me and you said your name was Finley Brown and you were new, from Oklahoma, and you hoped I had a great day. The doors closed before I could say anything."

I kept staring at her, because I didn't remember *any* of that. The whole day was something of a blur. Chunks of it I could recall. The tour of the campus by a woman in a khaki skirt and aqua Asics. Dad getting a ticket for illegally parking the Jeep as he broke a sweat hauling most of my stuff up the elevator to my then dorm room. Mom setting up my side, making it look pretty with some of the new things she'd bought from the Bed Bath & Beyond in Avon and me rearranging most of it after they left to drive back home.

But I didn't recall the exchange with anyone near the elevator.

"I don't expect you to remember," she said quietly. "You met so many people since then and I stay to myself. But I remember thinking you were nicer to me in that one moment than anyone else had been my whole sophomore year."

"Why?" I shook myself from my stupefaction to ask.

Plus, this was the most we'd ever talked, really talked, and it felt important.

I wanted it to continue.

"Partly because I barely go out. Partly because not everyone at Barrington is an Edgie, but enough are. There's no way for me to start over here, not authentically. You at least could."

I laughed, and not in amusement. "Yeah, that didn't exactly work out for me," I said, leaning my head back against the wall.

She watched me a moment. "I heard," she said.

"How? Is there some sort of community posting board?"

"No, that was disbanded about ten years ago."

I hadn't been serious, because real posting boards were so early 2000s, but good to know there wasn't one in active existence.

"Then how did you know about . . ." I frowned. "Whatever it is *you* know about *me*?"

Petra fidgeted again. "Last Christmas, I overheard a fight between Scotty and Bronwyn. I wasn't eavesdropping, so you know," she hastily added. "Scotty had her on a video call through the living room TV screen at our house in Edge Hill—he likes to work out while talking to her that way so she can see him shirtless."

Okay, gross. I'm so glad Ayisha dodged that bullet. I mean, yes, he was empirically good-looking and I had noticed his body was seriously ripped, but now I realized he was a shallow probable narcissist, which moved him squarely into the "Swipe Left!" category.

"They were talking about Josie Sutton's birthday party—"

My back immediately went up. I had to concentrate on keeping my breathing even.

"—and how she invited everyone except you."

I scowled. "Why would she tell Scotty that?"

"Because she was talking with him about Arthur. Ever since Hatcher met Lord Watercress, Bronwyn would taunt Scotty when they'd get in fights and say she was going to get Arthur Chakrabarti Watercress as her boyfriend and marry him and become a lady in England and forget all about Prescott."

Yep. I could 100 percent see her saying something that stupid.

"She guessed that Arthur had a crush on you so she excluded you from Josie's party so she could flirt with him. But I guess he didn't show up so she told Scotty she'd make her move when she got back to school."

There was so much to unpack in all of that my brain almost didn't know where to begin.

First of all, I'd been right! Bronwyn *was* high-octane flirting with Arthur! Both at Halloween and at the lockers, and all the other times.

Second, what kind of psychopath tells her boyfriend/ex-boyfriend about her plans to go after another boy?! That was some serious next-level evil-queen manipulation bullshit. I'd feel sorry for Scotty if he wasn't knowingly walking back into that relationship of his own free will.

Third, boy, had her plan backfired! If she hadn't excluded me, I wouldn't have had my feelings hurt enough to go back home for Christmas and I wouldn't have hung out with Arthur and fallen for him and we wouldn't be in this weird purgatory of romantic/platonic that, no matter how it was defined, kept Bronwyn out of the picture. If she hadn't been such a shit human, I would have challenged her to a game of chess because she was clearly terrible about thinking ahead with any degree of accuracy.

No way did she know about en passant capture.

"Anyhow," Petra said, looking almost shy. "When I heard Thea wasn't going to be here anymore, I thought . . . it might be okay to have a roommate if it was someone who was nice and had been going through the same kind of bullying I'd gone through, in a way. So I put in a request with Ms. Martinez, who was surprised."

I laughed. "I'll bet."

My short laugh seemed to calm her, and she came close to smiling.

"I wasn't sure it would happen."

"I'm glad it did," I said. I meant it, to my surprise. And hers. "Despite you giving me the icy treatment for the first few weeks," I needled.

"I know I'm not good with people."

"You're discerning," I said, thinking that was probably something Arthur would say.

It seemed to do the trick because, at long last, Petra Bergerac smiled. Nothing beaming or even showing her teeth. But the corners of her mouth curved up and her energy settled.

Close enough.

"You're just saying that because I blackmailed Bronwyn for you," she said dryly.

"Totally," I joked in return. Though there was some truth to that. I had more questions for her. Yet I sensed she was close to being talked out. I wasn't as much of an introvert as she was, but I leaned more that way than extrovert so I could empathize.

However, one question I still wanted to know the answer to was: "Do you want to hang up flyers with me tomorrow?"

With a laugh she said, "Absolutely not." And opened her book. A moment later, without raising her eyes from the page, she added casually, "Thanks for worrying if I was murdered."

My smile didn't dim. "Any time."

She nodded and turned the page.

Nothing more was said between us that night, but it wasn't uncomfortable. Most important, I was fairly certain I'd just made my first friend at Barrington who I hadn't kissed or known back in Oklahoma. Someone who, unbeknownst to me, had sought me out and who had my back when I least expected it.

And you know what?

It felt pretty darn good.

Progress.

Thirty

Gaines ended up being the one to help me hang the Valentine's Day Dance flyers around campus.

It was Saturday, and Arthur was having brunch with Esha in New Haven. Ayisha was working on a paper on the history of "the Black Belt" in the American South as it related to the Cretaceous Period and how massive deposits of plankton from millions of years ago helped create conditions that often affect voting demographics in the here and now.

I blinked several times when she told me that, then asked if I could read it when she was done. She said yes, but I had to leave her dorm room and get those flyers up first.

"Ticket sales are lagging," she informed me. "And I don't want to hear any crap about how last year was better when Buffy and Muffy were in charge."

Talk about ticket sales reminded me that I didn't know which of the many boys who liked Ayisha she'd chosen to be her escort. When I asked her, she just said, "I don't have time for that." Then she smirked. "I'll find someone when I get there."

Which made me laugh, mainly because of course she would. He'd probably be awesome, too.

She shooed me away and I left with my backpack filled with a large/heavy stack of Caldwell's flyers, a packing tape gun, a box of tacks, and a thermos mug filled with cinnamon coffee. Heading into a gray-sky day with a cold, sharp edge to the wind.

On the way to my Saturday morning flyer adventure-task, I got a text from Arthur.

Barrington was about an hour from New Haven and he was driving by himself, so, naturally, being the good *friend* that I am, I asked him to text me when he got there.

He pretended to be annoyed, but I had a feeling he liked it that someone cared enough to keep tabs on him. Friend tabs.

Arthur's text: I have arrived safely in New Haven and parked. Also safely. I am now going into the restaurant to have brunch with my auntie.

My text: Safely?

Arthur's text: 😐

My text: 🤓

Arthur's text: 🙄

My text: Have fun!!

Arthur's text: It's brunch with my aunt, not Disneyland.

My text: Have you ever been to Disneyland?

Arthur's text: Of course. The one in Paris a few times.

My text: What's your favorite ride?

Arthur's text: Hyperspace Mountain. It's a bit like your American Space Mountain.

My text: But hyper?

Arthur's text: 😑

My text: My favorite's still Pirates of the Caribbean. It's relaxing.

Arthur's text: There are "cannons" firing over your head!

My text: Not really. Plus, it's mostly dark and cool. And people are having dinner at the beginning.

Arthur's text: **You must try Hyperspace Mountain.**

My text: **Next time I'm in Paris . . . which so far is never.**

Arthur's text: **You've never been to Paris?!**

My text: **Hello? American from the middle of the country.**

Arthur's text: **You can't fool me, I now know for a fact there are such things as airports in the middle of your country. Indeed I've used one! Regardless, you simply must go to Paris. I insist.**

My text: **Yes, sir. I'll start saving now.**

Arthur's text: **I can take you.**

My thumbs hovered over the keypad as mind drew a blank on how to respond. Fortunately, before I did, he texted me again:

Arthur's text: **Ah! I see Auntie. I'll tell her you said hello.**

My text: **Thank you!**

No bouncing three gray dots followed on our text exchange, so I knew it was over.

I put my phone in the pocket of my jacket and hung my first flyer on the posting board at the bottom of Charity House. The first hour I handled everything by myself with confidence. But Barrington was huge! I wished I'd packed Advil.

Luckily, the Peddler—our campus store—was nearby so I ducked into the shop.

And saw Gaines.

He wore a knit cap and bomber jacket as he walked out holding a roll of Mentos and a bottle of Mountain Dew.

My first instinct was to ask if he was planning to combine the two and record the results as all boys seemed to have done at least once in their lives.

But then I remembered what Petra said and suddenly I was pissed.

I stormed over to him and said, "Did you do the hashtag thing about Petra?"

He stared at me, confused. "Come again?"

"Pound Petra ring a bell?"

He grew pale. "Oh."

"Yeah." Angry, I shoved him in the shoulder. "How could you do that?!"

"I didn't!" he insisted.

"Isn't creating hashtags your thing?"

"It's a lot of people's thing, not just mine."

"Then if you didn't do it, who did?"

"I don't know who started the hashtag, it was years ago. It could've been anyone."

"But you know who started the rumor about her, don't you?"

It was obvious by his expression that he did. He sighed. "Probably. But I told people it wasn't true!"

"Did you tell Bronwyn to stop spreading lies about Petra?"

"It wouldn't have done any good, Fin. She was on a warpath back then. She calmed down once Petra's mom married Scotty's dad and Mrs. B could become her mother-in-law." He rolled his eyes at the last part and popped a Mentos into his mouth.

"You know that's part of why Petra doesn't leave her dorm room, don't you?"

His pale face flushed and his chewing slowed. Apparently, guilt doesn't go well with spearmint Mentos.

"Is Bronwyn on a warpath now, spreading rumors? About me? Or Ayisha?"

He shrugged. "I don't know."

"Come on, Gaines. You always know what she's doing."

His cheeks grew redder and he looked down at his feet. "Not lately." Then he glanced up. "You're not the only one on the outs with her."

To my shock and his mortification, his voice cracked at the end

and he rolled his lips in, clamping down hard as if to keep anything else from escaping.

It was too late, though.

I realized then: "Oh my God, you're in love with her, aren't you?"

Now his whole head was so blazing red I should've looked
around for a fire extinguisher.

He clenched his jaw hard. "That's stupid. We're friends, we've
always been, like, friends."

"You can still have romantic feelings for your friend," I said,
not elaborating on how I could possibly be so certain. "And you
totally do."

"I don't, though," he insisted with zero conviction, to the point
even he heard how pathetic he sounded. He closed his eyes before
he let out a long sigh. "Look, there's only so many times you don't
get chosen before you gotta move on, you know?"

"But you haven't," I countered. "Moved on. Not really. You
said it yourself, she's not talking to you. You're still waiting to get
back into her good graces."

That hit a sore spot.

His brow knitted. "It's not easy, Fin. You don't know, you
haven't ever loved someone you can't have. It sucks! Watching
her flirt with basically *any* other guy! And Scotty, who's banging,
like, six girls at a time. But Bron's still"—he mimicked her higher-
pitched voice—"'Oh, Prescott, soooo cute and strong and he's
going into politics.' Or was it personal training? Then she catches
him with another girl for, like, the thousandth time." He scowled
at me. "Man, I just came out for a snack," he muttered, stuffing
the rest of the Mentos roll in his back jeans pocket.

"Don't act like a martyr, Gaines." I poked him in his shoulder
again until he looked back at me. "You chose to be a jerk to Petra."

"What? Are you guys besties now?" he snarked.

"Maybe I just think it's important to be a decent human being. Unlike some." I glared, then angrily brushed past him, deciding to forgo my need for Advil.

I got a ways down the pathway that led into the main part of campus before I heard him call out, "Fin! Hey, Fin, wait—"

Spinning around, I saw him jogging to catch up with me. Before he could utter a word, I deployed the Ayisha Finger Point. "My name is *not* Fin. It's Finley. Only my friends can call me Fin."

He rubbed the heel of his hand against his right eye and sighed roughly. "Look, you're right, okay? About, you know . . . about what happened to Petra. It was fucked up and it's bothered me for a long time and I . . ." He sighed again, dropping his hand to his side. "I don't know how to make it better."

"Have you tried apologizing to her?"

He was silent.

I rolled my eyes. "It's literally the least you should do!"

He nodded, but his eyes drifted off to the side and I realized, "You're worried Bronwyn'll find out, aren't you?"

"It's not easy to just . . . you know . . ." He shook his head helplessly. "Just stop having feelings for someone. Even when you know you should." He jammed his free hand back into the pocket of his bomber jacket and breathed out hard into the cold air. "You haven't ever loved someone you can't have so you don't understand."

Au contraire, Gaines.

Although, in my defense, I wasn't struggling against having a huge crush on a psychopath, albeit one who vaguely resembled Kate Middleton. If you ignored the dark cloud of evil hovering over her gorgeous auburn hair.

"I know you don't like her," he said then. "I get it. But, the thing is, I still remember her from way back. When she was ten years old and Grandpop died and I, like, couldn't stop crying. She was the only one of my friends who came over to my house and sat with me until I couldn't cry anymore. Then we ate pizza and watched *Elf* even though it was summer, because *Elf* made me laugh." He shook his head wearily. "I can't get *that* person out of my head." A sadness crept over him. "Even if I haven't seen her . . . in a really long time."

It was difficult for me to reconcile the girl he described with the one I'd met. Yes, I knew she couldn't always be riding on her broom and thinking of new ways to deploy Dementors for her personal gain.

It just felt like that most of the time.

I was still mad at Gaines. Maybe disappointed, too.

Yet I also felt a pang of . . . pity? Empathy? Sympathy?

Something.

He may be a jerk sometimes, but feelings were stupid and powerful and illogical.

And apparently weren't going anywhere anytime soon.

The weight of many flyers in the backpack hanging off my right shoulder made itself known. I had a lot of ground to cover and I wanted to be back at my dorm by the afternoon and have had a nap before Arthur and Esha returned. Which would be difficult if I did this all on my own. In theory it was a two-person job.

"What are you doing the rest of the morning?" I asked.

After all, he was technically still a part of the Valentine's Day Dance Committee, despite not having shown up lately.

He rubbed the back of his neck. "Uh, I don't know. Maybe putting Mentos in my Mountain Dew and filming it . . . ?"

Lord.

"I'm putting up flyers around campus for the Valentine's Dance. I could use help."

I saw him debating the pros and cons. The main con being if Bronwyn saw him with me, what that would mean for their dysfunctional friendship.

He took his hand out of his jacket pocket and held it out. "Hand me a stack," he said. I gave Gaines the ones in my hand. And we got to work.

Thirty-One

E sha Chakrabarti looked exactly the same. Short dark hair, perfectly styled eyebrows, and deep brown eyes that sparkled when she smiled. Which was often. Considering I'd only seen her a month ago, this shouldn't have been surprising.

It just felt like it had been a lot longer.

"Hello, Finley," she said to me in her lyrical English accent, opening her arms for my hug.

I smiled and wrapped my arms around her. "Ms. Chakrabarti!"

She smelled the same, too. Cinnamon, cloves, and pepper. Parts of her perfume that were warm and subtle. Like she was.

"Please. We're past that." She drew back to look at me. "You must call me Esha."

Despite already being "Esha" in my head, I said, "Okay. I'll try," with some reluctance. It was difficult for me to address adults by their first names.

We were alone together in the common room at the bottom of Charity House. The gas fire burned low in the fireplace behind the glass screen. Late afternoon light angled in from the tall, west-facing window, showering the area in golden shades.

With Gaines's help, I'd finished hanging the flyers two hours ago, leaving enough time for a quick nap, so I was refreshed. And happy to see her again.

"Come. Sit." Esha led me to one of the leather sofas. She faced me with a cheerful smile and keen gaze. "Now. How are you?"

"I'm fine. I didn't expect you to be here so early. Grandma Jo told me you were coming to the States for Arthur's birthday."

"Yes, that is part of what has brought me back this time."

"Are you going to see Grandma Jo while you're in the States?"

Her expression lit up with excitement. "I am. I'm leaving from here for Oklahoma to see Jo. And that is the other part of why I'm in America again so soon. Specifically why I'm here two weeks before Arthur's birthday." She blushed a little. "Jo and I are going on a trip to the Turks and Caicos Islands. I've always wanted to go, but not alone. Jo's never been."

I covered my surprise. Not that my grandmother had to clear her itinerary with me, but it was a reminder of how I was a long way from home and missing things.

I was happy for them. Their relationship was clearly working for them, despite the distance. After Grandma Jo's unofficial coming out last Christmas Eve, there had been some blowback from certain town members, particularly a couple on the Christmas Zoning Commission who tried to shoot down Grandma Jo's effort to expand her inn to include a separate building for a spa. Apparently, though, Dr. Raymond had given them a stern talking-to and threatened to not use as much nitrous oxide next time they came for some dental work. It worked. And now Grandma Jo is going forward with her plans. Though apparently she had a trip to take first.

"I'm glad," I chirped. "Grandma hasn't gone on vacation in a long time."

"Which is precisely why I insisted we take one immediately. Someplace warm." She smiled. "Given the blizzard of last month, she didn't need much convincing."

I grinned. No, probably not. "How was lunch with Arthur?" I asked.

"Quite a treat. We went to a charming seafood restaurant in New Haven called Shells and Bones. It's right on the water. Have you been?"

"No. I've barely left Barrington."

"Arthur should take you."

I blushed. "Oh, no. That's okay."

"Don't you like seafood?"

"I haven't really eaten a lot of it, not the East Coast kind, like lobsters and scallops. Oklahoma's totally landlocked. Restaurants have stuff flown in, but I'm sure it's not as good as what you had."

She waved off my hesitation. "Then you simply must go."

Images floated across my thoughts, of me seated across a table from Arthur beside the ocean, with candles and white tablecloths and maybe a well-dressed waiter named Rocco. I didn't know if Shells & Bones was like that. Probably not. But in my mind it was. *Romantic and totally out of bounds.*

"Maybe," I said with a smile, tucking my hair over my left ear. It would be never, of course.

"I told Arthur I wanted to speak with you before I flew out for Oklahoma." She took my hands and, though kind, the gaze she leveled at me stopped any of my natural fidgeting. "I wanted to know how you are truly doing. Beyond merely 'fine.' Which is a word that seldom reflects what the speaker is actually feeling."

I bit my lower lip. *I mean, where to start . . .*

She seemed to have an answer for that unspoken question, too. "I'm aware that you and my nephew have reconsidered your situation from our time together in Christmas and have chosen not to date each other, for the time being."

"Um . . . yeah."

I have no idea why I hadn't anticipated my conversation with Arthur's perceptive and empathetic aunt would not be easygoing. There was no way we wouldn't get into the heart of things. She was a barrister! Being unfairly perceptive was probably a requirement.

Then something stood out.

"Did he say that?" I asked. "The 'for the time being' part?"

"Not in so many words, but I know my nephew quite well."

"He adores you," I said, hoping to shift the focus.

"And I adore him. I shall never have a child of my own, Arthur is as close as I'll come. His well-being in all areas is a priority for me. But, Finley. I'm also concerned about you."

My eyes widened. "Me?" I squeaked.

She nodded. "Your feelings for my nephew have put you squarely in a circumstance that you never asked for. It's unfair, on a number of levels. I recognize that you're both quite young, you all the more so. However, that doesn't invalidate how you feel now."

For whatever reason, her saying that hit me hard in the center of my chest, and before I knew it, I had to swallow hard against a wave of regret. Not for what I'd done, but for the whole situation. The one boy I liked more than anyone else was the one boy I couldn't have.

"It's stupid," I mumbled, looking down. "We were barely together at all . . ."

Esha squeezed my hand. "'It is not time or opportunity that is to determine intimacy; it is disposition alone.'"

Quickly wiping at the corner of one eye with the back of my hand, I cleared my throat. "Is that a quote?"

"Yes. Jane Austen." Her eyes twinkled. "We Brits are duty bound to quote either Austen, Shakespeare, or one of the Brontës at least once when having a heartfelt conversation."

She winked and I laughed, feeling the tiniest bit lighter. "I see why Grandma Jo likes you so much."

"And I can see why Arthur likes you. Regardless of how your relationship with my nephew ultimately plays out, I appreciate that you care for him." Her dark eyes clouded. "He has not always experienced that as he should."

"I met his father."

"Mmmm, yes, I heard. From Arthur *and* Lionel."

I sat up straighter. "Lord Watercress mentioned me?"

"Oh, yes. You weren't at all what he presumed."

Drawing my hands away, I wrapped my arms around my midsection. "Really? We only talked for a few minutes. And I was mute through most of it. Or freezing."

"I think it was the part where you held out a bag of Arthur's clothes to him in the ski hospital that caught him most by surprise."

A pang of embarrassment hit me. "Oh, right. That." I frowned. "I don't know why he wouldn't take it. Arthur was using two crutches so it was awkward for him."

"That is a very American perspective, one I admire wholeheartedly." Then she chuckled, touching fingertips to her mouth. "How I wish I'd been there to see his expression!"

"He didn't really have one. He mainly stared."

At that, Esha practically guffawed. "How perfect!"

I wasn't quite as amused. In fact, I was now more nervous than ever about seeing him again. "He must hate, me, huh?"

Esha sobered up, shaking her head. "He doesn't. My brother-in-law is not entirely bound to tradition, he wouldn't have married my sister were that the case. Racism in the upper echelon of British society is quite entrenched, regardless of what those may say publicly. For Lionel to marry Bisha, it required more rebellion on his part than it should, or that he perhaps remembers."

"Did his parents not like her?"

Esha chose her words carefully and I could tell there was a whole lot of story there. "They were not unkind to her. My sister is absurdly accomplished. Makes me seem quite the shirker by comparison and I assure you, I'm not. Back-to-back vacations not withstanding." She winked. "Lionel and she were simply meant for each other, however. Both are focused, brilliant, and, when it comes to being a parent, not especially interested in the day-to-day intricacies of the task. More in the results. My niece Polly was fine with their laissez-faire attitude. Arthur was not."

I couldn't help noting, "Lord Watercress doesn't seem laissez-faire lately. At least when it comes to Arthur's next step."

"Quite true. There has been a shift. I suspect that is due to the fact Arthur is about to turn eighteen, and when he does, he will no longer be a child. Now what he chooses to do has real consequence, which, in turn, reflects on the family, and thus draws Lionel's attention."

"Is that where I come in?"

Her expression gentled. "Yes, dear, I'm afraid so." She soothingly rubbed my upper shoulder. It was nice. "Now. I ask again: How *are* you?"

This time I didn't try to pretend. "I'm incredibly sad," I admitted tremulously. "I really like him. A lot." The backs of my eyes prickled with the threat of new tears.

Esha once again took both of my hands in hers. "Then hold on to that for as long as you can. It may fade, as young love often does. Or it may hold true. There's no real way to tell other than to go through it. My advice is, don't make a preemptive decision on how you *should* feel or *might* feel. Allow yourself to simply *feel*, and cherish it for the gift it is."

"Gift?"

She nodded. "All love is a gift. Whether it lasts a moment or the entirety of your life, and every degree in between. Love is always important. Regardless of the outcome."

After we talked a bit more, Arthur drove Esha to the airport in Hartford. I didn't expect to see him again that night but to my surprise, a little before nine, he texted that he was downstairs in the common room. There was maybe an hour before one of the proctors came down to make sure the space was cleared of non-residents, mainly boys.

I found Arthur standing by the fireplace. Once more, he was in his puffy green jacket and pressed dark jeans. His hands were clasped behind his back and he seemed lost in thought. So much so, he didn't notice me at first.

The only other people there were three girls in sweats I recognized as underclassmen who were seated at a round table in a far corner, textbooks open, holding highlighters. Studying for something. I planned to do a little catch-up on one of the books I needed to finish for Mr. Poisson's class.

Right now, Arthur had my full attention.

By his posture, I could tell Arthur was slightly guarded for some reason. Even when he saw me, he only relaxed a little.

"Hello," he said. At least there was a hint of a smile.

"Hi." I stopped in front of him. "Everything okay?"

His head bobbed. "Yes, yes."

Clearly untrue. He seemed as nervous as a cat at a dog show. Before I could even draw breath to ask him anything—*How was the drive to the airport? Did you have fun with Esha? Why do you look like that?*—he abruptly moved one of his hands forward, proffering several sheets of white printer paper.

I was so puzzled. "What's this?" I asked, taking the pages from him.

"It's a story," he said cryptically, shifting his weight from one leg to the other.

I cocked my head at him. "Okayyyy . . ." Then I glanced down at the front page and saw only two printed words: *The Astronauts.* And for some reason, it clicked. My stomach clenched. "Wait. Is this something you—"

"Shhh!" He shot a furtive glance in the direction of the study circle.

I lowered my voice. "Wrote?"

He cleared his throat. "Yes."

"Oh!" He glared. I whispered, "Wow!" I clutched the pages tighter.

"I wasn't certain you'd be interested, since it's space-related, but then you mentioned having read *Solaris*, which, to be clear, this is nothing like. Particularly in narrative execution."

"Arthur."

He ignored my chiding tone. "Also, Auntie told me I should have you read something I wrote." His lips twisted in a self-deprecating grin. "And that I shouldn't be so fainthearted at the thought of showing my work to others."

"I'm really honored."

"It's not any good."

"Arthur!"

"It's not, though! I wrote it last year, not long after I'd arrived here in the States. Mainly to alleviate the boredom."

"Well, I can't wait to read it."

"Take your time. Or don't, if you'd rather not. It's up to you,

I shan't be offended either way." He waved dismissively, as if this wasn't the hugely important moment we both knew it was. The bright shine of his eyes betrayed him, though.

Gotta confess, it was strange and all kinds of adorable to see him like this, vulnerable and uncertain. So unlike him. This was important. I wanted him to know I'd be careful with his trust.

Reaching out, I laid a hand on his forearm. "I'll read it," I assured him.

He shrugged a shoulder. "Whenever," he said gruffly.

But he covered my hand with his own, holding it in place. Everything inside me fluttered and, when our eyes met, my mouth went dry in a way that had nothing to do with friendship. The searching impression in his dark eyes told me he felt the same.

He squeezed my fingers and we held each other's gaze for longer than was necessary.

Then he released his hold and I stepped back, pressing the pages to my chest and watching after him as he left.

Of course, I wanted to read the story right away, but a pang of nervousness *for* Arthur hit me and, by the time I'd returned to my dorm room, I couldn't.

What if it was terrible? What would I say then?

There would be no way I could fake it; he'd see through me in a second!

Suddenly I felt like I shouldn't have said anything. This was a very risky move on my part.

It was also a huge honor and I needed to stop being such a numpty. (Arthur had used that word once when referring to his roommate, Landon, and I loved it, even if it didn't fully apply here, though it mostly did.)

I stared at the pages, printed so nicely, stapled in the left corner.

The Astronauts

Of course, it would be about space.

Giving in to apprehension, I set it between the pages of my AP Calculus textbook, vowing to get to it tomorrow. I had to read Mr. Poisson's latest assignment: *The French Lieutenant's Woman.*

The man was on a romance kick, for sure. I just wished this one were a more interesting read and less idealized-woman-through-man's-perspective. Maybe then my mind wouldn't have been wandering over to Arthur's story . . .

An hour later, I admitted my defeat, set the novel aside, retrieved Arthur's pages, and read them.

Thirty-Two

It was Tuesday and the penultimate Valentine's Day Dance Committee meeting was almost over.

The day had turned out to be unseasonably warm, with skies the color of a robin's egg. Everyone voted to migrate our gathering out to the courtyard of the quad with its concrete tables and metal chairs bolted to the ground.

Ayisha looked like a badass future CEO/president as she reviewed everything we'd accomplished so far and what else was left to do in our second-to-last meeting. The last one would be next week and then our plan was to go to Nostos on the thirteenth to drop off all of the party essentials.

Even the ticket sales had started to tick upward.

I chose to believe the flyers posted at every turn helped. If the thumbs-up Gaines gave me after the announcement was an indication, he agreed. I was happy he decided to show up for the meeting.

We voted on which Valentine's Day/romance movies from the approved list we'd have playing in the background and wound up with three: *Valentine's Day* (because, duh, even though it's kind of boring), *Crazy Rich Asians*, and *Love, Simon*. The volume would be off so no one worried about editing out the profanity.

Ms. Martinez volunteered to keep the party decor at her house and then we adjourned the meeting.

I stayed behind.

Arthur had an AP Macroeconomics test today and had needed to focus. But now he was going to meet with me so we could finally discuss his story.

It was about a group of astrophysicists who encode the history of humanity onto the DNA of trillions of tardigrades then launch them into deep space in hopes of keeping alive the memory of their collective civilization since their sun was going supernova. One spaceship of tardigrades landed on the third planet from an unimpressive star twenty-seven thousand light-years from the center of its galaxy and they eventually merged with proto-humans, who then follow the course of history established in the coded tardigrades until about five billion years later when the Sun began to expand. So, new scientists developed space vessels for trillions of tardigrades encoded with the history of their planet and launched them into deep space, hoping to keep the memory-chain of humanity alive across the universe.

Basically, the directed panspermia theory combined with the rebooted *Battlestar Galactica* and an old-school *Planet of the Apes* ending.

It was *suuuuuuper* nerdy.

Here's the good news, though: it was really good! *(Thank God!)* He wrote it in such a way I honestly didn't see the "Earth *is* the new planet!" reveal coming.

I was excited to talk with him about it. And tell him he was talented.

However, right before our meeting, he'd texted me he would be late since he had to do an unexpected video call with his parents.

Once the dance meeting was over, everyone bolted, leaving just me and Ayisha. I had my feet up on the edge of another chair and my laptop open, killing time.

She nodded to me. "Are you going to stay here until your totally not boyfriend shows up?"

"That's the plan."

A soft *ding* heralded the arrival of new photos in the shared Brown family file we had going. Grandma Jo and Esha had sent a few from the white sandy beaches of Turks and Caicos—a place approximately a million miles from Connecticut in early February—but these new photos were from my parents.

Dad sent shots of Mom with her hand resting on her growing baby bump. He'd been uploading a lot of them since I came home from the ski trip.

I showed them to Ayisha, who smiled. "Your folks are so dang cute." Then she sat back down on the seat across from me, cupping her chin in her hand. "Do you think this'll influence you about college?" she asked thoughtfully. "Like, maybe you go back to Oklahoma so you can be closer to the Bean? Maybe help out?"

I bit my lip. "Does it make me a bad person that I never even thought about that?"

"Nah. It's still new."

I closed my laptop, then held it. Drummed my fingers on its red plastic topper. "I looked up the requirements for Yale . . ." I said as nonchalantly as I could muster.

She was surprised. "Not Oxford?"

I laughed. "I don't think that's going to be in my future." She nodded slowly, her expression growing pensive. Which got me curious. "What about you? Where were you thinking about going?"

"Until about six weeks ago, I figured I'd go to Utica Junior College, maybe transfer to OU later, when Billie and Linda were in high school and Mamma wasn't so worried about them being on their own."

"What about now?"

"Now . . ." She hesitated before glancing up at me. "I was thinking about Oxford. Or Cambridge. Maybe the University of London. Major in marketing." She shrugged and took a sip of her iced coffee.

I blinked. "That's a lotta England," I said.

"Yeah."

"Is this because of that guy in *Bridgerton*?" I teased, despite feeling an unexpected pang of panic at the thought of now losing her to the same country about to reclaim Arthur.

She gasped playfully. "Regé-Jean Page! Do not forget the name of the hottest man on the planet!"

"It'd be easier if I'd seen *Bridgerton*."

She clutched her chest. "How are we even friends?"

I bit my lower lip. "Are we?"

She laughed then realized there was more seriousness than not in my question. "Don't get insecure now," she said, swatting my shoulder.

"Too late," I half joked.

We shared a smile. But a part of me really wanted to know.

Our beginning had been so fraught, spent trading snark and scowls. Things had changed since she told me about having been admitted to Barrington before me only to have her mother force her to withdraw. We'd been acting like friends, and I considered her *my* friend. Maybe we didn't need a formal acknowledgment.

And yet . . .

"Yeah, Finley Brown," Ayisha said with a slow smile. "We're friends." She arched a brow. "Despite your shit taste in entertainment."

I grinned, relieved. "You can get me caught up when this dance is over."

She sighed and flipped her braids with deliberate drama. "Somebody's gotta give you a well-rounded education." She zipped up her backpack.

"So, wait. Why England?" It wasn't something I'd ever heard her mention to me as interesting her.

She paused, considering. Then, "When I was younger, I had a really intense dream that I was married and living there as an adult. I asked Arthur about all sorts of things when he first showed up at your grandmother's inn. And before that look on your face gets any more frowny, I wasn't *flirting* with him. I already knew you had a crush on him by that point."

"Um, I didn't like him when he first got there," I protested, feeling a blush come over me.

She snorted. "Oh, yes you did. Your cheeks got all pink whenever he was around. Kinda like now."

"Anyway." I drew out the word and looked at her expectantly so she'd refocus. "England."

"England." Ayisha toyed with the metal zipper pull at the top of her backpack. "My dad lived there for a while, when he was in his twenties. Mom used to have photos of him up from that time. You know, posing by a lion statue in Trafalgar Square or at the West End. Tourist places." A shrug. "I guess that stuck with me. Like, maybe that's where he wound up . . ."

This was the first time I'd heard her mention her father. He was always a mysterious figure in her life. I wasn't even sure about his name. Anytime I'd thought about asking a question about him, I hesitated. Instinct told me he wasn't an easy subject for her.

Before I could even form a question about him, she nodded over my shoulder and smiled. "Speaking of jolly ol' England . . ."

A glance behind me revealed Arthur walking toward us.

My pulse started to hammer and I sat up straighter, feet on the ground then, because I suddenly had an influx of energy. Funnily enough.

I stood. "Hey," I said as he arrived.

Arthur nodded to both of us. "Finley. Ayisha." His inherent formality made me want to giggle. Though I didn't. "I hope I'm not interrupting," he continued.

My urge to giggle quickly faded. There was something in his tone that put me on alert. It was off. And not in the same way as when he gave me his story to read. This felt much bigger.

Ayisha answered, "Nope. We're done. I was just keeping Finley company while she waited for you."

"How kind of you," he said.

I frowned at him, noticing his hair was mussed, as if he'd been running a hand through it, and his eyes could barely meet mine before dropping. Something he'd done a lot on the day he returned to Barrington.

Right before we broke up.

Uh-oh.

"What's going on?" I asked, not bothering to wait for Ayisha to leave.

He took a deep breath. "As you know, I spoke with my parents just now . . ."

I glanced at Ayisha, who had clearly picked up on the same vibe. "Everything okay?" she asked.

"The family is in good health," he assured, distracted.

"That's good," she said.

But I wanted to know, "So, why do you look like someone stole your pony?"

He wavered before disclosing, "My birthday party is canceled."

I gasped.

"Whoa," Ayisha said, equally surprised.

"Why?" was what I wanted to know.

"My mother was given a last-minute invitation to be a guest speaker at the International Astronomical Union's General Assembly. It's being held in Prague this year. Normally it's held in the summer, but they moved it to mid-February, wouldn't you know." He scratched the back of his head, distracted.

"And she's going there instead of being at your birthday?" I was incredulous.

"It's a great honor, you see. And, well, they'll have my party afterward."

There was something still cagey about his demeanor that I didn't quite get.

"Are you okay about this?"

His sigh spoke volumes. "I've never been keen on having a party of that size, as well you know." He looked at me. "However, that is not the most pressing issue at hand."

Foreboding hit me then. "What is?"

Dark eyes met mine and I saw in them a seasoned stoicism. "My parents have just informed me that . . . that I shall be returning to London to resume my studies there." His Adam's apple bobbed as he swallowed before solemnly clarifying, "In two weeks."

Thirty-Three

Everything was going GREAT.

Really.

It had been ten days since Arthur dropped the "two weeks" bomb, and my life had come into a sharp focus. Like tunnel vison when mortal danger approaches.

The planning for the Valentine's Day Dance was done and Ayisha was psyched to learn ticket sales were now a little ahead of last year. *(Take **that**, Muffy and Buffy!)*

Mom and Dad called yesterday and were happy as the Bean continued to grow.

Grandma Jo and Esha looked like they had the time of their lives on their epic vacation and were headed back to the States.

And my grades were rocking across the board, in every subject.

I'd gotten my paper back on Stendhal's *On Love,* and you know what? I got an A. Mr. Poisson had particularly found my pragmatic and jaundiced view on love "interesting." I may have written that I thought the flowers-and-love ideal of romance was a crock of shit (not how I phrased it) when all it ever led to was pain and disappointment. He patted my shoulder when he handed my paper back and told me, "It gets better."

I'd stopped by the planetarium a couple times, just to be out of my dorm room. I found Oswald and Poisson there each time so I guess they were still going strong. I was rooting for them. Along with Mom and Dad, Grandma Jo and Esha. Everyone seemed to have it figured out.

Unlike me and Arthur.

I only saw Bronwyn & Crew in class. Rumor had it that she and Scotty were on the outs. That gossip had come from Petra, of all people, via her mother (aka Scotty's stepmom).

A quick perusal of Bronwyn's Instagram showed a barrage of photos of her with Scotty until about a week ago, when she started posting pics of herself looking hot and pouty and writing what a great time she was having.

#LoveMyLife #SundayFunday #WeekendStyle #LoveYourself #PutYourselfFirst

Universal hashtag language of "you're going to regret this"!

If I'd been a better, bigger, more mature person I would have had a tiny bit of sympathy for her.

I didn't. And I wasn't remotely bothered by that.

What I did have were good grades.

Against all reasonable assumption, I discovered a new trick for not thinking about Arthur's impending departure: studying!

Turns out I was good at tuning out.

Sure, Petra initially gave me the side-eye since I maybe wasn't trying to engage her in conversation as much or being, you know, perky. Fortunately, Ayisha had stopped by and told her what happened so she understood.

That was another thing going better: Ayisha, Petra, and I had formed a study trio, albeit always in mine and Petra's dorm room.

Ay was fine with that arrangement since her roommate kept trying to drag her to her Evangelical Bible study group. The way Ayisha explained it, if she'd spent the first seventeen years of her life in a small town in the heart of Oklahoma as an Episcopalian, she sure wasn't going to convert to Evangelicalism *in freakin' Connecticut*.

A few days ago, I'd also found my dress to wear to the dance. Mom had okayed me buying one ("within reason") since it was universally known that my wardrobe was seriously lacking in that department.

Ayisha and I had grabbed a bus into Avon. We hit several stores before we located a red velvet dress with long sleeves and a nice A-line shape that Ayisha promised made me look "hot." The kind of hot that would make a guy "wish he wasn't flying to another damn country."

For instance.

I bought it.

Without discussion, Arthur and I had stepped back from each other.

We still saw each other in class and around campus. We'd nod or wave. But we didn't chat or text and the study sessions had ceased.

There were no hard feelings.

This time there was just . . . nothing.

And it was fine.

No. It was the *correct* decision. We knew it was going to happen eventually, of course. Now it was happening sooner than expected. A *lot* sooner. But life was like that sometimes. Apparently. I was determined not to make him feel bad. Brody had done that to me and it wasn't cool.

I would be cool.

Well, *after* I came to terms with what was happening.

At first, I'd been in shock.

Two weeks?

The words had hung in the air after he'd said them.

Ayisha had been the first to speak. "Seriously?"

Arthur had explained, "They were planning to tell me in person when they came for my party. However, since that is no longer taking place, Papa broke the news on our call."

I shook my head, trying to find a coherent response, wondering: *What about Astrid Blanchard's black eye and that dick Cory Goedert and being banned from UK schools?*

I couldn't ask those questions. Not without betraying his confidence about why he was at Barrington instead of his old school.

What came out instead was: "The semester's already started . . ."

"Class schedules are quite a bit different in England. I'll return to classes in upper sixth form at Jarrow Academy after the spring half term is over. Which is February seventeenth."

I'd barely understood most of what he said other than he was leaving in two weeks.

Two. Freakin'. Weeks.

Panic flooded my veins.

Ayisha asked, "Won't it be hard to transfer back at this point?"

"It would appear it's already in process. Papa started the ball rolling at my old academy once he returned from the ski weekend."

After he'd met me.

It hadn't been said, but it had to be—what else had changed? I thought things had gone okay in our talk outside my dorm.

Clearly, I'd been wrong. The kind of wrong that made a lord decide to take his son out of school months early and bring him back home.

"Papa and Cyril are flying out here on the weekend of my birthday," Arthur continued wearily. "To celebrate and help me move."

Ayisha frowned. "Cyril?"

Arthur explained, "My older cousin. Cyril Chakrabarti. Son of my mother's first cousin, Tasim, and my father's personal assistant."

Words could not accurately convey how little I cared about this Cyril guy. My brain felt like it was swirling.

"Is this what you want?" I asked, fighting against my distress. "Couldn't you still have a party or—or—"

His brown eyes conveyed sadness but also capitulation. "Finley, I don't have a choice."

That was when I lost my temper at him. "You keep saying that but you *do* have a choice! You're going to be eighteen, Arthur. You're an adult then; you can make your own decisions!"

"It's not that simple—"

"Not if you don't let it be!"

"And what should I do, Finley?" he shot back hotly. "I'm not independently wealthy. My college tuition will be paid for by my parents, as is everything else already. My life is set up for me to learn how to *eventually* make my own way in the world, but right now I'm far from being able to accomplish anything like that. As, frankly, are *you*. If *your* parents demanded you return to Oklahoma, what would *your* response be?"

"I'd at least try to make them understand!"

All the fight went out of him then. A heaviness took its place. "But you see, my parents *do* understand," he replied quietly. "They simply don't care . . ."

"They have to—"

He shook his head. "They don't. I love them as they are, in their own way. But I don't much like them, and I'm not sure they much like me. Not enough, really, to be honest. They're all I have, though." A small smile. "And Auntie Esha."

It broke my heart. To have the two people most responsible for you make you feel as if you were a burden or a pawn to move around on some imagined chessboard. *Go here, Arthur. No, wait. Go back here. No, no, back to the beginning, and no being with who you want or doing what you want.*

Being who you want to be.

I felt terrible. For him, for me, for the impossible "us" I still wanted. I hated all of this. Selfishly, because it took him away from me, but also because, deep down, I knew his mapped-out life wasn't what he wanted. I could see it, feel it.

What I couldn't do was change it. Because it wasn't my business. It wasn't my life or my decision. It was his. All his.

What I could do was give him a hug. A long one. He needed a friend right now and I would be that for him. And I would ignore how holding him, even for a moment and in the context of starting the countdown to our eventual good-bye, made me wish I could keep holding forever. Ignore how my heart hurt, my throat stung, how I had to swallow once, twice, three times so I didn't start sobbing right then and there.

After longer than necessary, I stepped back and we shared a sad smile.

Then he'd gone off to be by himself. I sniffed, my attempts to hold back the tears not fully successful.

Luckily that came later, after Ayisha had slung her arm over my shoulders in sympathy.

"I'm sorry, Fin Bear," she said, and I was so bereft, I didn't realize until later she'd given me a cute nickname.

Arthur and I hadn't spoken about "The Astronauts." Not the most pressing issue in light of . . . events. But I wanted him to know, before I forgot everything,

When I got back to my dorm that day, I'd written my thoughts about his story on some stationery, which evolved into me writing *to* him about him. About how much our time together had meant to me, how I admired him and thought he had more talent than he knew and how I hoped he realized it one day.

It wasn't flowery, but it was heartfelt.

Then I'd folded it and put it in an envelope and . . .

And didn't give it to him.

I would. I chose to wait a bit longer.

His birthday present arrived with today's mail.

The package was wrapped in brown paper and addressed to me from Vaughn Novak (Yale University label). I opened it while Petra was taking a shower and stared down at the hardbound book for a long moment before I retrieved the note I'd written, flipped to the back, and slipped the envelope in there. Then I did a quick wrapping job, opened the sliding drawer beneath my dorm bed, and tucked it between my sweatpants.

His birthday was tomorrow.

I'd give it to him later since I couldn't give it to him now.

Friday classes were over for the day, and I needed to find Ayisha. We were going to catch the afternoon bus into Edge Hill to meet up with the rest of the committee.

We had a dance to prepare for.

I stood from my bed, grabbing my coat. It wasn't especially cold now, but it would be by the time we got back from Edge Hill.

A glance out the window, however, stopped me. Because there was Arthur, outside below. Pacing. Then stopping twice. Before he shook his head, turned and strode away.

I was so *curious*. Why was he there? Was he coming to see me? Or, you know, not coming to see me, as it turned out?

The door from the hallway slammed open, hitting the concrete wall with a loud bang.

Turning quickly, I saw Ayisha there, holding her phone. Her eyes were wide and slightly panicky.

Ayisha *never* panics.

"Uh-huh," she said to whomever was on the other side of the call. "How can that be?"

I heard the sounds of the shower cease.

I focused on Ayisha. Who was now focused on me.

I raised my hands: *What's up?*

"Ms. Martinez? I'm with Finley now."

She hastily removed the earphones' wire from its phone port to I could hear too. Now I saw she was on a video call with Ms. Martinez, who was outside Nostos.

I waved. "Hey . . . ?"

"Hello, Finley." Ms. Martinez wasn't smiling.

"What's going on?" I asked both of them.

"Finley, when you were here a couple weeks ago, who was it you talked with about the dance?"

"Um, Mr. Tucker. He's the manager."

Ayisha's eyes briefly closed. Ms. Martinez's expression was grim.

The door to the bathroom opened and a bathrobe-wearing Petra stepped out, her expression curious as she dried her hair.

"Did he acknowledge the contract for the dance with you?" Ms. Martinez continued.

"Acknowledge? No. I mentioned it, but he didn't seem to care much."

Ay clenched one fist. "Did he show you the restaurant's copy?"

"No. But he let me take pictures of the place. He knew why we were there." Another look between them and I was growing concerned. "What's going on?" I repeated.

"Ms. Martinez stopped at Nostos ahead of us," Ayisha explained. "To drop off decorating supplies for the dance tomorrow."

"Okay . . . ?"

Ms. Martinez was concerned. "And the owner—a Ms. Fields—has no idea about the dance."

I stiffened in surprise. This had to be a simple mistake. "Ask Mr. Tucker," I said. "He's the manager. He'll know."

"Mr. Tucker quit last week."

Now I gasped.

"What?" I looked at Ayisha whose jaw was clenched.

Ms. Martinez said, "Apparently he left abruptly last week, which didn't endear him to the owner."

"She doesn't have his contact information?" Ayisha pressed.

Ms. Martinez nodded, but, "He didn't answer their calls while I was there."

"Are they going to keep trying?" Ayisha asked forcefully. "Because he knows about our booking. We have a contract!"

"Unfortunately, no one at Nostos has a record of it," Ms. Martinez said.

"They have to!" I cried, my stomach in knots.

This was crazy! I'd seen it. I knew I had because it had made my head hurt as I was trying to understand the legalese in the doc and came to the firm conclusion that I had no interest in being a lawyer. Or barrister. Or anything else that involved trying to understand what those attorneys had written.

"It doesn't matter, because Nostos has a Bat Mitzvah booked this Saturday and that *definitely* has a contract. They showed it to me."

The room felt like it was closing in. "What—" I took a breath. "What does that mean for us?"

"It means," Ayisha said, laying it all out bleakly, "the Barrington Valentine's Day Dance is tomorrow, and we don't have a venue."

Thirty-Four

Less than an hour later, the Valentine's Day Committee had assembled like anxious Avengers coming from all corners of the campus.

Ayisha had sent out a group text that said: Valentine's Day Dance in TROUBLE!! Come to Common Room of Charity House by 5PM.

People sat on the sofas near the fireplace, like Hawley, Pashley, and Caldwell, or, like Eadrich and Nolan, pulled up chairs.

Gaines leaned against a sofa's tall arm.

Ayisha stood in front of them.

I was closer to the window. A sliver of chilly air from the outside slipped in from a corner in need of a fresh caulking, but I didn't move. Given my body was boiling from the amount of panic I was holding inside, it felt kind of nice.

To my great surprise, Petra joined us. She'd seen the dismay on my and Ayisha's faces, and I guess she was either moved or curious how this would end.

Weren't we all, Petra. Weren't we all . . .

Everyone's confusion and concern turned to shock as Ayisha explained what we knew.

Which was very little. Except for the major detail of: "We don't have a place to hold the dance."

"How did this happen?" Eadrich asked—quite reasonably—once Ayisha was through.

Looks between Ayisha and I were exchanged. Then she admitted, "We don't know."

Honest, but it didn't exactly inspire confidence.

Noland scrunched up his nose. "What about the Tucker guy?"

"No one can get ahold of him," Ayisha said.

"Was he fake?" Hawley wondered.

"No," I said. "He was real."

"He's just *real* gone when we need him," Ayisha muttered.

"I thought there was a contract," Pashley pointed out.

Caldwell nodded.

"There was," Ayisha said.

"But it's missing," I finished.

We'd discovered that unfortunate fact after the call with Ms. Martinez ended. Ayisha brought over the pink binder with the pink hearts and excellent organization (I'll give Bronwyn that) only to find the tabbed section after the tab marked CONTRACT was empty.

Not good. The opposite of good.

Disaster.

I hadn't taken it out.

Ayisha hadn't taken it out.

But someone had taken it out because it was nowhere to be seen.

The only place the binder had been was either Ayisha's room or at the committee meetings.

While Ay and her roomie weren't the best of friends, no one thought Sable would go into Ayisha's belongings, find the binder, and steal a single contract. What would even be the point?

No. There really was only one suspect:

Bronwyn.

As soon as we realized the contract was truly missing, Ayisha, Petra, and I had the exact same thought. The threat had been hanging there since that night at the planetarium: *You won't* even *see it coming.*

But how?

She wasn't at any of the committee meetings since the ski weekend and we'd had the contract after then. Was she really capable of arranging all this? Yes, she was a terrible, awful human, but this was next-level/"uses *Pretty Little Liars* as a how-to guide" type of maneuvering.

Despite her calm exterior now before the group, I knew Ayisha was worried. I was, too. No. Actually? We were both freaking out. She was just better about hiding it.

I was alternating between chewing my thumbnail and chiding myself for chewing my thumbnail, then unconsciously going back to chewing my thumbnail.

We were in charge of this dance. The two newest girls.

Outsiders.

A lot of our time here at Barrington was riding on being able to pull this off. While we—and by that, I meant Ayisha—planned for every scenario, the one not counted on was losing the venue.

The day before the dance.

When finding a new one would be practically impossible.

I felt my throat closing, my breath going shallow.

Which was about the time a lilting voice said, "*What's* going on?"

And there was Bronwyn. Wearing a long red coat. White Barrington turtleneck and uniform skirt over leggings. Auburn hair perfect as it framed her unnervingly symmetrical face.

Having entered the common room from the outside, she stood

behind the group, looking at us. Oh so curious. Josie and Landon were with her, on either side. Like sentries.

Ayisha and I exchanged looks. Petra stiffened beside me. Without thinking, I rested my hand on her shoulder. She relaxed. Somewhat.

Pashley announced breathlessly, "The Valentine's Day Dance is being canceled!"

Ayisha held up her index finger. "No one said that."

"Yet," Pashley fired back with a flip of her long dark hair.

I hadn't been sure if I liked Pashley before. Now I knew. Hard nope.

"What else is going to happen?" Hawley piped up. "We don't have a place to hold it."

Bronwyn seemed puzzled. "What happened to Nostos? Didn't you get a contract?"

"*You* got the contract," I shouted. "It was in your binder you handed over."

She snorted. "Uh, no. *That* contract wasn't finalized. It was for *negotiation*."

"It was signed . . ." *Wasn't it?* Suddenly, I wasn't sure.

"Not by *me*." Bronwyn smirked in satisfaction.

"Yes, it was," Ayisha said forcefully. "I saw it."

I nodded. "So did I."

Bronwyn crossed her arms over her chest. "Prove it, then. Let's see it."

Uh . . .

"The contract's missing," Ayisha admitted with great reluctance.

But you already know that, I thought, the back of my neck on fire.

"How convenient," Bronwyn snarked. "This way no one'll know for *sure*." Gaines stood up straighter, staring hard at Bronwyn. She ignored him. Kept her focus on Ayisha. "But there's exactly zero chance I'm going to let you two blame *me* for *your* screwup."

"We didn't screw up," I asserted angrily.

Bronwyn ignored me to look back at the rest of the committee. "You all know if *I'd* been the *only* leader from the beginning, the Christmas Girls wouldn't be ruining Valentine's Day."

Several members exchanged looks and I could tell they were agreeing with her.

"Bron—" Gaines started.

She shot him a look. "Shut up, Gaines." He closed his mouth. Then she moved to face the rest of the group, assuming the position of being the one in charge. "I don't know *what's* going on, but, as I'm sure you all know, my parents own a restaurant. La Belle's. It's right across the street from Nostos. It was *supposed* to have a party there tomorrow, but that got canceled. We can move the Valentine's Day Dance there."

It was instantaneous. Everyone lightened.

"That's awesome, Bronwyn!" Pashley said enthusiastically.

Ever the fluffer, Josie gushed. "Bron, you're a-*mazing*!"

"It's perfect," Bronwyn continued with confidence. "Nothing much will have to change since they're so close to each other."

Eadrich's tone was more diplomatic, but relieved. "That could work . . ."

My heart was beating so fast. This had to be bullshit. But if we accused her without proof, we'd be spiteful failures.

"I'll call my parents," Bronwyn said, taking her phone out from her coat pocket. "Though I know my mother will want to do *whatever* she can to help out Barrington. She's an alumna here." Bronwyn shot Ayisha a superior look. "Guess that makes me a legacy."

What I wouldn't give for a table full of chocolate fondue and Jell-O shots right then.

Bronwyn stepped aside and placed a quick call.

Ayisha crossed over to me and Petra. "She for sure did this," she said in a low voice.

Ay was furious, but there was concern, too. Different than mine. The social situation wouldn't affect her the same way; she had a master's degree in knowing how to navigate the shallows of peer status and even if things blew up, she'd know how to put things back together. But how would this affect her future beyond Barrington? Would the faculty remember her part in the Valentine's Day Dance Debacle when it came time for college recommendations? Would that influence their view of her, impact her options?

Petra remained silent. Her focus wasn't on Bronwyn—it was on Gaines.

"He knows something," she said, certain.

A glance and I had to admit, there *did* seem to be something off with him. Scowling. Arms crossed tightly across his chest like he was trying to hug himself into feeling better.

Right then he looked up at the three of us. His gaze lingered on Petra.

My stomach clenched.

He looked . . . guilty? No, that wasn't it. Or it wasn't *totally* it. There was something else—yes!

Shame.

He looked *ashamed*.

Right then I knew: he'd done something. The question was, what?

You can't trust him, Petra had warned weeks ago.

When he dropped his gaze, I had a sick feeling she was right.

My heart sank. I'd trusted him despite what Petra had said. Because I'd wanted him to be a friend. But his heart had divided loyalties.

Bronwyn ended her call with a big smile. "We're *in*!"

A cheer from the group.

"Now all we have to do is make sure everyone *knows* about the change," she said, looking thoughtful.

Josie suggested, "We can have signs outside Nostos," in such a way it felt rehearsed.

Landon raised his hand. "I'll do that."

"We'll do it together," Josie cooed then kissed his cheek.

My eyes rolled so hard.

"Great!" Bronwyn beamed.

Fully in charge.

The heroine of the dance.

And maybe that's what she would have been, too, except . . .

"Tell them, Bron," Gaines said, his voice low and tight as if the words were being pulled from him with aching reluctance.

She frowned, confused. "That's what I'm *doing*." She turned back, preparing to speak.

"The truth," he said. Looking up. His whole face was taut.

She dismissed him with a laugh. "Gaines, are you drunk? *Again?*"

Josie and Landon joined in. Pashley snickered.

That seemed to loosen things up for Gaines. He dropped his arms. "Where's the contract?" he asked.

This time Bronwyn shot him a quick look of warning. "We've already talked about that, Gaines. The Christmas Girls can't find it, keep up."

"They can't find it because *I* took it out of the binder a couple of weeks ago and gave it to you." His gaze was pointed. "Like you asked me to."

My eyes flew open wide. Ayisha gripped my wrist.

Bronwyn spun to face him. "Shut *up*, Gaines!" she hissed.

He didn't, though.

He stood taller. "No. I think I've been quiet for too long." He looked at Petra and swallowed. "About a lotta things."

Petra watched him, her bright eyes not missing a thing.

Ayisha took a step forward, facing Bronwyn. "What did you do with the contract?"

"*Nothing!*" she insisted ferociously. "Don't listen to him."

"No," Petra said. Attention swiveled to her in surprise. "*Do* listen to him. He has something important to say."

Gaines swallowed hard, but there was a slight head dip.

Bronwyn sneered at her. "Who let *you* out of your cage?"

Though Petra's expression was neutral, I was close enough to her that I saw the slight tremble around her eyes. She pushed her glasses up her nose. "I did." She glanced at me and Ayisha. Unconsciously, I nodded my support.

Bronwyn rolled her eyes and flicked her wrist, shooing a fly. "Whatever, Boo Radley." She turned back to the group. "We don't have enough time to listen to the resident school shut-in and Guzzlin' Gaines. We have a dance to prepare for!"

This time, though, there was no accompanying cheer.

"Actually." Eadrich stood. "*I'd* like to hear more about the contract."

"So would I," said Ms. Martinez as she approached. She still wore her long camel hair coat and blue patterned silk scarf, having just now arrived back from her fruitless trip to Nostos.

Beside her, to my surprise, was Arthur. His capless hair was windswept. When he inclined his head toward me, our eyes lingered.

I'd been too focused on Bronwyn to notice their arrival.

If Ms. Martinez's grim expression was any indication, she'd heard a lot.

Bronwyn flinched and for the first time I saw genuine alarm in her pretty blue eyes.

Ayisha crossed her arms, her gaze steely before she nodded to Gaines. "What happened with the contract?"

Bronwyn leveled him with a look of warning yet also a quiver of pleading.

Gaines kept his focus on Ayisha and Ms. Martinez as the rest of us waited.

He drew in a deep breath. "Two weeks ago, Bronwyn asked me to get her the contract for Nostos out of Ayisha's binder. I'd forgotten about it until now. She said she wanted to make sure she'd done everything right so if anything went wrong, she wouldn't be blamed."

Bronwyn seized. "And I was *right*! I *am* being blamed for mistakes by these two!" She pointed at me and Ayisha, which was unnecessary. Pretty sure everyone knew who she'd blame for most anything in the multiple-choice section of her misdeeds.

Ayisha cocked an eyebrow and didn't flinch.

"The best way to settle this is to look at the contract," Ms. Martinez pointed out reasonably.

Bronwyn didn't hesitate. "I gave it back to Gaines."

"Bullshit!" he shouted, his face flushed.

I believed him. Because I knew how much he didn't want to go against her. And why.

"Enough, Mr. Alder." Ms. Martinez swiftly took control of the situation. "Clearly something potentially improper happened and I'll get to the bottom of it. But none of this affects the very real problem: we're scheduled to have the dance in twenty-four hours and have no place to hold it."

"What about La Belle's?" Hawley asked.

Ayisha stepped forward. "I don't think it's right to bring money to Bronwyn's family when it's obvious she caused the problem in the first place."

Several people, including me and Petra, nodded in agreement. Bronwyn's glare was laser hot. But she didn't fight back.

Arthur moved closer to me. This time I noticed. His eyes were on the unfolding drama.

"There's no place else to go," Nolan pointed out.

Arthur glanced at me, gave a small smile, then returned his focus forward. So did I. But not before I felt a surge of heat, the kind of surge that's always lingering between us. Even now.

I let out a soft breath and tried to think of something other than this boy I liked so much it made me dizzy.

"There has to be somewhere," Ayisha reasoned. "Anything anyone can think of. Someplace that can hold a large group."

Silence followed as everyone hunted for an alternate venue.

My brain searched and searched, feeling there was such a place. But coming up empty. Despite being in Connecticut for over half a year, my familiarity was still limited to the campus and half of Sheridan Boulevard.

I was about to give in to the idea of La Belle's because of the expediency when my glance landed on the gap in Arthur's unzipped jacket . . . allowing me to see his sweater beneath.

That ridiculous reindeer sweater.

The same one he'd worn the other day at—

"The planetarium!"

Everyone turned to me. My heart started to kick up in excitement as the idea began to coalesce.

I focused on Ms. Martinez. "There used to be events there, right? Before Oswald—"

"Dr. Oswald."

"—Dr. Oswald stopped having them?"

"That's right," she said, slowly nodding as she remembered.

"What if we open up the spaces there and create, like, a bunch of different areas as well as the dance floor."

Eadrich asked, "Is it big enough for the dance?"

Arthur stepped forward. "My mother has hosted events for her students and their families at the Royal Observatory Greenwich, which is a bit smaller than the one here at Barrington. Both have good spaces that, if properly utilized, could serve the purpose of a dance."

A rush of appreciation came over me for Arthur. Along with the urge to hug him or maybe hold his hand in gratitude for his support concerning an event he wouldn't attend. I refrained. Only just.

"Dr. Oswald won't go for it," Bronwyn pronounced. Which I thought was cheeky of her, considering the circumstances.

"I'll talk to Kiersten." Ms. Martinez cleared her throat. "Dr. Oswald. Impress on her the emergency nature. But that could work. And we'd save money on the booking. However, we need a full committee vote. If you're in favor of using the Barrington planetarium for the new dance venue, raise your hand."

Everyone except Bronwyn did.

Even Josie. Which earned her a death stare from Bronwyn. To her credit, Josie gave her a "what other options are there" look and head shake in return. Bronwyn seethed, her pale skin covered in deep red splotches like fresh hives.

Not a good look.

I loved it.

"Motion passed." Ms. Martinez looked at Ayisha. "I have the decorations in my car." She handed over her keys. "Start getting them out and bringing them to the planetarium."

"On it."

Ms. Martinez smiled. "I know." Then she looked over at Bronwyn and Gaines, her eyes narrowing. "You two. Come with me. Now."

She didn't wait for either of them to respond before she exited.

Bronwyn and Gaines moved to follow her. I heard Bronwyn whisper harshly at him, "We are *no* longer friends!"

He glowered back. "We haven't been in a long-ass time."

She recoiled. In surprise? Hurt? For a hot second, I wondered if she was thinking back to when she and Gaines watched *Elf* after his grandfather died and she had acted like a decent person. The person who was locked in Gaines's memory. The reason he clung to her way past the discard date.

Didn't matter now.

Thirty-Five

We got to work like field ants building a new nest. Even Arthur. Who confessed he was nearby my dorm because he'd been wanting to talk with me. Hence the (nervous, I now know) pacing I'd witnessed from my window.

When I asked him about that, he grumped/abashedly declared, "I was not pacing like some crazed stalker."

"You kinda were?"

I got the stink eye for that one.

But we didn't have time to discuss anything. We were put to task after task after task. Bringing boxes from Ms. Martinez's (very nice) BMW SUV to the planetarium and setting them in whatever spot was closest.

"Is there any point in my mentioning I was not an *actual* member of the dance committee," he asked as we made the third trip, our arms laden with boxes of decorative paper red hearts for hanging and boxes of candy.

"Member by association," I tell him with no pity.

He huffed but he also didn't hesitate to go back to get the next load of supplies.

Notices of the change of venue were sent out by school-wide text alert and email. To be on the safe side, Ayisha arranged to keep at least one shuttle going between Nostos and Barrington in case someone somehow missed the update. She also told Josie and Landon she was holding them to their earlier volunteering to be at Nostos, but now to make sure the shuttles were running smoothly for the dance's first hour.

They weren't thrilled. But they agreed.

As for the planetarium itself, it took Ayisha less than minutes to figure out that the main dance space would be in a large open area on the second level called "the Void," the rom-com movie screenings would take place in the dome, check-in would be at the entrance, and the best location for the food/beverage station was the half-circle lobby, because of the tile.

Ms. Martinez was still gone, as were Bronwyn and Gaines. Bronwyn I was fine with. I was curious about Gaines. His telling us what really happened had to count in his favor.

Petra was here. She didn't duck back to our dorm room. She was a full participant. When I checked in with her to see if she wanted to head back, she shook her head.

"You're a man down without Gaines," she said with infinite pragmatism.

"I can't believe he spilled the beans about Bronwyn," I said as we set up some card tables together on the lobby level. She was quiet. I knew I was risking it because it had been—and probably still was—a sore spot, but I added, "I'm proud of him."

It was the truth. He'd done a stupid thing. He should have known something sketchy was going on. But at least when the fan was getting pelted by excrement, he'd done the right thing. Though there was little chance Bronwyn would see it that way.

Petra paused. Her voice was so soft I almost didn't hear her when she said, "Me too." She glanced at me fleetingly then reached for the white linen tablecloth.

We put it over the card table.

I felt Arthur's eyes watching me.

When I looked up, he ducked his head and focused on working with Hawley and Eadrich to string red hearts attached to wires above one of the refreshment stations.

They were using ladders. I was glad Eadrich was the one who stretched his long frame while Hawley and Arthur kept the ladder steady. He was tallest so it made sense. Plus, this way Arthur would be safe from taking an unexpected tumble. Though, if he did, maybe he couldn't fly back to London so soon . . .

Which reminded me—I didn't know the exact date of when he was flying back home. I'd avoided him so much I didn't find out any of the logistics. Now that felt like a mistake. What if he was leaving tonight? Unlikely since he was here, helping, and it was already late. He probably wouldn't leave tomorrow since it was his birthday. Then again, who knew with the way the Watercress side of the family operated.

The answer arrived close to an hour into our activity.

A handsome guy in his early twenties wearing a dark blue suit with a yellow-and-blue-striped tie entered through the front doors and paused.

I didn't recognize him, though he felt familiar. He was of Indian descent, his inky-black hair cut and styled close to his head as if he'd tamed any inclination of it to curl. It was the tight carriage in his shoulders and ramrod-straight posture that were dead giveaways.

He took in the activity in bewilderment, as if he'd somehow wandered into Brigadoon instead of a prep school planetarium.

I walked toward him and he quickly noticed.

"I say, could you help me?" he asked in a sharp English accent, and I instinctively knew my first guess was right: Arthur's cousin.

"Cyril?" Arthur called out as he hurried across the lobby.

He smiled, and it was then I saw the resemblance in the cheek dimple despite the five-o'clock shadow along his square jawline. "Ah! There you are," he said to younger cousin.

Arthur stopped beside us. "What are you doing here?"

Cyril explained, "I've come to drop off some boxes for your packing, per Uncle Lionel's instructions." He flicked his sleeve back, and I caught a gleam of a shiny silver wristwatch. "It's nearing seven o'clock. He's at drinks and dinner with Mr. Campbell now, so you shan't be able to contact him. I also wanted to see if you wanted to go to dinner. I'm famished."

I glanced between them.

Arthur noticed. "Finley, this is my second cousin Cyril Chakrabarti. Cyril is also the lead executive assistant for my father. Cyril, this is Finley Brown, my . . . friend."

Cyril's impressive eyebrows rose. "Ah. So you're the famous Finley Brown."

"I don't think I'm famous," I said back.

What had Lord Watercress had said about me? Then again, maybe I shouldn't know.

"It depends on the audience," was his return.

Ayisha said as she approached, "I ordered fifteen pizzas for everybody. They'll be here in twenty minutes."

A flicker of relief flashed across Arthur's expression.

She held a sizable cardboard box in her arms. Her attention was zeroed in on Cyril. "Who are you?" she asked him directly.

He blinked twice. "Cyril Chakrabarti."

"Right. The cousin. Here." She didn't give him time to answer before putting a sizable box in his arms. "Help me carry these up to the Void."

Cyril was taken aback. "Void?"

She nodded. "Yeah, where the dancing's going to happen. Can't have a dance without dancing." She grabbed a box of her own. "C'mon."

Ayisha didn't wait for him to answer. She was several strides on her way to the stark white stairs with glass panes for a banister that wound up to the second level by the time Cyril looked at me.

"Who was that?" he asked, confounded.

"Ayisha Lewis," I said.

"She's in charge," Arthur added.

"I gathered."

He frowned, uncertain. Perhaps considering if he should let a teenager tell him what to do when he was already moving onward into his own young adulthood. Then he gave his head a slight "why fight it?" shake and followed after her.

"How old is he?" I wondered.

"Twenty-two. He graduated early last year from—"

"Lemme guess—Oxford?"

Arthur smiled. "Cambridge, actually. He's not a Watercress, much to his chagrin. Cyril went to work straightaway for my father." A curious expression came over his face. "He's here to help me get ready to fly out on Sunday."

"Oh," I said in a small voice.

And there it was.

Day after tomorrow.

Obviously, I'd known his departure was imminent. It was another thing to hear the exact time.

An uncomfortable silence followed.

Arthur broke it. "Do you suppose they'll take much time?" he asked, nodding after Ayisha and Cyril.

"Probably. She's good at getting people to do things," I murmured.

"Pizza will help," he said, patting his flat stomach. Which got me looking at his stomach. And its flatness. And the memories of how good it felt to touch that flat stomach. And—

My shoulders slumped.

"What?" he asked.

I shook my head. What was the point? I'd been over this a thousand times. Nothing was going to change.

Deep breath. Forced smile. "Let's hang up the twinkle lights," I said, and moved in the direction of the boxes of lights stacked against a wall.

He hesitated a moment before following.

Hours of work followed. Ms. Martinez and Dr. Oswald, with Mr. Poisson in tow, showed up not long after the food arrived.

Dr. Oswald looked like she was on the verge of a heart attack at the sight of open pizza boxes and twelve people taking a break to devour every slice. (Also, one vegan chicken wrap for Cyril, who had shed his jacket and tie and worked as hard as the rest of us despite seeming as if the whole experience was a trip to the *Twilight Zone*.)

Ms. Martinez spoke in soothing tones to Dr. Oswald ("It'll be all right, Kiersten . . .") while Mr. Poisson patted her shoulder.

In the end, three of the glass-cased exhibits were moved to safe storage elsewhere, which made sense. You only had to look at Prescott's food and beverage table to know how things can go really wrong *really* fast.

Ayisha told me later that Ms. Martinez had bribed Dr. Oswald by redirecting the money that would have gone to Nostos to the Astronomy Department.

Whatever worked.

When the committee took a break to eat, we were all exhausted to the point of loopiness.

It was also kinda fun. Lots of giggling. Reminded me of the group activities back home.

Even Josie seemed more laid-back. It was the first time I'd seen her anywhere other than Bronwyn's shadow. She initially avoided me, Ayisha, and Petra, but there weren't that many of us. After the first two hours an unspoken détente was reached.

I knew things would go back as soon as Bronwyn returned, but for this short time, it was a nice reprieve. I didn't hate her.

And Arthur . . .

It could've been because he was tired or because his cousin was there, or maybe me, too, but he was the most relaxed I'd seen him in a group setting. Even at the Halloween party he'd held himself apart from the others. At least for the blip of time I'd been there.

But I'd caught him a couple of times laughing at something Eadrich or Caldwell said, and as we all sat on the floor in a quasi-circle around the pile of food, tossing a bag of Flamin' Hot Doritos to his (soon-to-be-ex) roommate, Landon, with a borderline teasing, "Here. Your favorite."

Landon's eyes lit up before he ripped it open and devoured the contents.

Which earned a disgusted look between Arthur and Josie.

"Good luck with him later," Arthur said dryly.

Everyone laughed.

In between bites, Landon joked, "C'mon, CW, you know you're going to miss what we had together."

Surprisingly unperturbed by the "CW" nickname, Arthur retorted, "Cockroaches?"

That earned giggled groans and "Ewwwww!"

Josie seemed to sympathize, though. "You'd better not let the room go back to how it was before CW had the place cleaned," she said pointedly to Landon. "Because I will *not* go there if you do."

Landon pouted. The Doritos' dust around his mouth didn't help his cause.

Josie turned to Arthur. "I need the number of your cleaning service."

More laughter followed.

And a part of me was amazed at how natural it all felt.

Back in Oklahoma, when I'd be in my bed, anticipating what my time in Barrington would be like, I'd had big dreams, sure. Great grades propelling me into an awesome college was top of that list. But I'd imagined simple moments like this, too. Having a group of friends around me. Maybe a boyfriend all my own. Nothing life-altering or dramatic. And while Arthur wasn't my boyfriend anymore, for a brief moment, I could pretend . . .

Naturally, it couldn't last.

After the food break, several students thanked Ayisha for getting "some banging pizza!" according to Hawley, and we all went back to work for a few hours.

One by one, volunteers started peeling off afterward and I didn't blame them. Josie and Landon bolted around nine. Probably to get in as much "alone time" as possible before Arthur got back to the room.

Pashley was next to leave. Caldwell seemed like he would've stayed longer, but one hard look from his girlfriend and he was out the door with her.

Eadrich, Nolan, and Hawley lasted until eleven, but it was cleanup after that.

Which left Ayisha, Petra, me, Arthur, and Cyril, who had stuck it out to the end, pausing only to take and make a few phone calls with Lord Watercress once his evening with Mr. Campbell was done. Arthur had explained that it was a "makeup" dinner to apologize for the cancellation of the birthday party. Apparently a "big check" was involved.

I was sweeping up a section on the first floor with Arthur when the self-proclaimed "knackered" Cyril came up to us.

"Ayisha has kindly released me for the evening," he announced with a wry smile. He nodded to his cousin. "Shall we get together tomorrow after brunch to begin the packing?"

Arthur looked pained but nodded. They firmed up their plans to meet. Cyril was staying pretty close so it was easy for him to swing by.

Cyril turned to me and his smile was more genuine than it had been earlier. Maybe arranging umpteen boxes of red candy hearts in stacks on the various tables was an untapped form of bonding. We hadn't talked much, but I'd appreciated his attention to detail.

"Lovely to meet you, Finley. Will you be at the dinner tomorrow evening?" he asked.

I hid my surprise; this was the first hearing about it. "No," I said, not looking at Arthur. "But it was nice to meet you too."

Cyril sent Arthur a cryptic look, then gave me an air kiss near my left cheek—he smelled of pleasant cologne and light sweat from the evening's exertion—and exited the planetarium. However, not before shooting one last glance in the direction of Ayisha, who was with Petra.

She didn't acknowledge Cyril until he was gone and the doors clicked closed behind him.

Then she looked over to where he'd been.

And I saw the faintest smile.

Thirty-Six

This time, Arthur didn't ask if he could walk me back to my dorm. It was late, we were both exhausted from the setup and talking and all the emotional turmoil of the day. We just kinda wound up walking together. Side by side, our shoulders brushing sometimes, usually when I leaned into him like I'd been drinking.

He didn't seem to mind. Neither did I.

Ayisha and Petra went together to Ms. Martinez's residence to drop off her keys. I offered to go with them, but Ayisha glanced at Arthur then back at me and said it was okay. Petra agreed. We all left at the same time but veered off in different directions.

Too tired to disagree, I went with Arthur.

It was dark and cold on the path, which had some trees planted every few feet running the perimeter. They didn't have leaves this time of the year, so their branches looked much darker against the clear night sky with its waning crescent moon.

Despite the chill, we kept our pace at a slow stroll. I didn't want to get to my dorm quickly because that would mean it was over.

And I didn't want it to be over.

That's why anytime the thought of our impending finality

started to creep into my thoughts, I dodged it like Neo in the classic first *Matrix* movie.

"What's your favorite constellation?" I spontaneously asked Arthur when another spike of emotion threatened. My arms were crossed, my cheeks and nose already icy.

He gave it some thought. "I don't know that I have a favorite constellation. I've always found myself drawn more to the photos from the Hubble. Those I look at for hours."

"Astronomy Picture of the Day."

He glanced at me, and though it was dark, I could tell he was smiling. "Of course you would know that site."

"You too?"

"I've loved it for ages."

What a random thing to learn.

We walked along in silence. It was peaceful out. Even my heart was behaving for once.

I said, "Thanks for helping so much with the dance."

"It was surprisingly fun." He rubbed the back of his neck. "Though I may need an Aleve for the muscle aches."

"Too bad you won't be able to see the final result," I said. "Of the dance."

He was quiet for a moment. "Perhaps you could send me a picture . . . ?"

"Sure, absolutely." I tucked a strand of my hair over my cold ear and wished I'd thought to bring a knit cap.

"Maybe, you could . . . send one of yourself?" I shot him a look right as we passed beneath one of the lampposts so I caught his aghast look as he realized how that could be misinterpreted. "In your dress! For the dance! All very proper! Oh, God . . ." he groaned, mortified.

I laughed then. It's possible one of my very favorite things in the whole world was when Arthur Chakrabarti Watercress got flummoxed.

"I'll have Petra take a photo of me." That got me thinking. "We don't have that many photos together."

"That's true."

I thought we'd have more time.

Pushing my inner voice aside—because, seriously, what was I supposed to do?—I took my phone out of my coat pocket and stopped.

"Here," I said. "Let's take one now."

I didn't wait for him to reply. Much like I'd done on the light bridge back in Oklahoma, I looped my arm through his and pulled him close. He took my camera from me and held it out. We both knew his arms were longer.

"Ready?" he asked.

No, I thought. *Not at all.*

I nodded.

Snuggling unnecessarily close, we both smiled. The light flashed a couple times. We peered at the results, which happened to keep us close against each other . . .

It was a good shot. He looked amazing. His teeth always looked movie-star straight and white in contrast with his olive skin, but more so in photos. However, it wasn't until I was looking at my phone screen that I realized where we were.

The Bee Bridge.

Where, in a lot of ways, it all started. When I'd gotten hurt and frustrated and decided to go home to Christmas for Christmas.

He noticed, too. Then our eyes met. And my breath caught.

"I was coming to your dorm to tell you about the dinner tomorrow, and why I didn't want to put you through the experience of dining with my father," he explained softly.

"It's okay," I said, letting him off the hook.

"It isn't," he replied, pained. "It's my dinner, I should have whomever I want be there. I should . . . I should . . ." He swallowed. Let out a frustrated breath. We both watched it float. Our eyes meeting again. "I wish—" he started to whisper.

But I shook my head. "Don't," I said, cutting him off. "It'll just make us both sad."

He closed his eyes for several moments, his brow furrowed. Then nodded his assent.

Not wanting to leave him just yet, I blurted out, "I started researching the SATs."

"Did you? Good . . . good."

"Maybe, if I have any questions, I can still ask you . . . ?"

"Absolutely." This was more definite. His dark eyes softened. "I'd like that very much."

"And, um, Yale. I'm going to need your advice?"

"The essay, yes. Most assuredly." He smiled easier. "You know how much I like writing essays."

"Also, when it comes to Oxford . . . you'll send me photos once you're there?"

He dropped his gaze and let out a humorless laugh. "How dull that would be for you."

"Not if you're in them."

It just came out before I could stop myself. He looked back up at me. Our eyes locked and an unyielding intensity settled between us. The silence was deafening.

Too much. It's too much.

I stepped back right as he started to step forward.

We both stopped.

Right then the faint echo of a nearby, off-campus church bell echoed across the midnight sky.

Midnight.

Oh!

Holding up my index finger, I told him, "Wait here for a minute. I have something for you."

He nodded and I turned, running back to the Charity House dorm. Punched in my personalized coded entry—GGB's birthday (4-19-38). Raced to the elevator, which, thankfully, was on the ground floor. It took forever to get to my floor. I passed Farris Roswell, the proctor, who was in the TV area at the end of the hallway, watching a women's soccer game rerun while knitting. Went into my room, which was still empty (weird). Opened the drawer beneath my bed and took out Arthur's birthday gift. Super grateful I hadn't dawdled about wrapping it.

Then I raced back over my steps and back out to find Arthur right where I left him. Now he was colder and I was completely out of breath.

"H-he-here . . ." I held out the wrapped book.

He took it.

"Hap—" I cleared my throat. "Happy birthday, Arthur." My hands were on my hips as I worked to breathe normally again.

"Thank you . . ." His eyes danced over the colorful wrapping paper. Pink, covered in red and white hearts.

I blushed. "It was the only wrapping the Peddler had right now."

To my relief, he grinned. "Story of my life."

"Mine's close enough to Christmas that people still try to merge the two." I mimed my two hands coming together.

"The injustice," he murmured, though he was much more interested in examining the present. He felt the weight. "Hardback," he guessed. Accurately. "I'm so intrigued."

"You could unwrap it," I pointed out impatiently. Should've guessed he was one of those impossible people who didn't rip off the paper of their presents two seconds after it's in their hands. Which, I confess, was me.

"I'm savoring the moment," he replied.

Double meaning received.

Then he slid his fingers beneath the edges I'd taped down and carefully pulled it apart. Without a single tear! It was like magic.

I took the paper from him and held my breath as his eyes widened in surprise at the hardback first edition of *The Amazing Adventures of Kavalier & Clay.*

"Open it," I whispered, my breath dancing on the cold, night air.

He did. I bit my lip as he read the signed inscription that Mr. Novak had helped me get from the author:

To Arthur—
"Take care—there is no force more powerful than that of an unbridled imagination."
—Michael Chabon

Arthur stared at the page so long I started to worry he didn't like it and was trying to figure out how to tell me. But then he swallowed hard. His face tightened as he clenched his jaw so tight I was afraid he'd crack a molar. When his beautiful brown eyes met mine, they shimmered with tears.

My chest constricted and tears of my own blurred my vision.

He tried to speak, but no words came out. So, he closed the book with a snap and pulled me into his arms and kissed me. My mind went white. Blank. All I could do was feel.

His lips were cold at first but warmed quickly and were as soft as I remembered. There was a decisiveness in how he held me. Tightly. How he kissed me. Passionately. How our bodies pressed against each other. Intimately. I felt dizzy. Electric. Alive. I never wanted it to end. If the way he kissed me—over and over—was any insight, neither did he.

My arms fell naturally around his shoulders, one hand on the back of his neck, my nails digging in. *This* was what I'd wanted since he left me in Christmas, since the last time we were together.

And it came as we were saying good-bye.

I felt tears on my face. It took me a moment to realize they weren't mine. That just about ripped my heart out.

Pulling back, I rested my forehead against his. Clutching the lapels of his familiar green jacket. Neither of us spoke for a long time, our breaths coming fast and hard, mingling together before drifting off.

When I'd allowed myself to think of what this moment would be like, which hadn't been often, I'd always had something deep and meaningful to say. It was either poetic or pithy, capturing the moment, the emotions. Now that the moment was here, I couldn't think of a single thing. There were too many words, too many feelings.

I leaned away. Our eyes met and held. Reaching up, I gently wiped away the trail of his tears, then left my hand, cupping his face, and said the only thing that really mattered.

"I love you."

His eyes closed. I didn't want him to say it back to me, that wasn't why I'd told him, so I leaned in to place a kiss on his lips before he could start, if that had been in his thoughts.

Then I stepped out of his embrace.

His arms dropped to his side. He opened his eyes.

I paused. Took a mental picture. Which was how I would

remember him. Standing there, his lips slightly swollen from our kissing. The Bee Bridge behind him. Holding his birthday present.

Watching me as I walked backward.

Away from him.

Thirty-Seven

Believe it or not, I managed to get some sleep last night. You'd think I'd have gone to my room and sobbed my heart out into my pillow. But I didn't cry at all. As soon as my steps carried me away from Arthur and into the dorm, a numbness came over me. I could feel the tears inside me. They were for sure there. Waiting for the right time to unleash. Possibly on the fifteenth, when I knew he'd be truly gone.

I honestly didn't know.

What I did do was pass out two seconds after my head hit my pillow. I slept so deeply I didn't hear Petra come home. A first for us.

My body must've wanted to avoid dealing with the inevitable emotional tsunami that would come with morning because I slept in until after eleven.

I might even have slept longer if there hadn't been a loud pounding on my door that pulled me awake.

Jesus, what the—?

Groggy, I stumbled out of bed, my heart racing, and blinked twice. Kept one dry, crusty eye closed, but it was enough to notice that Petra wasn't in the room. Her bed was neatly made. Had she come home last night?

"Finley!" That shouty voice from the other side of the door belonged to Farris, the proctor who took her job *way* too seriously.

As much money as Barrington brought in, you'd think they'd have a more tech-forward method of notifying students in the dorms of guests, but nope.

When I reached the door, it took a couple seconds for me to notice there was a bright yellow Post-it there. Eye level. Petra's handwriting:

I'm out of our room of my own free will and not being murdered, so don't call the police.

I deserved that.

Pound! Pound! Pound!

Inches from my face. I opened the door to find Farris there. "What?" I demanded, my voice crackling from sleep.

"You have a visitor downstairs." Per usual, she gave no more information and was halfway back to the TV room by the time by my brain began processing normally.

My first thought went to Lord Watercress. Again. He was roaming around Connecticut free range so it was possible.

What could he want from me now?

He had Arthur.

Earlier than expected.

He shouldn't be mad.

I'd done exactly as I promised—stayed out of the way of Arthur's decision-making process. Such as it was. I mean, it was him giving in to his father's vision for his life. Not a lot of deciding appeared to be undertaken. Lord Watercress had the same lack of decision thrust on him when he was Arthur's age. And then his father before him and Watercress men ad infinitum.

I pressed the heel of my palm into my sleepy eye. Popped open. Okay. There. Felt better. Deep breath. Ran my fingers through my hair, hit about six knots along the way. Opted for a ponytail holder and put my hair up. Did a lightning-quick brush of my teeth—Dr. Raymond would *not* approve—and got dressed. Jeans and sweater. This time I wore an extra layer of clothing and warm socks then grabbed a puffy light blue vest from my narrow closet. To be safe.

When I got downstairs and went into the common room, I saw at once it wasn't Lord Watercress.

My heart caught.

"Grandma Jo!"

She smiled warmly and held out her arms. "Hello, darling Finley."

I didn't realize I had run across the room until I launched myself into her, wrapping myself in her loving embrace. I pressed my face against her soft, angora-sweater-covered shoulder, drawing comfort by how familiar she smelled and felt.

Home. She felt like home.

Which was when my tears decided now was the right time to let loose. She held me tightly as I wept. Rubbed her hand over my back. Staying silent, her cheek against the top of my head. I hadn't noticed any other students so I could be making a fool of myself. I didn't care. My grandmother was here and she loved me, which was what I desperately needed.

After a while, I'm not sure how long, I calmed enough to pull back and look up at her beautiful face, surrounded by her blondish hair and, for a woman who'd just spent over a week in the Caribbean, lightly tanned skin.

"Boy?" she asked, handing me a tissue.

I sniffed. "Boy." Dabbing my tearstained face.

She nodded. Slipped her arm around me, drawing me to her again. "How about you and I go for a walk around this glorious campus of yours? I passed a coffee shop on my way to your dorm. It was very busy. Do you suppose they have peppermint tea?"

"They do," I said, swallowing.

"Perfect. We'll go there. Get some much-needed sunshine along the way." She gave me a look. "Always try to get out for a little sunshine every day. Weather permitting. It does wonders."

"Yes, ma'am."

She smiled and kissed my cheek. Then wiped the inevitable lipstick smudge. Today's shade was a pearly pink.

Twenty minutes later we were holding our to-go cups of tea, sitting outside in one of those random social nooks created for conversation or solo contemplation that were scattered throughout the campus. Benches. Picnic tables. Small clusters of tables and chairs.

A sip from my cup. The tea was still too hot to drink, but the heat felt good in my hands and the aroma of peppermint soothed me.

I glanced at Grandma Jo. She was backlit by the noonday sun, creating a sort of halo with her hair. Back in Christmas, Arthur had confessed once that he thought she resembled Cate Blanchett, and I teased him for the rest of the day about his crush—which he strenuously denied—on my grandmother.

"I'm glad you're here," I told her, earning another smile. "Though, why *are* you here?"

"To surprise you for Valentine's Day," she replied with a teasing grin. "Did it work?"

"Yep."

"Good." She leaned into me, lightly bumping my shoulder. She sipped her tea—Earl Grey with a splash of low-fat milk—and let her gaze travel over the buildings in front of us. The library was the prettiest. Neo-Gothic. "Esha and I had also been planning to come to Arthur's birthday party. That would have been a surprise for you, too. Had it happened."

"Meeting the family already?" I teased. Which was something I wouldn't have been able to do before last Christmas.

She chuckled, her cheeks darkening with a faint blush. "Actually, a little," she confessed. "But mostly, to be a support system for Arthur." She met my eyes. "And for you."

That warmed my heart. "I'll be okay," I said, knowing it was true. Eventually. Though it felt a long way off.

"I know you will, honey." She squeezed my hand then took another sip of her tea. "Will we see you tonight? At Arthur's birthday dinner?"

The thought of both of them being there made me want to change my plans and go with them. But it wasn't possible; there were too many things in the way.

I shook my head but didn't elaborate. She seemed to get it anyhow.

"That's right. You have the Valentine's Dance. How is that going?"

I told her almost everything. From Ayisha and Bronwyn's power struggle, to Bronwyn dropping out. When I got to the part about, ahem, Prescott's food table, her eyes widened, then she grinned.

"I did something like that once."

Now my eyes widened. "You *did*?"

"Remind me to tell you about Mimi McGinley and the Okmulgee pig farm disaster when I was fourteen. Let's just say this Bronwyn got off easy." She winked and my eyes got wider. She rolled her hand. "But continue with your story."

I did and got her caught up, minus the details around my goodbye with Arthur last night. When she asked, I showed her the photo of me in my dress that Ayisha took when I first tried it on.

"Beautiful." To my surprise, tears glistened in her eyes. She put her arm around my shoulders. "It feels like Skip and Dana just brought you home from the hospital. And now you're a young woman, breaking hearts."

I scoffed. "Hardly. More like, getting *my* heart broken." I stared at the white plastic lid of my cup, which would probably be on this planet in some landfill long after I was gone, outliving me and my stupid issues. "He doesn't want to go back home," I said. "Or go to Oxford or run his dad's business."

"Did he tell you that?"

"No." A shrug. "I can just tell. How he reacts whenever it's mentioned."

Grandma Jo was quiet for a moment. "Esha thinks the same thing. For the same reason. That she can tell by looking at him."

"Then why can't his parents?"

"People see what they want to see, and ignore what they don't."

"Parents shouldn't."

"True. But we're all human, with human faults and failings and blind spots. But you're right. If Arthur *doesn't* have the same goals, Lionel and Bishakha should honor his wishes." She sent me a loving but firm look. "Of course, *he* has to be the one to speak up. No one else can do it for him."

"I know." I flicked my fingertip against the sharp edge of the eternal plastic lid. "He won't, though. That's not how he was raised."

A thoughtful look came across Grandma Jo's face. "Going against your parents' wishes is . . . a challenge."

She was thinking about GGB then, I could tell. And how her mother's subtle and, I'd guessed, unsubtle homophobia kept Grandma Jo in the closet for decades.

Until last Christmas.

Which didn't make me feel better. Was I supposed to be hopeful that Arthur would come to his senses when he was in his fifties? When half our lives were already over?

She gave me a wry look out of the corner of her eye. "I don't think Arthur will take as long as I did," she murmured, guessing the trajectory of my thoughts. "Times are different now." A small smile. "Even for the English."

Needing to switch the subject, I asked her about her vacation with Esha. The way her face lit up as she talked about the sunsets, the beach house hotel where they stayed, the food, and their time together, the easiness and pure joy in how she held herself made me so happy for her. It made me want a time machine to go back to fix things with her younger self. I'd tell her to have courage, and make GGB see the light, too, or try.

At least Grandma Jo figured it out and found her "true north" as the books liked to say.

Not everyone did.

Yeah . . .

"We're thinking of going to London this summer," Grandma Jo continued. "To meet the whole family. After the new baby is born, of course."

The Bean was due sometime in July. She would want to be there for the new arrival. At least this time she'd be closer to the average age for grandmothers, even if she still didn't look like one.

Elbowing her in the side, I teased, "Things are getting serious, huh?"

Her smile was circumspect. "They are. I've waited a long time to know when it's time to stop waiting." Then she took another sip of her tea. "If you'd like to tag along to London as my chaperone . . ." Her eyes danced with mirth. "The invitation is open for you."

I blinked several times, my heart suddenly beating faster. I knew what she meant. She knew that I knew what she meant.

Whoa . . .

The opportunity, if I wanted to take it, was there. Go to London. Go to Arthur.

Risk is also there, my ever-present contrarian side reminded me.

Months would pass between now and then. Anything could happen. Arthur could return to England and forget all about Barrington, and me, like we were from another world. Because we *were* from another world.

And yet . . .

Hadn't I just thought about how much I'd wished for Grandma Jo to have been braver when she was younger . . . ? Easy to do since I knew her outcome.

It was a lot different not having a guarantee going in.

Scarier.

So much scarier.

And also, so much more exciting.

"Maybe I will," I said at last, then took a sip of my tea to hide my smile.

Thirty-Eight

Petra zipped up the back of my dress. Red velvet. Long-sleeved. It felt wonderful. My hair was loose around my shoulders and given a good once-over with a wave wand.

"There," Petra said, stepping back.

From the other side of the dorm room, Ayisha gave me an appreciative nod. She wore a black, A-line, pearl-beaded, off-the-shoulder midi dress, the hem hitting her just below the knees, with high black heels that would probably send me to the hospital. She could be a movie star.

"Lookin' hot, Finley Brown," she decreed.

"Says the girl destined to be the hottest person in the room." I laughed, blushing.

"So you know I'm telling the truth," she shot back with a confident smirk. Then winked.

Petra sat back down on her bed, taking up a book and holding it in her lap. For later, after we'd left. Looking super comfy in her navy sweatpants and soft gray Barrington pullover. Despite all efforts by me and Ayisha, Petra was not going to the dance. And believe me, we tried.

For a brief moment I wished I could take the dress off and join her.

But I caught my reflection in the long mirror attached to the bathroom door, and I realized I'd already put in a lot of the work; I should at least reap some sort of reward.

Plus, Ay would kill me.

I reminded myself that this wouldn't be like the Halloween party, I wouldn't show up alone and afraid. Or need to drink wine beforehand.

Ayisha and I had agreed to be each other's dates. It made the most sense; we'd be working part of the time. But there was a relief, too. For me, having someone by my side who knew what I was going through and how to deal.

She'd already caught me zoning out a couple times as we got ready, thinking about Arthur, wondering how he was doing. Checking my phone over and over, hoping to see a text or anything from him, maybe an acknowledgment of the "Happy Birthday" text with a GIF of a shimmering cake I'd sent this morning, despite my better judgment. Swallowing my disappointment when there was none.

She'd put her hand over the screen.

"None of that," she'd said.

And there was no more of that.

In its place was a surprisingly girly glam session—with dinner ordered in because none of us had transportation to take us to a local restaurant—between me and Ayisha and Petra, who had gamely played along when Ayisha broke out the "good stuff" makeup and insisted on "doing up" Petra's face.

Really, I think Ay was mostly eager to get some mascara onto Petra's pale eyelashes.

The transformation of Petra had been nothing short of makeover-reveal-show worthy. Even I, the least-savvy reality TV–watching person, had seen my fair share of those. We'd been mindful not to force anything on her—a woman's beauty doesn't come in foundation and eye shadow—but Petra had been amenable. And, look, I'm pro—natural beauty, as my daily presentation to the world proved, but I'm not going to deny that there's something exciting about taking extra steps when the right event called.

Tonight was such a night.

Despite Petra choosing not to go to the actual Valentine's Dance, Ayisha told me later she wanted to have her "at least be prepared in case she changes her mind."

"You have a whole Jess Glynne vibe going on now," Ay proclaimed.

Mine wasn't the only blank expression staring back at her. Petra was right there with me.

Ayisha rolled her eyes. "Great. Now I gotta teach two pop-culture virgins."

When it was time to go, Ayisha caught me looking at my phone.

I quickly explained, "I was checking in on Gaines. I sent him a text earlier to see if he was okay."

"Bronwyn's suspended until a hearing before the school board. Gaines is on probation," Petra announced. We both zeroed in on her. She shrugged. "I texted him, too."

"Is he okay?" I asked.

"I think so." There was a faint glimmer of concern in her green eyes.

Ayisha wanted to know, "Is he coming to the dance?"

"He didn't say."

"*Can* he?" I wondered.

Petra considered. "I would think so." Then an expression close to smug appeared. "Bronwyn can't, though. Gaines said she admitted to having her mom hire Mr. Tucker away from Nostos and then getting him to go radio silent before Valentine's Day."

Ayisha and I exchanged astonished looks.

"She's toast," I said.

"Burnt toast," Ay agreed.

Petra smiled and picked up her book.

Fifteen minutes later, Ayisha and I were walking to the planetarium. It wasn't as cold as it had been last night. Which was a good thing since it took us both twice as long to make the trek in heels. We were arriving about an hour before the dance officially started, to make sure things were exactly as they should be.

As we made our way, I brought up Grandma Jo's visit earlier that day. She's specifically asked me to tell Ayisha "hello." An idea popped into my mind as we were strolling.

"What are you doing this summer?" I asked.

She gave me an incredulous look. "We're only halfway through February."

"I know, but . . ." I bit my lip. Lightly, because I was wearing lipstick, which was still a new experience for me.

"But what?"

"Grandma Jo and Esha are talking about going to London in the summer and I might, you know, go with them, and . . ." I knew my cheeks were flaming. Putting myself out there, even with friendship, came about as natural for me as understanding cryptocurrency. "I thought it'd be cool if you, um, maybe . . . came with me?"

Her brows lifted and lips pressed together. She was quiet for several paces. "Mamma might need me to be there for the twins . . ."

"Billie and Linda are on their own now," I pointed out. Ms. Lewis said they were flourishing at their new school. Surely, they could handle being on their own for a couple of weeks over the summer in Oklahoma while their sister went on vacation.

"Unless you don't want to go." I realized that might be the case. "Which is totally okay—"

"No, that's not it. Actually, going sounds . . ." She bit her lip, then confessed, "It sounds like something I'd really like to do . . ."

Then her eyes met mine and she smiled.

It was a Valentine's wonderland.

Are there actually such things?

Who knew?

But if there *were*? The Barrington planetarium had become exactly that.

The path up to the entrance was lined with white paper bags with red hearts, each one containing a battery-operated tea light to give it a magical aura. At the entrance itself was an archway of red and white balloons and twinkle lights.

The first-floor lobby doubled as check-in—with Caldwell and Pashley manning that until Josie and Landon returned from Edge Hill—and had the food and beverages, plus two of the five photo stage areas. Ms. Martinez had managed to guilt Nostos into donating cupcakes, chocolate strawberries, and a ton of heart-shaped cookies in a variety of flavors, as well as one of their line cooks (whose name, according to their badge, was Lotus) to keep things going smoothly.

Each Valentine-themed photo area was staged differently and they were huge hits, with the cell phone flashes going all night.

After a bit of creative thinking, the audio-visual storage area had been transformed into a coat check. The Theater Department had loaned us four rolling clothes racks and Baxter Pringle, a freshman who, thankfully, took his job watching coats *very* seriously.

The Void was a void no more.

Otherwise empty space had been filled by red heart balloons, disco lights from above, and white gauzy curtains with strips of fairy lights along the two walls.

Behind it was the setup for DJ Bronze, a ripped Latino man in his late twenties with an impressive collection of piercings and smooth musical mixes, albeit the "clean" versions. Dr. Oswald was ever-present and no doubt she would not approve of unvarnished Lil Nas X or Doja Cat.

And I was excited to see the variety of different words, expressions, and occasional doodles that followed the *Love Is . . .* name sticker students could wear.

Ay's was *Love Is . . . Philautia.*

Eadrich had written *Love Is . . . Family.*

Caldwell had written *Love Is . . . Kissing!*

Hawley had written *Love Is . . . The Red Sox!!*

Pashley's had been *Love Is . . . My Mantra!*

Nolan's had been *Love Is . . . Like a Box of Chocolates, Some Are Caramel Some Are Coconut.* (He must've used a different Sharpie to get that to fit.)

I'd chosen: *Love Is . . . A Gift.*

Like Esha had said.

The three rom-com movies were set to play on a loop in the dome, where Ms. Martinez and Mr. Mehdi were stationed so nothing got too out of hand in a quiet, darkened room housing comfortable seats and horny teens.

Josie and Landon had made it back to the planetarium from Nostos via the shuttle with three couples who had somehow failed to get the messages about the change of venue.

But it all worked out.

By eight thirty p.m., it was clear the dance teetering on the precipice of disaster had pivoted into a full-fledged success thanks to the committee's teamwork. Even Ayisha had relaxed the tension she'd been holding between her shoulders since the moment she burst into my dorm room yesterday. Not enough to go dancing whenever any of the boys or girls had tried to get her into a one-on-one dance, though.

After I saw a boy from the senior class be turned away, I came over to where she was creating busywork with one of the "kissing booth" photo stations.

"Don't you want to dance?"

She shot me an amused look. "Are you asking me?"

I laughed. "No. But I'm about the only one who isn't."

She paused then to survey the scene, hands on hips. "Boys, boys, boys, as far as I can see. Uh-uh. I'd rather wait until I'm able to find someone mature and interesting. No more Brodys or Scottys." She shook her head.

I pursed my lips. "Like, maybe a guy about four years older than you who went to Cambridge?"

"That'd be nice."

She nodded to the next duo who were in line to get their photo taken.

"Once you're legal, of course," I said.

She laughed. "Yeah, there's that."

"When's your birthday again?"

"July twenty-third." She was suspicious. "Why?"

Affecting my best aura of innocence, I said reasonably, "Because maybe you're in London for your eighteenth birthday and maybe you meet up with a handsome older-by-an-acceptable-margin guy who went to Cambridge? Named Cyril? For instance."

She stopped straightening the photo backdrop after the duo were done. "Are you trying to set me up with your ex-boyfriend's cousin?"

I faced her. "Are you saying you *don't* want me to try to set you up with my ex-boyfriend's cousin? Who you all but kidnapped yesterday? For hours? And made him do work for a dance he's not even attending?"

For once, Ayisha didn't have a comeback. If possible, she even seemed embarrassed. Followed closely but hesitant. "Did he say . . . anything? About me?"

"Not that I heard." Disappointment flitted across her expression. "But I'm sure he liked you. *Every* straight guy likes you. Assuming Cyril's straight."

"He is," she said with an assured dismissal, as if she had a superpower for knowing such things. Unless—

"Did he hit on you?!"

"No." Her brow furrowed slightly, as if presented with a difficult puzzle. "He was a total gentleman the entire time."

"That's a good thing. Isn't it?"

"It is. It . . . totally, totally is." She continued to frown. "He's single, though, right?"

"I have no idea. But I can ask—"

I shut my mouth hard.

No, you can't ask Arthur.

Not anymore.

She got my dilemma, placing her hand on my upper shoulder. "It's okay. It doesn't matter," she said kindly. And she was about to say something else when her attention shifted to over my shoulder. "Well, well, well . . ."

I turned to see Petra enter the dance area, wearing a deep-purple shimmering dress with a matching sheer evening wrap, her hair up, glasses still on, and sporting matching purple corset heels.

What was even more of a surprise beyond her venturing outside her comfort zone was who she was venturing with: Gaines

Alder stood beside her. In a pressed red wool jacket, red tie, and black jeans. His hair had been combed back, gelled in place.

Ayisha and I moved to them as they moved toward us.

"I thought I'd come after all," Petra said, keeping it casual.

But we all knew what courage it took for her to be here.

"I knew the makeover would work!" Ayisha said with a huge grin.

"You look beautiful," I said sincerely then turned to Gaines. "And you . . ." I saw him brace. I smiled. "Did the right thing yesterday."

He turned red but nodded. "Yeah, well . . ." Then shrugged. In his eyes, though, I saw relief.

Ayisha pointed between the two of them. "So, does this mean you two . . ."

"No," they both said at the same time. Then looked at each other and smiled. It wasn't entirely an easy vibe between them, but you could tell they were working on it.

"We're going as . . . friends?" Gaines looked at her questioningly on the last word. Petra nodded. Which earned a smile from him in return.

Beaming, he reached into his jacket pocket and took out a *Love Is . . .* sticker and his own pen, and handed both to Petra. His own sticker was already on his lapel with the word "Freedom" written in dark letters. Petra quickly scribbled "Philia" then handed him his pen with an easier smile.

She then explained to us, "Gaines came by our room after you'd left and insisted I go with him."

He grinned and nodded, though I suspected there was more to that story.

Maybe for another time.

For now, though, there would be dancing. And while Ayisha

had resisted earlier, once it was the four of us, she was the one to lead the way onto the tightly packed dance floor. Loud music seemed to surround us from all angles. Despite not being a fully enclosed space, the temperature rose from everyone dancing close and having fun. I was in the middle of it all, and I didn't feel like a fraud. I felt, in this moment, like I belonged.

And for that, I was grateful.

As the time drew closer to nine, I knew, as much fun as all this was, I needed a break. Dancing wasn't my specialty. Plus, after a while, looking around at the couples holding hands and being cute got to me.

It wouldn't always be this way, but for tonight, given all the variables, it was.

Needing to take a breather, I told Ayisha where I was headed then slipped off on my own.

One of the benefits of being a co-organizer of the dance was that I'd been able to explore the planetarium during the setup in a way I hadn't when I'd come with the class a few weeks ago. To my delight, I'd found the door that led to the upper deck, where, under different circumstances, I could go with a telescope to gaze at the stars. And while I obviously didn't have a telescope, the idea of looking up at the night sky suddenly called to me.

I found, then took, the narrow flight of stairs to the rooftop deck.

It was cold. I knew it would be. But after the heat of the dancing, I welcomed it. Lifted my hair off my neck and let the air cool me down. I moved to the edge of the deck, holding on to the railing and turning my gaze upward.

To the stars.

Tonight's was still a waning crescent moon, a sliver of curved silver high in the sky. The stars and planets weren't as clear as they would be when the new moon arrived in a couple of days, but they were still out in droves. Dotting the inky sky.

I closed my eyes. Let the peacefulness wash over me. Even though the wind was mostly blocked by the stair-enclosure structure, I knew I wouldn't last long out here. What I really wanted was the chance to send up a little prayer. For Arthur to be safe. And happy. Most of all happy.

I don't know how long I stayed up there. Until it grew too cold. I was considering dipping back into the dance to either warm up or maybe grab my peacoat and return when I heard something on the wind that made me pause.

"Finley?"

My heart stopped.

The familiar voice was faint at first, and hesitant. Searching.

"Finley."

I spun in the direction of that voice and found myself face-to-face with—

"Arthur?"

And it was!

Despite the thick shadows that surrounded us, I knew at once who was there. I would always know. Having come around the stair enclosure, now walking toward me. As he neared, I could make out what he was wearing: a pressed button-down white shirt beneath his black jacket and dark jeans. His hair was a wild mess, blowing in the wind.

"What—" I halted, my voice catching. Reaching back to grip the railing behind me for balance, I collected myself as best I could. "What are you—?"

Nope. Power of speech still not working.

I swallowed hard. *Three . . . two . . . one . . .*

He stopped in front of me. There was enough light from the

windows of the stair enclosure that I saw his face, saw when it did the thing where he stared at me in such a way I forgot about the other thing called breathing. Until I bit down on my lips and sucked in lungfuls of bitterly cold air, which burned, and I wished I could be remotely composed.

"What are you doing here?" I finally asked.

"Trying to have a dramatic entrance," he said with a hint of mischief. "But apparently Gaines and your roommate already achieved that." He tipped his head to one side. "And you weren't here to witness my arrival, so I had to go looking. Ayisha told me where you were."

I knew he was speaking words and they were likely coherent under other circumstances, but none of it made sense to me right then.

"Why aren't—? Your birthday dinner—?"

"It's done." His tone was resolute. "There wasn't much left to say after Papa and I had our row."

My heart stuttered. "You fought with your father?" The last thing I wanted was for him to be at odds with his family. Theirs was an already complicated relationship. Adding drama could bring no good. Selfishly, I was also worried I'd somehow get blamed.

Glancing aside for a moment, he seemed to search for the correct wording. "More that . . . I expressed my feelings to him. For once. He expressed his disagreement. Not new. Then he left the dining table and went up to his room." His mouth pulled to one side. "All very civilized," he murmured drolly.

My grip on the railing tightened. "Okay, but you realize you left out, like, a huge amount of detail in there, right?"

He laughed. "I did."

I rolled one hand in impatient agitation.

He crossed his arms and leaned his back against the railing.

"I told Papa I wanted to complete my term here at Barrington. Which, as you know, is paid for at the beginning of each new semester, so were he to attempt to force me back home by stopping my tuition, he would be forced to ask Barrington to reimburse him, which he will not do."

"Are you sure?"

"Very. It would bring family disagreements into the open, which he considers . . . undignified. And since as of today I'm legally in charge of my life's direction, he can't use parental rights as a means to force me to return to England with him." A small smile. "Which you rightly noted."

My mind spun. Was I hearing correctly? Or had I imagined the part where, "You're staying at Barrington?"

"Yes. Until I graduate in May."

He said it so casually, but I knew better. I could feel the intensity in his gaze. He was waiting for my reaction. Problem was, I had too many taking place. I couldn't settle on one!

"And then what?" I whispered, biting my lower lip.

He reached out to tuck a stray lock of my hair behind my ear. "I'm working on that part. For the moment, Papa and I've agreed I'm going to take a gap year to consider my options."

I gulped. "How was he about that?"

"Not great," he said in clear understatement. Then he grinned. "But when I threatened to go to Yale, he was suddenly up for a compromise."

Despite Arthur's self-possessed attitude, I was still worried for him.

"Arthur, I—I think . . ." I released a big breath, shaking my head at myself at what I was about to say. But honesty was important between us. And this situation was important for him. Which meant it was important for me. "Oxford is extraordinary," I said quietly. "And that's without the whole Watercress legacy part. It's the kind of opportunity that most people dream about having."

"Oh, I quite agree. That's why I'm still going to Oxford. At some point. It may or may not be right after my time here at Barrington is over, or later down the line, if possible. But I'd be a fool not to attend one of the world's greatest institutions." His eyes danced. "Particularly one that has an outstanding master's program for creative writing."

"Writing?" I echoed.

He nodded, his expression turning serious and sincere. "I read your note." He took my hand, holding it tenderly. "It meant . . . It meant the world to me that you liked my silly story."

"It wasn't silly. And it meant so much to me that you trusted me with what you wrote." I squeezed his fingers. "I liked it a lot."

He gazed at me as if I was something of a marvel. "I don't have many people who believe in me," he said softly. "That's undoubtedly my fault for keeping most people at arm's length. But when I read what you wrote, I knew that you did. That you were with me. It gave me a kind of . . . power. One minute I was moving blindly forward, doing what was expected of me. As always. And the next, it was as if I felt this force come from within me, giving me strength. Your words were that force. You." He shook his head, as dazed with what happened as I was learning about it. "After that, I knew what I had to do. So I did."

The wind blew between us. I stepped closer, took hold of his other hand. They were still warm. Warmer than mine. Soft and warm and wonderful.

"What happened then? With your father?"

"He was furious, but we both knew he wouldn't cut me off completely. Tuition's a done deal. And the basics. Food, health care, et cetera. Auntie gave me a check for my birthday. It should be enough for a while. Especially since I plan to get a job! Take care of myself!"

He puffed up a bit, almost excited by the idea.

My expression must have matched my inner incredulity, because he arched a brow. "I'm perfectly capable of working, you know."

I turned our hands so they were laced together; the growing euphoria of him staying made me near-giddy. "Will you get one that makes you wear an apron?"

His eyes narrowed. "Do you have a thing for aprons?"

"Maybe," I teased. "You looked pretty cute in that one when we baked Christmas cookies together."

"*Burned* Christmas cookies together." We shared a smile before he turned serious again. "The key word is 'together.'" His eyes were fixed on me. "Every time I thought of leaving here, I couldn't breathe. I tried to pack, but . . ." He shrugged his shoulders helplessly. "I couldn't. Because, if I packed the bags, they could be taken, and if they were taken, I'd have nothing, and if I had nothing, I might be forced to leave. And I don't want to leave. Because you're here."

I shook my head emphatically. "Don't stay for me."

"I'm not," he insisted. "I'm staying for me. For what's best for me. *Who's* best for me. And that, Finley, will always be you."

His eyes never left mine as he raised my hand to kiss it then. It was the most romantic moment of my life, there beneath the stars, looking up at him on a day dedicated to love and romance. He'd said before that he could be romantic as long as it was real. *This* was real. *We* were real. And he had everything right.

I shivered. He noticed.

"We should go back inside," he murmured, his voice low and intimate.

I nodded, we should, but didn't move. "One thing first," I said.

Then I stood on the tips of my toes and pressed my lips against his. He didn't hesitate before he pulled me close against him, one hand in my hair, the other at the small of my back, and I wasn't cold anymore.

After kissing for I don't know how long, I drew back to stare up into his eyes, staying within the circle of his arms. Part of me still wasn't sure this was real. The other part didn't care. I loved this boy. This was what love was for me. Right here. And we would find a way, through all the challenges ahead of us. Somehow. I felt it to the depths. I knew it. *I knew it.*

When he took a step back, he kept hold of both my hands. Watching me with a soft smile.

Which was when I finally noticed the white-and-red badge stuck against the left lapel of his jacket, over his heart. A soft gasp caught in my throat. Tears filled my eyes. I looked up at him. He nodded and reached up to lightly touch the sticker, which said:

Love Is . . . Finley

Acknowledgments

It's a blessing that there are so many people to whom I owe a debt of thanks for helping me get *So, This Is Love* from a germ of an idea to print: Rhonda Bloom, Claire Tattersfield, my friends and family who've helped keep me relatively sane over this past year, which was not easy. There have been births and deaths, accomplishments and losses, agonizing frustrations, exhaustion, hilarity, annoyance, delight, and, most of all, love. All manner of love. So to each and every one in my life I say thank you.

But I specifically want to acknowledge two people who've helped me bring Finley and Arthur and the rest of the crew to life: Eileen Kreit and Regina Hayes.

Making the transition from screenplay writing to writing a novel isn't easy. Being able write in one field absolutely does not guarantee you'll be able to do well in another. What you need is someone who believes in you and, most importantly, fosters that same belief in yourself until, slowly, step by step, it becomes a reality. That's what Eileen Kreit does for writers. She makes you believe you can create a story that others will actually want to read, then she surrounds you with the tools you'll need to make that belief a reality. All the words in the world wouldn't be enough to express the depth of my gratitude for her reaching out to me back in 2019 and ultimately allowing me to transfer my dreams onto these pages. Thank you, Eileen. You're a superstar, as your long list of accomplishments within the publishing industry attests, and I'm so thankful—and amazed!—that you chose to take a chance on me.

One of the biggest gifts Eileen provided to help me on this journey was convincing Regina Hayes to be my editor. Kind, wise, hilarious even in the middle of a raging pandemic, Regina has been my North Star throughout the writing process. When she would say, "This works," I always felt a surge of pride, and when she also said something needed to be reconsidered, I knew she was right. Because I trust her completely. Thank you, Regina, for all of your suggestions, guidance, and encouragement. It means so much.

Both women are legends in the publishing business, as they should be. And both women have my deepest appreciation.

Read more about Finley and Arthur in

So, This Is Christmas!